ELYSE LARSON

For Such A Time

BETHANY HOUSE PUBLISHERS
MINNEAPOLIS, MINNESOTA 55438

For Such a Time
Copyright © 2000
Elyse Larson

Cover by Dan Thornberg

War poster images in the cover montage courtesy of the National Archives and Records Administration.

Published by Bethany House Publishers
A Ministry of Bethany Fellowship International
11400 Hampshire Avenue South
Minneapolis, Minnesota 55438
www.bethanyhouse.com

Printed in the United States of America by
Bethany Press International, Minneapolis, Minnesota 55438

Library of Congress Cataloging-in-Publication Data

Larson, Elyse.
    For such a time / by Elyse Larson.
        p.   cm. — (Women of valor)
    ISBN 0-7642-2355-0
    1. World War, 1939–1945—France—Fiction. 2. World War, 1939–1945—Women—Fiction. 3. Americans—France—Fiction. 4. Women—France—Fiction. 5. France—Fiction. I. Title.
PS3562.A7522235 F67   2000
813'.6—dc21

00–008270
CIP

ELYSE LARSON is an author, photographer, and writing instructor. *For Such a Time* is her third published novel. Elyse and her husband live in Gresham, Oregon. They have three children and eleven grandchildren.

DEDICATION

★

To my sisters,
Dorothy Kilber, Edith Bates, Alice Parker,
to our mother,
Annabell Wagner Douglas,
1894–1985,
and to all
the strong women before us.

ACKNOWLEDGMENTS

———⋆———

Special thanks to editor Sharon Asmus, whose expertise made this book so much better than it would have been, to editors David Horton and Sharon Madison, who believed this book should be published, and to editor Lonnie Hull Dupont, who could see potential from the beginning and encouraged me over the long process of development.

Special thanks to my many writer-friends, too numerous to name, who critiqued again and again and never failed to encourage me. This is your book too.

Special thanks to Edetha Keppel, who served at the station hospital in Govilon, Wales, and shared her memories and journals with me. I'm so sorry she didn't live to see this book published, so I thank her family in memory of her. Thanks to the families of Bruce Keppel, Geoff Keppel, and Steve Keppel.

Special thanks to Lucie Aubrac, a woman of the Resistance in Lyon, France, who courageously wrote a book in defense of all resistants when the work of the Resistance was under attack by collaborators during the trial of Klaus Barbie, "the Butcher of Lyon." And thanks to the University of Nebraska Press for publishing in 1993 a translation of Aubrac's book *Outwitting the Gestapo*.

CHAPTER ONE

December 1943
Lyon, France

As Giselle Munier led her daughters across the city street, she positioned herself between Jacqueline and the two Nazi soldiers they would soon pass on the corner. Although Jacquie was only eight, Giselle worried about her attracting attention and hated that worrying was necessary. More and more, everything she and Claude did with the girls was overshadowed with fear for them.

The vibrant city of her own happy childhood had grown dismal under the occupation. No one washed the streets or planted flowers, or applied fresh paint to shutters and doors. Streets of Lyon that once had sung with the voices of shoppers and vendors now lay mute. One walked or bicycled and only went out for necessities. The few sputtering civilian automobiles reminded Giselle of mice dodging through the yard of a hungry cat.

Many families had sent their children to live with relatives in the country. Soon Jacquie and Angie would have to go.

Normally Giselle never took the girls along when she acted as a courier for the French Resistance, but today she had found no one to care for them, and the message was too urgent to delay. Having them with her this time had made the delivery easy. Now information for tonight's changed rendezvous was safely in the hands of Landine, Claude's contact from Dardilly.

There was no way for her and the children to walk quietly past the soldiers. Their wooden sabots clacked against the pavement. Leather for growing feet had disappeared in the first months of the German occupation back in 1940. The hand-carved clogs, worn with thick socks, were comfortable for the children, who could not remember shoes with flexible soles. Although Giselle still had some good leather dress shoes in her armoire at home, she clopped along in sabots too, as did most people.

As she approached the curb, the two Nazis in their shiny black boots and spotless pressed uniforms glanced at her and turned away, their narrow lips twisted in contempt. Good. She had learned early to darken her glossy blond hair with a tea made from boiled onion skins, nut hulls, or tree bark and to arrange it in a straggling, unattractive bun whenever she went out.

She stepped up onto the sidewalk. The girls, without coaching, had stopped talking, but Giselle could see they were staring at the men in gray-green uniforms. She tightened her grip on six-year-old Angelique's small hand. Angie glanced up at her and smiled.

Giselle smiled back, then setting her face to a well-rehearsed calm, she avoided eye contact with the soldiers. *As one does with vicious dogs,* she reminded herself. While her quickening heart urged her feet to hurry, she feigned the innocence of a housewife trudging home from the market with the usual half-empty bag. Should these two SS men stop and search her, they would find nothing to connect her with the Resistance. Still, she didn't want to attract attention.

Too many times strangers had volunteered comments about Jacquie's beauty. Without a conscious decision, she had begun months ago to dress the girls to look younger than they were. When she realized what her protective instinct had led her to do, she put careful effort into maintaining the fiction. So far it had been easy, because both girls were small for their age. She kept Jacquie's hair in a tight, little-girl braid and the hems of her worn dresses shorter than the more dignified length that her age normally deserved.

Last night Claude had affirmed her unvoiced worry. Looking at the girls after they were asleep, he'd whispered, "They are so beautiful. There are men—no, beasts—who like children. Pray we win this war before our girls invite attention—"

With a shudder, Giselle had interrupted him. "Don't even say it," she whispered, pulling him by the hand to the front room. To her shame, she had burst into tears. Claude held her in his arms while she cried against his shirt. "I hate them! I hate them!" His arms tightened around her, but he didn't speak. When she regained control, he kissed her, and she felt his cheeks as wet as her own.

Regret over her emotional lapse formed a tight lump in her chest. "I'm sorry. You have enough to take care of without having a weeping woman on your hands."

"Don't say that! You and the girls are my life. I fight for you. If only I could be sure you will be safe . . ."

"We will be. If there's a God in heaven, we will be."

"Yes. God."

He sighed, and she knew what he meant. His Jewish parents had been hauled away in a boxcar to only God knew where. And yet she knew he kept praying, hoping they were still alive and safe somewhere.

She prayed for them too. Mother and Father Rose had welcomed her, a Gentile, into their family with kindly affection. When Petain—an elderly French general the Nazis had selected to rule under them—had announced that all Jews must register, in the same loving way, Father Rose had insisted that Claude take Giselle and the girls to a large city where they could lose their identity, even though it meant they would not see them for the duration of the war. Giselle prayed daily for Claude's parents and for his young sister. She also prayed that his changed surname from Rose to Munier and his forged papers would continue to protect him. They had moved to Lyon with the falsified documents in time to avoid the registration of Jews. With those papers he had easily acquired his job of repairing the runways of the Bron airport. As everywhere in France, the pay was low, and like everyone else, he worked long hours and took care not to draw attention to himself. With his arms still around her and his chin resting against the top of her head, she couldn't see Claude's face when he revealed a growing danger. "I just learned that yesterday five resistants in Avignon were betrayed by one of our own countrymen who collaborated with the Nazis."

"Oh no!"

"It's time to send the girls to the Leveques' farm." He let go of her and stepped back, keeping his hands firm on her arms. His steady gaze seemed to command her to stay strong. "It's best for them. They'll be all right."

She nodded, not trusting herself to speak.

He had turned away then and raked back his thick black hair

from his forehead with his fingers as he always did when he was thinking. "With the invasion surely coming soon, the Gestapo and that puppet Petain will work harder than ever to stop us. I hate to think so, but we may already have a traitor in our *réseau*. Lately a few coincidences have made me uneasy. I've asked Martin to go and make sure the Leveques can take Jacquie and Angie."

Evyette Leveque was her mother's cousin. Before the occupation shut off communication with her mother and father in Paris, her mother had arranged for Giselle and Claude to hide at the farm with Evyette and her husband Emile. She and Claude had chosen instead to save the farm as a safe hiding place for the children if the need arose.

Now it was time.

"Yes. Good." Giselle bit her lip to stop its trembling and to hold back a cry of *It's not good! Nothing is good under the Nazis!* Her rage and hatred of them had always given her strength to do whatever was necessary. And so with the safety of her children at stake, she would take this next painful step.

Emile and Evyette Leveque lived in the hills west of Lyon. Although she hadn't seen them since the beginning of the occupation, she trusted them utterly to care for the girls as if they were their own.

As Giselle led the girls up Avenue Berthold, across from the column-lined courtyard of the Terminus Hotel—now the Gestapo headquarters—she glanced down at their innocent profiles. Dread for them became a physical weight in her chest. No wonder people talked of the heart breaking. If she and Claude were arrested and the children taken ... she couldn't allow herself to imagine that. *The girls must leave us.... But what will the separation do to them? How will they change before I see them again? Oh, how can I let them go?* She struggled against tears the children must never see.

"Ooh, *Maman*, look at the little dog!" Angie exclaimed.

From the side street a thin, gray-haired woman walking a shaggy terrier approached. Not many people could still afford the luxury of pets. The woman smiled at the girls, so Giselle turned the corner onto the lesser street to let them pet the dog.

"My petite Francine, she requires not much food," the woman said, "and she is all I have left to care for. My husband— God give him rest—died soon after the occupation." She glanced nervously over Giselle's shoulder toward the Gestapo headquarters and then relaxed a little.

"I'm glad you have Francine," Giselle said. "Thank you for letting my children pet her. They've been wishing for a puppy of their own."

"Ah, it is so hard for the children." She smiled at Angie. "After the war, little one, all will be better." Again she peered beyond Giselle at the square gray building with its constant traffic of green and gray uniformed soldiers. This time she moved to leave. "A good day to you, madame."

"Good day to you, madame."

They had never met before and probably never would meet again, but they had cautiously brightened each other's day. *And this is how it is all over France. People afraid to speak freely, yet our spirits stay strong.* Pride in her heritage brought tears to Giselle's eyes again. *We will win. We will do whatever we have to do to win. And so will our children.*

She drew in a deep breath. "Come, girls. Let's go home." Now out of sight of the Gestapo headquarters, she strode along with her head high, slapping her sabots against the sidewalk with each step as if she were a schoolgirl again. Her hair slipped free from its clumsy bun and bounced onto her shoulders.

The girls laughed and skipped beside her, tapping out a counter rhythm with their flying feet.

Giselle quietly closed the apartment door behind Martin and hurried to the window to watch him leave the building. From behind the curtain, she saw him stride to the sidewalk and on down the street. No one stopped him. No one followed him. As the afternoon sun flashed briefly on the river *Saône*, he crossed the bridge and disappeared into a narrow street on the other side. Slowly Giselle let her breath out.

The girls, playing in their bedroom, had not heard him come and now gave no sign of hearing him leave. The less they saw, the better.

He had confirmed that the Leveques were ready to take in Jacquie and Angie. Martin would be the only one besides her and Claude to know the location of the children's sanctuary. And Jeanie, of course. Long ago she had sent a message to Jeanie in case she and Claude did not survive the war.

Giselle lingered at the window, thinking about her cousin so far away yet always so near in her memory. Although Jeanie had not met the Leveques, she would remember much about the western hills where their farm was located.

When Jeanie was ten, Giselle had persuaded their uncle Al to bring her to Lyon for the summer.

Jeanie had blossomed, but the next summer, when Giselle went to Oregon, Jeanie seemed quieter than ever—too introspective for her age. It had taken Giselle two more years to prevail upon Uncle Al to let Jeanie come to Lyon again. Finally, the summer Jeanie was fourteen, he agreed and let her stay for the whole school year. In addition to attending a girls' secondary school in Lyon, Jeanie explored Paris, visited Versailles and the Louvre, played in the snow of the Alps, and bicycled endlessly.

Giselle's instinctive reasoning had proven correct. The longer visit had drawn Jeanie out of the loneliness and reserve that had throttled her since the death of her brother. Just as Giselle had imagined, Jeanie loved being in France, and the experience had set her free. *She even loved our language and spoke with scarcely a hint of accent. How sad she will be when she sees Lyon after the war. . . .*

War. The very word jolted Giselle back to the present. Claude felt that neither he nor she should accompany the children to the farm. For the past month, ever since the *Milice* had arrested resistants in Bourg-en-Bresse, he'd stopped taking the girls out in public, feeling his presence endangered them.

She hated the idea of not going with them. *They're hardly more than babies. They scarcely know Evyette and Emile, or Martin for that matter. How can we send them with a stranger to a strange family? And yet any minute, a knock on the door could . . .* She pressed her fist against her mouth and squeezed her eyes shut in a futile effort to blot out the possible disaster she so easily pictured. *Claude and I must get out of this apartment too.*

Claude had rented a tiny apartment in Vieux Lyon, the ancient part of the city, where cobblestone alleys and old courtyard apartment buildings dated back to the sixteenth century. Because the Gestapo seldom entered the maze of tiny streets where poor and elderly people lived, Claude conducted some of his underground activities from that neighborhood. Bit by bit he had stocked the apartment with nonperishable foods, in the event they should have to hide, but his intention had never been to care for the children there.

Now, as he'd planned, tomorrow morning Martin would bring an automobile and take Jacquie and Angie to the Leveque family. *I have to tell them, and they mustn't see me cry.* Raising her chin, Giselle marched to the kitchen where Martin had laid the freshly slaughtered chicken and a neatly wrapped ball of butter from the Leveques. Such generous gifts comforted her. For them to send food was not only a sacrifice, it was risky. Farmers were as hungry as city dwellers, what with the Nazis requisitioning almost all they produced. If any farm failed to meet its quota, the Nazis burned it to the ground.

She opened the butter and dropped a spoonful into the steaming bisque she'd made of two potatoes, an onion, and a carrot—the latter two ingredients a surprise from an elderly greengrocer who had grown fond of Jacquie and Angie since they'd moved here. He saved fresh vegetables for the girls whenever he could. After tomorrow, he would be the first in the neighborhood to miss them, but he would know better than to ask questions.

She dipped a wooden spoon into the bisque, blew it cool, and tasted. One more spoonful of wine from the bottle Claude's cousin in Dijon had given them and a pinch of dried basil would give the final touch.

Even without bread, we'll feast tonight. Maybe I should wait until after supper to talk to the girls.

She cut off the head and feet of the chicken, washed the lean body and placed it in a pot to boil, then added wine and a dab of butter.

Her thoughts wandered back to Martin. *I don't even know his real name!* Neither did Claude. And to Martin, Claude was known as Armand, and Giselle was Julie. In the beginning no one had bothered with false names. Now, not only their personal safety but the security of the Resistance depended on not knowing real names. Other resistants maintained only a few trusted contacts. Of necessity, she and Claude had come to know everyone in the Lyon réseau and many far beyond Lyon, because Claude had fallen into leadership after the betrayal and execution of Jean Moulin, General de Gaulle's man in France. Their broader knowledge made their circumstances more dangerous.

From the children's bedroom came a ripple of giggles, then Angie let out a squeal of delight.

Giselle supposed they were still playing paper dolls. Fortunately, they could spend hours with their homemade dolls cut from ads in prewar magazines. *How wonderful,* she thought, *to hear them enjoy small moments, trusting us to hold their world together.*

She dreaded letting them go to the country, yet at the same time prayed that she and Claude had not waited too long. Soon after the occupation, she had begun to teach them at home. The few hours she spent with them each day had become her connection to the happy past, when France was free and at peace. *And the way it will be again someday, please, God.*

She paced back to the front room and peeked out the deepset window to the street below and the river beyond. The river's silken surface cast the last light of the winter afternoon back at the sky. Time to close the shutters and turn on lights. Curfew would bring Claude home soon.

She smiled, thinking how surprised he would be at the oldtime fragrance of chicken simmering in the kitchen. Sometimes she'd had to offer a bribe of black-market cigarettes to get even a fish head to stew. Since Claude did not smoke, she used their ration of two packs every ten days to trade for black-market items for the girls, such as extra tins of condensed milk, sardines, and occasionally a bit of chocolate.

She opened the windows, pulled the paint-encrusted shutters into place, then closed the windows, the black-out shades, and finally the old curtains. Their worn fabric softened the prisonlike feeling that the blacked-out windows gave to their apartment. Moving on into the girls' room, she closed their shutters and curtains.

Jacquie jumped up to help. "Maman, when will *Père* take us to the park again? I'm so tired of staying indoors."

"You know he would take you often if it were safe."

"Yes, but—"

Now was the time. She had to tell them. "Angelique, if you please, go set the table. And if you are very careful, you may use the dishes of *Grand-mère*. We shall have a small party."

"I will be careful!" She jumped up from the rug where they had been playing and trotted to the dining room. The sight of her thin legs moving eagerly below her threadbare pinafore gave

Giselle a pang. The girls never went hungry, but they never had second servings or even the quality of food that growing children need. Getting taller had smoothed away all of their dimples.

Angie had taken her coloring from her mother—straight hair, blond as sun-bleached wheat straw, and blue eyes—a porcelain doll of a child. On the other hand, Jacquie, their firstborn, had delighted her mother by looking like her father from birth, with long-lashed dark eyes and black waving hair, which she wore like Angie's in a thick braid down her back.

"Maman?" Jacquie's forehead puckered with unchildlike concern.

"Yes?"

"Can we go up to the cathedral for Christmas?"

"Jacquie ... I have something to tell you ... and I want you to be brave about it and help Angie not to worry."

"What is it, Maman?" Her eyes became triangles of anxiety. "Is it too dangerous to go to church?"

Giselle slipped one arm around her thin shoulders and hugged her tightly against her side. "Come. Sit beside me on your bed."

While Jacquie got settled on top of the down-filled quilt, Giselle pondered how to begin. "Jacquie, I have always told you the truth, so you know there is danger. But you know Père and I will take care of you. Remember when I said you might go to the country to live? Our cousins Evyette and Emile have invited you to live with them on their farm. We have decided you should go."

"Will you and Père come too?"

"No, dear. Remember? I told you if this should happen, we could not go."

Jacquie sat as if frozen to the bed.

"Sweetheart. We can't even promise to visit. I'm sorry. I know it's hard."

"I don't want to go."

"Jacquie, you must. You know that some of your friends went to the country a long time ago. I'm counting on you to help Angie understand and not be frightened. Can you do that for me?"

"But, Maman—"

Giselle pressed her finger against the child's lips. Gently she ordered, "No buts. You must obey and be brave."

Jacquie's mouth trembled. Her effort at self-control stained her cheeks pink. Chin down, she nervously fingered the yarn ties on her comforter.

Giselle pulled her into her arms and held her close. "My brave little soldier. It will be only for a while. Very soon the Americans and the British will come to drive out our enemy, and once again you will play and run in the park and have picnics along the river and visit Grand-mère and Francine."

Jacquie sniffed but didn't give way to sobbing. After a bit, she pulled away and rubbed her eyes. Carefully she said, "We will see Aunt Jeanie again, no?"

"Yes. We will see Aunt Jeanie again. It is her turn to come to France." Giselle had kept the memory of Jean alive for the girls by showing them snapshots from Jeanie's year in France and from her own summer visits to Salem, half a world away. She told them the name Salem meant peace, and that someday they would visit Oregon together. The girls always had nodded, believing. Anecdotes about Aunt Jeanie and Great-Grand-mère often had served as their bedtime stories.

Now, with Angie noisily setting knives and forks on the table in the other room, Jacquie threw her arms around Giselle's neck and clung to her. Holding her close, swaying side to side, Giselle rocked her without benefit of a rocking chair as she had soothed her when she was a baby. Finally, she released her and said, "Now go and help your sister set the table but don't say anything about going to the country. Let me tell her."

"Yes, Maman." Jacquie left, and soon the childish sounds of teasing and arguing suggested she had accepted her responsibility, as she always had done. Giselle sighed and stood up, feeling heavy and exhausted.

She trudged to the kitchen to make sure the chicken was bubbling at a good rate and then called the girls to sit with her on the divan. She couldn't delay any longer talking to Angie about going to the farm. She wondered how her mother would have handled a situation like this when she herself was six years old. Both of her parents had protected her from adult worries as long as she lived at home. Now she felt unprepared to help Angie and Jacquie to understand the necessity of the separation without frightening them.

With both girls snuggled close, she told Angie about going to the farm, but she did not say it would be tomorrow. She wanted

Claude present for that. He knew best how to reassure them.

An hour later, Claude still had not come home. Giselle tried to keep a cheerful face, but anxiety made her feel like a tightly wound toy, ready to fly apart in front of the children. When the plodding minutes stretched beyond an hour, she fed them, for they were always hungry, and especially so with the delicious smell of chicken filling the apartment. After supper, seated again together on the divan, she read to them from their favorite fairy-tale book.

Suddenly a loud rap on the door stopped her in midsentence. Even if Claude forgot his key, he would never knock like that knowing how such pounding frightened her. She rose to her feet and put her finger to her lips. "Stay quiet," she whispered and tiptoed to the door to listen. The stone walls of their apartment, the heavy shutters, and the solid door had muffled the sound of approaching feet. Who and what waited on the other side?

She motioned for the girls to go to their room. They moved quickly, silently, their faces chalky masks of fear.

When their bedroom door was safely shut, Giselle casually called, "Who is it, please?"

"Julie! It's Martin," his familiar voice called, using their Resistance names. "I've brought Armand. Open! Hurry!"

She turned the key and peeked out. Claude stood propped against Martin, his right arm draped over Martin's shoulders. His face, tense with pain, looked gray. Giselle darted to him and tried to slip her shoulder under his other arm.

He flinched and gasped. "No . . . it hurts!"

His clothing was wet and cold, and the shoulder of her dress where she had touched him came away wet and streaked with blood. She pushed the door wide so Martin could half carry him inside.

Martin kicked the door shut. "Lock it."

She did.

"Bedroom," Claude ordered through clenched teeth.

In seconds Martin laid him on their bed and began to strip off his wet clothes. "He's been shot. Do you have hot water?"

"Yes. I'll get it and some towels."

"Fill bottles and jars with hot water, heat blankets—anything to warm him. What do you have for antiseptic?"

"Iodine."

"Bring it."

"What about a doctor?"

"We can't risk having anyone come here. Tell you later."

"He's right, Julie." Even weak and in pain, Claude remembered to use her Resistance name. "Do as he says. And don't let the girls . . . see me like this."

She nodded and ran to spread a woolen blanket on the kitchen chair close to the stove and set the flatiron on to heat. Ironing was the only method of sterilization they had, and although the homemade bandages had been heat pressed before she stored them, they must be done again. Then she hurried back to Martin with a basin of hot water, soap, washcloth, and towels. Now that Claude was bare to the waist, she could see the dark hole oozing blood below his left armpit. Her ears began to ring.

Don't faint! She quickly set the basin on the floor beside Martin and kept her head down until the ringing stopped and her nausea subsided.

"Hurry with the bottles to warm him," Martin said.

By the time she returned with a hot water bottle and two full jars, Martin had cleansed the wound area. "Got to turn you over, my friend. Can you help?"

Claude tried, and Giselle pulled on the sheet under him. Blood trickled from an exit wound below his shoulder blade.

"You are very lucky!" Martin exclaimed while gently washing the area. "No slugs to dig out, and it missed your lungs. The bleeding had almost stopped until we turned you over. Now the iodine."

Giselle placed the heated bottles around Claude and wrapped him mummylike in the warmed blanket, leaving only the wound area uncovered. Then she fetched the iodine. "I'll iron the bandages."

"Maman!" came a whimpering cry from the girls' room.

Giselle jumped. "Oh, the children!"

Martin nodded while trying to pour iodine into Claude's wounds. "Go to them and keep them quiet, but hurry with the bandages."

Again Claude gasped, "Don't let them see me."

CHAPTER TWO

Giselle awoke to the sound of a clock chiming six. For a moment she wondered where she was and then recognized her own parlor. She had slept on the divan to avoid disturbing Claude. With burning eyes and aching back, she lowered her feet to the cold floor and stood. The day when they must say good-bye to the girls had arrived. Claude had decided she should accompany them. She was relieved for the girls' sake but hated to leave him.

She peeked into the bedroom. He was sleeping. What a blessing they had saved a few precious tablets of a painkiller in their emergency supplies.

She washed in cold water, dressed quickly, and started the coal stove with a few sticks of dry wood. After setting water on to boil for their roasted barley coffee, she laid out the last of the cheese and cut the last chunk of bread into five slices. She'd have to trade cigarettes for more bread. While Claude was healing, he would need the comfort of daily bread.

Too soon the clock chimed seven. She opened the curtains and shutters to let in the gray light. Appropriate to her mood, black clouds draped the sky. She retreated to the door of the children's room and called softly, "Jacquie! Angie! Time to get up." They both mumbled a reply.

Looking in on Claude again, she found him still asleep and breathing evenly. She closed the door to let him rest as long as possible, knowing that once he was awake, he likely would not sleep again. He was at his keenest in the morning. Fortunately, she had learned to be so too.

Martin arrived with Andre, a resistant who had come recently from the Cannes réseau.

Seeing Andre, Giselle felt better about leaving Claude. Twice that she knew of, Andre had put himself in danger to protect her and Claude. She greeted him lightly, as she normally would, so as not to worry the girls. He smiled and patted the sleepy girls on the tops of their heads as they trudged past him to the kitchen. With a wave of his hand at Martin, he went into the bedroom to Claude. While the girls nibbled at their bread and cheese, muffled voices came from the bedroom.

The girls couldn't finish their food. Giselle let them go without urging. They ran to Claude for good-bye kisses. They had seen him briefly last night with his bandages successfully concealed under the comforter. He had told them about leaving in the morning. As usual he'd helped them accept the trip to the farm as both an adventure and their part in helping win the war. Now, although they were quieter than usual, they were calm.

Giselle kissed Claude, touching his forehead lightly to check for fever. His skin felt warm but normal. "Stay in bed all day," she ordered.

He feigned meek submission. "Yes, madame."

She kissed him again.

To Andre she said, "Coffee and bread are on the kitchen table for both of you."

He nodded. "Good. Thanks."

She hurried out to the old Renault and climbed into the front seat. The girls and their bags filled the backseat. Martin tinkered a bit, and with a coughing start the auto rumbled down the street.

The drive out of town and into the hills was happily uneventful, and they reached the farm by midmorning. The stone house, set on one side of a courtyard across from the stable and flanked by the poultry house and the cow barn, seemed ageless. Giselle knew it had been home to more than three generations of Leveques. Martin parked beside the neatly swept entry, and before they could climb from the car, a boy near Jacquie's age and an angular young woman burst out the door.

Evyette's oldest daughter, Louisa, introduced herself and her son Pascal. Then Evyette came out wiping her hands on her work apron.

"Come in, come in," she said, giving the girls a welcoming smile and a hug. Turning to Giselle, she said, "I'll show you where to put their things."

After Giselle had unpacked the girls' clothes and put them in the armoire that had been emptied for them, Louisa and her young sister Nannette called them to lunch, which proved to be a generous meal that reassured Giselle her daughters would be well fed at the Leveque farm. When finished eating, Martin left the table to work on the Renault's brakes. Giselle followed the children as Nannette, who was fourteen, and Pascal showed them the cows, sheep, goats, and chickens. Then they all trooped back into the house, where Pascal pulled out a worn picture puzzle for Angie and a small tray of watercolors for Jacquie. For himself, he opened a small box of carving tools and set to work on a partially carved wooden duck.

Giselle went to the kitchen and helped Evyette knead dough for bread. "I haven't had good bread for so long. How did you get white flour?"

"A neighbor who likes my cheeses mills it for his family. He's often able to hide away a bit for us. And we do the same with our cheese. Then we trade. When our cows produce much more than our quota for the Germans, we put some aside. Emile says we must, of course, give the Germans a little extra or they'd suspect us."

A shiver of fear ran through Giselle. "You mustn't attract their attention."

Evyette smiled and reached across the table to pat her floured hand. "Don't you worry. We won't take any chances with the girls here. Emile would not risk anything happening to our children either."

"I'm sorry. Of course you wouldn't! It's just so hard to leave the girls and not be able to come see them. But I know they are safer with you." Giselle kneaded the dough more furiously.

"I will teach them to make bread," Evyette said with a gentle smile, "as I taught their grand-mère. Your mother always loved my homemade bread. She used my recipe to teach you. I wish we knew how things are with her and your father. I'd feel better if they had been able to get out of the city when Paris fell."

"Yes. It's been a long time since Claude heard anything from Paris. He keeps saying that most people there are safe enough if they simply obey the Nazis' laws. I'm sure Père and Maman would not get involved in anything dangerous."

Evyette finished her dough and laid it in a large bowl, covering it with a cloth. She set out another bowl and cloth for Giselle's dough. Straightening, she said, "Yes. Of course you are right, but I often wish they had been able to flee and stay with us. The Germans came here only once at the beginning of the occupation to tell us what we must deliver to them. The same with other farmers here in the hills. The roads are not good, and our superior enemy thinks we are not very smart, so we've had no more visits."

Giselle nodded. "They do not understand the French, and that is to our advantage." Giselle shaped her dough for the first rising and plopped it into the bowl. "It would almost be worth violating curfew to stay and have some fresh baked bread."

"No curfew out here where they never come. What time must you be indoors in Lyon? Same as Paris?"

She grimaced as she said, "Eight o'clock Berlin time. It's funny how such a little thing can rankle so much. Claude gets up in the dark most of the year to go to work. And even though sun time may say dinner hour, it is curfew time and blacked-out windows." She looked out the kitchen window. "I know it's cloudy, but it's getting dark already. Maybe I should see if Martin is done tinkering with the car."

As if on signal the kitchen door swung open, and Martin strode in. "I think we should be returning to Lyon. It's best to drive in the city while everyone else is going home from work."

"Yes." She turned to Evyette.

"I'll get the girls," the older woman said, "so you can say good-bye."

A few minutes later they all stood at the front door. Evyette assured Giselle that she and Louisa would remember all the special instructions that would help the girls adjust.

Finally Giselle knelt to hug the girls. They clung to her, crying. She struggled to conceal her own grief. Holding them close, she kissed one and then the other. They would not let go. She pulled away and stood up. "Be good girls. Be brave for Père and Maman. And always remember we love you!" She turned and ran to the chugging, shuddering car where Martin waited.

As Martin drove down the bumpy road, Giselle turned in the

seat to wave. The children stood frozen, but when they saw her wave, Jacquie raised an arm in response, then finally Angie lifted hers.

When the car descended into a ravine, the children and the hilltop farmhouse disappeared behind the winter-brown hill.

Giselle pressed a fist against her mouth to keep from sobbing aloud.

Martin handed her his big handkerchief. "You are doing the right thing," he said firmly. "They will adjust and they will be safe."

She nodded. "Thanks."

"I took my children to the country last year."

Martin had never mentioned his family before. "Did your wife go with them?" Giselle asked.

"My wife died in the first year of the occupation."

"I'm sorry."

He kept his eyes on the road, his face impassive. "It was a blessing. They would have taken her soon to a concentration camp. Her mother, father, and little brother all went. We could not help them. . . . Her grandfather was Jewish. My wife's heart was weak . . . shock and grief killed her."

"I'm so sorry." If he had intended to stop her weeping for Jacquie and Angie, he succeeded. Quieted, she said, "Thank you for helping us with our girls."

He smiled briefly, warmly. "No need. It is nothing. You would do as much for me if you saw opportunity."

"Yes. I would." Emotionally she was drained but able to focus on the present. Her mind turned to Claude. As soon as he felt able, she would take him to the hideaway apartment in Vieux Lyon. Soon her lack of sleep last night caught up with her. She turned sideways, rested her cheek against the worn seat back, and closed her eyes.

She didn't think she slept but jumped when Martin said, "Best to sit up and watch with me. We are entering Lyon."

She obeyed.

They crossed the *Saône* and the *Rhône* rivers without seeing either the Milice or the Gestapo. Martin slowed the car a few blocks from Giselle's home. "You should walk alone from here."

"Yes." She tugged the door handle and let herself out. From the curb she leaned inside and said, "Thanks. Thanks so much."

He nodded. "My pleasure, Julie. When you approach your apartment, be watchful. If anything at all seems unnatural, don't go in."

She stopped breathing. "You think they could have. . . ?" She had been so concerned about the girls and about Claude's wound becoming infected that she had almost forgotten the daily danger of being betrayed by a collaborator.

Martin's expression didn't change. "Just be extra careful."

"Yes. Yes, I will."

He turned his attention to the street as she slammed the door. He shoved the Renault into low gear and drove away.

Giselle glanced at the dark sky and then at her watch as she started toward home. With curfew less than two hours away, it would be too risky to move Claude to the hideaway tonight.

Approaching the apartment building, she covertly studied every detail of the street, the alley, their unshuttered apartment windows, and all sides of the building. Everything seemed normal. Still on alert, she entered the building and tiptoed up the stairs to their second-floor flat. Inserting her key, she thought for a moment the latch was not locked. But no. It gave the familiar click. She pushed the heavy old door open and stepped inside.

She knew instantly that Claude was not there. Motionless, she held her breath and listened.

Cautiously she entered. It took only a few seconds to confirm her first impression that the apartment sheltered no one but herself. Giselle checked each room, searching for evidence as to why. On the unmade bed the comforter lay folded back. No sign of any struggle.

The bedroom reeked of Andre's cigarette smoke. He had almost filled an ashtray with broken cigarette stubs. For him to smoke that many, they must have been here most of the day. She touched Claude's pillow, half expecting it to feel warm. It was not.

If the men had gone out for a normal reason, wouldn't they have left her a note? She lifted all the covers and looked under the bed but found nothing.

Quickly she opened the hidden panel in the back of their armoire. Leafing through the forged papers for Claude's various identities, she found them all except those he used as "Armand." She went to the bathroom and felt his shaving brush. Dry. She saw no soiled bandages and no trace of blood in the basin or on the towel. Maybe Claude had asked Andre to take him to the hideaway. *If he did, then I'm not safe here either.*

Giselle stepped out of her sabots and pushed her feet into the soft-soled leather shoes. Leaving the apartment as she had found it, she let herself out, locked the door, and hurried downstairs. She had less than an hour before curfew to create a false trail and then make it to the hideaway. Surely Claude and Andre would be there waiting for her.

She reached the sidewalk without the concierge seeing her. Once outside she wondered if she should have found an excuse to knock on the garrulous woman's door and ask if she had noticed or heard something. *No! Calm down! Speak to no one.*

Giselle walked down the sidewalk and then turned casually into a smaller street that led behind the building. From there she climbed the cracked concrete steps to the street above, pacing herself as though she were simply on her way to visit a neighbor. At the top, after making sure no one was watching, she hurried to a narrow curving cross street and trudged higher up the steep hill. A Gestapo car drove slowly by, its engine purring on gasoline the French could not obtain.

Without showing that she noticed the sleek black car, Giselle entered the courtyard of an old hotel that loomed beside her. She went inside. The old man at the desk appeared to be deaf, for he never looked up.

With practiced poise, she strolled down a long corridor and exited through a service door at the rear of the hotel. Immediately she began running and didn't stop until she reached a private path to the next street. On this street some mothers with children and a few older folks were trudging home in the evening darkness. She made her way up the hill close behind them, yet not close enough to involve them should she attract unfavorable attention. Each step led her farther from the hideaway in Vieux Lyon.

Finally, when she was certain she had not been followed, she circled back and entered the ancient streets of Vieux Lyon from the hill above, which meant another long stairway but going downward this time. She glanced at her watch. Woman or not, she could be shot for being on the street after curfew.

At the bottom of the stairs she seemed to be the only one out in the whole length of the dark cobblestone street. Best now that she assume her old woman identity to appear like most of the other residents. Hunching her shoulders, she leaned forward a little and changed her straight stride to an unsteady slower gait.

Early in the war she'd learned to imitate the movement and stance of an elderly woman whenever she wanted to become invisible. As if out of breath, she stopped, leaned against a stone door casing, and fumbled at an ancient wooden door that looked as if it hadn't been opened for a hundred years. But the latch lifted smoothly. She hobbled inside and closed out the modern world. Only then did she allow herself to worry. *What if Claude and Andre are not here?* She had no answer.

In front of her in the dim moonlight lay the broad stone-paved courtyard, entirely enclosed by three stories of ancient apartments fronted by balconies. This Romanesque-style building had been closed before the war after a balustrade cracked off and two children fell to their deaths. Now the poor and elderly had moved into the lower rooms, and city officials chose to ignore them. Even the Gestapo seemed to avoid the labyrinth of Vieux Lyon. Claude had said there were just enough unimportant old men and women coming and going that a properly disguised resistant would not be noticed.

He had brought her here, excited about the seclusion of the upper room he'd rented. It possessed a panoramic view of the courtyard. No one could enter without being visible from their window. Also, he had shown her two exits downstairs that faced a vacant hillside covered with vines and bushes. But the exterior stone steps were narrow, without a balustrade, and ended in a drop to the ground that Giselle hoped never to have to make.

She stood inside the silent courtyard for a moment, then hobbled in a practiced arthritic gait down the left side to a weathered door that retained the tint of old rust-colored paint. She swiftly struck a match and shielded the light as best she could with her cupped hand. She saw no threads caught near the latch where they should be if no one had opened the door. Who had opened the door? Claude or a stranger? Or had Claude simply neglected to set up the signal the last time he left? Should she chance it and go in?

She blew out the match and stood poised, waiting for some inner knowing to guide her. Nothing did, but she slowly unlocked the door anyway and entered. She felt for the flashlight, then closed the door. Aiming the beam left to right, she saw nothing disturbed in the downstairs room with its simple old chairs and lamp tables. Giselle listened intently. Hearing no sound, she locked herself inside, crossed the dark sitting room, and lifted the faded tapestry behind the sofa.

Undisturbed dust coated the narrow stairs. If anyone else had come in, they had not gone upstairs. She climbed to the empty upper room. Now curfew made it impossible for her to look further for Claude. With her flashlight off, she quietly opened one shutter and looked out at the dark courtyard. She sat on a wooden chair by the window and stared at the dark entrance. *Where is Claude? If he returns to the apartment, will he guess I'm here?* From out toward the river about three blocks away, a Milice siren blatted, louder and louder, then faded away.

Giselle shivered. She drew in a deep breath, squared her shoulders, and got up to look for a candle and something to eat. This was going to be a long, long night.

Giselle slept fitfully and finally awoke just before sunrise. She made a quick breakfast of hot water and a black-market chocolate bar from the larder. As soon as she dared, she covered her head and shoulders with a large black kerchief and hobbled out into the stone streets of Vieux Lyon. As she crossed the bridge into modern Lyon, wind from the Alps gusted down the Rhône Valley, whipping her threadbare wool coat against her body. By a circuitous route, she returned to the street of her home. One could not be too careful despite past successes.

After four years of intense observation, she knew the Gestapo expected only naïve submissiveness from women. Apparently they could not imagine a French woman courageous enough to defy them or smart enough to deceive them. Their arrogant attitude allowed women like herself to complete Resistance assignments where no man would dare.

Once she had faced the Gestapo commander Klaus Barbie in his own office. He believed she was a simple housewife pleading for a pregnant friend who wanted to marry the imprisoned father of her baby. Her pleas had delayed the execution of the man just long enough for a group of resistants to rescue him while he was being transported from the prison to Gestapo headquarters. And Barbie had never connected her visits with the escape.

She smiled to herself, remembering, savoring again the heady sense of striking back at the enemy.

Across the street from her apartment building, she entered a café that recently had changed ownership. Sitting at a table by the window, she ordered a cup of roasted barley coffee from the *serveuse*. Beyond giving her order, she did not converse with the other woman. Talking to strangers was not safe, and although this woman may have noticed Giselle walking about in the neighborhood, it would be understood that neither of them would acknowledge the fact. She forced herself to maintain a calm, unhurried appearance despite her fear for Claude. Would he be in the apartment now? What if he wasn't? She could imagine the worst. Men often disappeared without a trace. Dread tied her empty stomach in a knot.

When the coffee came, Giselle sipped cautiously, barely managing not to shudder at its bitterness. She could only hope that whatever the cook had roasted in place of barley, it would not be a laxative, as were some concoctions she'd recently been served. Slowly draining the cup, she watched her apartment while pretending to read the newspaper, a propaganda piece put out by collaborators.

In the beginning of the occupation, the Nazi take-over of the papers and magazines had triggered the first acts of resistance all over France. She and Claude had helped print and distribute an underground paper containing the BBC news they'd heard on hidden radios. From that first desire for truth had grown the present carefully organized Resistance. It had taken only a few months to become a force against the enemy.

Giselle finished the cup of hot brew and stood up. To linger might attract attention. She left the café while the serveuse waited on another patron. Her walk to the end of the block before crossing the street gave her a few more minutes to survey her surroundings. Seeing nothing amiss, she crossed and entered the apartment building. She climbed the stairs, remaining alert as if walking through a minefield and proceeded quietly to her apartment door.

If Claude still is not here, I will go to the office of Dr. Remarque. Maybe Andre has taken him there. Even as she thought this, she realized the doctor could not let Claude stay after treatment. By this time he would have to be hiding somewhere else.

She listened at the apartment door. No sound came through. Quietly she fitted her key in the lock and turned it. Just as the door opened for her, the concierge called from the other end of the hall in a strained voice, "Ah, Madame Munier, you are home again at last."

Conditioned not to reveal surprise or fear, Giselle put a smile on her lips and turned around casually. Two uniformed men stood behind the concierge. Giselle's heart leaped and then fluttered like a trapped bird.

The men marched down the faded rose-patterned carpet toward her. The shorter one said in awkward French, *"Bonjour,* madame."

CHAPTER THREE

———— ★ ————

Late December 1943

An icy wind gusted through the man-made canyons of New York City the day after Christmas and fingered its way along the sheltered tracks at the train station. It did not, however, fully dispel the heavy odor of coal smoke and oil. Jean Thornton, in the dark blue winter uniform of the American Red Cross, edged forward in the slow line to the railroad car she was to board. Her large bags had been checked, and so all she carried was a musette bag, her overnight luggage.

Her friend, Mary O'Leary, who had been her roommate when she taught school at Tulelake Internment Camp in the wilderness of northern California, marched in front of her. They had volunteered together for Red Cross work, and so far, except for their internships, they had stayed together. Jean hoped they might end up at the same military station hospital.

Jean shivered and wished she could break the Red Cross dress code and tie a wool scarf over her head. Her military style cap offered no protection against the bitter wind. Mary's home was in upstate New York, and she seemed oblivious to the pervading chill. Jean called to her, "Is this freezing cold typical of New York winters?"

Mary nodded cheerfully. "With one variation. It also comes with sleet, snow, or freezing rain. It even comes with sunshine occasionally."

"No wonder you never complained about the cold at Tulelake."

"I told you I grew up on ice skates."

"What did you do in the summer?"

"Waited for winter."

"Well, you should be happy if we land in Scotland. I've heard it's a cold place."

"Ladies!" snapped an army sergeant in the next line. "Do not discuss destinations. Not even wild guesses."

"Yes, Sergeant," Jean said, stricken that she could have forgotten. Several of the soldiers with him stared at her with a not unfriendly gaze, but she was glad their two lines separated. She and the other Red Cross personnel boarded the coach to the right, and the sergeant and his men moved on to the left.

The car Jean entered was nearly full of soldiers, probably also headed for troop ships in Boston. Mary marched down the crowded aisle ahead of her. Her porcelain-fair skin and black hair inspired wolf whistles from soldiers they passed. Mary obeyed standing orders not to fraternize with the noncommissioned men, but Jean could see by the rounded curve of her cheek that she couldn't keep from smiling. At last they reached the middle of the car and sat down with the other Red Cross women.

Within minutes, the train lurched and rolled slowly out of the station. Jean leaned back to rest.

Mary, sitting beside her, with her usual directness, said, "You feeling okay? You sure look beat."

"Well, thanks! You look great too!"

"You know what I mean. You're always pretty. It's just that you look almost as tired as when you had pneumonia last winter."

Last winter, when I first realized I loved Tom. Without raising her head from the back of the seat, Jean turned her face toward Mary. "I guess I am tired. I haven't told you that Tom and I . . . that nothing is going to come of us. He . . . he's backed out."

"Oh, kid! I'm so sorry. That jerk!" Her expression hardened. "Why did he lead you on like he did?"

Jean shook her head. "I can't be angry. I wish I could, but I have to admit I lost my head . . . and I never gave him a chance to back out gently."

"Men! You must feel awful."

Jean forced a smile. "Well, you warned me about the danger of falling in love with a Japanese man, and you were right. Nothing could come of it."

Mary groaned. "I wish I'd been wrong."

"I wish I'd taken you seriously. No. That's not really true. I wouldn't trade anything for the moments when I thought he loved me."

Mary wriggled her feet and cleared her throat. "At the risk of sounding heartless, I have to say I think you're better off without him. I worried about you being insulted or even abused when you went out with him."

And I was, Jean thought. Not mindful of how she would sound to Mary, she snapped, "I really hate bigotry!"

Mary jumped and said, "Well, sure, kid. I didn't mean it that way."

"Oh, not you! You're not a bigot! I was thinking about my last day with Tom. When I kissed him hello in the train station, a soldier made a disgusting remark. I thought Tom was going to deck him, and I was so angry I wanted him to. Fortunately the guy's friends pulled him away, but only because they noticed that Tom outranked them." Remembering the ugly scene made her feel squeamish, as if she had touched something filthy. Tom had warned her such slurs would happen, but she hadn't wanted to believe him, just as she hadn't wanted to believe he didn't love her enough to marry her until he finally convinced her by cutting off contact with her. She sighed, unutterably tired. Her head felt as if it were swathed in thick rubber bands. "Please, let's talk about something else."

"Okay." Mary paused only for a moment. "I've been meaning to ask what you hear from your uncle Al, the late great senator from Oregon. Is he happy not being 'Senator Moore'?"

Jean welcomed the glimmer of laughter Mary's unexpected words provoked. "The Late Great is fine. I think he misses the Senate, but working for the State Department in London satisfies his desire to be more active in the war effort. He can't tell me anything about what he does, but he sends me a running report on life in London. He loves the British people."

"I hope you're saving his letters. They'll make good family history some day."

"You're a natural born teacher! What are you doing in the Red Cross anyway?"

Mary didn't laugh. "I'm serious. If he were my uncle, I'd save every letter."

"Well, I guess I have saved them. I just didn't think about it as a project. I've saved Dad's few letters too, even though he doesn't say much that anyone else would care about."

"And even though he hasn't cared enough to write very often."

"Well, that's Dad. He still doesn't write, despite the fact he has avoided alcohol for several years. I only write to him when he writes to me. I sent him my overseas address, but I doubt I will ever hear from him.

"Uncle Al was my father while Dad neglected me, and in some ways, Uncle Al still is. If he could have obtained permission from my father, he would have adopted me. He and Aunt Esther had no children. They loved my cousin Giselle too as if she were their own. Her mother Ruth was Aunt Esther's youngest sister. After Aunt Esther died, I went to live with Grandmother, but Uncle Al still spent time with me . . . in ways I'd always needed from Dad. Being my mom's only brother and she his only sister, I guess Uncle Al naturally felt close to me. He says I look a lot like my mom. She had green eyes and blondish brown hair too, and of course the black Thornton eyebrows. I think the resemblance stops with those three traits. She was pretty and Grandmother is handsome, but the combination didn't work as well on me."

"For pete's sake. Have you ever really looked in a mirror? You're beautiful."

"Cut it out! I was not asking for a compliment."

Mary gave her hard look. "I cannot let you get away with stupid remarks like that." She shifted on the seat and stretched her legs. "How old were you when your mother died?"

"Eight. I wish I could remember her better."

"Yeah. That's tough."

"Grandmother has lots of photos of Mom before she married Dad. After she was married, I guess they were too poor to take many. Dad must have been drinking then too."

"You sound a lot more forgiving than I could be."

"Do I? I don't know. Dad came back into my life when I was fifteen. Then I couldn't seem to get close to him." She had tried desperately at first. "Maybe it was my fault. Maybe I didn't really forgive him. All those years when I needed him so badly, he didn't even send me a postcard. And then when we were finally together, he yelled at me a lot. I kept thinking I could make him feel better. One day I told him he shouldn't blame himself for my brother Jimmy's death, and he really blew up at that. He said I didn't know anything about it, that he had given Jimmy the gun and had taught him to use it, and of course it was his fault. Then he yelled, 'Shut up.' So I did."

Mary's eyes widened and her mouth hung open. "You never told me you had a brother! No wonder it hit you so hard when you lost your fiancé, Dave, at Pearl Harbor. You had already lost so many people you loved!"

Jean drew in a deep breath and let it out slowly, hoping to clear her fuzzy thinking. "I'm sure you're right. I think new grief does rouse old grief."

"And now Tom. Knowing all this makes me all the angrier that he gave you the come-on and then hit the road."

Jean shook her head. "It wasn't that way at all. Really."

Mary glanced at her and asked hesitantly, "How old were you when you lost your brother?"

Jean had never discussed Jimmy's death with anyone but Giselle. Maybe talking about it would be a good thing. Lately she'd had some of the old nightmares. "I was nine. It's so long ago. I hadn't thought about him much until just lately. With the war on, I've been glad he doesn't have to be fighting in it. . . ." She straightened up in her seat and gazed out the window at soot-stained buildings passing by. "He was thirteen when he accidentally shot himself. I realize now that Dad couldn't get over Jimmy's death on top of losing Mom, but at fifteen I didn't understand that. I shouldn't have given up on him. But I did . . . then he started drinking again."

"But you've saved his letters."

"The three he wrote after he finally broke away from drinking—not many since. He apologized for abandoning me but insisted I was better off with Grandmother. He may be right, but she didn't have the memories of Jimmy and Mom that Dad and I could have shared. Even if he couldn't talk about them, it would have helped me to be with him. Grandmother couldn't bear to talk about Mom or about Jimmy. It was as if she'd never had a daughter or a grandson. I don't know what I would have done that first year after Jimmy died if it hadn't been for Giselle.

She was barely a teenager, yet she understood that I needed to talk about Jimmy and cry."

Mary looked about to weep. "You poor kid," she said, her eyes filling.

Mary's sympathy brought tears to Jean's eyes. She bit her lip to steady it and turned away. Shrugging out of her topcoat, she rolled it up and placed it in the small of her back before continuing. Clearing her throat, she said, "I hope it's normal for a kid to forget. After that first year, I stopped thinking about Jimmy all the time. Now, hard as I try, I can't remember much about him ... or about my mom. I only remember that Giselle, my cousin by marriage, became my big sister. I don't know how I would have managed without her."

"For pete's sake, I can't imagine how you managed at all, even with Giselle. But what about Giselle? Have you heard anything from her?"

Jean slowly shook her head. "Not a word. I can't bear to think that she could be in trouble...." As if fear could make bad things happen, she mentally pushed away the dread that always crouched on the edge of her thoughts of Giselle. "It must be that it's too dangerous to use the shortwave radio. Claude is very clever. He'd never take unnecessary risks."

Mary didn't say anything, but her silence spoke her doubts.

Jean leaned back and closed her eyes, wishing she could sleep. *Mary thinks I'm trying to whistle away my fears, and maybe I am, but I know Giselle is alive. I just know it.*

The *clackety-clack* of the railcar's wheels broke into Jean's thoughts, and she remembered that when she was a child, she had pretended that the rattling made words. She listened now, and the rhythm seemed to sing, *Giselle's alive. Giselle's alive.*

Yes! Jean agreed.

After a bit, she welcomed the drowsy feeling that crept over her in response to the repetitious sound.

Sometime later she awoke, hoping she hadn't cried out in her sleep. She had dreamed about Tom again. She was back at Tulelake Internment Camp, visiting him in the military jail. Only this time he knew the truth—she had spied on him and his friends for Uncle Al. In her dream Tom looked hurt instead of angry.

How could I have been so blind? she wondered. *Uncle Al was so sure the Japanese in the United States were a threat to national security, even though interned, and I went right along with him.* Early on, before she knew Tom, she had placed his name on a list of suspects and then could not get it removed. The dream brought back her guilt and grief intensified. She wished she could talk about it. Talking would get her back to reality, but Mary had never known that Jean was spying, and according to Uncle Al, she must never be told. *If I could talk to Giselle, I could tell her everything. More than anyone, she would understand how I feel about hurting Tom and about losing him.* Jean blinked her eyes to clear them and sat up straighter. Outside the train window, she saw warehouses and storage buildings.

"Providence, Rhode Island," Mary remarked. "It won't be long now." Her tone was pure groan.

"*C'est la guerre*," Jean teased. She could always get a rise out of Mary with a few French words, and Mary needed the distraction. She feared deep water and crossing the ocean by ship.

"You and your French! I prefer plain American. 'Kilroy was here' has a good ring to it. Anyway, it's an American's right to gripe. Keeps us in good fighting form."

Jean chuckled, grateful for Mary's dependable humor.

The next morning on the dock in Boston, Jean and Mary stood fully outfitted and ready to board ship. In addition to their winter uniforms with military style topcoats, they now wore GI combat helmets and web belts to hold their gas masks.

A local Red Cross volunteer offered them coffee and donuts. Jean set down her bedroll, musette bag, and suitcase and gratefully accepted. Sipping slowly, she warmed her hands on the cup. The hot brew seemed to seep into her veins and fortify her against the damp sea air.

At last orders came to board the ship. Jean trudged up the gangplank behind Mary and the dozen other Red Cross women. The USS *Argentina*, a converted cruise ship, would carry them with the army troops to the British Isles. They would not learn their assigned destination until after they docked on the other side of the Atlantic.

Within an hour, the ship weighed anchor, and tugboats eased it out into the harbor. Jean stood at the rail on the top deck, with Mary on one side and some of the ship's officers on the other, watching the receding skyline of Boston. The historic city seemed to back away and change from a real city to a flat cardboard stage prop. Then heavy gray clouds crushed the skyline until the sea swallowed it.

The throng of soldiers on the decks below grew so quiet Jean could hear the cry of the gulls flapping overhead. Their silence made her chest feel heavy and full of gray clouds too. It hit her hard—many of the men on this ship would not be coming home. She glanced at Mary. "It gives me a lost feeling to be going this way."

Mary tilted her head to one side. "Yes. It's more than leaving our families. It's—"

From the troop deck below, a soldier with a strong baritone voice began to sing, "God bless America. . . ."

More men joined in. Unpolished, untrained, they sang the popular Irving Berlin song the way he must have meant it to be sung. The last note hung in the air for an instant, and then a spontaneous cheer erupted and broke the emotional moment.

The women on the top deck blinked and swiped tears from their cheeks as the Red Cross supervisor called, "To quarters, ladies! Follow me."

Jean and Mary marched to the tiny rooms that would be their home at sea.

After they stowed their baggage in their cabin, they reported for orientation back on deck. A sailor handed a life preserver to each one with orders to keep it and a canteen of water always within reach. Then he took them to their assigned "abandon ship" station. "No matter where you go on this ship, you gotta know how to get back here fast," he warned. "And dress warmly at all times. That means you sleep in your clothes."

Jean thought she had the location clear in her mind, but a couple of hours later when they were called to abandon ship in the first practice drill, she couldn't find her station.

Afterward in their cabin Mary collapsed on her bunk and moaned, "I'm a born landlubber. I'd rather remain unprepared and try to forget I'm on a ship."

Jean laughed. "I'm just hoping our drills are always just for practice."

Four days out, the ocean turned rough, throwing the ship at the sky one moment and threatening to dash it to the depths the next. Sometimes Jean's stomach felt as if she were going down on a fast elevator. To her surprise, she didn't get seasick, but poor Mary retreated to her bunk too ill to even talk. Nothing Jean did for her gave Mary any relief.

The next three days ran together in a blur of continuous lunging, tipping, rocking, and falling. The ship seemed utterly at the mercy of the wind and mountainous waves. The stench of vomit spiraled up every stairwell from the troops below, and their own cabin wasn't a whole lot sweeter. Jean longed for fresh air, but it was too rough to go on deck. Whenever Mary slept, Jean retreated to the empty recreation room.

She was the only woman who ate in the officers' mess. The second day of rough sea the first mate lurched against her table and caught himself on its railing. All the dishes slid to the far side of the table. Through the rain-washed windows, Jean could see only angry gray. The next minute only dark foam-streaked water was visible as the ship dropped into a giant trough, and the tableware and dishes slid and banged on the opposite side.

The first mate laughed. "You must have sailing in your blood to be able to eat during this storm."

Jean smiled. "I don't know, but I'm glad for whatever keeps me from getting sick. Are we making any progress bobbing around like this?"

He nodded. "More than it may seem. But one good thing is that we make a lousy target for U-boats."

"Are we in submarine territory?"

"Technically speaking, we always are, but the closer we get to Britain, the greater the risk. Don't worry, though. We're not sitting ducks. We've got good protection in this convoy."

"Thanks for telling me. It's reassuring to know the storm has its good points."

When she returned to the cabin, she told Mary.

Mary only groaned.

Late the third day, the wind finally stopped and the ocean gradually settled to more normal swells. The next afternoon a misty calm flattened the sea. Mary began to feel a little better, but her naturally pale complexion accentuated the dark circles under her eyes.

"You need some fresh air. Come out on deck with me," Jean said.

Reluctantly, Mary agreed.

They had walked for only a short time when one of their escort destroyers suddenly put on speed, veered away, and turned back into their ship's wake. Another escort ship moved closer to the troop ship to fill the gap. Looking back at the retreating destroyer, Jean saw a line of white foam inscribed on the dark sea. She pointed. "Look! Is that a periscope?"

Mary turned paler than ever. "Looks just like what I've seen in newsreels!"

As they watched, the white line suddenly faded and disappeared. The destroyer raced to the area where the sub had dived and circled. White geysers burst from the ocean in its wake.

"Depth charges," Jean said, breathless from an adrenaline rush.

"Yeah!"

They clung to the rail, uncertain where the safest place would be if a torpedo struck. An officer ran by and shouted them off the deck. Wondering if at any moment their ship would be rocked by an explosion, they hurried to the recreation room.

The floor sloped as the ship turned hard. Soon it tilted the opposite direction.

Mary pressed one hand against her stomach. "I need to go out on the deck again."

"Soon as the ship hits a straight course, we'll pretend we don't know any better and go out."

Minutes passed. Evasive maneuvers continued. Mary gave up and staggered to the cabin.

Jean went along. "You've got to keep your life jacket on."

Mary groaned but didn't argue. Jean helped her lie down and pulled a blanket up over her. "Your canteen is here where you can reach it. Don't forget it if we . . . have to leave in a hurry."

"Right." Mary did not open her eyes.

Jean grabbed her hand and guided it to the canteen.

"Got it," Mary said with eyes still closed.

"Will you be okay if I go out again?"

"Sure."

Jean quietly let herself out into the companionway and sneaked back on deck. In a niche over an air duct from the engine room, she crouched in the warm draft, hidden from the view of tense-faced sailors who ran from task to task. The faint odor of engine diesel was more comforting than offensive. She waited and watched, ready to dash for Mary if anything happened.

After dark Jean went to dinner. Again she was the only woman eating. The men came in small groups, gobbled their food, and left.

The first mate paused beside her. "You know there was a U-boat out there."

She nodded. "I think I saw its periscope."

"Word is that we've scared it away. We'll probably still change course a lot during the night, but don't let the movement worry you. It's just a precaution."

She smiled, knowing that might not be the case but appreciating his concern for her. "Sure. Thanks." Her voice came out calmer than she felt. Soon Jean sat alone. All hands were on alert, watching and ready to act.

Returning to the cabin, she felt her way around in the dark and ran her fingers over the black-out cover on the porthole to make sure it was secure. Then she clicked on her flashlight, taking care to aim the beam at the floor. Mary, surprisingly, seemed to be sleeping. Jean placed her canteen beside her bunk and lay down fully clothed and wearing her life jacket.

Instinctively she felt for the small gold locket around her neck. Tom had given her this small oval embossed with wild roses and had refused to take it back. She still wore it because it was so lovely. At least that's what she told herself. Her fingers closed around the metal, as warm from her skin as if it had a life of its own. *If only we could have continued. . . .* Continued what? He did not love her. And yet, right now, if her life should end here on the high seas, it was somehow important that she loved him. To comfort herself, she thought about the way his whole face had seemed to light up with delight when he smiled at her. *If I could feel his arms around me now, I wouldn't be so scared.* She remembered the way he had talked about praying, as if talking to God were as natural as talking to her. The few times she'd heard him pray, he had sounded as though he were conversing with a good friend.

An army chaplain had said there were no atheists in foxholes, but Tom had good, strong, everyday faith, while she—she didn't mean to be a person who only called on God when facing death, but she had not been to church or a chapel service since breaking up with Tom. Whenever she prayed, God seemed so far away. Tom would say it was she who was away from God.

She pulled her grandmother's Bible from the shelf beside her bunk. By the glow of her flashlight she opened the leather-bound book and began to search for words that might help her feel closer to God, less scared, if that were possible. Her grandmother had taken her to Sunday school and church, but it wasn't until she met Pastor Ichiba at Tulelake that she had grown in her own faith. Tom and Pastor Ichiba both had prayed as if they were conversing with someone right beside them.

Grandmother was more reserved about expressing her belief in God. However, she often said there was a psalm to fit every problem. Now Jean read the Twenty-third Psalm. It had been her favorite after Jimmy died. It had comforted her to imagine Jimmy in the House of the Lord, which she thought must be the most wonderful castle, filled with everything a boy could want.

When she finished the Shepherd's Psalm, she noticed a thin slip of paper barely visible marking another place. She opened to that page and read a carefully underlined verse. *"If I take the wings of the morning, and dwell in the uttermost parts of the sea; even there shall thy hand lead me, and thy right hand shall hold me...."*

How beautiful! Did Grandmother mark this for me? In her mind's eye she could see Grandmother's dignified expression soften the way it often did when Jean had given her an unexpected hug or kiss. *Thanks, Grandmother!* Without thinking or trying, she prayed. *Oh, God, please hold us close—Grandmother, Giselle, Claude, the girls, Uncle Al, and Tom, wherever he is.*

Jean closed the Bible and laid it back on the shelf, then rested her head uneasily on her pillow. She tried to think of God the Father surrounding them all with His care. Yet she knew that in wartime many people prayed for their loved ones, and still many died. She must learn to accept that whatever happened God was with her and from God's viewpoint, dying was not the worst thing that could happen to her. She wanted to believe this, but every part of her being cried, *No, I want to live! I want to see Tom again!*

Staring into blackness with the distant throb of the ship's

engine vibrating the metal hull close to her ear, she imagined that somewhere in the depths below there were men in a submarine who were listening and waiting for the first light of dawn to illuminate their target.

CHAPTER FOUR

But the convoy lost the submarine in the night and so without threat sailed on to Glasgow, Scotland. Once safely docked, it took four days for the troops to disembark.

For some reason Jean did not understand, there was no hot water for bathing now that they were in port. Neither was there normal dining. They ate cold food, same as the troops who were gradually being moved to trains. Tempers among the young Red Cross women frayed. It reminded Jean of her college days and the tiffs that went on in the dorms before spring finals. She and Mary escaped to the deck as often as possible.

One day they managed to get some war news from a deck-hand who had been on shore and brought back a Glasgow newspaper. They read it quickly while leaning against the railing. Soon he returned and took the paper to give to his buddies.

As she watched the slow disembarking of troops, Jean said, "I had hoped the invasion of Italy would go easier after the Italians surrendered back in September. After that one city joined the Allies and fought nearly to the death, I thought the whole country might be ready to help the Allies when they landed."

"Well, I guess many still wish they could. Looks like the Germans were running the show the whole time, and you and I will have our jobs here in England helping with the wounded for quite a while. I wonder when the second front will start."

"I'm sure Hitler is contemplating that very thing."

"*Ja. Der Fuehrer.*" Mary pulled her black hair down across her left eyebrow and held her finger under her nose to suggest the dictator's mustache. She assumed a foolish pose that created a startling resemblance to some caricatures of Hitler they'd laughed at in the States.

Jean giggled. "You'd better not do that when we get off this ship. Some angry Brit might take a potshot at you. Are you ready to go check in with our supervisor again?"

"No. But we'd better."

Reluctantly they returned below deck.

The next day they finally disembarked and boarded a train. Here Jean learned their destination was Abergavenny, a market town in Wales close to large military station hospitals. The station doctors gave immediate care to the wounded, then decided which patients needed to be sent home for more care than they could give, and which ones could stay in Abergavenny to heal and be returned to battle.

The train traveled all night with black-out shades pulled down, so Jean saw nothing of Britain or the British people. Finally at six in the morning the train stopped, and a conductor walked through announcing their arrival in Abergavenny. Jean climbed off the train behind Mary and welcomed the fresh air of hill country as rain-washed as Oregon. Her eyes burned from lack of sleep. She'd scarcely dozed in more than twenty-four hours. She didn't know what she needed worse, sleep or a good hot bath and some clean clothes.

On the boarding platform, a Welsh woman with graying blond hair tucked under a knitted cap smiled warmly and called, "Welcome to Wales! We're so glad you've come!" Her breath made small puffs of white in the cold air. On a trolley beside her sat large pots of coffee and tea and trays of donuts and cookies.

Jean walked over. "Thank you. We're glad to be here. Oh, how I need a cup of tea." She reached for the mug the woman held out and took a sip. As she drank, the warm steam from the tea soothed her sleepy eyes.

"I do hope the ride was not too rough," the woman said. "These wartime trains..." She ended with a sympathetic shake of her head and gestured to a tray of cookies. "You'll be wanting some biscuits with your tea. Not as good as a hot breakfast, but they'll give you a bit of a lift."

"Thank you. Do you often meet the trains?"

The woman nodded. "Someone from our congregation usually comes. It's the least we can do."

"Your congregation?"

"Presbyterian. I'm the minister's wife, Elizabeth MacDougall. Please come for tea at the manse when you can. The door is always open."

Jean glanced at Mary, wondering if she, a Catholic, would feel all right visiting a Protestant manse. Mary smiled. "I'll be looking forward to that."

At Mary's signal, Mrs. MacDougall poured her a mug of coffee. "You'll be missing a real home. Those Nissen huts can't be that comfortable, made of corrugated metal like they are, and looking like an oil drum cut in half and laid open to the ground."

"Oh," Jean said. "They must be like our Quonset huts. So that's what we'll live in."

"Aye, from what I've seen. Don't understand why they couldn't have constructed brick barracks for you, same as they have for the hospital wards."

"We'll be fine, I'm sure. This hot tea is wonderful. Thanks again."

"Here, lass, have some more." Mrs. MacDougall's tone softened. "You have a look my daughter Nella gets when she's worn to a frazzle."

Her personal concern warmed Jean. She had an uncanny feeling that she already knew this woman. Hoping to extend the conversation, Jean asked, "Is your daughter living at home?"

Mrs. MacDougall, glancing down while she filled Jean's mug, said with undisguised pride, "Our Nella did her part in the WAAF. That's the Women's Auxiliary Air Force. Before the war we wouldn't have thought to let her go off like that at her age, barely eighteen, but we're all doing things we never thought we would, aren't we?" Smiling, she gazed at Jean again with friendly warmth. "Will you come by the manse to visit? Nella's husband was killed in action, and she's home now with her baby. She gets a mite lonely and would love to meet you."

Still wondering why she felt so drawn to this Welsh woman, Jean said, "Why yes. I'd love to." As an afterthought she added, "My name is Jean Thornton."

"Miss Thornton, a pleasure! When you get settled, just do come."

Mary, a few feet away, called, "Jean, our ride is here."

With a final thank-you, Jean hurried to the personnel carrier and climbed aboard. As they drove down the hill and across a wet, winter-green valley, she felt oddly settled, as if she had come home instead of having just arrived in a foreign country. Was it because Wales looked a little like western Oregon? Or was it because of the friendly welcome from Elizabeth MacDougall? She found herself looking forward to meeting the lady of the manse again.

Jean was astonished at the size of the military station hospitals. About two miles from Abergavenny, hundreds of brick barracks formed vast communities much larger than the villages they surrounded and covered acres of pastureland. Jean settled into a Nissen hut with six other Red Cross women at Govilon on the banks of the Brecon Canal where long narrow barges carried coal to Newport. Mary was assigned to an identical hut two miles away below the village of Gilwern on the banks of the Usk River.

Jean decided right away that when she could, she'd meet Mary and hike along the river. Because of her art background, she habitually studied land, details of vegetation, and the lighting of the sun at different times of the day. She looked forward to bringing along a sketch pad as soon as the weather was favorable.

One day while they were hiking, Jean remarked to Mary, "Wales is much tidier than Oregon. These stone walls and trimmed hedgerows are lovely. Around Salem farmers use a lot of barbed wire and no one would think of taking time to trim wild bushes at the edges of fields."

"Same with my part of New York. Have you noticed there are no evergreen trees here? I wonder if there ever have been."

"You're right. I haven't seen any at all!"

While Mary wasn't into drawing and painting, she was alert to the possibilities for Jean. Each time they walked, they discovered both new and familiar trees and bushes, but no evergreens of any kind. Jean wondered if they had evergreen trees at Christmas. Surely they did. She'd ask Elizabeth MacDougall the next time she saw her.

Jean hitched a ride to the gray stone manse in Abergavenny the first time partly as a courtesy and partly because she wanted to get acquainted with Elizabeth MacDougall and her daughter. Driving took only ten minutes. On her old used bike it would have taken more like twenty or thirty. A young woman opened the door at Jean's knock. Her face brightened with friendly surprise when she saw Jean. *This must be Nella,* Jean thought. With her curling reddish blond hair in a short halo around her face, she looked like a schoolgirl. Her baby stood shyly just behind her, clinging to a fold of her woolen skirt. About two years old, the little one possessed the same fair skin and pink cheeks and paler red-gold curls. She could imagine them as mother and child in a Renoir painting.

"Hello. I'm Jean Thornton from the military hospital. I met your mother at the train station when I arrived."

"Oh, Miss Thornton. Do come in," Nella said, throwing the heavy door open wide. "Mum told me about you, and I was so hoping you'd visit us. I'm Nella Killian." She turned to the baby. "Livie, this is Miss Thornton. Miss Thornton, this is our Olivia, but we call her Livie."

"Hello, Livie. I'm happy to meet you," Jean said.

The baby smiled a small replica of her mother's bright smile and then shyly tucked her chin down.

"Please come in, and I'll tell Mum you're here then."

She escorted Jean into a roomy parlor off the center hall and gestured toward an upholstered chair near a large enameled heating stove, which radiated comfort after the blustery rain outside. "Let me hang your coat, and please be seated. Can you stay long enough for a cuppa?"

"Yes, I'd like that. Thank you." Jean handed her coat to Nella, then held her cold hands out to the stove.

Nella nodded. "You soak up some warmth, and I'll be right back with the tea." As she left, Nella whisked the baby away too, leading her by the hand and calling, "Mum, we've a guest. Miss Thornton has stopped by."

Jean leaned back and let the quietness of the manse soothe her. This formal room with its high ceiling felt like an island of peace after the hubbub of settling into the Nissen hut with the other women and learning her way around the sprawling station hospital. In this solidly built home, she could barely hear the distant voices of Nella and Elizabeth. She thought about Nella, who looked so young to be a widow. She wondered how old she was. Twenty? Surely no more than twenty-one.

Elizabeth hurried in and held out a welcoming hand. "My dear, I'm so glad to see you. Nella is bringing us tea. Tell me, are you comfortable enough in those terrible huts? Is there anything we can provide for you and your friends?"

"Oh, we're fine. Quite comfortable, really. But thank you for asking." Jean already knew she had access to more food and personal items from the post exchange than the British had. It touched her that they wanted so much to help when they possessed so little themselves.

Nella returned carrying a tray of cups, cream pitcher, sugar bowl, small muffins, and what looked like a jar filled with honey.

"Set it on the trolley, dear, and roll it all over here near the stove. Did you bring a bit for Livie too?"

Jean could hear a subtle change in Elizabeth's voice—a switch to the tone mothers use when addressing a child. She glanced at Nella and saw the sunbeam smile fade, but the girl answered cheerily.

"Sure did, Mum." With Livie following like an eager puppy, Nella loaded an ornate wooden tea trolley and pushed it close to Jean's chair. "I'll be right back with the tea. Livie, you stay with Gamma, please."

"Yes. Bring your chair over here, dear."

The toddler trotted across the room carrying a miniature chair over to her grandmother's side and sat upon it.

Elizabeth smiled. "She's such a dear—so much like her mother. It's a joy to have them here despite the sad reason." She lowered her voice. "Nella seems hardly able to get over her loss. I worry about her.... But there, I didn't mean to talk about us. I want to know all about you and your work and how things are going at the hospital. Our church tries to help out the soldiers any way it can."

Nella returned and poured them steaming cups of tea. For Livie she poured a few drops of tea into a half cup of milk. Then she poured for herself, drew up a chair, and sat.

Jean chatted with the two women as comfortably as if she'd

known them for a long time. After a few minutes, a sturdy man with closely clipped curly gray hair appeared in the doorway of the parlor.

"Hallo. I was sure it was time for tea. We've got company, I see."

"Ian, come meet Jean Thornton from America," Elizabeth said.

Nella stood up and lifted the tea cozy from the china pot. "I brought an extra cup, Daddy, thinking you might be coming."

"Ian, this is Jean, the lovely young lady I told you about meeting at the train recently. She works for the Red Cross at the military hospital." She turned to Jean. "Which one is it, dear?"

"At Govilon. How do you do, Reverend MacDougall?"

He walked over and clasped her hand with a firm warm grip. "Just fine, thank you. How do you do? You're a long way from home, lass."

"I am at that. My home is on the west coast of the United States in Oregon."

"Well, I hope you'll soon feel at home here. We're so glad you've come." He took his tea cup from Nella and sat in a nearby upholstered chair. Settling back, he let out a sigh of comfort and then said, "What do you do in your position with the Red Cross?"

"I'm a recreational therapist. There are several of us here, and we assist the injured men in their recoveries. When they arrive, we give them packages of personal items and help them notify their loved ones that they are here. In a way, we are like a bit of family for them while they're away from home. For those who are disabled, we write letters, make phone calls, even send cablegrams. And our staff provides activities like movies and special music for the men in the wards confined to their beds. When patients become ambulatory, we hold daily activities in the recreation hall. For the guys who are nearly well, we become tour guides for excursions to places like the White Castle and Tintern Abbey."

"Well, now, you sound like you're a nurse for the soul," Ian declared.

"I wish I were a nurse. I was a schoolteacher, but the Red Cross gave me the opportunity to do something more directly helpful for the men, and I've been glad to do it."

"Good for you." Ian had finished his tea while she spoke. Now he stood up. "Please let us know if you need anything. Our parishioners are eager to help. We have some fine singing groups if you want a bit of music on an evening."

"Thank you. I'll remember that."

He knelt beside Livie. "How's my big girl this afternoon? Got a kiss for Gumpa?"

She kissed him and he kissed her back. Smiling, he rose to his feet. "Well, ladies, thank you for the tea and biscuit. Elizabeth, I'm going with Colin to Newport. He thinks he can get us a used fan to circulate the heat in that downstairs Sunday school room. I'll be past supper, no doubt. Jean, I'm very pleased to have met you. Please come again. And if you're free and of a mind to, we'd all be happy to see you at church services on Sundays."

"Thank you. I will come when I can."

"Do take care, dear, with the blackout and all, and that old car," Elizabeth cautioned.

"Bye, Daddy," Nella called, then grew quiet, seemingly lost in her own thoughts. Her mother made a failing attempt to draw her into the conversation again.

Jean wished she wouldn't. Having known deep grief herself, she felt Nella needed the freedom to be quiet when she felt like it. Then she chided herself. How could she know about a Welsh woman she'd just met? She had no right to put herself in Nella's place. Feeling a bit awkward but hoping to get attention off Nella, she asked about some of the plants and trees in Wales that were new to her.

Nella returned to herself, exclaiming, "You notice these things then? So many people don't. They only notice the castles and old pubs and bridges. Me, I love the growing things too."

"I like to draw and paint, so I'm always looking at details. Growing things fascinate me. My biggest surprise when I arrived was how much this part of Wales looks like western Oregon where I grew up ... except for the lack of evergreen trees, like pines or fir or spruce. I haven't seen any even in people's yards as ornamentals."

"That's so," Nella said. "In other parts of Britain, you'll find some evergreens, but they are rare here. And for Christmas an evergreen tree is an extravagance. Last Christmas we worked hard to set up such trees for the hospital wards, but mostly we decorated leafless branches and holly."

Elizabeth handed Livie a piece of muffin and said, "I hope you won't be getting homesick for your Oregon trees."

Jean shook her head and laughed. "I don't think so. I love these serene hills and valleys, even though the leaves are all gone right now."

"Well, now, I'm glad of that." Elizabeth's caring attitude reminded Jean of Giselle. Her cousin and this woman had much in common and would like each other if they ever could meet. On impulse Jean told her about Giselle and that she had not heard a word from her French cousin in weeks.

Elizabeth sobered, her kind face lined with concern. "She's in occupied France?"

"In Lyon. At first she sent messages with men who escaped to England. Then through the Resistance, her husband Claude sent shortwave messages to operators in England. But last fall the shortwave messages stopped. I've been really worried."

"I should say so!" Elizabeth exclaimed. "Would you like our church to be praying for Giselle and her family?"

"Oh, would you? I'd be so glad." Jean mentally stumbled over her own doubts, thinking, *Pray for what? Pray how?*

Nella sipped her tea and said nothing.

Hesitantly Jean admitted, "Sometimes when I pray, I really don't know what to say."

"God doesn't always need our words," Elizabeth said. "He answers our heart messages too. Remember Dunkirk, when the British army was trapped on the beach and every floating vessel in Britain crossed the channel to rescue our men?"

"Yes. I listened every day to the radio."

"Well, everybody in Britain prayed for our trapped men, and we were so distressed, I think we just babbled to God. Yet He protected and saved our men. Beyond that, I had a very personal answer."

Nella stood up abruptly. Suddenly she looked much older than twenty. "Excuse me. I'll go get more tea while you tell Miss Thornton the story."

"Dear, I know how you feel about losing Rob, but God did do something that night for our Charles. And while I've no answer for why he didn't do the same for Rob, still I must attribute this one thing to God's hand."

Jean wanted to ask Elizabeth to tell her some other time, but courtesy demanded that she remain silent. Nella left and Elizabeth turned to her.

"Our Charles was at Dunkirk, or at least we thought he was. But on the night of the second day our boys were stranded there, I woke up with a terrible fear for him. I had dreamed he was alone and lost. In my dream I saw him about to go into a village for help, and I could also see a truck full of German soldiers entering the village from the opposite direction. It was so real, I woke up my husband and said, 'We must pray for Charles! Right now!' Ian climbed out of bed and knelt with me. We didn't know what to pray or how to pray. We just agonized over our boy. After a while we both felt we could stop. It was about two in the morning.

"Two days later, Charles called from London. He said he had been separated from his squadron when France fell and had walked alone for two nights through fields and pastures, hiding in the daytime. Then, two nights earlier—the night we prayed— he discovered that he had been walking in a great circle. He would have to ask for directions. He started toward a dark village, then suddenly stepped into a deep hole of some kind. He injured his knee so badly he couldn't walk. He dragged himself to the side of the road, hoping he would not be found by the Germans.

"Soon a man appeared at his side. He was a farmer from the other side of the village. The man splinted his leg, helped him hobble to a nearby barn, brought him food, and found someone to drive him to the beach. Charles said to us, 'Can you imagine a tired French farmer waking up in the middle of the night and deciding to walk a few kilometers to a certain road without knowing why? That's how the man said he found me. He had to have left his home at least half an hour before I hurt my leg!'"

Excited, Jean said, "You believe your prayers awakened the farmer then?"

Elizabeth nodded. "God awakened the farmer. And God saved our men at Dunkirk. And for reasons I don't presume to understand, in both cases I'm certain God wanted us to pray."

"Even though you were scared, you had faith."

"Faith is turning to God for help. Fears are only feelings."

Jean nodded slowly. "That makes sense. I've been afraid that my fears for Giselle might somehow cancel out my prayers for her!"

Nella returned and poured them fresh cups of tea. Elizabeth stirred in canned milk and sipped her tea while Nella sat down again. Then the mother quietly responded to Jean's remark. "It's easy to start thinking that God is notional, like us. Scary thought, that."

This woman's faith amazed Jean. She blurted out, "But have you ever prayed and then something bad happened?" Suddenly she realized that must have been what happened for Nella. She wanted to apologize, but Nella had turned to help Livie with her tea, and it seemed best to let the gaffe go.

Elizabeth didn't seem to notice her blunder and answered Jean's question. "Well, I thought so at the time, but good always came in the end."

Jean thought of Jimmy's death. Nothing good had ever come of that. "Even things like children being killed?"

Pain flashed over Elizabeth's kind face. "Aye, that's the hard one. That's where faith must work."

"I lost my brother Jimmy when I was nine."

Nella straightened from tending Livie and gave her a stricken look.

Again Jean wanted to take back her thoughtless words. How could she have been so inconsiderate as to mention the death of a child?

"I am that sorry!" Elizabeth exclaimed. "How did it happen?"

"For Jimmy's birthday Daddy had given him a small shotgun for shooting pheasants and quail. We lived in a rural community where he could hunt in the nearby woods. Daddy had trained him carefully. We were poor, and it was a treat to have fresh game."

She moved her thoughts away from why they were so poor. Her father had spent most evenings at the local tavern. "The day of the accident, Daddy wasn't home, and I begged to go hunting with Jimmy when he picked up his gun. He didn't want to take me, but he knew how I hated being left alone. We had to go through a barbed wire fence. When he bent over to hold the wires apart for me, he leaned his gun against a tree trunk. It started to fall toward me. He grabbed for it and must have clutched the trigger. It went off and hit him. . . ." The memory still hurt. She began to feel the cold horror somewhere deep in her chest. Hurriedly she finished. "I stood there paralyzed, unable to run for help." She pushed the scene from her mind and said, "His death made me hate guns."

Nella, gazing at Livie, said, "Sure and it would."

"I'm sorry. I didn't mean to bring up this story," Jean said. "It happened long ago, and I've had a good life. It's just that the war has made me think more about Jimmy than I have in years. I'm glad I'm a woman and don't have to decide whether to take up arms."

"I've thought of that myself," Nella said, "but in a war it becomes easy to hate."

"Yes," Jean agreed.

"And if you hate, you can kill."

Jean suppressed a shudder, but her face must have shown her aversion.

Nella looked at Livie. "I think I could kill if someone threatened my child. Sometimes I even think I could kill any German soldier if I had the chance."

"I think we cannot know what we would do, but war changes people, even us women," Elizabeth said. She reached out and patted Jean's shoulder. "We are thoughtless to be talking about hate and killing, with you remembering your brother like that." She turned to Nella. "I'm that sorry that my girl can think of killing anyone. It's not a woman's place to pick up a weapon. But to want to—that's another tragedy of war."

"I hope I never shall face the need, Mum. But it's a fact that sometimes I'm so angry I feel I could kill." Then she smiled. "Don't worry. In Abergavenny I'll sure not be seeing a need. Jean, tell us about your brother. What was Jimmy like?"

"He was a good big brother. Our mother died when I was eight, and he took care of me when Daddy had to be gone." No need to mention that her father was sometimes home in bed drunk. "I thought Jimmy was handsome and could do anything. I always went to him for help. He mended my doll when her arm came off. Once he made me a doll buggy out of old tricycle wheels and an apple crate. I . . . I'm sorry I can't remember as much as I wish about Jimmy, but he was my hero."

"That's how I felt about my Rob. My hero—he'd do anything for me. I'd say you remember what is important."

Jean sipped her tea and sorted her thoughts. When she set her cup down, she said, "After Jimmy died, my cousin Giselle helped me get through the intense grief by remembering the happy times I'd had with Jimmy. I hope you can do that too, Nella."

"I do. Most of the time. Yet for Livie's sake, I must never forget how he died for our country—for us."

"Have you written down anything for her?"

"Well, I'm not much of a writer, but I do have a diary I keep adding to."

"That's good." Jean glanced at her watch. "Oh!" She straightened and stood up. "This has been wonderful, but I have to go meet my ride. Thanks so much for the tea. I'm indeed renewed."

Nella and Elizabeth walked her to the door, and Nella followed her to the front gate. Elizabeth waved and closed the door.

"Do you ever have time off to go walking?" Nella asked. "I could tell you about the trees and plants, you know."

Her offer caught Jean off guard, but she said, "Why yes. I do have some free time. I could ring you up and meet you somewhere. I'd like that." The more she thought about it, the better she liked the idea. She had taken to Nella the same way she'd taken to Elizabeth. And Nella obviously needed someone to talk to besides her mother.

Later, while her driver Eddy escorted her back to the station hospital in an ambulance—the only available conveyance at the time—Jean thought again about how Elizabeth had responded as Giselle would have. Although much older, the minister's wife was like Giselle in some ways. *That's why I felt I already knew her,* Jean concluded.

Jean attended the Presbyterian church every Sunday that she could. Elizabeth and Nella introduced her to many members, and she quickly felt at home among the congregation. The service was more formal than in her grandmother's church, yet at the same time there was more warmth.

One Sunday afternoon when it wasn't raining, Jean stayed for lunch in the manse and then went with Nella to walk along the Usk River. They hiked upstream, climbing over stiles and crossing farm pastures. There was no real trail to follow. Beside them the river flowed dark and swift. Nella paused, picked up a broken limb, and began to remove the small twigs to turn it into a walking stick. She glanced shyly at Jean. "I'm real glad you took me up on the walking."

"Me too! I love it out here."

They walked on in a comfortable silence awhile. Then Nella asked, "Do you ever wonder about death and why some are spared and others not?"

"Yes. I wonder about it a lot. When I lost my fiancé, I was very angry for a long time. It seemed so unfair."

"You lost your fiancé!"

"Yes. Just three weeks before our wedding. He was killed during the bombing of Pearl Harbor."

Nella turned toward her with a compassionate look. "I'm sorry."

"Well, it was hard, but different from you losing Rob . . . and leaving you with Livie to care for."

"Livie . . . well, she gave me the heart to keep on." Nella tested her walking stick, tapping it on the grass turf. "It hurts to have no one to talk to about Rob. Mum thinks I grieve too much, but I just want to remember him, like you said."

"Of course you do! I'd love to hear about how you and Rob first met."

A dreamy look came over Nella's face. "It was in the winter after the London blitz began. Mum and Dad had let me join the WAAF, and I'd finished my training. I was a driver in Suffolk. One day I had orders to pick up some pilots in Portsmouth and transport them to an airstrip east of Westminster. It was my first assignment alone, and I was that nervous."

While Nella talked, she took a path that led closer to the riverbank. She flashed Jean her wide smile. "The men, they saw how easily I blushed, and they were for having a bit of fun with me. But there was a tall sandy-haired man with a gentle smile who, seeing I was quite rattled, made them back off. He had the bluest of blue eyes."

She talked about dates with Rob, their secret marriage, and that when she learned she was expecting Livie, she'd had to leave the WAAF. And then Rob's plane went down.

Nella paused beside the fence they were about to climb over and poked at the rickety stile to test it. Suddenly she exclaimed,

"Oh, I promised to tell you about the trees and growing things, and here I've just been going on about myself."

"That's okay. Please go on. I love hearing about Rob."

Nella obeyed, obviously hungry to have someone listen who would not be distressed. As they walked, she talked. Finally she turned back toward Abergavenny.

Despite Jean's interest in Nella's memories, her thoughts repeatedly strayed to Tom and to her fiancé, David. She loved them both. She always would love David, but he was gone, and Tom had filled empty places in her soul. She wasn't the same person as the one who had been about to marry David. He seemed now like a tenderly remembered childhood sweetheart.

For a while after Tom had broken off from her, she'd clung to the hope that he might change his mind and at least write to her, but now she knew he never would. Her undying need of him had tormented her one moment with sorrow and the next with anger over the prejudice that had separated them. Jean forced her attention back to what Nella was saying about her tiny apartment near the Royal Air Force airstrip. Then her thoughts returned to Tom again. Was he overseas now?

No! She would not dwell on Tom. One way to push Tom out of her thoughts was to think about Giselle. Sometimes she wished, crazy as it sounded, that she'd been living with Giselle when France fell. She nearly had been, but Uncle Al had changed his mind about letting her study another year in Lyon. He'd had his mind set on her finishing high school in the States. Later he said he'd been right, what with the stories coming out of France about the imprisonment, torture, and execution of civilians, as well as the thousands being sent to concentration camps. The news had filled Jean with such rage that she envied Giselle's opportunities to work with the Resistance.

Now here she was with Nella in this peaceful Welsh valley, safe and a long way from the war compared to what Giselle was facing. She wished again that she could do more.

Nella's words penetrated Jean's wandering thoughts. "It's been hard lately, when I find myself angry at my father's God."

"Your father's God? Don't you believe in God?" Jean asked gently.

"I can't not believe, but I'm so angry I want to yell and scream, 'Why doesn't God stop this war?'"

"I've felt the same way."

"You don't now?"

"Well, I've found some peace."

"How? How can I find peace with the way things are? How can I help Livie find faith and peace when I feel so abandoned?"

"It takes time." They had reached Abergavenny, and Jean came to a halt at the steps of the Swan Hotel where she would catch a ride back to Govilon. "Nella, don't let anyone hurry you about getting over the grieving. Feel what you have to feel. Then slowly your pain will ease."

"Thanks for not preaching at me or trying to encourage me. It really helps. Will you go walking with me again sometime?"

"Sure thing. I'll telephone you when I have time off."

"Bye, then. Thanks again."

"You're welcome. Thank you for showing me your country."

As she watched Nella stride on up the narrow street and disappear around the curve, Jean thought again of Giselle, this time about what a comfort her cousin had been when Jimmy died. *I wish I could help Nella that much,* she thought wistfully.

That evening after the men left the rec hall for mess call, Jean put away the board games, moved card tables to the side of the long room, and arranged chairs for the movie.

She set up the screen and the projector, turned off the lights, and gave *They All Kissed the Bride* a brief test run. Then she rewound the film, got it ready to start, and switched the lights back on.

The door behind her opened. She didn't turn, supposing one of the men had returned for some forgotten thing.

Then she heard a familiar voice.

"Jeanie . . ."

"Uncle Al!" She whirled around.

He didn't smile. He was thinner and dark half-circles under his eyes made his face look gaunt. Two men in uniform stood respectfully beside him.

"What is it?" Her heart began to race. "Have you heard from Giselle?"

He shook his head. "Not from her . . . but news about her."

CHAPTER FIVE

Jean's mind froze at Uncle Al's words and the look on his face. She made her feet move toward him. "What? What have you heard?"

"She's in hiding."

"Oh, thank God." Her thoughts began to connect rationally again.

His face remained somber. "She and Claude were captured... and tortured before the resistants freed them."

Jean almost choked. "Oh no! Is Giselle okay? What about the children?"

Uncle Al reached out and took her hand. "The children were safely hidden before the arrest. As for Giselle—she's alive and in a safe place. We can be thankful for that."

Slowly she said, "Then she's not okay."

"She..." In a gesture that said more than words, he gripped his forehead and closed his eyes for a moment. Then he shook his head as if to clear it and said, "Let's sit down."

One of the other men reached for a chair beside a game table and pulled it out for Jeanie. The two strangers sat down across from her. For the first time she realized one wore a French army uniform. The other was British army.

Uncle Al slumped into a chair beside Jean. Visibly struggling to pull himself together, he said, "Let me introduce my friends." He gestured toward the Frenchman. "Lieutenant Georges Crozet, recently from France and now in de Gaulle's Free French Army. Because of his work in the Resistance, he's been assigned temporarily as liaison to British Special Operations."

He turned to the other man at the table. "Captain Harry Lloyd, British Special Operations. They have army business in Abergavenny but kindly came with me to tell you about Giselle and Claude."

The dark-haired, dark-eyed Frenchman studied her with such a probing look she wanted to back away. In contrast, Captain Lloyd, a fair-skinned Englishman, seemed friendly but distant.

"I'm glad you could come with my uncle," she said, meaning both of them, but avoiding the Frenchman's eyes.

Lieutenant Crozet, however, spoke first. "As your uncle said, we have other duties here, but we are glad to be of assistance."

The Englishman said nothing.

"Georges, please tell Jean what you told me about Giselle and Claude," Uncle Al said.

Lieutenant Crozet leaned forward, one arm on the table. "Your cousins knew me as Martin." His English, though good, was heavily accented. "I knew Claude as Armand and Giselle as Julie. I can talk easier if I refer to them by the names I know best."

"Yes. I understand." Not wanting to insult him but eager to hear in fluent detail, she added, "I speak French if you wish."

"Thank you, but no. I prefer to use English." At her nod, he proceeded at a reasonable rate. "Most of us knew no more than two or three resistants—our partners and contacts—but Julie and Armand, because they were leaders, they knew ... many other leaders. Many resistants stayed at their home. To catch Julie and Armand was for the Gestapo a great good fortune. Although your cousins do not know true names or addresses, what they do know could expose many, many resistants for arrest.

"We managed to—I think you would say *ambush* the Gestapo when they brought Armand and Julie from their different prisons to Gestapo headquarters for interrogation. This took much planning because the two ambushes had to happen just so— Julie's rescue moments before Armand's. Our attempt to save Armand was only partially successful. We had him, but we were discovered. Two of our men were killed. Armand and one other man ... we could not find. We know only that the Gestapo, they did not capture them because I have reports that they continue to search for Armand.

"I was with the men who rescued Julie. For her safety, I alone hid her." He stopped as though his report were finished.

"She is all right then?" Jean persisted.

Lieutenant Crozet's thin Gaelic face turned grim, but then his eyes softened with sympathy. "Julie ... by now her wounds will be healed, but she is ... shattered in other ways. She is receiving most tender and professional care."

Jean had read about Nazi torture. Horrified, she cried, "Is she out of her mind?"

"No, no! The doctor is certain her stability will return."

Uncle Al caught her hand. "Jeanie, she simply has endured too much. Her mental condition is sure to be temporary."

"Oh, Uncle Al!" She wanted to scream but instead began to cry.

Uncle Al threw an arm around her shoulders and pulled her close. She pressed her face against his shoulder. *Giselle, Giselle!*

Finally she quieted, and Uncle Al slid his handkerchief into her hand. As soon as she could control her voice, she asked, "Is she truly in a safe place? What's to keep them from finding her?" She detected a wordless message in the glance Captain Lloyd gave Lieutenant Crozet. "She's not that safe, is she?" Jean stated flatly. She turned to Lieutenant Crozet. "Why can't somebody get her and the children out in the same manner you left France?"

He immediately became defensive. "I would have brought them with me if that were possible. But Julie was too weak. And there was not time. Most dangerous of all ... her face. She would be quickly recognized by the collaborators in Lyon. I did not dare go to the children, but they are safe with a family in the country. I could only hide Julie and then by myself leave."

Jean exploded. "She's still in Lyon?"

"It was all I could do."

Captain Lloyd spoke at last. "Miss Thornton," he said gently, "our special agents in France tell us Lieutenant Crozet has saved your cousin's life by leaving her. And it was he who helped her hide the children."

Suddenly Jean could hear how she must sound. "I'm sorry, Lieutenant Crozet. I didn't mean to suggest you had not done the best you could. I'm so upset, I forgot to thank you for rescuing her!"

For a moment Crozet lost the tough look that seemed most

natural to him. "I understand. It is for you shocking, mademoiselle. For this I am sorry."

Getting a firm grip on herself, she said, "But you also brought good news. She's alive and in the safest place you could find. Uncle Al, isn't there some way to get her out of France?"

"I've wracked my brain and come up with nothing," he said wearily. "The State Department can't do a thing."

Jean turned to Captain Lloyd. "What about British Special Operations? I've heard you have agents in France. Can't your people help Giselle get out when she's stronger?"

He shook his head. "It's British Special Operations Executive, the French arm of our secret service. We're an army operation, so we're involved only with military objectives."

Crozet brusquely interrupted. "Is not the Resistance of military value?"

"You know I believe the Resistance is very important," Lloyd snapped. "It is *your* general who says the Resistance must remain separate from us."

"So why am I assigned to you?" Crozet prodded back. "I have to tell you, sir, that Madame Julie can give away the largest Resistance groups in France if the Gestapo should find her. She hasn't the strength to resist more torture."

With a sympathetic glance at Jean, Lieutenant Crozet argued passionately. "Do you think, with the invasion soon coming, that they will stop searching for her? They know what the Resistance can do when the second front begins. Mademoiselle Thornton is right about getting her out of France. The Nazis would keep her alive somehow until they had the information they know she holds. In the name of mercy, sir—"

His eyes, burning with anger, met Jean's. "I hated leaving her there! I know that someone close to Armand betrayed him and probably is still in Lyon, watching and searching." He slapped his hands flat on the table and leaned toward Jean. "Mademoiselle Thornton, I'm afraid I lied to you. Julie is not safe. I did what I could, but she will never be safe in France. If I could, I would return for her, but it would mean her death. They know me as well as they know her."

Jean turned to Captain Lloyd. "Can't someone get into France the same way Lieutenant Crozet came out?"

"I have no one to send. All my agents are assigned. Even the women."

"You have women agents?"

He nodded, but before he could speak, Uncle Al pushed himself to his feet and broke into the conversation. "Jeanie, we've taken as much time from these busy men as we dare. They have to get on with their jobs. Unfortunately Giselle's plight is our personal problem."

Jean's temper flared. He had managed, as he'd done so often while she was growing up, to get a jump ahead of her. It was as if he could read her mind. She was about to ask if she could be trained to go. As she had done ever since her rebellion over spying at Tulelake, Jean rose to her feet and confronted him. "You mean that as far as the United States and France and Britain are concerned, Giselle is expendable."

Grief etched his strong features with angular shadows and deep lines. "She's only one family's sacrifice to the war, Jeanie. I'd do anything to protect and save her, but I am helpless."

For the first time she noticed that his previously iron gray hair had turned almost white. She held back raging words that would hurt him more. "I'm sorry. I'm not thinking clearly. I know you would do anything for her." She hugged him. "Will you return to London tonight?"

He held her tightly for a long moment. When he released her, his mouth was working for control. In a forced voice, he said, "First thing in the morning. They've found us rooms at the Swan in Abergavenny for tonight. Can you get away for supper with me?"

"I'm afraid not. I'm on duty at the rec hall, and it's too late to get someone to fill in for me." She spun around to face Lloyd and Crozet and offered her hand, first to the Frenchman and then to the Englishman. "It's been a pleasure to meet you. Thanks again for coming with Uncle Al. I really appreciate it."

They responded formally, but their faces telegraphed compassion and ... what? Questioning? No. More like calculating. She wished she could read minds as well as Uncle Al.

On the way to dinner she realized she hadn't asked Uncle Al if he had learned anything about Giselle's mother and father.

Her mind had been so focused on Giselle. But surely he would have said something if he had heard anything about Aunt Ruth and Uncle Paul. She would ask when she talked with him next time.

Meanwhile she must find a way to speak privately with Captain Lloyd and Lieutenant Crozet. She hoped her quick answer about not being able to get out for dinner with Uncle Al was not prophetic. If she could persuade Betty Lou to take her shift in the rec hall, maybe she could find someone to drive her to Abergavenny.

Whatever she did must be utterly concealed from Uncle Al. She didn't want to worry him but also knew he had the power to stop her and would do so if he learned that she planned to enter occupied France.

At the officers' mess where the nurses and American Red Cross workers dined, Jean drew her roommate Betty Lou away from the others and quietly asked, "Could you please take my place and manage alone at the rec hall if I get the movie going?"

"What about the super? Is it all right with her?"

"She's at a meeting in Gilwern and probably won't return before ten. I'll be back by then, but if I'm not, just tell her my uncle is in town only for tonight, and I went to see him. I'll work your shift on Sunday, if you'll trade."

"Well, sure. Okay, kid."

"Thanks! Thanks a lot." Jean ate quickly, excused herself, and left to search for her driver, Eddy. She found him outside the noncom mess hall.

"Hi, kiddo. What can I do you for?" he joked.

"How are you at covert operations?" she asked.

He bounced his eyebrows up and down in imitation of Groucho Marx. "Just try me, sis."

"This has to be very covert. Can you get away right now and deliver notes to two men staying at the Swan and then bring me back their replies?"

"Say, you are turning into one fast worker!"

"Eddy, this is serious. My uncle from London, Al Moore, is staying there, and he must not know you are doing this for me."

"How will I know your uncle?"

"Well, he's about five feet ten, thin, with thick silvery hair and bushy black eyebrows. And he may be the only civilian staying the night there."

"Okay. So where are your notes?"

She handed him the two small envelopes she'd prepared before supper. "Lieutenant Crozet is wearing a Free French Army uniform, and Captain Lloyd is wearing British Army. In the notes I've asked them to simply give you a verbal yes or no. They may or may not be rooming together."

"I'll find them. Just leave it to me, beautiful damsel." He placed one hand over his chest and raised the other high. "I go, but I shall return! Uh . . . where will you be when I return?"

"In the rec hall helping Betty Lou. If either of them gives you a yes, can you then drive me back to town by eight?"

"Sure thing."

"Thank you!"

He ran to his jeep, quickly started the engine, and roared away.

Jean hurried to the rec hall and again tested the movie and projector. When Betty Lou arrived, she explained as much as she could and then took a seat near the door while men filed in for show time.

Someone snapped off the lights, and the camera began to roll. *They All Kissed the Bride* began with the familiar Hollywood music that they had listened to a lifetime ago in their hometown theaters on Saturday afternoons.

In just a few minutes the story had captured everyone's attention. Jean pulled on her coat and slipped out. Glad that it wasn't raining at the moment, she strode to the parking area beside the rec hall to wait there for Eddy. Soon he drove up in his jeep and stopped beside her. "Climb in," he said. "You got two yesses! Where do you want to go?"

"Back to Abergavenny. You can drop me off at St. Michael's Canteen in Pen-y-pound. I doubt that Uncle Al will venture that far from the Swan."

Eddy shifted gears, stomped on the accelerator, and away the jeep bounced. The wind made Jean's eyes water. She turned up the collar of her topcoat and tied her scarf over her Red Cross cap to cover her ears.

"Sorry I couldn't get an ambulance to give you some shelter," Eddy shouted.

"This is fine," Jean yelled back.

In Abergavenny they chugged slowly through the narrow streets to Pen-y-pound, and Eddy pulled up at the canteen. "How long you think you'll be?"

"I don't know. I asked them to try to be here at eight o'clock, which is pretty soon. Could you come back in an hour?"

"I'll lay low at the USO and be back here at nine," he promised.

She climbed out and blew him a kiss. "Thanks, Eddy!"

Before she reached the canteen, Captain Lloyd and Lieutenant Crozet stepped from a nearby doorway to meet her. "We thought we could talk more freely in a friend's home. Do you mind a bit of a walk?" asked Captain Lloyd.

"Not at all," Jean responded quickly. "Lead the way."

Captain Lloyd's friend lived in a row house in an ancient stone and oak-timbered building on Castle Street. Lloyd let himself in with a key from his pocket. Although a lamp lighted the room and the coal stove gave off warmth, no one seemed to be at home. "Make yourself comfortable by the fire, Miss Thornton," said Lloyd.

She sat in a worn red upholstered chair near the stove, then wriggled out of her coat to enjoy the warmth. The men took places opposite her on a Victorian couch covered with faded red velvet. Neatly crocheted needlework protected the arms and a hand-knit white wool afghan lay folded at one end. It didn't look like a single man's home, but there was no sign of any children.

Apparently Captain Lloyd followed her eyes, for he remarked, "My cousin is out on some Home Guard mission. She gave me the key when I told her I needed a private spot for a meeting."

Lieutenant Crozet took an envelope from his breast pocket and withdrew notepaper she recognized as her own. He reviewed its contents and then waved it at her. "I found your message most intriguing. What can either of us do for you who are in the Red Cross service?"

"I want to go to Lyon, prepare Giselle for escape, then bring her and the children here to England."

"Whee-oo!" responded Lloyd. "You are most direct."

"When I have to be."

"And most naïve, I'm afraid," added Crozet. He leaned back in an attitude of dismissal.

No longer surprised by his confrontational attitude, Jean decided to challenge him. "I think you already may have considered whether I might fulfill just what I'm proposing."

He raised one black eyebrow and the hint of a smile tugged at the corner of his mouth, but he said nothing.

Captain Lloyd also leaned back, folded his arms across his chest, and stretched his feet toward the stove. "You ask the impossible. What made you think you could attempt such a thing?"

His smooth English face had subtly acquired aggressive angles. Looking into his sharp blue eyes, she wondered why she'd initially thought he was the friendlier of the two. Straightening in her chair, she said, "First, I spent the past year doing undercover work for Uncle Al. I can't tell you what it was, but I can tell you I lived a secret life and kept it all hidden, even from my roommate. From that experience I learned I can play an assigned part convincingly."

Switching to French, she said, "Also, I have spoken French since I was nine years old. Giselle spent every summer with my grandmother and me. By the time I was twelve, Giselle said I spoke French like a native. And I've lived a year in France—went to school there when I was fourteen."

Neither of the men moved or said anything, but they eyed her with an alertness that reminded her of a blue heron she'd once seen peering into the water waiting to catch a fish. She plunged ahead, this time in German. "I also speak passable German, because of my aunt Esther and her German cousins."

Crozet pulled a cigarette box and matches from his breast pocket. He shook out a cigarette for Lloyd and one for himself. Methodically he lit Lloyd's and his own with the same match. Then reaching for a heavy milk-glass ashtray on an end table, he placed the ornate dish on the floor between them and dropped the matchstick into it.

Jean read the smoking ritual as a stall. Not a bad sign. She had made him take her seriously. She hid her impatience while he inhaled and blew a leisurely cloud upward.

Finally he said in rapid French, "Being qualified for a secret mission does not mean you are qualified to rescue Julie from occupied France. You would not only lose your life, but also you most surely would lead her and her children to their deaths. No.

I must find someone more experienced and tougher than you could be."

Jean slid forward in her chair and responded in French. "So you *have* been wanting to send someone to rescue her!"

He blew out another cloud of smoke. "Of course, but if I cannot send an expert, Julie is safer left alone."

She resisted his understandable caution. Continuing in French, she said, "Then there is a way to get someone into and out of occupied France?"

He drew on his cigarette and shook his head.

Jean turned to Captain Lloyd and asked in English, "How does British Special Operations send their agents into France?"

"It's very complicated. It takes months to prepare an agent for a drop." His tone said, "Forget it," but his watchful eyes compelled her to go on.

"When you say drop, do you mean they parachute in?"

"Yes."

Her mouth went dry. She had hoped she could be taken by submarine or small boat to a deserted beach in southern France. She knew she could find her way up the Rhône River to Lyon. With confidence she did not feel, she said, "You mentioned that you have women agents in France."

"Yes. We've been criticized for sending women, but they volunteered and have been more successful in some cases than our men. The Gestapo seems unwilling ... or unable ... to suspect that a woman could be a threat." He leaned over and jammed his cigarette into the ashtray to snuff it.

"I'm volunteering," she said firmly, "and I am partially trained."

He gave her a calculating look, then muttered, "No. It would never work."

With a tense gesture, Crozet snuffed out his cigarette too. "Harry, I'm beginning to wonder...."

"I can do it!" Jean exclaimed. "I know I can if you'll prepare me and get me into France."

Captain Lloyd snapped, "Georges, stop right now. There's no way she could do the job. She was only a schoolgirl when she was in France."

Jean turned on him. "I could be coached well enough to make my way. I know I could."

Abruptly the Frenchman leaned over toward Captain Lloyd. "Why don't you give her a try, Harry? Her French is good enough to pass. If she got a little coaching, her slight American accent would not be noticed. You could call it all off if she doesn't do well in the training."

Captain Lloyd exploded. "There's no time! We don't know when the invasion will begin, but it will be soon. She could be caught in a battle zone. We'd be unable to help her or bring her back. No, it's better for your Julie to stay in hiding."

Crozet rose to his feet and began to pace the floor of the small room. "Long ago I promised Armand I would take care of Julie if he could not." He paused to touch a dried rose in a vase on a shelf. "I did my best, but she may not live until the invasion."

He swung around and glared at Lloyd. "We do not know who betrayed us, but we believe the betrayer remains in Lyon because the arrests continue. They still watch for Julie and search for her." He shoved his fists into his pockets and stood hunched like a tethered falcon. "I tell you Harry, Julie knows too many Resistance leaders to be safe anywhere in France. If the Nazis break her, they could cripple our plans of sabotage—sabotage that will purchase time for your troops when they land."

"This one woman is that critical?"

"Man, I've been telling you, it is so!" Crozet's face flushed with anger.

They seemed to have forgotten Jean was there. She watched and waited, sensing that her best chance now lay in remaining silent. She willed Crozet to win.

CHAPTER SIX

Jean watched the two men with silent passion. Her cousin's life was on a balance scale. Because she was willing to risk everything to save Giselle, she felt Crozet's side of the argument carried the most weight. But this Englishman was stubborn.

Captain Lloyd thumped the arm of the couch with his fist. "We are army. We train British army volunteers. This girl is neither British nor army."

Standing above him, with both hands clenched into fists, Crozet said in a surprisingly controlled voice, "For the sake of the Resistance and your own troops, you could request an exception. After all, your British army agent helped me to escape from France."

Lloyd glanced at Jean.

She gazed back at him, poised and ready.

"You really want to give it a try?" he asked.

"Yes!" She wanted to add, "With all my heart," but she bit off the words for fear she might sound girlish.

Looking from her to Crozet, Lloyd dipped his head in a curt nod. "I'll see if I can get permission." Once persuaded, his mind moved swiftly. "Georges, you must provide a Frenchwoman for Miss Thornton to live with while she's in training. Someone from Lyon—"

He broke off, and Jean saw indecision creep back into his face. "Is Miss Thornton's French truly good enough to sound native?"

Crozet smiled at her for the first time. "It will do."

"Then gather all the latest information on living conditions in France, so Miss Thornton won't walk into a shop and ask for something they haven't had on the shelves for months. About clothing—you'll have to get her authentic clothing. And the present train schedules ... But first I must obtain permission."

Lloyd turned to Jean. "Miss Thornton, can you leave your post with the American Red Cross without raising questions?"

"We're allowed emergency leaves. There's one problem, though. Uncle Al must not know about this, and I can't just drop out of touch. I'll have to think of something to satisfy him."

"Knowing your uncle, that won't be easy. I leave the solution of that problem to you." He stood up. "When were you to be picked up at the canteen?"

"Nine o'clock."

"We'll walk you back. You'll just make it."

They strode down the narrow street, one on each side of her. Neither spoke. Upon reaching Pen-y-pound, they escorted her across the street to the steps of the canteen.

"I'll be in touch," Captain Lloyd said. "Plan as if you will be going. Then you can move swiftly if permission is granted."

"Thank you. And thank you, Lieutenant Crozet."

Crozet sobered. "If you do this and succeed, many people will be thankful. If you try and fail, it may cost us more lives than if you did not try."

"I understand."

His expression turned grim, and he shook his head. "No, you don't. Not yet."

Neither of them smiling, the two men said good-bye and walked away.

The next day Jean began to lay the groundwork for taking an emergency leave from the station hospital. She confided to her supervisor that her uncle in London had fallen ill. She wrote to Uncle Al that she'd had a bout of flu, which had left her extremely tired, and she planned to ask for a leave to recuperate if she did not feel better in a few days. He would forgive the deception once she succeeded in getting Giselle and the girls out of France.

Three days later Uncle Al sent a telegram. "Go rest. Am wiring money. Uncle Al."

Jean had not anticipated that he'd send money, which showed her how unperceptive she had become since her spying days at Tulelake. Her survival in France would depend upon her ability to read people and anticipate their reactions. *I must watch and deceive better than I ever did in the internment camp!*

She didn't want to accept Uncle Al's money, but she couldn't refuse without having to answer questions. Writing a short note of thanks, she said she would let him know where she would be staying to recuperate after she decided. In the same post she mailed a note to Captain Lloyd, reporting what she had done. "I hope you can arrange for regular communication to Uncle Al from the place where I'm supposed to be resting."

Several days passed. Jean grew jumpy from wondering and hoping, but when anyone noticed her edginess, it was easy to pass it off as the result of worry over her uncle.

That same week in Lyon, Giselle awoke in a strange room in a clean bed and covered with a warm down comforter. A shaft of sunlight spilled from a high narrow window. *Is it morning?* she wondered. *Afternoon? It's so quiet.*

She tried to raise her head but felt as if it were glued to the pillow. Above her arched a high ceiling, dingy as a church vault darkened by centuries of candle smoke. *Where am I? Where are the girls?* Her heart began to hammer against her ribs, taking her breath away. *How long have I been here?* She couldn't remember yesterday. But she remembered something about the Gestapo. . . . Yes! The man with clubs for fists . . . the pain . . . the blood . . .

But the resistants came and snatched her from the Nazis.

Slowly memories surfaced. The girls were safe, but Claude . . . The rendezvous with Claude went bad. SS men came from everywhere. . . . She had seen Claude dive for cover—or had he been shot? Martin had grabbed her and dragged her into a building, and they hid in a dark basement.

Where was Martin? First she must locate Martin. He would help her search for Claude. She must get up . . . get out of here . . . and find Claude. She sat up in bed. The room swirled around her. Her ears began to ring. She flopped back down on the pillow so as not to faint. *What's wrong with me?*

She raised her hands to her face and felt unfamiliar lumps

and lines where smooth skin once had been—tender scars across her cheeks, even on her head. Someone had cut her hair short like she had worn it as a girl. Exploring further, her fingers fell on a stubble of hair growing back where one spot on her head had been shaved. In the shaved area lay a scar—a surgical scar? Yes. Of course. She remembered the blinding headache and the physician who had told her he would have to operate to relieve the pressure. She had survived! But that must have been days ago. She tried again to sit up, raising herself slowly, pausing at intervals until the room stopped spinning. Cautiously she swung her feet out and down onto the cold clean floor. *I'm moving like an old woman,* she thought. Pain shot from her back down her leg as she stood up. A few steps away stood a dressing table. She shuffled to it and looked in the mirror. Before she could glimpse herself, the image of a stranger appeared. Where had that woman come from, poor thing, with such a grossly crooked nose and her hair chopped off and tangled into a mat?

We have that in common, Giselle thought. She raised her hand to her own hair, and the stranger mirrored her action. The stranger was her! She had not imagined the scars could be this bad. Shaking, she grabbed the edge of the dressing table for support.

Suddenly her own grotesque reflection disappeared, and she saw only the vision of a man's raised fist, shiny with her own blood, about to smash into her face again. She covered her face with her hands and tried to scream, but her heart began to hammer too hard and too slow, and she couldn't get her breath. Everything faded into darkness.

When Giselle awoke again in bed, she felt she was supposed to do something, but she couldn't remember what. She didn't know where she was or how she had come to be here. She did not even know her own name.

On Sunday, when Jean strolled out of the Presbyterian church after the morning service, Captain Lloyd stood waiting on the steps. He said in a sympathetic tone, "Miss Thornton, I've come from your uncle in London. He's worse and is asking for you. Can you grab a few things and come this afternoon?"

Jean's pulse began to race. It was easy to let anxiety crumple her face and raise her voice. "Oh yes! I'll arrange for an emergency leave."

"I've already told your supervisor. That's how I learned you were here. I'll take you back to your quarters, and you may pick up what you will need."

Nella, standing nearby, came to Jean's side. "Is something wrong? Anything I can do?"

"It's my uncle Al, very ill in London. I'm going to him."

Elizabeth hurried over. "What's wrong?"

"My uncle in London is very ill. I'd appreciate your prayers . . . for him . . . and me too." Inwardly she cringed at asking for prayer for a false situation, but she quickly stifled her guilt. Soon Giselle's life and her own would depend on her ability to pass off lies as truth.

"You shall have my prayers every day," Elizabeth promised. Her expression assured Jean she had carried off the deception convincingly.

Jean introduced Captain Lloyd to the mother and daughter and explained that he had come to escort her to her uncle.

"I pray travel mercy for the both of you," Elizabeth offered.

"I hope you find your uncle getting well by the time you get there," Nella said.

"Thanks. I hope so too. Bye for now." She felt their eyes following her as she hurried down the steps with Captain Lloyd.

An hour later on the train with Captain Lloyd, Jean was glad she'd asked Elizabeth to pray. No one else who cared about her would know she needed special prayer.

Captain Lloyd sat silently across from her in the private compartment he'd somehow managed to procure and gazed out the rain-washed window at the hills surrounding Abergavenny. His proper British profile gave her no clue to his thoughts. When the train began to roll, he pulled a large manila envelope from his attaché case and handed it to her. "Read all of this. Memorize the details of your new identity and personal history. From this moment on, you will answer to Marie or Madame Fauvre. You are now Madame Marie Fauvre, widowed mother of a young boy and girl."

"Beginning right now?" Jean repeated.

"Yes. You must be Marie even in your dreams before you can leave England. Can you manage a French accent when you speak English?"

"Yes. I . . . hadn't thought this far," Jean admitted.

His slight frown dug in between his brows. "You told us you were experienced. Your coaches will do their job, but in the end, over there, it will be up to you. You must foresee a multitude of possibilities at any given moment and still be uncomplicated Marie on the outside," he lectured.

Jean resented his attitude. She determined she would show him. She said briskly, "I will do my part, sir."

He stared back at her, then pulled out more papers from his briefcase and bent his head to attend to them.

She opened the envelope and began to study the life of Madame Fauvre. While she read, darkness fell. Captain Lloyd lowered and fastened the black-out curtains and turned on the light. He stretched and pulled a copy of the *Daily Telegraph* from his briefcase and leaned back to read.

She glanced at the page facing her. A lead article reported that eleven hundred planes had flown against the French invasion coast in daylight raids today. Another said the Russians had driven fleeing Nazis into a wilderness of swamps in the Pripet Marshes. She noted the date. If she lived to tell it, she wanted to remember that January 14, 1944, was the day she became Marie Fauvre and began her journey to help Giselle. She was glad the war news held encouragement on those two fronts at least.

The train rumbled on with few stops toward . . . where? No matter. Jean leaned back and recited her new life history to herself. From time to time she searched the papers for a forgotten fact. Her mind slipped into a near dream state. She dozed off and then jumped awake when the train stopped at the next station. Drifting off again, she relaxed and slept.

She heard Captain Lloyd before she realized the train was stopping again.

"We're here, Madame Fauvre," he said.

She opened her eyes and sat up straight, wondering where here was.

He reached for her overnight case on a rack above her head and stood back for her to precede him down the aisle. They stepped out onto the passenger platform of a small station comparable to the one in Abergavenny, but the air was much colder.

A steady wind blew rain against Jean's legs. "Where are we?" she asked.

"York," he said. "Too small to be a priority target for the Germans and yet large enough that you won't be noticed while you are in training. Crozet feels we need to practice security from the start. We'll drive you to a nearby airfield for jump practice. Come along. This way." He nodded toward the left and guided her into the station and then out the other side to the street. At the curb, he beckoned to a parked army sedan. The car rolled to them. A soldier jumped out, took her luggage from Captain Lloyd, placed it in the boot, and opened the rear door for Jean. Captain Lloyd walked around and let himself in the other side.

Jean glimpsed the approach of dawn on a distant horizon before the car passed between the buildings of the blacked-out town. She must have slept quite awhile on the train, for she felt wide awake. The auto's dimmed headlights showed only a few yards ahead and illuminated only hints of rain-washed sidewalks and buildings on either side. After making what seemed like a half circle through the town, they turned down an alley and stopped. In the thinning darkness, Jean could see a tall line of weather-beaten row houses looming on either side.

Captain Lloyd took her suitcase and led her into the miniature walled garden of one and banged the knocker. The old door opened. A streak of yellow light splashed across the steps and into the dooryard. What should have been garden was old cobblestones and cracked cement, the only growing object, a scraggly, leafless climber rose on one side of the steps.

A woman with a French accent called, "So she is here. Your British trains are most reliable to stay on time even now!"

The captain introduced them. "Madame Marie Fauvre, this is Madame Thibault, who will be your teacher as well as your hostess."

"I'm delighted to meet you, Madame Thibault," Jean replied in French.

With outstretched hands, the short buxom woman exclaimed in French, "But you must be tired, my dear. I have your bed ready. A little hot soup, a hot bath to soothe you, and pouf!— you will relax and rest for the morning. Captain, leave her to me for today. We will get acquainted and practice our speaking." She took Jean's case in one hand and Jean's arm in the other and led her into the hallway of the old Victorian row house.

The house had been a high-class home in its day, but now the carpets were faded and threadbare. A bowl of dried flowers on an old stand near the door gave the entry a mournful air. Jean compared the house to her grandmother's. It was probably the same age, but Grandmother's was light and filled with welcoming cheeriness.

In contrast to the mausoleum effect in the hall, however, a wonderful aroma of chicken soup drifted from a distant room. Jean's mouth watered at the thought of good homemade soup. Her thoughts were interrupted by Captain Lloyd.

"Sorry, but Madame Fauvre has no time to lose in taking naps. She must begin work immediately. Remember to speak only French with her," he reminded. "I'll return at ten this morning to brief you, Madame Fauvre," Lloyd called to Jean.

Jean smiled and answered in French. "Thank you, Captain Lloyd, for everything."

He gave her a half salute and let himself out.

"Come, dear, and please call me Eve. May I call you Marie?" She hesitated only long enough for Jean to nod and then she rushed on. "Marta will take your luggage to your room while you have some soup and tea. Come. We dine in here." She led the way through a modern parlor made cozy with upholstered couches and chairs arranged around a large fireplace and into a dining room that contained a huge sideboard and buffet of gleaming dark wood and a long polished table that could easily seat a family of twelve. This comfort and beauty was in stark contrast to the faded dark entrance and hallway.

"This is lovely!" Jean exclaimed.

Eve gave her a pleased smile. "Thank you. I do require beauty and comfort, and I persuaded the powers that be that everyone learns more quickly in pleasing surroundings. We leave the entry and the garden to match the rest of the neighborhood for security reasons. Most of the buildings have been let go, and the few tenants do not visit me to discover the changes here. It is better that they consider me an unfriendly widow lady."

"I should think you might get lonely."

Eve nodded. "But it is my contribution. I do what I can for my country. And Edna and Marta are good company."

As if summoned, a young woman, neatly dressed in a dark skirt and sweater, appeared in the doorway that led into the kitchen. She curtsied. "Shall I serve now, madame?"

Her demeanor seemed like something from the last century, but Eve acknowledged it naturally. "Please do, Edna, and then tell Marta to take our guest's luggage upstairs to the room in the middle, nearest the bath."

The girl curtsied again. "Yes, madame." She disappeared into the kitchen.

"Come. Be seated, and I will join you for a cup of tea." She beckoned Jean to a chair and for herself took the one at the head of the long table.

Eve, with her tiny waist, full bust, and pink-and-white complexion could have come from the days when dresses were long and skirts were hooped. She resembled the woman in the painting above the dining room fireplace. Her black hair swept up in a chignon, although a modern style, added to the illusion that she could have stepped out of an earlier time.

"Are you warm enough?" asked Eve, noticing Jean's gaze toward the fireplace. "These great fireplaces do not heat so large a room, so we have the hot water heat. Sometimes that is barely adequate."

"I'm fine," Jean said. She was glad, however, that she had worn a wool skirt and sweater and had brought several more with her.

The maid returned and placed a steaming bowl of soup and a plate of crusty home-baked bread before Jean along with a large pot of tea insulated by a thick tea cozy.

"Do go ahead and eat while I pour our tea," Eve urged.

"I am hungry," Jean admitted.

A short time later with her hunger satisfied, Jean followed Eve upstairs to the room that would be hers. An old crystal chandelier provided soft light. The room contained a modern desk and lamp, chairs, and a sofa upholstered in dusty rose and powder blue. A deeper rose comforter lay on the four-poster bed, plump and inviting above spotless white dust ruffles. A plush wool rug, ornate with oriental blue- and plum-colored flowers brightened the floor. Lace curtains could not conceal the blackout blinds, but the blinds were finished in soft blue on the inside.

Eve opened the blinds to let in the morning light. Jean looked down on the street. The row houses were indeed in disrepair. The front gardens were barren and cluttered with broken stones and bits of trash.

"Sorry about the view," Eve said. "I guess they had to choose a place that looked as if nothing important could happen there."

Jean turned and smiled. "It does look that way."

"When you go out, you must keep a watchful eye about you. Most of our neighbors want to be as private as I do, so there's no telling who they are or what they might do."

"Really? You mean robberies and the like?" Jean had never worried being out alone at night in Abergavenny any more than she had in Salem, Oregon.

Eve nodded. "It has happened. Just keep an eye out and your wits about you. Now if I were you, I'd take a good hot bath and lie down awhile. I'll call you in plenty of time to be ready for Captain Lloyd when he arrives at ten."

"Thanks. I'll do that."

The bed had a goose down tick on the mattress that nestled up around Jean when she slipped under the covers. The sheets and pillows smelled of sunshine, like her grandmother's freshly washed laundry. The plump comforter settled over her as softly as the wing of a mother bird. Jean closed her eyes and fell asleep.

In Lyon, Giselle had tried for several days to remember something that would lead her to knowing who she was and where she was. How could she, a thinking, comprehending person, lie here and not know? Who had brought her here? And why? She had pestered the nun who seemed to have no duties but to sit with her. She thought she recognized the habit worn by the sister, but she could not name the order. She could not remember anything about her life before waking in this strange place a few days ago, and that woman would tell her nothing.

And she did not know the doctor who was pressing a cool stethoscope against her ribs, telling her to breathe deeply and listening with a frown to the messages her chest sent. Finally he rolled up his stethoscope and shoved it into his black bag.

In a hearty voice he said, "You ran a very high fever, madame, and except for the fine nursing of Sister Therese, we would have lost you. Now be a good patient and continue to obey her. To-morrow you may sit up in a chair for a while. Sister," he said to the nun, "call me if any untoward change occurs."

Giselle burst out, "Doctor, do you know who I am?"

His face grew fierce. "Madame, it is not safe for me to know who most of my patients are." Then he relaxed a bit and sadly shook his head. "No, this you must wait for patiently. In time, your life will come back to you."

Frightened and feeling abandoned, Giselle watched him leave. Why was she here, and why would they not even let her comb her own hair? What kind of a hospital was this?

They treated her like a child, but she knew more than they thought. She knew there was something important she had to do. As soon as her legs grew stronger, she would leave this place and find someone who could help her remember.

CHAPTER SEVEN

When Jean awoke, she was lying in the same position as when she had climbed into bed. She squinted at her watch. Nine o'clock. Her robe and slippers had been laid out on the chair beside her bed. She put them on and padded across the room to open the black-out curtains that Marta had closed. Heavy clouds scudded across the morning sky.

A light rap sounded on her bedroom door. "Come in," she called. "I'm up."

Marta entered. "Madame Thibault asks that you join her in the dining room as soon as you are dressed. May I lay out your clothes?"

Jean had packed so few things, she wanted to laugh at the thought of needing help. Instead, she said, "No, thank you. I'll manage."

"Yes, madame. You will find them in the closet." Marta bobbed her head and backed out.

What a curious combination, thought Jean. *She looks and acts like a local serving girl, but she sounds like a native of France.*

Jean opened the old-fashioned closet and stepped back in surprise. The pungent scent of leather leaped out at her. On the floor sat sturdy high-top boots and next to them a leather flyer's cap. Beside her clothes hung two pairs of wool khaki trousers, two wool shirts, and a warm jacket minus insignias. They were evidently for her jump practice. She bent and touched the boots with one finger, then grabbed her own skirt, blouse, and sweater, and slammed the closet door.

As she quickly dressed, she felt she could smell the leather boots right through the closed door. *This is it,* she thought. Her stomach fluttered with dread. *Will I be able to overcome my fear of heights?* She remembered all too well the time she'd climbed high up a fir tree, then froze there in terror and had to be rescued by Uncle Al. Worse than that was the time she'd peered over the edge of a cliff on the Oregon coast into the surf swirling below. Just looking, she'd felt as if she were falling. The reality that she would have to jump from a plane made her light-headed. She collapsed onto the edge of the bed and pressed her face into the sweet-smelling pillow. With her face in the pillow, she forced her mind away from parachuting and thought instead of Giselle, hiding, suffering from brutal treatment by the Gestapo and probably worried sick about Claude and the girls.

A few deep breaths calmed her stomach. *If I can keep my mind on Giselle, I can do it.*

What comfort Giselle had been when Grandmother had not understood her. *I wanted to visit Giselle again in Lyon, but not like this.*

One summer day in Oregon when Giselle was still in secondary school, they'd sat side by side on a moss-carpeted rock, dangling their feet in the water at Silver Creek Falls State Park. Upstream, the south fork of Silver Creek tumbled in a five-hundred-foot drop with a foaming rumble, then spread out in a crystal pool before sweeping past them where they cooled their feet. Arches of mossy branches threw shadow stripes across ferns and salmon berry bushes.

They chattered in French, as was their habit when they were alone together. For Jean, speaking French was more fun than the pig Latin her classmates enjoyed. French belonged to her imaginary world where fathers didn't disappear and brothers did not get killed.

At the end of summer, however, pretending didn't work with only one more week until Giselle would have to go back to Lyon. Jean said hopefully, "Grandmother has plenty of room. Couldn't you stay and go to school here this year?"

Giselle looked up from the stream, her forehead puckered in sympathy. "I shall miss you too, Jeanie, but I must go home. When we grow up and can choose for ourselves, we will be together as much as we wish, is it not so?"

As usual, Giselle's affectionate response made Jean feel better. "Yes! I'll come visit you again, and you can show me all the places I missed before."

"Ah yes. You would love the valley of the Loire, Mont Blanc... and Father may show you the cave paintings at Lascaux.... Oh, there is so much you haven't seen yet."

The sunlight had flashed up from the water onto Giselle's face, lighting her blue eyes and making a luminous halo of curling strands of hair around her face. Jean understood in that moment that her cousin would never choose to live anywhere but in France.

When she visited Lyon again, she fell in love with all that Giselle had promised and wanted to return again and again.

Neither she nor Giselle had realized that grownups may not be free to go anywhere they please. *We could never have imagined how I will return now to Lyon ... or what Giselle would endure because of her love for France. ...*

Remembering Eve waiting downstairs, Jean sat up and smoothed her hair.

When she opened the door to the upper hallway, a man's voice came from below. Captain Lloyd had arrived.

Jean hurried down the carpeted stairs and stepped into the parlor. "Good morning," she said in French.

"Good morning. I hope you rested well," Eve responded.

"Wonderfully well, thanks."

"Madame Fauvre," Captain Lloyd greeted Jean in French, "let me brief you on what you may expect this week."

Jean smiled. "Please call me Marie."

He blinked. "Yes. It would be simpler if you call me Harry too." He returned to business. "I'll take you out to the airfield this morning. Your biggest hurdle will be learning to parachute in such a short period of training. So we've got to get on with it. You'll have—"

Eve interrupted. "Really, Captain, you must let her at least have a cup of tea before starting this."

"Thank you," Jean said to Eve, "but I do have a lot to learn." To Harry she said, "I'll get my coat."

He nodded. "First, did you find the trousers and things I ordered for you?"

"Yes."

"Have you tried them on for size?"

"Not yet."

"Well, go try them now. If they fit, keep on the trousers, shirt, and jacket. You'll begin conditioning and get an introduction to jumping today."

"Jumping?" She almost yelled the word. Lowering her voice she said carefully, "Today?"

"Not real jumping. You've got to build up your strength and learn how to land first. The final thing you'll do is an actual parachute jump. But it's too bad you can't try it first," he added. "If you're going to wash out, the sooner we know, the better."

Through stiff lips, she said, "I'll go try on the trousers." Chin up, she marched out the door.

Behind her, Eve's voice rose. "Are you trying to help or hinder her?"

"You think I like this? We haven't time for normal training . . . but she volunteered. The choice is hers."

Jean ran upstairs and threw open her closet door. She yanked the khaki garments from the hangers, stripped off her own clothes, and pulled on the itchy wool. At first glance she'd thought they were men's clothing, but now realized they must have been designed for a woman—for some British service, she guessed. The jacket radiated warmth back at her. Before returning downstairs she went to her purse and withdrew a billfold-size photo of Giselle and gazed at it for a moment. *I'm coming, Giselle. Please stay safe.*

She tucked the photo into the jacket pocket and marched back down to the parlor. "I'm ready. The fit is fine."

Harry's eyes flicked over her with an expression bordering on distaste. For a second she thought he was going to tell her to go change into her own clothes again. Instead, he nodded toward the door. "Let's go then."

In the car he proceeded to lecture as he drove. "In this neighborhood you must speak to no one. And let Madame Thibault shop for you. At the air base I've arranged for an American to conduct your training. To him you may speak English, but don't forget the French accent. It's important you habitually maintain a French attitude. You have to eat, drink, and gesture like a Frenchwoman. Madame Thibault will critique and coach you in this."

As they passed U.S. troop trucks, jeeps, and British lorries on the narrow road, she learned that her mornings would be spent conditioning her body for the rigors of parachuting. Afternoons, Eve would coach her on French behavior and attitudes and the precautions she must take when in France. Every evening Georges Crozet would come to test her knowledge.

"How long will my training take?" Jean asked.

"That depends on you," Harry answered, "but Georges and I think you must be ready to leave England in about four weeks, by the time of the next full moon—if the weather cooperates, that is."

"I'll do my best," Jean said quietly.

He nodded. Around the next bend in the road he turned into the air base, stopped for the guard, and then drove on between brick barracks. "That barrack straight ahead will be your classroom." Beyond the building he indicated, she could see a hangar, and in the distance stood a line of tall towers. They reminded her of the guard towers at Tulelake.

Harry parked near the entrance to the barrack he'd pointed out, and they went inside. Beyond the simple office, several small rooms seemed to be outfitted for briefings and lectures.

A sergeant sitting behind a desk greeted them. Jean suppressed a smile. If he were to squint one eye, he would look like Popeye in the comic strip. Harry introduced him as Sergeant Ainsworth, her American trainer who did not speak French. Without explanation to Ainsworth, Harry said, "Fortunately, Madame Fauvre speaks English. I'll return for her at fourteen hundred hours." And then he left.

"Mrs. Fauvre," Sergeant Ainsworth barked, "we will begin with a movie, giving you an overview of what you'll need to know for jumping. Then I'll show you how the chutes are folded."

She felt like saluting. He sounded as if he surely had eaten his can of spinach for the day. She wanted to laugh at her private joke. Instead, she said, "That will be fine, Sergeant."

Without any change of expression or tempo, he continued. "We'll go over the jump film a second time, and I'll add my own commentary and answer questions. Any questions now?"

"Only, one, if you please. Would you call me Marie?"

A slow grin softened his square face. "Would make things

easier . . . if anything can. You call me Sarge. I hate to see a girl doing this, but I guess you got your reasons."

"Yes, very good reasons, Sarge. I shall much appreciate anything you may show to me."

"Right. Let's roll that film."

Jean watched the film intently. Trainers showed men how to fold their own chutes, how to get into and out of their gear, how to jump from towers and planes, and how to land correctly when they reached the ground.

After the movie Sarge took her to a large room, hoisted a heavy parachute pack onto the table, and explained each buckle clip and strap. Then he opened the chute pack and spread the chute out on the floor. "You won't be doing this, but I figure you need to know the what and whyfor anyway. Only trained personnel are allowed to rig the chutes. This here's the log book." He pointed to a small record book attached to the parachute pack. "The log book gives the rigger's name and the date each time this parachute was folded." He then explained each step of the folding. "These big rubber bands on the cords keep them from tangling, and they pop off when the chute opens."

Jean watched with interest, and her fears briefly retreated while she focused on the way the parachute functioned.

"We'll leave this for a rigger now and get you back to work," Sarge said as he led her into a room with mats on the floor and some basic weight lifting equipment. "I'm not gonna beat around the bush with you. I've never trained a woman to jump. All I know is what works for the men. I know you won't be able to do as much as a man, but your life will depend on doing as much as you can. You've got to build up strength in your upper body—arms, shoulders, neck, and back. From now on whenever I say 'Down on your face,' you drop and do ten push-ups. Today you'll run a mile. Tomorrow, two. Before long you'll carry the weight of the chute for at least an hour a day. Right now, though, you start with lifting weights. I hope I can build you up, not tear you down."

She raised an eyebrow and smiled. "Thank you so much, Sarge."

He stared at her for a second, then barked, "Down on your face!"

Jean immediately dropped and managed five push-ups before

her quivering arms gave out. Awkwardly she scrambled to her feet.

Without comment, Sergeant Ainsworth turned and led her to the weight lifting equipment. He removed all the weights from the long bar before handing it to her. He picked up a bar with weights for himself. "Do everything I do," he ordered.

She obeyed, lifting, pressing, working out with bars minus their weights. She kept up with him but grew very tired.

Finally Sarge grunted, "That's enough for today. Tomorrow you'll do it with weights."

Her face was dripping wet. She laid the bar beside his and watched his face for a hint of how she was doing. His expression gave her no clue.

"Let's go to the mess for lunch. While you eat, you can read this manual and review how to get in and out of your harness and about the basics of parachute landing falls—PLFs."

Her growing hunger fled at the mention of PLFs. Nevertheless she smiled as she took the book and said, "Thank you."

In the chow line, men did a double take and then made way for her. One even offered to carry her tray. "No, thank you," she replied with a smile but did not encourage conversation.

The food was a thick beef stew served with bread and canned peaches for dessert. She ate a little and studied a lot. At a quarter to one she returned her tray to the clean-up counter and headed back to the classroom.

Sarge quizzed her about what she had read and then said casually, "Now you need to get into the jumping gear."

She gulped. Surely he would not ask her to jump from anything today!

Sergeant Ainsworth took her to an open shed filled with parachute harnesses suspended from the rafters. "Do what I do," he said. He wriggled into one of the harnesses.

Jean climbed into a harness. She managed to get the front fastenings in the correct arrangement on her front side. A strap went around and under each of her legs. A wide belt attached to the leg straps snapped around her waist. Other heavy straps went up and around her arms and over her shoulders.

"Okay," Sarge said. "Now let your weight go onto the harness and see how it feels."

She did. It did not feel good.

"Can you release yourself from the harness?"

She did so and climbed out.

"Tomorrow wear your boots, and I'll find you coveralls to wear over those clothes. Then we'll have you practice PLFs."

"From a tower?"

"Naw. Just a platform. But you gotta have your boots to protect your ankles."

"Oh," she said, not at all reassured.

"Down on your face," he suddenly ordered.

Jean dropped to her stomach and managed only three push-ups this time. She rose to her feet exhausted.

Frowning, Sarge looked her in the eyes and said, "I hate putting you through this, but it's the only way I know."

"Most certainly your method is fine, and I must learn."

He nodded, and his gesture, although polite, seemed to express doubt about her ability. "Well, you're done here for today. At home, take a two-mile hike before supper. It'll keep you loosened up." He led her back to the office where they first had met.

Harry was waiting. "How did she do, Sergeant?"

"She's got a long ways to go. I think you're asking for a miracle to get her in shape in just four weeks."

"Righto, but a miracle is what we need. Isn't that right, Marie?"

"Oh yes," she responded quickly, "but Sarge does not beat around the hedge with me." Harry stared at her. She'd definitely caught him off guard with her portrayal of a typical Frenchwoman who could not remember the correct English idiom. Though wanting to laugh, she soberly returned his startled gaze.

Sarge guffawed. "She means—"

"I know what she means, Sergeant," he said brusquely and marched to the car ahead of her.

Eve had filled the bathtub with hot water and ordered Jean to soak in it. Jean happily obeyed. While immersed in the penetrating heat, she sipped from the cup of tea Edna had placed on a chair beside the tub. Jean's arms, legs, and back cried with fatigue. No amount of hiking would ward off the soreness that had already begun. *When this is over, I won't ever do another push-up in my life,* she promised herself.

By the time Jean dressed, Marta came to say Eve wanted her in the parlor.

Jean navigated the stairs down more carefully than she had gone up. Every muscle seemed to beg for bed rest.

Eve began the afternoon by giving some history. She said that in the beginning of the occupation, part of France had been designated "Unoccupied France." Hitler had promised some autonomy. Lyon was in the unoccupied zone, now called Vichy France for the city, Vichy, that housed the puppet government of Marshall Petain.

"Petain's armistice with Hitler stripped France of everything. The Germans took over our factories to build their war machines and ammunition. They shipped our food to Germany. Now our people live on the poorest subsistence, especially in the cities where they cannot grow a small garden or have chickens."

"In cafés and hotels where I may eat, will I order or simply request what they have?" Jean asked.

"You may be given a menu if they can offer a choice, but probably they will just tell you what they are serving for that meal. We will prepare you as best we can, but changes happen so frequently we can't be certain we've heard the latest. Wherever you go, avoid unnecessary conversation. At the same time, you must blend in and not appear secretive. You must never show surprise when you come upon an unexpected circumstance. Make a joke on yourself if you discover you have asked for something that has not been available for a long time."

Jean nodded. "I think I'd better take notes so I can review what you've said."

"Good idea. Don't think, however, that you can memorize all you'll need. That is a false security. Only your quick wits and inventiveness can protect you. Am I frightening you?"

"Yes."

"Good. In France, fear is rational and necessary."

"Poor Giselle," Jean murmured.

"Did your cousin tell you anything about her life after the occupation?"

"No. She couldn't write much after France fell."

"Then I will fill you in briefly," Eve said. "The first thing we lost was communication. Every newspaper, magazine, book publisher, movie studio, and radio station—all of our media fell under strict control of the Germans. Owners, managers, producers, editors, writers, and artists either collaborated with the Germans or lost their jobs. In less than six months the normal vehicles of communication in France produced only German propaganda.

"People were so hungry for the truth that underground newspapers sprang up and printed everything they could hear from BBC on their hidden radios. Those underground papers were our first steps of resistance. The publishers risked death, but people helped to hide them if the Gestapo came close."

Jean nodded, trying to imagine an occupied United States with all papers, magazines, books, and movies controlled by Nazis. She couldn't. Yet Giselle would have said the same thing about France ten years ago.

Eve poured them both more tea and continued. "Next the Germans ordered all Frenchmen of working age to report for deportation to Germany to work in factories and on farms. Men by the thousands fled from their homes, hid, and then later joined the Resistance. The Germans continued to plunder France, sending everything back to Germany. We have no gasoline. Cars have been converted to run on gasses from heating wood in a crude device that looks like a small boiler, similar to a steam engine."

"Gas from wood! How can they run a car on that?"

Eve smiled. "Poorly, but it is very clever. They build a small fire to heat either wood or grasses in this special container. As the material heats up, it gives off a gas, which is then piped directly to the engine's carburetor."

"So 'warming up the car' means something quite different in France."

"Everything in France is quite different." The light went out of her eyes. She picked up her tea, drained it, and set the empty cup down. "Work shifts were made to match German time, even though we are in a different time zone. If anyone violated curfew, they were liable to be shot on sight, and many were."

Eve frowned and shook her head. She murmured, as if to herself, "I need not tell you all the suffering. . . ." Her voice turned businesslike again. "Trains still run, but schedules change frequently. We can't guarantee what you may find when you get there, but it will be imperative that you do not ask many questions. Even if you see a printed time schedule, train runs may have been dropped or changed long enough for local people to wonder why you do not know.

"You cannot trust anyone. Some of the French are collaborating with the Gestapo. The Milice, Petain's military police, are as dangerous as the Gestapo. They have became the French SS. Petain has commanded them to destroy the Resistance. Everywhere you go, they will check your papers. We will give you good identification, but it will be your task to conform flawlessly to your assumed identity."

Jean's mind raced to absorb all this. Raising her head from taking notes, she drank the rest of her tea. That small movement revealed soreness in her back and shoulders. She stretched, shrugged to loosen her muscles, and settled back to making notes.

Eve spent another hour giving Jean detail upon detail about eastern France and the city of Lyon. She described the people, the terrain, the customs, and finally what the rail trip might be like from Jean's drop point to Lyon.

At last Eve stood and said, "This is enough for today. After you've taken your walk, we'll have dinner, and perhaps you can rest until Georges comes. Oh, I almost forgot to tell you—when you write to your uncle, put this address for your return address." She handed Jean a slip of paper with an address in Scotland on it. "Harry has arranged for your mail to go through his office there. Give him your outgoing mail. He will see to it that it is sent from there. He said to put this London address on all your mail back to Abergavenny, and he will see to that postmark too." She handed Jean a second slip of paper.

"Good," Jean responded. "I hope my mail catches up with me soon."

On the way upstairs to dress for her assigned two-mile hike, Jean thought of Tom. The mere mention of mail brought him to mind. Would she ever get over this chronic hunger for him? How could a man, in such a short time, so capture her? She wanted to forget him, truly, but sometimes instead of struggling against thinking about him, it was a relief to just give in and remember.

Tom had shared her concern about Giselle. Of all people, he

would understand her wanting to go to her, even though he would not approve of her taking the risk. *Heaven help me, I miss him more than ever!*

By now, he could be overseas. She swallowed hard.

CHAPTER EIGHT

Before supper Jean pulled on a sweater, knit cap, and jacket, and set out to do her required two miles. Clouds scurried overhead, but the breeze felt dry. Her hike led her through the old walled city of York, past the cathedral, and down narrow cobblestone streets where the upper stories of some buildings almost touched. Walking briskly, she glanced in shop windows that displayed a sparse, wartime selection of household necessities, modern in contrast to windows that looked as if they belonged in a Charles Dickens novel.

She hiked on through town, out a gate in the ancient city wall, and into more modern architecture, first finding a business district and finally a pleasant residential area. Here dooryards—those small treasured spaces between the front gates and the houses—were carefully tended, expressing the Brits' love affair with gardens. Purple, white, and yellow crocuses and multihued primroses were just beginning to unfold bright petals. Clumps of violets sent sweet perfume over low stone walls.

Why, spring will come soon! She'd almost forgotten such beauty would return despite the war. Early February always brought out the violets and primroses in her grandmother's garden in Oregon. At the memory a twinge of homesickness swept over her. At the same time, the glimpse of new life here in a carefully tended garden gave Jean an energizing burst of hope as she turned to retrace her steps back to St. Mary's Lane and Eve's old row house. This spring she would be with Giselle.

By the time she reached her destination, her feet were

weighted with fatigue. Quietly letting herself in, she wished she could soak again in a hot tub and go right to bed, but two hot baths in one day was a luxury she wouldn't dare ask of her hostess. Without looking for Eve, she forced herself up the stairs to get ready for the evening schedule.

When Jean sat down to supper that night, she and Eve listened to the BBC. Everywhere, except for the Russians on the eastern front, the Allies were making little success. The battle raged in Italy at Anzio, where a second landing had been made. Fierce fighting continued around Cassino with little progress. She looked at Eve.

Eve shrugged and turned off the radio. "It's time we began our own work."

While Jean ate, Eve watched and coached her every action. Jean listened, obeyed, and tried to imagine what Giselle's life had been like as a resistant. By the time they finished eating, Marta was ushering Lieutenant Crozet into the dining room.

"Georges! Will you have coffee?" Eve asked, speaking naturally in French as she had been doing with Jean.

"Please," he responded. He took a chair at the table and asked, "How has it been, your first day of training, Marie?"

"There is so much to learn. After listening to Eve, I'm more concerned about how I'll do when I reach France than how I will get there."

"That is my concern also," he said soberly. "When you have finished your meal, Eve and I will take turns acting like people you may encounter in everyday situations. You will respond to the best of your ability. Then we will have a critique session in which Eve and I will advise you how to do better."

"Sounds good! I'm ready as soon as you finish your coffee," Jean said.

A few minutes later in the parlor, Eve became a storekeeper from whom Jean wanted to purchase food. Georges was a café owner, and Jean practiced ordering an evening meal. Another time he played the part of a station agent of the railroad. Then he became a local policeman requesting her identification papers. Next Eve was a crotchety landlady, snooping for personal information about Marie.

In each instance Jean reacted as best she could from what

she'd learned. Afterward Eve and Georges gave her more detailed information, which she now found easier to remember. They also pointed out dangerous mistakes she'd made if she should be talking to a collaborator. And they corrected her pronunciation of certain French words that revealed an American accent.

Finally Georges said, "Enough. You are tired from this long day. Do not worry that we find so many faults. By your mistakes you will learn well. Now, Eve, can you have Marta draw a nice hot bath for Marie?"

Jean was so glad he thought of the bath that his manner of treating her like a child did not offend her as it usually would have. She sighed. "Oh, thank you."

Eve and Georges laughed.

"You go on up. Marta will be along in a moment to help," Eve said.

Halfway up the stairs, Jean glanced back into the warmly lighted parlor. Eve stood beside the fireplace with her hands clasped tightly at waist level. Her voice did not carry, but her face telegraphed distress. Georges also spoke too low to hear. He shook his head slowly, sadly, and his shoulders lost their military correctness.

Are they talking about Giselle? Jean wondered with dread. She gave herself a mental shake. The way things were in France, they could be talking about any number of other people.

At the hospital in Lyon, Giselle insisted on getting up to sit in a wheelchair as soon as the doctor permitted. At first she was so light-headed, she swayed unsteadily even while gripping the chair's wooden arms.

Sister Therese hovered beside her. "Madame, certainly I should put you back into your bed."

"No! I'm fine. I must stay up to regain my balance."

"Yes, that is so, but—"

"I'm better already. See?" She let go of the chair arms and sat straight and still.

"Yes. That is good."

"If you please, wheel me out so I may see the rest of the hospital."

Sister's soft, round face grew anxious. "You are not strong enough."

"Surely if I can sit here, I could sit in a hall and look out a window," Giselle retorted.

"I'm not allowed to say. Only Mother Agnes can permit it."

"Go then and ask her. You see I am steady, and I'm not tired."

"I must not leave you alone."

"Would it take so long? Please. . . ."

Still the nurse shook her head.

Giselle, peering up at her, realized she was very young. *Younger than me? I don't even know how old I am!* Giselle had seen no other nurse, night or day. At least she couldn't remember seeing anyone else. She'd questioned Sister Therese endlessly and had found no discrepancy in the nun's statement that she knew nothing about her. Her attention dropped to the thin new skin encircling her wrists like pink bracelets. What had made these scars? Maybe whatever had erased her memory made her so wild that the sisters tied her down. No, surely hospital restraints could not leave such marks. She ran her finger over the ragged welt on her left wrist. "Sister, did I have these marks the first time you saw me?"

The nun's mouth trembled. "Please do not ask. I am not to say. You are not well enough."

"I am well enough. I demand to know!" Giselle's heart began to hammer so hard she could feel the thumping against her ribs. Startled, she pressed her hand against her chest.

"Madame, please don't excite yourself. Here, you must lie down again."

Giselle did not argue. Weakness consumed her, and the chug of her heart frightened her. For several minutes her heart continued to beat abnormally, as if trying to send great gulps of blood instead of a steady flow. Finally, to her relief, the pounding sensation eased. She looked up at Sister Therese. "Why did my heart pound so?"

"The doctor says it is only because you are so weak. You have been very ill. He says your heart will be all right once you regain your strength. In the meantime, you must not strain yourself." She reached down and took Giselle's hand. "I am sorry not to be able to help you more, but the doctor says you will get well. Try to believe and be patient."

In response to her sympathetic touch, Giselle's eyes filled with tears. "If only I could remember, I know I would get well faster."

Sister's hand tightened on hers. "Sometimes the loss of memory is for your protection, to help you get well."

"You think something so terrible has happened to me?"

"I cannot say, but there is the war, and we are an occupied country."

Giselle's heart speeded up. "And the enemy?"

Sister's face flashed worry again. "I have said too much. Please. Lie quietly while I go for your lunch tray." She let go of Giselle's hand and left swiftly.

For the first time Giselle was aware of the click of a lock after the door closed. Had they always locked her in? Why?

She looked around the room again, searching for any clue that would tell her about the hospital. This long room provided much more space than one patient and one nurse needed. There were no windows except for some up high, set into the sides of the ceiling. The high ceiling, finished in ornate tiles that appeared to be very old, soared upward from the windows in a manner that almost stirred a memory. She struggled to capture a clear thought from the nebulous feeling.

On the edges of her mind, she sensed this room did not suit a normal hospital. But how could she know? The wheelchair, the bed, the side table, the wash basins, Sister's narrow cot—all seemed appropriate to a sickroom. The desk, upholstered chairs, and small bookcase at the far end of the room looked different, less starkly functional. The white stone floor was immaculate, the yellowed plaster walls barren except for a large bronze crucifix above the desk.

The rasp of a key in a lock announced the return of Sister Therese. She entered with the food tray. An older woman in a simple black habit followed on silent feet. Her tall shape seemed made up of three parts, delineated by a heavy gold crucifix suspended from her neck and an ivory-colored cotton rope looped around her waist, from which dangled a cluster of keys. As she closed the door, the keys clinked together, making a cheerful jingle. The tall woman seemed familiar to Giselle for a moment, but the feeling of recall immediately slipped away.

The older nun stepped to her bedside and said, "Madame, I am Mother Agnes. Sister tells me you are distressed. How may I help you?"

Again Giselle could not hold back tears, proof, she supposed, of her extreme weakness. "Please, Mother, can you tell me anything about who I am? Where I am? How I got here? What's wrong with me?"

Mother Agnes motioned with her head toward Sister Therese. Sister set the tray on the bedside table and left the room, closing the door quietly.

"My dear, I'm sorry. I can tell you very little. First, please rest easy about your health. The doctor says you are recovering now and will regain your strength quickly. As to where you are, this is the Sisters of Mercy Hospital. You were brought here by a man who told me only your first name: Julie. Does your name awaken any memory?"

Giselle frowned and desperately tried to own the name. Defeated, she shook her head. "No. Did the man say anything more?"

"He said he could not return for you, but that someone else would come."

Giselle's heart began to race again. "How can I ever go with someone I don't even know?" Her voice rose toward panic. "Isn't there something you can do to identify me? Someone who could help me remember?"

"Madame, you have forgotten the war. The Nazis ... Germany now occupies all of France. No one can safely search for identity or relatives."

"Nazis?" The strange word pierced her mind and quivered there, but she could remember nothing. "Was I hurt in the war?"

"Yes. This much I know."

"Strange that I can't remember a thing as big as a war."

"Not so strange. In some cases, memory loss is a blessing—God's way of protecting us. As you grow stronger, your memories will return. Do you believe in God, my dear?"

Suddenly angry, Giselle cried, "How can I know what I believe when I don't even know who I am?"

The nun held her hand tightly. "Please try to be calm. I know this is very hard to bear, but you must stay peaceful to speed your recovery. You will be all right."

Giselle pressed her lips together and throttled the scream of frustration that tightened her throat.

The nun smoothed her hair and then gently cupped her forehead. Her hand felt warm and strong and sincerely caring. Giselle closed her eyes and let go of some of her fear.

After a moment, Mother Agnes said, "Could you not eat some of your lunch? Doing normal things may help bring back memories of normal things."

Giselle opened her eyes. "I will try."

"Let me call Sister Therese to help you." Before Giselle could beg her to stay, she left. The clinking of her keys faded with the click of the door latch.

At the air base, in addition to frequent drops to the floor for ten push-ups, Jean was supposed to learn a proper PLF—land on the balls of her feet, flex her knees, and not *splat*—Sarge's term for a bad PLF.

She practiced by jumping from a height of about ten feet to the ground. To Jean the height of the platform might as well have been fifty feet. It was much farther than any sensible person would try to jump.

The first time, Sarge, standing beside her, gave the same signal to jump he said he would use in the airplane. He slapped her on the back of the helmet and barked, "Go!" With clenched teeth she leaped. She splatted, but at least she had jumped and had not broken anything. He ordered her up to jump again ... and again.

By the end of the week, she could do ten push-ups, shuffle-jog one mile, and splat only about half the time. Although she had acquired new aches daily, her soreness from the first day's excesses decreased.

The second Monday Sarge took her to a tower. Once again she thought of the guard towers at Tulelake. Sarge said these were twenty-nine feet high. With coveralls over her trousers and jacket, but minus the parachute pack on her back, she climbed zigzagging steps to the top. Sarge clipped her harness to a ring on a cable that descended at a steep slant to the ground. The cable would let her fall at the speed she would drop in a parachute.

A man stood below at her fall location while Sarge stood beside her. He checked her harness back and front. "In a plane," he explained, "we always check the harness of the trooper in front of us as we head for the door, and the guy behind us checks ours."

This information did nothing to calm Jean's panic. Gazing at the ground, she froze. *I can't do this!*

At her side, Sarge said quietly but firmly, "You gonna quit now, Marie?"

No! her will silently cried. "No!" she yelped.

"Okay." He slapped her on the helmet. "Go!"

She launched herself. The ground leaped up at her. Flexing her knees and preparing her feet, she hit and made a good PLF.

Sarge beckoned her back up again. He ordered one jump after another, until fatigue made her splat with painful regularity.

As they walked back to the office to meet Captain Lloyd, Sarge said, "You're ready for a drop with a chute from a higher tower, like at Fort Benning, Georgia, but we ain't got any high towers here. Too bad. The high practice with a chute would set you up better for the real thing from a plane."

Silently Jean thanked God she was not at Fort Benning.

A few minutes later when Jean climbed into the front seat of Harry's army car, she saw a large brown envelope on the seat beside him. In heavy black letters her French name, Marie Fauvre, stared up at her. "Do I have mail?" she exclaimed.

"Yes indeed. A handful. Sorry it took so long for me to get it rerouted." He smiled, appearing more relaxed than she'd seen him since their leaving Abergavenny.

Jean picked up the envelope and held it, savoring the feel of several envelopes inside.

"Sarge says you're progressing pretty well," Harry said. "Faster than some of the men he's trained."

"Nice of him to say so, but that's hard for me to believe."

"He's a good judge. I have to tell you it eases my mind. I've really regretted letting Georges talk me into allowing you to try this. But now ... it's still as dangerous as ever, but I feel our training may see you through."

"May?"

"That's the best we can hope for when we send someone over." He gave her a reflective look before returning his gaze to the road. "I would have pulled you out of this in a minute if Georges' colonel hadn't corroborated his statement that your cousin knows enough to make a difference for the Allies if the Germans get their hands on her."

Jean's fingers tightened around the thick envelope in her lap. "I will get her out," she said firmly.

He nodded. "It's good you feel that way. You'll need all the confidence you can marshal. I have a man lined up to train you in the use and care of the small handgun you'll take. You'll meet with him tomorrow afternoon and every day from now on for target practice."

Dread ballooned into her mind, crowding out reason. "A gun?" Fortunately her voice stayed even and low.

"You can't have imagined we would send you in unarmed. . . . I say, I think you did. What kind of spying did you do for your uncle, anyway?" He stared at her until she worried about him driving off the road.

"Nothing that required a gun," she said stiffly.

"Well, you'll not go without one this time."

Jean searched desperately for a reason not to carry a gun. "What if I'm searched and they find a concealed weapon? Won't that put me in more danger than if I were unarmed?"

"That's a risk all agents take," Harry said. "You'll have to find a quick way to dispose of it or tell a good story." His lower lip shot out, and his blue gaze challenged her. "If the gun is a problem, we can stop this now. You're out, and I'll get on with other things."

"It's not a problem!" she snapped, hoping her staged anger would cover the trembling that had started in her larger muscles and was now clutching at her vocal chords.

"Righto."

While he drove on in silence, she fought for control. *How can I ever learn to handle a gun? Maybe Georges can convince him it wouldn't be right for this operation, for who I am as Marie Fauvre.*

Harry interrupted her thoughts. "In that envelope with your mail I've also placed detailed survey maps of the Saône river valley as far north as Dijon and the city of Lyon and the outlying hills. A sheaf of photos show daily life in Lyon, including uniformed Milice and Gestapo and the Gestapo headquarters. Memorize as much as you can. Have you memorized the details I gave you on Madame Marie Fauvre's life and family?"

"Yes," she said, relieved at the change of subject. "I go over the material every night before I retire."

"Do the same thing with this new material. You'll be receiving more photos and maps as Georges obtains them. Look carefully at the old stone Sisters of Mercy Hospital for the Insane. Giselle is hiding there."

"In an insane asylum?" Jean gasped.

"Nuns oversee the hospital as humanely as possible. The Mother Superior has hidden others for the Resistance."

Jean mused over that fact for a moment and then asked, "Is the hospital in Lyon?"

"Georges will tell you where it is and answer your questions. So far, he has not told me, or anyone, except your uncle."

Jean clutched the envelope more tightly.

Back in her room at Eve's house, Jean threw her coat on a chair, opened the envelope, and spread out its contents on her bed. She had letters from Grandmother, Uncle Al, Mary, Nella . . . and Tom!

CHAPTER NINE

With her heart racing crazily, Jean sat down at her desk and slit open Tom's letter.

January 25, 1944
Dear Jean,
I know I'm being selfish to write to you, but my sister tells me you are still writing to her. I miss your letters so much, and suddenly, with the war and all, it seems stupid not to let you know how I feel and to ask if you might write to me, just as a friend, like you write to her.
I won't blame you if you don't want to have anything to do with me. I've treated you badly, and now I may be doing so again by writing. I mean, I'm so sorry I hurt you, and it seems crass and wrong to ask if we can still be friends. But can we?

Very sorry and hopeful,
Tom

P.S. As I write this, we're still on maneuvers here in Mississippi, but my mail will find me wherever I go.

Jean bit her lip and hugged his letter to her breast. *Tom! Oh Tom, I love you! How can I be just a friend?* She closed her eyes, and on the dark screen of her lids she could see him smiling, saluting, moving toward her in the station at Brownwood. *No. Grow up,* she told herself. She opened her eyes and laid his letter on the desk. He was asking too much. It was unfair. She should be outraged, but she wasn't. Without touching the opened page, she read his clear, strong handwriting again. *I miss your letters so much, and . . . with the war and all, it seems stupid not to let you know . . .*

With the war—with him going to the front and with her about to parachute into enemy territory, it did seem stupid. Why not settle for what he wanted, when she so badly longed for any possible contact with him? *Think about this,* said her head. *No, do it,* cried every other part of her. She wished she could talk to Giselle or even to Elizabeth.

Sighing, she pulled the photos from the large envelope and thumbed through them until she came to a Romanesque stone building showing two nuns on the broad front steps beside a woman in a wheelchair. Wrought-iron grilles covered all the narrow, deep-set windows. Heavy wooden shutters on every window stood ready to be bolted shut. With compressed lips, she studied Sisters of Mercy Hospital. *Oh, Giselle! Shut up in an insane asylum. Separated from Claude and the girls. How do you stand it?*

She didn't need to talk to Giselle to know what she'd say about Tom's request. Sure as anything, she'd say, "If you love Tom, write to him while you can."

Jean reached for her stationery and pen, then sat and stared at the blank paper. Her last letters to him had been love letters. How should she start? What should she say? She couldn't tell him anything about what she was doing now. And while she was in France, out of touch for no telling how long, what would he think? *Can I prepare him for that without revealing anything?* Having decided to write, she determined she needed time to prepare herself.

Next she opened Uncle Al's letter. He wrote he had no news about Giselle. Jean already knew that from talking to Harry. The rest of his note expressed his concern for her health. *Poor Uncle Al. He'd be a lot more worried if he knew the truth!* She laid his fatherly letter aside, then opened the thin envelope from Nella.

> *Dear Jean,*
>   *I can scarcely make myself write this but know you would wish to hear—my brother Charles was killed in action in Italy. Mum is devastated. So I'm writing for her as well as me. Daddy carries on, but he feels as bad as Mum. You know how I feel. I try to pray, but inside I can't believe God takes special care of any one person. Now I wonder if this made my prayers for Charles meaningless. I hope not. Please pray for Mum and Daddy, and me too.*
> > *Your friend,*
> > *Nella*

Grief overwhelmed Jean. Leaning her face on her crossed arms, she sobbed. She cried for the MacDougalls, for Giselle and Claude, for all the young men who had left the station hospital to return to the battlefield, and for Tom—for all that she had lost when she lost him.

At last, emptied of weeks of postponed tears, she wiped her eyes, blew her nose, and then picked up her pen. She wrote a note of condolence to Elizabeth and Reverend MacDougall and then a separate note to Nella.

> *Dear Nella,*
>
> *I'm so sorry you've lost Charles. Please don't ever think that how you feel makes a difference about your prayers. God hears us, but so many times we can't understand why He chooses to let such painful things happen. We can't see the whole picture. I believe He wants us to pray even though He may say no or not now or not this time. This is so hard, Nella. I am praying that you will find the comfort Jesus promised when He said, "Blessed are they that mourn, for they shall be comforted."*
>
>
>
> *With deepest sympathy and love,*
> *Jean*
>
>

She sealed and stamped each envelope, and then she took a fresh sheet of paper and began writing to Tom.

> *Dear Tom,*
>
> *I've missed getting letters from you too. Yes, let's be friends and write.*

I love you so much!

> *I've found that the Red Cross prepared me well for the work over here, and I really enjoy my job.*
>
> *The British are brave and enduring. When I watch them and our GIs, I know we will win this war.*

Darling, please take care of yourself!

> *I've seen Uncle Al only once, but that's once more than if I'd stayed in the States.*

She rambled on about daily life in the station hospital. At the end she chose her words even more carefully.

> *If you don't hear from me for a while, it won't be because I*

don't want to write. Mail delivery often gets interrupted here—a transport problem, I guess.

Would he believe such a lie? She signed *Your friend, Jeanie*, then immediately sealed her message in an envelope so she could not be tempted later to add a word of affection.

The day after the visit from Mother Agnes, Giselle insisted on bathing and dressing herself. Sitting on her bedside chair, she tried to brush the snarls out of her hair. "Sister, how can I do my hair with no memory of how it should be and no mirror to see what I'm doing. Can't you please bring me a mirror?"

Sister Therese smiled as she tugged the sheets from Giselle's bed and quickly tucked clean ones over the mattress. "I must take these sheets to the laundry. When I return I will arrange your hair."

"I can do it myself if you will bring me a mirror."

Sister left without making any promises.

Giselle brushed until her short hair felt smooth and sleek. She started to part it with a comb but stopped. She desperately wanted to see how it looked. She could not remember hearing Sister turn the lock when she left. Maybe there was a mirror nearby in the hall. She cautiously rose to her feet. Her legs felt weak but not shaky. One step, then two—she moved to the door and tried the knob. It turned.

Swinging the door open, she halted in surprise. Instead of a lighted corridor, she faced a windowless, oppressive room. With her next breath she wanted to vomit. The dark room breathed out a strong chemical smell. She couldn't remember why, but she knew evil and horrible pain went with the odor. She stumbled backward, panic welling in her throat. Instantly a greater terror made her hold back her scream. If she made a sound, she would be discovered. And this was not a hospital!

She closed the door and leaned against it, panting. If this wasn't a hospital, then what was it? Would the nuns lie? *Are they really nuns?* The horror triggered by the vile odor warned her not to trust anyone.

As quickly as she could, Giselle returned to her bedside chair and collapsed upon it. She felt certain she wasn't supposed to have seen that room. Terror sharpened her senses. *I must not let*

them know I can walk that far. And I must find some way to escape.

When Georges came that evening and had settled into a chair at the dining table with his cup of coffee, Jean said, "Harry has selected a man to teach me how to use a handgun."

"Good! Then he feels you are progressing satisfactorily."

"Sarge says I am, but I can't help wondering—would a French mother of two children carry a concealed gun in occupied France?"

He frowned and his brown eyes took on the hard expression that had intimidated her when they first met. "No. Not likely, but you must take that risk. You must become an expert. The gun should be an extension of your hand, and your automatic reflex must be to shoot to kill."

She shifted her weight to the forward edge of the Queen Anne dining chair and did not let her gaze waver from his. "If you are sure this is necessary, of course I will learn."

"You will not go into France unless you become an expert marksman with a handgun."

"I will learn, and I will go." She was surprised at the honest anger in her voice. Her rage at being forced to violate her principles lent validity to the emotion she had intended to fake.

Georges turned to Eve. "So what shall we demonstrate tonight?"

"I think a typical ride on a train and the usual inspections, for a start," Eve said.

Jean watched, listened, and then became the passenger while Georges declared her identification card out of order. Eve played another frightened passenger in the next seat. They kept Jean so busy with possible problems that she had no time to think again about learning to shoot to kill the next day—not until bedtime.

Sitting up in bed, she studied the maps and photos and reviewed the details of Marie Fauvre's life just before falling asleep. The reality in the photos steadied her. She had been naïve to think she could go into France unarmed. Now she must show Harry and Georges she could shoot with deadly accuracy. Her stomach gave a queasy contraction.

The next morning on the way to the airfield Harry handed her a small angular handgun tucked snugly in a leather holster. Her mouth went dry, but she said, "It looks like the ones I've seen in movies in the hands of mobsters or detectives."

"It's a pocket-size MAB—the gun your U.S. Women's Army Corps personnel carry for self-defense. Fortunately it was manufactured in France before the occupation, so it won't be out of place."

She accepted the gun as casually as she could manage. It was surprisingly heavy.

"That size is not good for much unless you are very close," Harry said, "which is why you'll have to become very skilled. If there's any hesitation on your part, an enemy could grab it and turn it on you."

She closed her fingers around the gun, outwardly accepting and cradling the thing in her palm. Jean wished she could throw it out the window, but nothing was going to keep her from going to France.

"I see," she said calmly.

That afternoon when Jean finished jump training, Corporal Haines, a young man with a prickly GI haircut showing below his cap, took her in a jeep to the firing range. He set up a special target for her, much closer than the ones already in place. "This is a point-and-shoot gun, ma'am, kind of like aiming your finger. It doesn't give much kick, so you can just raise your hand and pull the trigger. You load the clip like this."

Haines pulled the clip from the handle, pushed in small bullets one by one, then removed them. He shoved the empty clip back into the handle. "Always be sure the safety here is on before chambering a cartridge. Even when you know the safety is on, treat the gun as if it has no safety. To chamber a bullet you pull back this slide." Under his fingers, it looked to her as if the whole top portion of the gun slid backward to reveal a short barrel with an open hole into the firing chamber.

He released his grip, letting the slide snap back to its original position, and then turned his hand so she could watch the fingers of his other hand. "Keep a good grip on the handle and outside the trigger guard, like this. Never let your finger go near the trigger. And be sure the barrel is aimed down, away from yourself or anyone else." He pulled the slide back again. "When you fire, the spent cartridge ejects through this hole." He let the slide close again and handed the gun to her. "Now let's see you load your weapon."

The blue metal of the snub-nosed gun sent a chill from her hand to the fear in her mind. The roughness of the knurled flat handle felt as dangerous as a hand grenade. Awkwardly she removed the clip and tried to load it. She fumbled so badly several bullets fell to the ground. Starting to scramble after them, she felt Corporal Haines lift the gun from her hand.

"Never forget where the barrel is aimed, even when it's not loaded!" He scooped up the last two bullets and handed them back to her. "You really are new to this, aren't you?" he said not unkindly. "Just go slow. Think before you make any move. Never, at any time, take your mind off where the gun is aimed. And never touch the trigger until you intend to shoot. Okay, now. Go slow and concentrate."

Jean felt as if she were handling a time bomb about to go off. With trembling fingers she finally loaded the gun.

He then demonstrated how to aim and shoot and said, "Now see if you can come near the center of the target."

She slowly raised the gun as he had done. When she squeezed the trigger, she was relieved to feel firm resistance. The gun could not be simply jolted and go off. Pulling the trigger took effort. The loud report made her jump.

Corporal Haines ordered her to fire again and again. With every squeeze of the trigger, she told herself in a silent singsong, *It's only a target . . . it's only a target. . . .*

Most of the second clip hit the target. He coached her on reloading and firing for about twenty minutes. By the time he let her quit, sweat was trickling down her front and back, making her clothes uncomfortably sticky.

"You're doing good," he said as he drove her back to Sarge's barracks where she was to meet Harry.

Jean hoped she was smiling and wondered what he would call poor. In her assumed French accent, she said, "Thank you very much. It is difficult, but I will learn."

The gun jabbed against her ribs under her coat. She shifted her position to ease the unwelcome pressure. It seemed to taunt

her. She had so little time to become an expert, and she feared she would never be able to use the gun against a person, even in self-defense.

At the airfield and at home Jean began to hike with a weighted backpack. She jumped from the tower until her PLFs were consistently good. While being suspended from the ceiling of the harness shed, dressed in her chest protector—which made her feel like a turtle—and her jump suit, she practiced handling the riser straps. The risers, taking off from her shoulders, were supposed to guide her fall when she pulled on them.

Sarge watched her with a worried look on his face. "You gotta get more power in your hands and arms," he said.

After that, more frequently than ever, he barked out, "Down on your face."

Soon her arms and shoulders increased in strength. Ten push-ups became easy, except at the end of the day. Mornings when she climbed out of bed, she felt a new energy. She began to run for twenty minutes before breakfast—*slog* was a more fitting word, because she plowed through rain-muddied streets more days than not.

At the firing range, she was now hitting the center area of the target, and occasionally the center of the bull's-eye. Still, she did not feel the gun was an extension of her hand yet. Corporal Haines said it just took time.

And Jean's undercover training with Eve continued nonstop. Georges had brought to her more detailed maps of the districts of Lyon and their outlying areas and also more photographs. He still had not told her exactly where Giselle was located, but Jean surmised she must be in Lyon somewhere.

One night, contrary to Corporal Haines' instructions to never point a gun at someone she didn't intend to shoot, Georges insisted that she practice defending herself with her unloaded gun. To draw and aim at him nearly made her faint. From his expression, she knew he read the horror she could not hide. But he didn't say anything. He made her defend herself over and over, drawing her gun and holding him at bay. After each of her awkward responses, Georges and Eve critiqued, then Eve would demonstrate the appropriate reaction.

Finally Eve exclaimed, "Enough for tonight, don't you think, Georges? Marie will do better after a rest. Let's have a bit of tea and then say good-night."

But Georges scooped up his coat. "Sorry. I can't stay for the tea. Give her a little more advice while you sip your brew."

Eve saw him to the door and then fetched cups and a pot of tea. Discouraged and heartsick, Jean slumped on her chair, wondering how she would convince Georges she could defend herself or Giselle.

Eve poured her tea and added milk and a dash of sugar. "Here. Drink up. You'll feel better."

Jean sipped slowly.

"It's difficult to act out a violent situation when you are not a violent person," Eve said. "Georges knows that. He doesn't expect perfection. He only wants to expose you to different possibilities."

Suddenly Jean's control slipped. "Oh, Eve, I will never be able to aim that gun to kill anyone—not to save myself. What if I fail Giselle? What am I to do?"

"You can never know how you will do before the time comes. You will be able. I know you will."

"How can you say that? You don't know how I feel—" The expression on Eve's face stopped her. "Have you ever had to shoot someone?"

"Had to? I thought I had to." Eve sipped her tea and then drank deeply of it. "I shall tell you, and you decide.

"One day two resistants were with me at the train station when the Milice began loading Jewish women into a railcar. It made me sick to see Frenchmen acting like Nazis, rounding up people as if they were animals. Then I saw that they were separating mothers from their children, putting them in different cars." Her face suddenly contorted, and she pressed her hand over her eyes.

In a moment she apologized. "I didn't know it would hurt so much. The memory is always with me, and I supposed I was hardened by now." She cleared her throat. "There was nothing my friends and I could do, but without a word to each other, we determined to be witnesses who someday could testify to this crime. As we watched with a group of helpless bystanders, one very young mother, carrying a tiny baby, couldn't negotiate the high step into the car. She reached up for help, but one of the Milice grabbed the baby from her and threw it down on the concrete. I couldn't tell—" Her voice cracked, then she continued. "I couldn't tell how badly the baby was hurt. The man then tossed it into the car with the other children."

Eve's story hit Jean like a sledgehammer. *Oh, God. Oh, God!* her crushed heart cried.

"I had a Luger, a long heavy German handgun, hidden in my shopping bag. I had taken it the night before off of a dead German guard, and I had not yet turned it over to the leader of our réseau. In my outrage, I pulled out the Luger and shot the man who had hurt the baby. My friends then grabbed me and dragged me behind a group of older people. We escaped only because those onlookers created much confusion that sent the Milice on a false trail."

"Did the man die?" Jean was surprised at how emotionless her voice sounded. She felt ill. Eve's distress, the vision of the mother's anguish, and the baby's suffering all fused into a single stab of agony.

"Yes. I am an excellent shot. I do not regret killing the man, but I do regret losing control and placing others in danger. This you must not do, which is why we train you so intensively."

"I understand. I will try to be a good student."

"I can see you still doubt you could shoot anyone. But I believe you will never let anything happen to your cousin or her children."

Stripped of all need for pretense, Jean said, "I pray you are right."

In the middle of the third week of February when Jean walked into Sarge's office with her jump suit, boots, and the rest of her gear, Sarge said casually, "The weather's good. There's no wind. I got us a plane for today."

"I'm going to jump from a plane?" Her ears began to ring. She bent over and pretended to tie her boots tighter, hoping the blood would return to her head.

"You're ready," Sarge said.

Jean struggled to breathe slow and easy to control her skyrocketing pulse rate. *I'll never be ready, but I've got to do it.* "I'll get into my gear and be right back."

Deep muscle trembling set in. By the time she returned to Sarge, wearing the jump coveralls and parachute, her teeth were chattering. The heavy layers of clothing concealed her shaking. As long as she didn't have to talk, he wouldn't notice her uncontrollable terror. She clenched her teeth and silently followed him out to the airplane.

CHAPTER TEN

The rumbling British de Havilland Mosquito circled the jump area. Jean would jump out the bomb compartment, located in the plane's belly, taking the same route as a bomb.

"You know what to do," Sarge yelled. "I've checked your harness, and everything's fine. Your release is clipped to the cable. When I slap you on the helmet and say 'Go,' jump exactly like you've been doing in practice."

She quickly nodded, unable to trust her voice.

Sergeant Ainsworth motioned for her to step to the edge of the open bay. She moved to obey, willing herself to pretend she was on the practice tower, but the roar of the plane's engines and the bumpiness of the air foiled her game. She had studied this procedure many times in the training film, and Sarge had coached her well, but nothing could have prepared her for standing there in the plane ready to leap. In France she would jump from six hundred feet. Today she was higher, which Sarge insisted was safer. It looked worse than the thousand feet he'd mentioned. The wind and the noise raged at her senses. *Oh, God, help me!*

Sarge slapped the back of her helmet. "Go!" he ordered.

Jean lunged forward and dropped.

The wind smacked her, but she got away from the plane safely, plummeting downward with her eyes squeezed shut. A released riser slashed across the back of her neck, making her see stars. She had forgotten to keep her chin tucked down. The parachute snapped open and wrenched her whole body to a slower descent. She floated toward the drop area, swinging from side to side like a clock pendulum. She seemed to be to the right of the drop area where men waited for her. Pulling hard on the left risers, she was able to alter her course slightly toward the drop site. She pulled again but couldn't see that it helped, because she was swinging too much.

The ground rushed up at her. She flexed her knees for the PLF and splatted yards from the ground crew. Grabbing the lines, she struggled to deflate the chute but could not. The billowing chute began dragging her along the ground on her side. But soon a soldier caught up with her, grabbed hold of the lines, and collapsed the parachute.

Jean clambered to her feet and released her harness. Two men started gathering the chute while the one who helped stop her asked, "You all right, ma'am?"

"I'm okay," she said.

Across the airfield the de Havilland touched down and taxied to a stop.

"Sergeant Ainsworth said to take you back to the hangar." The soldier gestured toward a jeep at the edge of the field.

She set out with him on legs so weak that she staggered and almost fell. Fortunately he didn't notice. Instead, he squinted at the de Havilland.

"You must be real important for them to designate an entire plane just for you."

She forced a grin. "Well, I don't know about that. I just have a job to do, like you do."

He gave her a look of camaraderie. "Were you scared?"

"Yes! I wish I never had to jump again."

He nodded. "You'll make it all right. We've all felt that way."

At the hangar, Sarge slapped her lightly on the back. "You did it, girl. If you were a Joe, I'd take you out for a beer."

"Thanks, Sarge. I can't believe I really jumped."

"Believe it. You really did. There are a few things I want to go over with you, and then while the weather's still okay and we've got the pilot and plane here waiting, I want you to jump again."

Jean took a deep breath and let it out shakily. "Sarge, if I live through your training, the rest of my mission will be easy!"

"I hope so," he said gruffly.

In all the hours they'd spent together, they had never dis-

cussed the reason for her learning to parachute, but Sarge's tone indicated he knew it would be hazardous.

On Jean's second jump, she was no less terrified, but she landed a little better and collapsed the chute by herself. Riding back to the hangar with the same paratrooper, she silently prayed she would hang together if Sarge ordered her up again today.

He did not. He gave her a brief critique and sent her home.

That night Georges brought her a box of chocolates along with his congratulations. Harry had told him about her jumps from the plane. "If Julie could know what you are doing, she would be so proud," he said.

"Thank you, but I've scarcely made a beginning."

He raised an eyebrow. "True, but we must celebrate successes whenever we can."

She smiled her agreement and then asked what had been on her mind all afternoon. "When is the earliest date I may be dropped?"

"Harry tells me the first week of March."

"That's less than ten days away!"

"Yes."

In a little over a week she would make the last parachute jump of her life, she hoped, and she would be on her way to Giselle. Something inside of her speeded up and, like a spinning gyroscope, steadied her and held her calm. "Then I guess we'd better get to work," she said.

Giselle had done nothing to make her keeper suspect her plan to escape, yet she could hear the careful click of the lock every time Sister Therese left. Still, Giselle always got up and tested the latch to see if the door was in fact locked. Surely one time it would not be or Sister would forget, as she had before. When she did, Giselle would be ready.

She had been behaving as trustingly as any patient might. She concealed her growing strength and asked for assistance she no longer needed. She begged to know when she could be wheeled outside to see the rest of the "hospital." Sister always gave a rational reason for not taking her out, and Giselle did not plead with her nurse beyond what she hoped would seem normal. Instead, she watched and waited. An opportunity to escape would come, she knew, because Sister did not know the full capabilities of her patient. By now Giselle had come to know her keeper very well.

Mother Mary Agnes did not come again, and Giselle did not ask for her.

Secretly Giselle worked to build up her strength, a challenging task with not much time alone and only her room for exercising. *Like learning to swim in a bathtub,* she thought and smiled, for she had not seen a bathtub here, yet remembered how one particular tub looked.

One evening her long awaited opportunity came. When Sister Therese left to take her tray back to the kitchen, Giselle did not hear the lock click. She hurried to the door. Steeling herself against the horrid odor she remembered, she turned the knob. *I must not scream. I must not run. I must . . . walk right through. . . .*

In front of the open door stood a stack of wooden containers, blocking her view of the dark space beyond. The only light came from her room. The odor grabbed at her and made her wretch. *I won't be sick . . . I won't! Go! Go!* she commanded her rebellious body. She stepped out into the storeroom and closed the door behind her. Taking quick shallow breaths, she fumbled her way around the boxes and along a long shelf at about shoulder level. A break in the shelves! She swallowed convulsively and ran her hands across a brick wall. At last a door! Her searching fingers closed on the large round knob. Turning it, she pushed. Dim light leaped in and she leaped out, shutting the door on the nightmarish stench.

Now she was in a vast room. A *basement?* Yes! She remembered the word. Many pipes and wires hung overhead. Before her in the slanted shadows created by a distant light bulb lay a vast array of neatly stacked boxes, barrels, cartons, and a tumble of bags, old desks, beds, broken chairs, and bedside tables. From the lighted end of the basement, she heard the sound of a door closing and then light footsteps. That would be Sister returning.

Giselle ran from the sound and the light and ducked down between dusty boxes. She heard the footsteps pause, a door scuffed against the stone floor as it opened and then closed.

After a few moments of silence, the door banged open and running feet slapped the floor until a door slammed, cutting off the sound. Knowing her escape had been discovered and praying there would be one more unlocked door somewhere at the dark end of the basement, Giselle moved swiftly away from her pursuing keeper. She banged her shins on low obstacles that felt as hard as stone. She could not find a wall, let alone a door. Her legs threatened to give way from fatigue. A distant door opened, letting in more light. She crouched behind a large wooden crate.

Sister's voice, sharp with distress, sliced the dead air. "She can't have gone far, Mother. Oh, I'm so sorry. If anything happens . . ."

The lower voice of the Mother Superior carried as clearly. "Hush. Compose yourself. She can't go far. Could she have fainted and fallen behind the bed or even in the storeroom?"

Again the dungeonlike door to the storeroom opened and closed. Giselle crept from her hiding place and now, at last, spied a door behind the next row of boxes. Rushing to it, she tugged the latch handle, and with a desperate yank she escaped into a lighted corridor. On each side many doors with small windows beckoned. She darted to the first one and peeked inside. In a small square room, a woman dressed in a shapeless gown like her own, sat on a cot. Her tangled short hair stuck out in all directions. She stared blankly at Giselle for a moment. Then her face came alive. She stood slowly and stumbled to the window. Her face twisted piteously as her howl of anguish penetrated the glass between them. Her cry was more animal than human. She pounded on the glass window with clenched fists.

Giselle flinched. Then she noticed for the first time the iron bars on the single window in the small room—proof that this was indeed a prison. Giselle began to tremble. She wanted to help the poor woman, but she raced down the hall instead, looking neither left nor right. More cries of pain and rage broke out from behind other doors. At the end of the hall Giselle crashed against a closed door, gasping, her own throat aching. Had she screamed with them?

She shoved fruitlessly on the door. She was trapped unless she could get back into the basement and find another way out. Gasping for breath, she retraced her steps.

To her great relief, the door that had let her in also let her out. She collapsed onto the basement floor too exhausted and weak to move.

Again Sister's high-pitched voice reached her. "She could have gone out when I came for you or while we were in her room. What shall we do?"

"You stay here in her room and wait," Mother Mary Agnes said. "Leave the doors open. She may wander back here. I'll look upstairs. If she is seen, she will expose us all!"

Expose them for what? Giselle wondered. She must evade these two who pretended to take care of her but were in fact her jailers. For all she knew they had caused her loss of memory. She waited in the shadows until she was certain Mother Mary Agnes had gone and no sound came from Sister Therese. Then she tiptoed the length of the basement, taking care to stay in the shadows as she passed the open storeroom door.

Being so careful took several minutes, but soon she was facing another door. She cautiously opened it and peeked out into a clean, well-lighted corridor. The odors of cooking food and laundry soap engulfed her. No one was in sight. Giselle spied a hiding place halfway down the hall—some carts full of folded sheets and towels. She ran and ducked behind them and leaned her head on the wall while she tried to catch her breath. She was exhausted.

Two sisters rushed by. She could see their feet pass on the other side of the cart that concealed her. The women walked fast, not speaking. Were they all searching for her? Whatever their intent, they hurried on. When they were gone, Giselle crept out and ran to the end of the corridor where there were double doors that might lead to freedom. Before she could push them open, a familiar voice stopped her.

From the other side, Mother Agnes said, "This door leads to the kitchen and laundry. Do you want to look there too?"

"We wish to inspect all the facilities," a man's voice growled.

Giselle looked frantically for a hiding place. There! On her left was an alcove marked "Toilette." She ran, wrenched it open, and closed herself inside, leaving the light off. She felt for a lock but found none. This small cubicle offered no concealment if the door were to be opened. She flattened herself against the wall, where she would be screened by the door itself.

Near the door now, the man said, "You religious women cannot fool officers of the Third Reich with your pious manners, so do not try."

Upon hearing his guttural pronunciation of French more clearly now, Giselle's chest tightened with dread. *I've heard this accent before....*

Suddenly another voice with the same accent superimposed itself over the arrogant voice outside her hiding place. A razor-edged voice that slashed at her will! A voice connected with hate-filled eyes and hands like clubs!

"You will tell me their names," the razor voice promised, then came crushing agony....

My face. Oh no, my face ... She tried not to scream. Everything turned red, then black.

Giselle slowly opened her eyes. She was very cold. *Where am I? Am I blind?* Then she saw a streak of light. Sliding her fingers across a cold, smooth surface toward the light, she came to a solid barrier. Light was seeping in under a door. She was lying on a floor.

Suddenly she knew where she was and who she was. She remembered the torture, the escape, that Martin had brought her here. The man she'd heard with Mother Mary Agnes was a Nazi. Now she understood why Mother Agnes had said if she, "Julie," were discovered, they all would be exposed.

There were no voices in the hall. Perhaps the German would not come back this way. She sat up, tucked her gown around her, and hugged her knees to her chest to try to get warm.

She remembered more. The last moment she had seen Claude, he had fallen from her view under a barrage of gunfire. Was he alive? Had he escaped? If he had not escaped, she hoped he was dead and would not have to endure more. She pressed her fists against her mouth to stifle the moans that wanted to come with each breath. Alone and in the dark, she labored over the rebirth of her memory.

CHAPTER ELEVEN

How long Giselle waited in the toilette listening for some hint of when it would be safe to come out, she did not know.

Suddenly the door opened, and she threw her arm over her eyes at the burst of light.

"Oh no!" a woman gasped. "Are you ill? How did you get here?" To someone else the woman cried, "Quick! Call Mother Agnes!"

Gentle strong hands pulled her to her feet. Pain shot through her stiffened knees. She slumped against the door casing. An arm gripped around her waist and held her up. "Get a wheel-chair! Hurry!"

In a few moments a chair rattled into the hall, and Giselle could now bear the light and see the two sisters who were helping her.

"Please, madame, be seated."

Gratefully she obeyed. Remembering the Nazi inspector, she peered nervously all directions and asked, "Is Mother Superior busy with guests?"

"No, no. We have no one this time of night. This is her prayer time, but we sent for her."

"You're sure she is alone?"

"Most certain. Ah, here she comes."

Like a tall clipper ship under full sail, Mother Agnes glided through the double doors. "Madame," she exclaimed, "I have been searching everywhere for you!"

"I'm so sorry to have distressed you. Mother, I can remember—"

"Of course you can. Now come. Let me take you to your room." She leaned close to straighten Giselle's gown and whispered, "Do not say any more."

One of the sisters offered, "We can take her, Mother, if you tell us which room. Then you may go back to your prayers."

"Sisters, I charge you to utter silence about this patient. You must never tell anyone you saw her. You understand?"

"Yes."

"Yes, Mother."

"Then go on about your work as usual until I can decide how to protect you from the risk of knowing too much."

"Thank you, Mother." They hurried away with bowed heads like frightened children.

Mother Agnes wheeled Giselle quickly through empty corridors, making many turns and passing through four sets of doors. Silence in every corridor suggested it must be a very late hour. At last at the end of a narrow hall, Mother paused to open an elevator. The lower level was the dimly lighted basement. In another moment they entered the storeroom. Giselle involuntarily held her breath.

Now she understood her horror of the smell of carbolic acid, which permeated the closed area. The Nazis had not used the acid to sterilize. A fellow prisoner, her prison garb saturated with carbolic acid and blood, had died in Giselle's arms. If she had lived she would have been blind and her face dreadfully scarred from the burns.

Memory of the cold, filthy prison cell engulfed Giselle. She had held Imelda in her arms, in agony herself because she could do nothing to ease the woman's suffering. Their cell had been like a tomb, and Imelda had prayed for death. Then the click of the guard's shiny black boots on the stone floor outside their cell door had signaled they were about to be raised to live in hell again. . . .

In the large clean room beyond the storeroom, Mother Agnes turned on a light.

Sister Therese sat up on her cot, squinting. "Oh, you found her!" She rushed to Giselle and smoothed her hair with nervous fingers. "Madame Julie, we were so worried about you! Mother, is she all right? Did anyone see her? Where was she?"

"She's chilled," Mother Superior said. "Get hot water bottles. I'll get her into bed. And Sister, she has regained her memory. We will not have to worry about her wandering out again. Isn't that so, Madame Julie?"

Giselle murmured, "Yes," knowing that as soon as she was strong enough she would go, with or without their permission, to search for Claude.

A few miles from York, Jean ended her parachute jump with a bone-jarring splat, crashed sideways, and skidded. Ignoring the blow to the side of her face, she clenched her teeth against the pain in her shoulder and yanked on the chute lines. Fortunately, the parachute started to collapse on its own. Her tugs brought it down before the men reached her. She stumbled to her feet, released her harness, and brushed her hand against her stinging cheek. Her hand came back wet and red.

Unfastening the earflaps on her cap, she pulled it off. The catch crew, ignoring the chute, ran to her. Their faces telegraphed concern.

"I must look a lot worse than I feel," she said lightly.

"You need to get that cleaned up," said one. "Here. Press this against it." He handed her his handkerchief and led her to the jeep.

At the base infirmary an army doctor checked her for head injuries and broken bones. Then he began the painful process of cleaning grit from her cheek. Her eyes were scrunched shut when she heard Sarge burst in.

"You okay?" he demanded.

Opening her eyes and trying not to flinch under the doctor's ministrations, she said, "Yes, I am okay. However, I do not intend to splat again."

"You better not," he said gruffly. To the doctor he said, "What are the damages, sir?"

"Nothing broken or sprained. I need to suture the cut near her eyebrow. She'll be ready to leave here in about fifteen minutes."

"I'll come back then," Sarge said.

"She can't go up again today," the doctor said angrily. "She could get hurt worse. The bruise on her shoulder will slow her down for a couple of days."

"Yes, sir," Sarge acknowledged. "I'm on my way to dismiss the pilot."

"I am all right," Jean protested. "I can jump once more today."

The doctor frowned and scrubbed her cheek harder. "Young lady, I ought to ground you permanently. Women have no business jumping out of planes. I don't know what's going on, but there are plenty of other ways you could help the war effort."

Jean clamped her lips together and said nothing lest she irritate him more. She didn't think he could ground her permanently, but he might delay her training.

By the time the doctor finished, Harry stood at the door of the infirmary waiting with Sarge. "How is she, Doctor?" he asked.

"In good shape for what she's been through. So she's another one of yours? I might have known. The army has no business sending women over there."

"Doctor, the only women we've sent have volunteered for the job and have been as highly qualified as the men. Madame Fauvre has made this choice and is more qualified for her assignment than a man could be."

The doctor grunted. "Harrumph!" Turning his back, he scrubbed his hands at the sink.

Harry escorted Jean to the car and headed for Eve's house. He drove silently and faster than usual until they reached the city limits of York. When he finally turned into St. Mary's Lane and pulled to a stop, he said, "You can quit, you know. Your cousin will probably be all right if she stays in hiding."

Jean opened her mouth to protest, but he held up his hand. "No! Don't say anything now. I told Sarge you wouldn't be in tomorrow unless you need to see the doctor again. And I'm going to tell Georges to stay away tonight. For the next twenty-four hours, I want you to reconsider what you'll face if you go through with this. And I will be doing the same."

"Harry—"

"That's an order," he warned.

Before he could get around to open her door, Jean had climbed out and marched to Eve's row house. Inside, she met

Eve's shocked look with a laugh. "It's nothing, but school's out for today. Do you have any liniment to keep me from getting stiff?"

"I have. You get into your chemise and robe, and I'll bring it along with a hot water bottle."

A few minutes later Eve spread strong-smelling salve on Jean's back and neck and then covered the area with a soft wool flannel wrapping.

"My right knee too," Jean suggested.

Eve rubbed the liniment around her knee. "Now lie on this hot water bottle, placing it where you ache the most . . . except where you're bruised. I wish I had some ice for that."

"This is fine. Smells to the heavens, but it feels tingly warm, as though it should help. What is it anyway?"

"You wouldn't like to know."

"Yes, I would."

"I had a friend who raised Arabian horses—"

"Horse liniment!"

"François took better care of his horses than some people care for their children. When I saw him draw out the swelling and pain from a sprain almost overnight, I made him give me some of his concoction. We'll see if it works on you."

"Haven't you tried it on yourself yet?" cried Jean in mock horror.

Eve shrugged a classic French shrug. "Me? I haven't needed it. Now rest, and we shall see."

Tension began to ease out of Jean's back, and she drifted into a light sleep.

When she awoke, the hot water bottle was cold. She stretched experimentally. Not bad. She got up, ran a bath, and soaped away the strong smell of the liniment. Thirty minutes later, in jacket and cap, she let herself out the front door, hoping a walk would ward off some of the stiffness.

Along the route she usually hiked, spring flowers were appearing more than ever. Patches of blue sky opened between the moving clouds, and the musty odor of leaf mold rose from a freshly turned community garden.

Jean reflected thankfully on the fact that she felt pretty good. Even her bruised shoulder was only a dull ache. She could just as well have jumped tomorrow, but maybe a rest would do her good.

Harry had asked her to reconsider what she was getting into. Of course to injure herself on the jump into France could doom the whole mission. They told her men had broken legs in that crucial jump and had to be brought back home. She wasn't as worried about the jump ruining everything as she was about the gun.

Jean was still afraid she wouldn't be able to use it if it became necessary. She handled the MAB smoothly and effortlessly now, and she consistently hit near the center of the bull's-eye, but she still dreaded the thought of aiming it at a person. Whenever she remembered Jimmy's accident, she nearly missed the target altogether. She had told no one about Jimmy. She was afraid Eve might decide she should not go if she knew. Her fear of failure was a heavy secret to bear alone.

But Giselle could never be safe in occupied France. She *had* to rescue her. *I am not going to let anything stop me now. I can do it, and I will make them see that I can.* With renewed determination she headed back to Eve's house.

At bedtime Eve applied more liniment to Jean's sore places.

The following morning Jean hiked again to work out the stiffness. Then she studied the latest maps and notes Georges had given her. After lunch Eve made her lie down for another application of liniment and heat. Afterward, she walked two miles again. By late afternoon her soreness had retreated to a few stubborn bruises.

Harry and Georges arrived immediately after supper. When Eve seated everyone in the parlor and brought in the tea trolley with biscuits and tea, Jean realized this would not be a typical work evening.

Harry took a winged chair close to her and fiddled with a magazine lying on the lamp table at his side. Speaking in English, he said, "Jean, we need to take our bearings. We've all had time to think."

Jean's spirits sagged. Was the fact he spoke in English and used her real name a sign that her mission was to be scrubbed . . . all because she'd made a clumsy PLF and hurt herself?

"You can't—"

Harry held up his hand. "No, listen . . ." He paused and sighed. "Georges, you tell her."

"We both feel we've allowed ourselves to be swayed too much by your urgent wishes. We feel you aren't suited for this operation."

"Because I made one lousy landing?" she exclaimed in Sarge's American English.

Georges raised both hands to hush her and answered in French. "No, not only that. Your injuries gave us opportunity to pause and reconsider. Getting Julie and her children out of France would be difficult enough for a professional. And your French is *not* flawless—"

"But you already said I could pass as a native!"

"I said your accent probably would not attract attention," he retorted firmly. "If that were all, it would be worth a try. Your great liability is that you are a novice. You have not faced the risk of torture and death. You cannot imagine how many ways one human can abuse another. Those of us who have seen the Nazis' ways—who have lost loved ones and our way of life—our grief and our hatred serves to empower us. It makes us sharper, quicker, and wiser than we were before the occupation.

"You do not have that edge. You are a brave woman yet a gentle lamb. You probably could not kill, even to defend yourself. How then could you protect Julie? We feel we made a grave mistake when we agreed to train you." He turned his hands palm up and shrugged in a gesture of dismissal.

Jean glared at him and then at Harry. Neither one would look her in the eyes.

She stood up. "So you're going to write me off without giving me a chance. You're going to write off Giselle and two little girls . . . and maybe many of our fighting men if Giselle is captured."

Georges broke in. "I was wrong to press you about her importance. She is—"

"No!" snapped Jean. "That's not where you're wrong. You're wrong for buying into the Nazi way of doing things! You believe hatred gives you an edge. Well, I don't need that kind of edge. My love for Giselle and the children will make me sharper and faster and wiser than hatred of the Germans ever could. And if it doesn't, I will still be the victor, because I won't become one more Nazi!"

The men glanced at each other blankly.

"I see you have been thinking," Harry said mildly.

"You bet your life I have. I know what I'm risking, and I know what I'm willing to pay. And don't give me any of that business about Giselle probably being safe. You've told me enough that I know her odds."

Eve said nothing, and Jean took her silence as encouragement.

Georges folded his arms across his chest and shifted his attention to the rug under his feet.

Harry glowered at her. "You're so naïve! If we all decided to stop Hitler with love, where do you think we'd be? Under his thumb, that's where!" He rose to his feet and stomped across the room to the fireplace. With his back to her and his thumbs hooked in his belt loops, he stared at the French painting above the mantel for what seemed to Jean a very long time. Finally he swung around with a look that reminded her of Uncle Al when she'd frustrated him but had made her point. "Perhaps," he said, "your idealism might pull you through in ways that Georges and I can't imagine. What do you think, Georges?"

Georges studied her with troubled eyes. "I think she is utterly foolish, but I wish she was correct."

Harry returned to his chair and slumped into it. "Me too. The question is, shall we be party to her idealistic foolhardiness?"

Staring at the rug again, Georges rubbed his chin.

Jean tried not to guess at what flashed in his mind to bring on such a hostile-looking frown.

At last, without looking up, he said, "I say let's proceed as we originally planned. Let's see if she can complete the training to our satisfaction."

CHAPTER TWELVE

After the day of rest Jean returned to training with renewed passion. The horse liniment had helped even her black-and-blue shoulder. Sarge reduced her jumping to once a day, and Jean managed not to hurt herself again.

At last the doctor removed the stitches from her eyebrow cut and remarked grudgingly, "It probably won't attract attention in another week. If making it noticeable would keep you out of Harry's operations, I'd have been tempted to be less skillful."

"Well, thank you, anyway," Jean said with a smile. He was a lot like Uncle Al on the issue of what women should and should not do.

On two different days strong winds prevented jumping, but Harry obtained more time for her on the firing range. Corporal Haines introduced her to heavier handguns in case she should need to use one. These she could not just point and aim. She had to hold them with both hands and brace herself for the hard kick. The noise was deafening. To Jean, all guns were ugly, but these larger calibers gave her the shivers. Even so, she listened attentively to everything Corporal Haines told her and worked hard to make them familiar tools.

On the first of March Harry came to Eve's at his usual time in the morning and said, "No jumps today. No more practice. If the weather holds, you go tomorrow night." He set a military duffel bag by the hall coatrack.

"To France?" Jean asked, needing to hear the word.

"To France. School's over. We sent a coded message over the

BBC last Thursday night to our agent in the Dijon district, and he has responded in the affirmative for tomorrow night. Eve, may we sit in your dining room to go over the details? I'd like a table to lay out papers and small items."

"Certainly. And I'll have Edna fix us a fresh pot of tea." She went to the kitchen.

Harry hoisted the duffel bag and carried it to the dining room. "Your wardrobe, recently imported from France," he said, "even to the soil on the shoes and the dust in the pockets."

From the military bag he pulled a simple white blouse, a gray wool sweater, a navy blue skirt, a rusty brown dress-length coat—slightly threadbare on the cuffs and front edges—resoled brown leather walking shoes, and used wooden sabots with thick, well-darned wool socks tucked inside. "Many people have returned to sabots because they can't get new leather shoes. Wear these around the house to get the feel of them, but not out-of-doors. You don't want English earth on them. Because you'll be wearing jump boots, you'll carry these and the other shoes, along with the purse, in a pouch attached to your harness."

Dipping into the duffel bag again, he produced a money belt. "Here's money. You'll leave most of it in this belt under your clothes. Hidden in the coat lining are the forged identity cards for Giselle and the children. Eve will show you how to best conceal the belt. You should have enough cash for food, lodging, and any unexpected expenses for several weeks. Here." He handed her a worn brown leather purse. "Madame Fauvre's purse. In it you will find your identity cards, worn gloves, head scarf, and other items French women normally carry in their purses, minus the prewar niceties such as makeup and perfume."

Eve returned from the kitchen and examined each item. "Excellent," she said at last.

Then Harry laid out a map and showed them the drop location outside a small village east of Macon. "I've arranged for our agent Henri to meet you at the drop site. He'll take you to a nearby safe house and then transport you the next day to the rail station in Macon. This is a photo of Henri. His other physical characteristics are listed on the back. Memorize his face because you can't take the photo with you. If for some reason he doesn't meet you, you will then go to the château near the drop field and wait for him or one of his men. You'll find a detailed description of the château in these typed instructions as well as an aerial photograph." He handed her several typewritten pages.

Jean took the papers and glanced at them. "I suppose I must leave these here too."

"You'll give them back to me when I pick you up tomorrow night. Now, back to the general plan. In Macon you will buy a railway ticket to Lyon. Once Henri drops you at the station, you are on your own until you can return to Macon with Giselle and the children. When you get to Macon you will go to Café Coq Rouge at this address and ask for Anton. This is Anton's photo with his physical description on the back also. He will arrange for your pickup time and place and will deliver you there.

"Of course you'll have code phrases for greeting each of the agents, which they must answer correctly. That's all written in your instructions too. I've tried to keep the process as simple as possible, but certain precautions are always necessary."

Jean nodded. "This is all in writing for me?"

"Yes."

"What time will you pick me up tomorrow night?" she asked.

"At twenty-two-hundred hours. If everything is cleared for takeoff, you'll leave by twenty-three-hundred hours. I suggest you read through all of this tonight, and Georges and I will be by in the morning to answer any questions."

She swallowed. Her mouth was dry. "All right," she managed.

"Nervous?" Harry asked.

"Yes."

"Even a veteran would be. Try to get a good night's sleep, because you'll lose a lot tomorrow night. Now I'm going to get out of here so you can get to work."

Eve walked him to the door.

Jean removed her shoes and tried on the wool socks and wooden shoes. They fit. Harry must have obtained her shoe size from Eve, for he hadn't asked her. She took a few steps. The thick hand-knit socks made the rigid shoes surprisingly comfortable. She kept them on while she studied the map and began to read and memorize what Harry had called her "briefing."

At the end of the day, Eve suggested she take a warm bath before retiring. "I'll rub your back if you like," she offered.

"Thanks, but no. I have some letters to write. Don't know how long it will take." Realizing this could be her last night in

Eve's house, she added, "I can't say a big enough thanks for all you've done for me, but thank you anyway."

Eve smiled, and in a gesture reminiscent of Giselle, she waved one hand as if to brush away the idea that she had done anything unusual. "It's a small thing. I'm happy to help," Eve said. "I want you to know that I believe you are doing the right thing, and if God still loves his children, which I believe He does, I think you make Him smile right now."

"Thanks." Jean gave Eve a hug. The intense demands created by the war and her mission had drawn them close, even though they knew very little about each others' personal lives. "I'd like to bring Giselle to meet you someday."

Eve's eyes sparkled with delight. "Oh, my dear, you must! I will look forward to seeing you both."

Jean gathered up all the materials Harry had scattered on the table and carried them to her room. After changing into her pajamas and robe, she sat at her desk with pen and stationery.

First she wrote friendly letters to Tom, Uncle Al, Grandmother, Mary, and to Nella and Elizabeth. Then she wrote good-bye letters in case she didn't make it back. Harry had promised he would keep those in a safe place and deliver them personally.

She wrote Tom's good-bye letter last, for it was the most difficult.

> *Dear Tom,*
>
> *If you are reading this, you know I have not survived my attempt to help Giselle escape from France. I want you to know that this was something I had to do, or I felt I would lose not only Giselle but an important part of myself. Maybe your need to be in the Nisei Combat Team is like that. Going for Giselle is my way of defying war and all its destruction.*
>
> *Keep on being your own sweet, honorable self and know that even from heaven, I am praying you may find much joy in life.*
>
> *Still your loving Jeanie*

Jean brushed away the tears that rushed down her cheeks and sealed the note in its envelope. She placed her good-bye letters in the large envelope Harry had provided with his name on it and sealed it. The others she stacked on the corner of her desk where she could not forget them tomorrow.

As she settled into the comfort of a hot relaxing soak in the tub, she tried to tell herself this was just another night. For all

she knew, the fair weather would not hold through tomorrow night.

Wearing a skirt and blouse instead of a hospital gown, Giselle leaned toward the dressing table mirror that had appeared in her hidden hospital room shortly after she regained her memory. *Will I ever be beautiful for Claude again?* She smoothed on the ointment Sister Therese had given her.

"Sister, what did you say is in this? It smells like beeswax and turpentine or some kind of tree resin."

Sister Therese looked up from mopping the floor and said, "Yes, something like balsam or myrrh, my maman said, with honey and olive oil. Can you tell if it is helping?"

"Some of the scars are fading, but maybe they would anyway. At any rate it's very soothing." Therese had offered her mother's salve after the doctor had given up on her scars.

"Maman says it takes time."

Silently Giselle cried, *But I don't have much time.* Aloud she said, "Yes. I suppose that's right."

Maybe the Gestapo would not recognize her now. Maybe no one would if she could cover some of the scars with makeup and make the rest look more like the result of an accident. But how could she obtain makeup? Maybe one of the resistants could help her with that. Or even Mother Agnes. Mother must know some of the resistants, because Martin had trusted her. She wondered where Martin had gone. Could he still be in Lyon? No, Mother Agnes said he could not return for her. He must be far away. With de Gaulle in England?

Claude would never go to England and leave her and the girls here. Before long she would search for him. She would sneak to the farm first, before anyone could possibly recognize her. She had to know that the girls were all right.

Should she discuss her plans with Mother Agnes, or just leave at the first opportunity? Sister still locked the door to her room but said she did so to prevent anyone from coming upon her hiding place by accident. She and Mother Agnes ought to be glad to be rid of her.

Giselle picked up the hand mirror to study her profile. The doctor had said her crooked nose could be repaired, but not now, not in occupied France. Until she could have it fixed, she would have to live with the deformity, which gave her a harsh, unfeminine appearance. With one hand she covered and lifted the darker dyed ends of her hair. If Sister clipped her hair to a boyish length, back to the natural blond roots, she might pass for a man.

"Sister," she called, "what would you think of cutting my hair back to my natural color? Then I wouldn't look so piebald."

Sister dropped her mop, wiped her hands, and came to look. "Oh, I'm afraid it would be much too short. You must either wait or dye it."

"I'd like it cut."

Sister lifted her hair, pulled it back from her ears, and studied the effect. "No. I cannot do it. You would look like a . . . a fallen woman . . . or even like a man."

Giselle laughed. "More like a man, don't you think?"

"Madame, how can you laugh at such a thing?"

"I don't know. It's been so long since I've laughed, I've almost forgotten how. Sister, when you go out, would you ask Mother Agnes to come see me when she can spare a moment?"

Night skies had darkened the high windows in Giselle's room by the time Mother Agnes let herself into the hidden room.

Sister Therese had gone to evening Compline in the chapel, and Giselle had given up and gone to bed. Seeing her guest, she sat up. "Please come sit, Mother. I need to talk to you."

Mother Agnes took the chair beside her bed. "How may I be of service?"

"You know I'm strong now. The doctor says he's done all he can for my face. I want to leave the hospital. I want to search for my husband."

"My dear, the doctor does not feel you should leave yet. And your friend who brought you to us begged me to keep you hidden until someone came for you. He said you would be taken again by the Gestapo unless someone could get you out of France."

"You know this? It is dangerous for you to know so much about the Resistance."

"I am French. I do my part."

"It would be better for you and for the sisters if I left."

"We are in God's hands. Do not worry about us. You must try to be patient a little longer. If no one comes for you after the doctor judges your health to be solid, then we will talk about how to help you leave. In the meantime, there is something you could do to help us."

"What?"

"Do you sew?"

"Yes. I made most of my children's clothes."

"The hospital suffers the same shortages as everyone else these days. Some of the sisters spend many hours cutting old sheets and blankets to make slippers, robes, and gowns for our patients. Could you perhaps help in this? Sister Therese can bring the material right here to your room."

"Yes. I'd be glad to have something to do."

"Very good." She rose to her feet. "Now I must go. I will pray daily for your husband and that you may soon be together again."

"Thank you, Mother."

After the door closed behind her, Giselle lay back down and stared at the distant ceiling. If she decided not to wait for someone to come for her, kindly Mother Agnes would understand. At least she had been forewarned.

For Jean in York, the next morning brought continued good weather, and everything looked clear for the flight that evening.

Harry and Georges arrived before lunch to give her a last briefing. When she could think of no more questions to ask, Georges handed her a soiled gray triangle of cloth that had been jaggedly slashed from a larger piece. "You will need this," he said. "Do not lose it. I cut it from the hem of Julie's blouse when I left her. The Mother Superior has the blouse and will know it is safe to talk to you when she matches this piece to the rest of the blouse."

Jean caught her breath and closed her fingers over the bit of cloth. "I wondered how I would persuade her."

"I thought it best to leave this until you needed it. Less risk of misplacing it."

"Thanks. Thank you both for letting me go, for helping me do this."

"Thank us by coming back safely with your cousin and her children," Harry said brusquely.

"You'll do fine," Georges said. "If anyone can bring them out, it is you."

On that optimistic note, they left, advising her to rest and try to sleep in the afternoon.

After they left, she tried to nap but couldn't.

At twenty-three-hundred hours, on the tarmac with the de Havilland's engines deafening them, Harry and Georges stood in front of Jean. Each man soberly shook her hand. Then they stepped back. Harry motioned for her to board.

With coveralls and jump boots over her French clothing—the skirt, sweater, and woolen street coat—she climbed heavily into the aircraft. Pausing in the door, she turned and waved. They gave her smart military salutes. She tried to salute, then laughed at her clumsiness and blew them a kiss. In the dim light she glimpsed their smiles before the man holding the door closed it.

In seconds the plane began to roll.

The man beside her locked the door and straightened. Despite the dim light, she recognized his familiar face and form. "Sarge! I'm so glad to see you!" she shouted over the engine noise. "I didn't know you would be the one to go with me!"

The plane's engines roared, preparing for takeoff.

He yelled his reply. "I couldn't tell you because Harry wasn't sure he could pull enough strings to get me here."

The plane began to bump down the runway. Jean dropped to a hard seat and fastened the safety strap across her lap. Sarge belted himself in across from her and pointed at some army blankets beside her. "It's gonna be cold. I thought you might need those."

"Thanks!" She wrapped one around her legs. Moments later the de Havilland lifted off, and they flew low over England's gently rolling land.

It was difficult to talk because of the noise. *I guess we've already said all there is to say,* Jean thought. *The reminders . . . the warn-*

ings . . . the good-byes. Now I'm Marie Fauvre, mother of two, widowed wife of Emile, who became a prisoner of war when France fell and died at the hands of the Nazis.

She leaned back against her parachute pack, closed her eyes, and prayed that no German planes would spot them from above. Harry had said the drop planes were seldom spotted while flying low all the way. The danger was greatest at the drop site. They could be shot at without warning. Or they might receive a signal not to drop, and they'd have to fly for home and try again later. *Please let me get down this trip,* she prayed.

Over and over she rehearsed the details of her assigned identity, the code words, and the landmarks she must look for as she parachuted to the ground.

The plane droned on. Moonlight coming secondhand from the nearby cockpit provided just enough light to see Sarge. After a while he leaned toward her, tapped his watch, and then pointed downward.

"France!" he yelled.

A jolt of adrenaline shot through her. She nodded and gave him a thumbs up. Soon she would be down there on French soil. For a moment the whole situation seemed impossible, unreal. *How can I be here doing this?* A pocket of bumpy air brought her back to reality. She felt the pressure of the plane banking sharply. She could tell by the weight of her stomach that they were climbing and then descending. Yet the plane flew on with no suggestion of preparing for the drop.

The night sky remained blessedly free of searchlights and gunfire. The cold was seeping through her layers of clothing and the blanket. She added another blanket.

Jean was wearing every stitch of clothing she would use in France except the women's shoes and purse. Sarge had clipped a shoe bag for those to her waist belt. She would drop the bag just before landing.

Sarge stood up and stepped forward to the cockpit.

It must be nearly time. *Oh, dear God, help me. We've all done everything we know to make this work. Please help me now.* She snapped the earflaps of her flying cap snugly under her chin.

A few minutes later Sarge returned and with his flashlight directed her to the bomb hold door. As she followed him, she could hear the lowering pitch of the engines as the pilot slowed the plane to begin a glide to the drop site.

Sarge doubled-checked her harness and clipped her static line to the cable. His pat on her back was a welcome break from standard procedure. He yelled in her ear, "You're a great paratrooper, Marie! You can do this!"

"Thanks, Sarge. Thanks for everything!"

"Sure!"

The door opened, and he motioned her forward. Six hundred feet below, the shadowy French countryside rushed past her view. Keeping a tight grip on the plane, she eased her feet to the edge and stood ready. In the moonlight she could recognize trees, fields, a sleeping village, and a huge private home. The château that was a safe haven? She must not close her eyes when she jumped. She had to get her bearings.

The plane quieted and slowed even more. Below in a field a tiny light blinked three times.

"The signal," Sarge yelled. He slapped the back of her helmet. "GO!"

Jean leaned forward and jumped out, her arms wrapped around the reserve chute on her chest and her chin tucked down. Her body cut through the air. The countryside rushed to meet her. Then with a snap the harness yanked her to a swinging, floating descent. The sound of the plane's engines quickly moved away and faded.

Where was the château? There! To the right. She saw the brief wink of a flashlight directly below. Releasing the bundle containing her shoes and purse, she flexed her knees for the landing.

CHAPTER THIRTEEN

The balls of Jean's feet touched the ground just as Sarge had trained her. Pulling on the lines with strength born of fear, she collapsed the chute and released herself from the harness.

Someone ran to her side and helped to fold the telltale pale fabric of the chute into a compact lump.

"What did you drop?" a woman's voice asked in a stage whisper.

"My civilian shoes and purse," Jean whispered back. She looked around and saw no one else. "Where is Henri?"

"He couldn't come. He sent me—Isabelle."

Jean stiffened. "March storms will blow in soon."

"Not on a night like this. Hurry, we must hide your parachute." Henri would have answered, "Yes, but sun follows the rain." If he had sent this woman, wouldn't he have told her the code? Or had he not had a chance to do so? And Harry had said three people would meet her and help her get into a safe house.

"Where are the others?" Jean asked.

Isabelle worked feverishly to tie the lines around the chute. "Same place as Henri. Lift the other side of this chute and help me carry it. Dragging it would leave a trail in the frost."

"I must fetch my shoe bag," Jean whispered and jogged to where it lay about fifty feet away. Should she try to escape from this woman? Or would she run into worse trouble alone? By the time she reached her shoe bag, she decided to go along with Isabelle, but she'd watch for a chance to lose her and go it alone. She returned to the woman, looped her small bag over her shoulder, and hoisted her share of the parachute.

Without a word, the woman led the way toward a thick stand of nearby trees. Under their feet the frost-covered grass crunched. Their mouths puffed out little clouds of fog, clearly visible in the moonlight. If anyone was watching, there was no hiding under the full moon.

The woman stopped frequently, raising a hand for silence, and listened. Jean felt as if someone would leap out from the shadows at any moment and it all would be over. She was then led straight into the woods. Far away a dog barked. *How far?* Jean wondered, shivering. She was nearing panic. She must calm down. Isabelle finally stopped beside a dark shadow at the base of a very tangled tree. No, it wasn't a tangled tree, but the root system of a large tree that had blown over.

"Here," Isabelle said, "help me scoop out the dead leaves."

Jean hesitated. "When will Henri come?"

"Look," Isabelle snapped, "I came when I saw Henri wouldn't make it back in time. You either trust me or go on alone. It is nothing to me. I only did it for him." She stood with hands on her hips, waiting. The moon softly lighted her face. A man's stocking cap down to her eyebrows could not detract from the feminine appeal of wide-set large eyes and softly curved lips above a firm chin. She looked incredibly young and very pretty.

Jean stalled. Hoping to learn something that would help her know what to do, she asked, "Are you in love with Henri?"

"Love! You are a naïve one. Here there is no time for love," she hissed. Isabelle knelt down and scooped out leaves from the hollow. "Are you going to help or just stand there?"

Defensive anger, Jean decided. *I touched a sensitive spot. If she cares about Henri, she could be telling the truth about coming here for him.* She jumped into the hollow and helped Isabelle clear a space in the deepest crevice under the roots. Together they lifted the chute and wedged it into the hole.

Hoping to learn more about this unexpected person, Jean whispered, "Does Henri know you love him?"

"You ask too many questions," Isabelle muttered. "Do you let me help you, or do I go home and get some sleep?"

"I want your help." Jean climbed out of the hollow to level ground where she could move more freely, pulled off her jump suit, helmet, flyer's cap, and boots, and tossed them one by one to Isabelle, who hid them with the chute. While Jean put on her French walking shoes, Isabelle poked the empty shoe bag under the roots also. The sabots had been left behind because they were too bulky to carry. Then Isabelle spread twigs and leaves over the cache until nothing could be seen but natural woodsy debris.

Jean hoped that was all that could be seen. They had obviously disturbed the frosty surface leaves, although down in the hollow there had been no frost. She brushed herself off, thankful for the frozen ground that kept her shoes from getting wet and muddy. From her purse she pulled the bandanna, tossed it over her head, and tied it snugly under her chin.

With a nod Isabelle said, "Good. Now you look like any Frenchwoman around here. I dare not take you to my home. I will take you straight to the château. When Henri returns, he will look for you there." After a glance at the moon, she set out.

Jean followed, wondering why she had even mentioned her home. The château had been the plan. Her gun pressed against her under the worn coat. She hoped she would not need it. Twigs and leaves crunched and snapped under their feet. If anyone heard, they would surely be detained and questioned. "Will you tell Henri where I am?"

Isabelle stopped walking. "I may not see him," she whispered. "You'll have to trust his experience in knowing where to look. The Germans came this evening to arrest the Duvalls—the family of the château. Henri staged an unplanned diversion to help them get away. He had asked me to help him meet a drop, but he didn't tell me anything about it. When he did not return by midnight, I decided to meet you myself. Under the circumstances, you would be safer at my home until he returns, but my family—what I do tonight or any night, my family must never know. Surely you know that."

"Yes," Jean said and discovered she was beginning to shiver so much that her voice trembled.

"We must not waste time talking. Come," Isabelle whispered and hurried on. Again the crunch of their careful steps seemed to echo through the whole woods and beyond.

At last they reached the edge of the trees, and Isabelle halted. "Shh! Stay here. I'll see if the house is guarded." Without waiting for Jean to respond, she darted across an open expanse of lawn toward an imposing château.

Jean hoped its tall shuttered windows blinded anyone inside to Isabelle's approach. She studied as much of the mansion as the moonlight revealed. The high roofline, gables, and chimneys matched the château in Harry's photo. Beyond the great house stood a couple of cottages, and at the edge of more woods stood a long low building that must be the stable.

Tired and cold, Jean listened to her doubts. What if Isabelle was simply a good liar and brought back the Milice? Jean edged back under the leafless trees and stood behind one with a thick trunk. If she ran now, could she lose pursuers who probably knew the terrain better than she did? On the other hand, if Isabelle was telling the truth, running from her could place the mission in jeopardy. Jean decided she must wait long enough to see whether Isabelle returned alone.

At last a single figure ran from the far side of the château and made straight for Jean. Jean stayed behind the tree trunk and waited.

"Psst, where are you?" Isabelle called softly.

Jean stepped out of hiding.

"What's your name?" Isabelle demanded.

"Marie."

"All right. I found no trace of the Gestapo. Henri must have succeeded in misleading them. You may rest in the stable. Stay away from the house and cottages. The Germans will surely return in the morning, and they will search the dwellings first."

"Then I will have to leave before daylight."

"No. Your best chance is to wait for Henri. Quickly now, to the stable." She set off across the frozen turf.

Jean followed, thinking fast. She would do as Isabelle asked, then, after she left, consider whether there was a better place to hide.

Isabelle pulled the stable door open. Something small darted out, brushing Jean's leg. Jean clamped her teeth against a scream. The creature fled without biting, scratching, or growling.

Isabelle, without comment, pulled her inside and closed the door. "Hold on to me," she whispered. "I know the way, and we must not light a torch."

Jean reached toward her voice and found her shoulder. Isabelle moved forward. Although the odor of horses lingered, Jean heard no hint of animals. Isabelle stopped and opened a creaking door. The smell of leather permeated the place—a tack room?

Isabelle bent over and bobbed back up. "Here, carry this," she said in a low voice. She thrust a horse blanket into Jean's hands. "I'll carry one too. Can you still hold on to me?"

"Yes."

"Just a few more paces to the stairs. Up there you can make a bed in the hay. Step up now."

Jean felt with her toe and found a rustic step. Hugging the blanket tightly, she groped her way up steep steps, keeping her free hand on the worn railing.

At the top Isabelle put the second blanket in her arms. "If Henri does not come by dawn, you better go and do the best you can alone. The Germans will come early. If you awaken and see them at the château, try to get into the woods behind the stable and put kilometers between you and the drop site."

Jean wanted to trust Isabelle. She seemed sincere. At a loss to know what to say, Jean stammered, "Thank you. . . ."

"It is nothing. Stay alert. Good-bye."

Jean heard a stair board creak under Isabelle's weight, and then seconds later the stable door rattled open and shut. She then fumbled to the hay, spread out a blanket, and curled up on it, wrapping the other one around her to make a cocoon for herself. She was so cold. She would rest awhile and then decide whether to move into the woods to watch for Henri, or the Germans.

Gradually warmth began to seep into her chilled arms, legs, and finally her feet. Against her will her eyes closed, and she dozed.

With a jump she awakened, knowing instantly where she was and sensing she had heard a noise. It wasn't yet morning, but it was lighter inside the stable. She could see shapes in the dark.

Jean rose to her feet and brushed the hay off her clothes. She pulled her bandanna up from around her neck and tied it again over her hair. Gathering up the horse blankets, she cautiously descended to the ground floor. As best she could from memory, she retraced her steps, found the tack room, and hung the blankets on pegs. In the tack room a window showed as a gray rectangle. She crept to it, taking care not to get close enough to be seen from the outside. The moon had gone down, but dawn was approaching. Everything appeared in shades of gray, looking life-less.

Wait! There! Across the frosty expanse of grass a figure moved away from the shadow back of the château. It was a man, moving slowly at first and then striding purposefully toward the stable!

She could not tell if he was in uniform. She jumped back from the window. Jean knew she couldn't leave by the door she'd entered without him seeing her. Oh, why hadn't she asked Isabelle to show her another way out? There was no time to search. She raced up the stairs to where she'd slept. She could be trapped if he came up, but she didn't dare hide in a stall near the door where she wished. If he was coming to search, he might look there first.

So she squeezed behind a stack of barrels and bags of grain near the top of the stairs. If he did climb up, he might search along the walkway that ran the length of the loft above the stalls. And the minute he was far enough from the stairs, she could sneak down undetected.

Jean now heard him below, opening one stall after another, obviously searching. How could he know she was here? Or was he looking for something else? The movements below stopped. Minute after minute, she waited, scarcely breathing. Had he gone out? Or was he listening for her, just as she was listening for him? And then, directly below in the tack room, she heard him again—light footsteps and then no sound. Had she left evidence there?

A stair squeaked under his weight. Then his voice came from so close he had to be at the top. "Hello!" he called in unaccented French.

Jean's heart jumped to her throat. When he remained and said nothing more for several minutes, she realized he didn't know for certain whether she was there. He sounded French, but she had been warned to trust no one. She crouched mute and motionless, poised to run if he proceeded down the walkway.

He did not move away. Presently he said, "I know you're still here. I saw your footprints under the new frost, and no prints lead away from the stable. Also now I see the depression in the hay where you slept."

Jean silently groaned. She had forgotten to fluff the hay. She peeked through a crack between the barrels, hoping to see the man.

She couldn't. She was trapped. If he was not Henri, she'd have to brazen it out. "Please, sir, I was walking, thinking I could get to the village and find a room, but I got lost. I was so tired. March storms will blow in soon," she ventured.

"Yes, but sun follows the rain," he responded.

"Henri!" She stepped out from behind the barrels. "I was afraid you were someone else."

He stood less than two yards away, medium height, curling brown hair, and the face she had memorized from his photo. He smiled. "Good morning, Marie. I'm sorry to have worried you. Even though Isabelle said she hid you here, I had to be sure also that you were the person I was to meet."

Jean was so relieved she wanted to throw her arms around him. Instead, she said, "I didn't know whether I could trust Isabelle."

"A bad time for you, I know, but I never had a chance to tell her the code. I was off and running, and I thought I could get back here in time. Isabelle is quick and competent, hardly more than a child, but she's saved my neck more than once."

"Are the Duvalls safe?"

"I think so. When I learned their cover had been broken last night, it was too late to warn you by wireless." He paused. "The Gestapo or the Milice will likely be here soon. Were you able to hide your parachute?"

She told him where they had stashed it.

"That's good. Then come along. I have a car of sorts. We've got to get out of here." He headed downstairs.

She trotted behind him. "You mentioned my footprints. Won't the Germans see them too?"

"Yes, unless the sun melts the frost or the growing clouds give us rain or snow before they get here. Either way, if your chute is hidden well, they won't know how you arrived. They will have the Duvalls on their minds, and when they reach the château's wine cellar, they may be willing to stop looking for a time."

"How did you delay them from coming for the Duvalls?"

"A matter of bombing a bridge close enough to call away men assigned to come here. After all, where could the unsuspecting Duvalls go while they caught the culprits who blew up the bridge? We left a very hot trail westward—for a while."

Henri's auto, an old Renault, was hidden among trees near a small road that led away from the main entrance to the estate. Jean stared at the stack of wood strapped to the car's running board. She could barely climb around it to get in the front seat.

"That's for heating our fuel," Henri explained. "When we couldn't get gasoline after the occupation, we converted our cars to use the gases from heated wood. Not bad when it works." He opened a little burning box and stoked it with a few more short pieces of wood. "This won't take long. She didn't cool much." He fanned the fire for a minute, then hopped into the car and stepped on the starter. The groaning vehicle finally gave a mechanical cough and shuddered to life. He put it in gear and away they bounced on the unpaved road.

Jean wondered what they would do if they ever had to make an unplanned quick getaway but decided she really didn't want to know.

Henri turned behind the stable and followed a rutted farm road that twisted through woods and around a vineyard. At last they pulled out onto a public road. He glanced at her and said, "You can take the scarf off your head."

She obeyed.

He studied her. "Fasten your hair up on top of your head—in braids or something. It will give you a more matronly appearance."

"If I can find something to fasten it with," she agreed. She emptied the contents of her purse onto her lap. Eve had slipped in a used red French lipstick and enough hairpins and combs to hold her hair up in a chignon. Guided by feel, Jean twisted and fastened her shoulder-length hair, then tucked in the loose ends. "There. Is that presentable?"

Henri glanced at her and raised one eyebrow and shook his head. "Can't you ugly yourself a bit?" he said with a smile.

"A mother of two children does not have to be ugly."

"No, but a mother of two should look as if she has finished school."

"So what do you want me to do? Take it down?"

He laughed. "No. Just remember to keep that nice ugly frown."

She sniffed and looked out the side window at the farmland. "You seem awfully carefree for a secret agent."

"I find very little to laugh about, but you yourself have brought me a smile."

She turned to him again. He had pleasant eyes and a friendly smile. "Your work must be hard. I'll do what I came to do and then leave, but you're here for the duration, isn't that so?"

His smile vanished and he focused on the road. "If I'm lucky. If I'm not, my remains will stay here. I don't allow myself to think of anything but the battle against the Nazis. You must acquire that skill too. Look! Here come the *Boches*."

A large black car raced toward them and zipped past, followed by a military sedan full of German soldiers.

Jean held her breath.

None of the Germans glanced at Henri or his battered auto. Henri watched them in his rearview mirror for a few seconds and then said, "I think we have good fortune. Without a doubt they are on their way back to the Duvalls. I saw the informer in the lead car."

"You know the informer?"

"Yes. We have our informers too."

"You seem awfully calm about it, just driving on as if nothing had happened."

"That is the life here. You will get used to it."

"Do you know why I came?" Jean asked abruptly.

"No, and do not tell me."

"Right."

In a detached voice he continued. "In fifteen minutes we will be in Macon. I will let you off a couple of blocks from the train station, and you will not see me again. This way I can tell no one who you are or where you went. And you can tell no one who I am, where I came from, or where I have gone." He chuckled. "But I shall remember how you made me smile."

Soon they had reached the outskirts of a small town. "Macon," he said with a wave of his hand.

Henri drove the narrow streets watchfully, making several turns. At last he slowed and pulled over to the curb.

"Please tell Isabelle thanks for me," she said.

He nodded. "I will. Straight up the hill on the left is the station. I won't help you with the door. That way it will look as if I just gave a stranger a ride. Whatever you do, act confident. God go with you!"

"Thank you." She climbed out quickly, and as she supposed a stranger would do, she called again, "Many thanks!" and slammed the door.

The car lurched forward. Henri did not look back.

Jean walked briskly to the station, marched to the ticket counter, and asked for a ticket to Lyon.

"Your permit, please."

She handed him her forged travel permit along with her official identification card.

CHAPTER FOURTEEN

The railway ticket man studied her permit and identification papers, then scooped up her money and handed her a ticket. Relieved, she proceeded to the boarding platform and wove her way through the growing cluster of passengers.

Anyone meeting her gaze quickly looked away. No one smiled except at the few children present. This was an aspect of Marie Fauvre's life that Jean had not totally anticipated. She must curb her inclination to smile a greeting if she was to blend in with these troubled people.

At first she couldn't locate the schedule board. When she did, she wondered whether to believe anything so stained with months of smoke and dirt.

A small gray-haired woman stood near the board. Perhaps she would know. Just as Jean was about to ask, two German soldiers approached, inspecting the crowd with narrowed eyes as they walked. The waiting passengers seemed not to notice them, yet as the Germans strolled by, most people turned their backs on them.

Jean moved away from the woman, not wanting to involve her or be involved if anything should go wrong.

The soldiers passed slowly, and from the corner of her eye, Jean could tell that they gave her no more than a glance. After they were beyond hearing, she returned to the little woman. "Will the train to Lyon arrive on time, do you think?" she murmured.

The old woman's lively dark eyes peered up at her from

under still black eyebrows. Her smile crinkles deepened, and she said wryly, "Who can say? I wait here hoping. My daughter in Lyon is ill, and the children need their grand-mère."

"I'm sorry."

"Well, life is hard for all of us, is it not? If my Pierre were alive, life would be easier. He knew how to get along no matter what the circumstance." She glowered at the backs of the Germans as they paced on down the platform.

"I hope your daughter gets well soon," Jean said as a good-bye and stepped away.

The woman nodded and let her go, but Jean could see she was lonely and wanted to talk. Resolutely Jean headed up the track. The woman had indicated this was the correct boarding platform, but waiting too long in one place seemed more risky than to keep moving.

The black-booted soldiers returned and stood like predators, surveying the vulnerable passengers. No one talked much. Jean unobtrusively worked her way into a mixed group and took her cues from them. At last a train huffed into the station. A trickle of people climbed off, and the group around Jean began to board. Jean quietly asked a woman with a little boy, "Excuse me, is this the train to Lyon?"

"Yes," the woman said without taking her eyes from the child or slowing her pace.

Jean followed her and found a seat, the last one available in that car, beside a middle-aged man. He kept his face turned toward the window and said nothing when she sat next to him. His broad hands, callused and cracked, retained the stains of his work, possibly a mechanic or a farmer.

Soon the aisle filled, and those who had luggage sat upon it. The conductor pushed through and climbed over the packed bodies to check train tickets, identification cards, and travel permits. When he came to Jean and her seat partner, she handed him her ticket and papers. He thumbed through the lot, punched her ticket, and gave everything back without questions.

Turning to the man, he said, "Your ticket, monsieur."

The man reached over Jean to present his cards.

The conductor studied them and then said abruptly, "These are out of date."

The man received them back. "Oh, I must have taken my old ones by mistake."

"I'm sorry, monsieur." The conductor beckoned to a hawk-eyed German soldier posted in the doorway at the end of the car.

The soldier pushed his way to Jean's side.

"This man has outdated papers," the conductor said.

"Come with me," said the soldier in poor French.

The man's ruddy face turned gray. He stood up and gripped the back of the seat in front of him with trembling fingers.

The soldier turned to Jean. "Are you with him?"

"No."

"Of course she is not with him!" came the scolding voice of an old woman nearby. "She is my niece, who could find no other seat by the time she boarded."

Jean turned and looked into the knowing eyes of the gray-haired woman she had met on the platform.

The woman continued. "We are on our way to her home in Lyon. Widowed as I am and at my age, I can no longer live alone. Without my sister's dear girl, I don't know what I'd do." She smiled and leaned forward to pat Jean on the shoulder.

Jean smiled back with what she hoped was an affectionate expression.

The woman shook her head mournfully. "I tell you since my husband died, life has not been easy—" She suddenly began to cough with an asthmatic wheeze that sounded terminal.

Jean then joined in the deception. "Please, Auntie, don't strain yourself!"

The old woman coughed harder, gasping for breath.

In genuine sympathy, Jean reached for her hand.

The German soldier turned to the man with the outdated papers. "Come with me! Let this old lady sit by her niece." He grabbed the man by the arm and dragged him through the people standing in the aisle and out the door at the end of the car.

With a jolt and clanking the train began to roll.

Jean grieved for the frightened man, but she had to continue to play her part. "Excuse me, please." Standing up, she helped the woman to her feet. "Come, Auntie. Do you want to sit by the window?"

The woman shook her head and motioned for Jean to move over. After she collapsed onto the aisle seat, she wheezed, "My pills. In my purse. Little green bottle."

So her cough is authentic. Jean found the bottle and handed it to her. Her new auntie placed a pill in her mouth, leaned back, and closed her eyes.

"Will you be all right?" Jean asked softly.

The woman nodded without opening her eyes.

Jean leaned back, pretending to rest also.

Presently the woman leaned close and whispered, "What is your name?"

"Marie Fauvre."

The woman repeated, "Marie," but did not raise her head or open her eyes.

"Good thing that soldier did not ask you for my name," Jean whispered, beginning to feel shaky. "You took a great risk. Thank you."

The woman opened her eyes and shook her head. "Not very great. Many times I have put my cough to good use." She chuckled, coughed again, but managed to stop. "They never suspect an old lady who is gasping for breath. The cough is real. I have had asthma for years. It took the arrogant Germans to show me the value of such a malady."

"You have distracted them before?"

"Yes, but not often for a total stranger. That was a risk, I admit."

"Should we continue to play our parts?"

"But of course, although the conductor probably will not check our papers again unless he forgets who we are before we reach Lyon. When he comes by again, I'll remind him by a coughing fit." She smiled mischievously.

"You are very brave."

"No, no. Just very stubborn. My Pierre, now, he was brave. He died in the first war in the battle of the Argonne. I still miss him," she murmured and closed her eyes again.

Jean feigned napping while listening to the rise and fall of French voices in the crowded car. She could hardly believe she was actually in France, so close to Giselle. Suddenly the fear Jean had fought for days loomed larger than ever. *What if I can't find her? What if she isn't strong enough to travel?* Her eyes flew open as if they had a will of their own. She studied every detail of the railcar and observed the behavior of the people. For a few minutes a glimpse of the vineyards of Burgundy captured her interest, then she covertly watched the people again.

Everyone looked weary and tense. Some faces bore the lines of chronic anger and some the frozen look of fear. Two women, one a young mother holding a toddler, sat across the aisle. Two thin men sat on their battered travel bags beside the mother. One of the men leaned over and began to play finger games with the baby. The baby's carefree innocence captivated every adult nearby. As Jean watched the interplay between the child and the adults, she took courage. Traveling with children could be easier than she'd imagined. Until now the thought of caring for Giselle's children had seemed to be an added risk.

When the train stopped at different towns along the way, Jean watched the manner in which people left and how new passengers boarded. At Villefranche-sur-Saône, a larger town, many people came aboard. She expected the conductor to forget he had checked her papers, but he passed by them without a word and moved slowly on to the next car. At last the train huffed out of the station.

The asthmatic woman shifted in her seat and opened bright eyes. "You see. I didn't even have to cough again," she whispered with a smug little smile. "The secret is to make a memorable first impression."

Jean wanted to laugh but restrained herself, as the woman had, to a quick conspiratorial smile. "I shall remember that."

By the time the train pulled into Lyon, the afternoon was nearly gone. Jean walked with the old lady to the busy platform and said a quick good-bye. For safety's sake, friendships could not be established, but she said, "Thank you. I will never forget you."

The woman's unconquerable smile made her eyes sparkle again, and she said, "Nor I you. We will win this war, you know. Good-bye, madame."

Jean set out on foot from the train station, trusting her memory of the map Georges had provided. She was glad she carried only a purse, for she would have to search on foot for a room. Georges had advised her to stay on the west side of the river Saône, which would place both the Rhône and the Saône rivers between her and Gestapo headquarters.

Beyond Notre-Dame de Fourvière, the exotic white basilica

she remembered on the edge of a cliff above the city, the land fell into steep hills surrounding a broad bowl of a valley. There, according to Georges, the Gestapo seldom ventured. The community, Tassin-la-Demi-Lune, was a suburb of Lyon, but geographically separated from the city by the cliff. The asylum where Giselle was hiding was located on the far side of Tassin-la-Demi-Lune. Georges had advised Jean to purchase a bicycle as soon as possible in order to cover the distance in a reasonable time.

Jean's memory of maps served her well, for she found she couldn't remember much about this part of town from her visit when she was fourteen. A fifteen-minute walk brought her to Place Bellecour, the municipal park that was like a giant town square. From there she turned left and in a few blocks reached the Saône and crossed over to the ancient St. Jean district.

Walking through the cobbled streets, she found a number of old hotels and apartment buildings. She felt conspicuous among the gaunt, poorly clad people who stared at her from doorways or furtively hurried around her. Soon she reached the river and walked for several blocks along the street fronting the water before seeing what she was looking for—an old hotel that contained a large number of rooms with exit doors at each end of the long building and several on the back facing away from the river. The stone building with deep-set windows and heavy shutters stood near an intersection that led to one of the several bridges crossing the Saône.

Jean entered the dim lobby and rang a bell that was marked with a handwritten note, "Concierge." A graying woman who was missing a lower front tooth greeted her. "Good day, mademoiselle."

"Good day, madame. Do you have a vacancy?"

"Perhaps. What do you require?"

"Only a single room."

"I will show you what I have," said the concierge. Taking a key from the pocket of her smock, she led Jean down a dark hallway, up a narrow flight of stairs, and down another dark hallway. She paused and unlocked a door near the end. "This room is small but provides a view of the courtyard and the river, and you have quiet neighbors on either side. It was vacated only yesterday. The toilette with a shower is two doors down the hall. You would share it with only five other residents."

Jean was surprised at the cleanliness of the room. For such an old building, it harbored no offensive odors. It contained a bed, dresser, couch, table, a tiny sink, and a counter with a plug-in hot plate. "This will do," she said.

"Very well. Come down, and I will register you."

Jean followed her back to the lobby. On the guest register she signed Madame Marie Fauvre and paid for a month's rent.

"Do you need help with luggage?" asked the concierge.

"No, thank you. I will bring it later."

The woman's sharp gaze flicked over her.

Jean stared back. "May I have my key?"

"But of course, madame. I beg your pardon."

Jean took it and went back up to the room. While she was unlocking the door, a slight man in a black beret and heavy black eyebrows stomped down the hall. He halted beside her. "You have rented that room?"

"Yes," Jean answered, wishing it were light enough in the hall to see him better.

"Bah! Why am I surprised? Of course the old woman would rent his room even before his body grew cold," he muttered and thumped on down the hall in his sabots.

In Giselle's room at Sisters of Mercy Hospital, the doctor folded his stethoscope and poked it into his black bag. When he straightened, he said, "You are very fortunate. Your heart is as strong as ever. For a while I was afraid you would not live to see your children."

Instantly wary, she said, "My children? What made you think I have children?" She had not even told Mother Agnes about the children. The safety of Jacquie and Angie depended on no one connecting them with her, even someone who did not know her true name. "I have no children."

His expression changed from surprise to sympathy. "Pardon me, please. When I first examined you, I could not miss the evidence left by childbirth. I'm sorry if you have lost your child, but with this war, hard as it may sound, you may be the lucky one. A family with children suffers more now than the rest of us, don't you think?"

"Yes. I suppose so," she said cautiously. Was he probing for information? What did she know about this man after all? Though Mother Agnes trusted him and he had kept the secret of tending her, she could not trust him to know about the children. The fewer people who knew about them, the safer they would be. *Maybe I shouldn't go to see them after all, when I get out of here.*

The doctor picked up his hat and bag. "Madame, you won't require my services any further. I want to give you some final advice. Mother Agnes tells me you wish to leave the hospital soon. I have to warn you that to do this too soon can be disastrous."

"But you said I was strong."

"Physically your strength is near normal. Your emotions are another matter. A shock could conceivably send you into amnesia again, or at the very least, give you a temporary loss of reality. You've been very ill, and life is harsh in Lyon right now. The streets are full of shocking, horrible surprises."

He hesitated and cleared his throat. "Madame, I can't order you, but I beg of you, please stay here longer. Mother Agnes says, if you are willing, she can give you work for as long as you would wish, even until the war is won. She is short of hands and so you would be a great help. Also, you would have food, shelter, and far more safety than on the outside."

Giselle did not wish to discuss her plans or defend them. "Perhaps you're right. I could live and work here awhile."

He raised an eyebrow and shook his head again. "Madame, you are not deceiving me. Well, at least I have warned you."

"Yes. Thank you, Doctor. Thank you for everything."

He raised a hand in a half salute. "Farewell, madame."

When he was gone, Giselle paced the long room nervously. She didn't like the idea of his suspecting she planned to leave soon. *Will I ever trust anyone again?* She stopped in front of the mirror. Her still alien face looked back at her. She ran her fingers over the scars on her cheeks and touched her lumpy nose. No, she could never trust a friend again, let alone a stranger.

She had told no one that her mind did play tricks on her, casting her back into the prison or Gestapo headquarters. Simple things like a sound or a smell could send her back, sometimes only for moments, but horrifyingly real moments. And the nightmares still came, trapping her for agonizing minutes in a world she wanted to forget.

Only last night she had awakened, and this room did not look like it does now. She was in prison again, and when Sister tiptoed in without switching on the light, Giselle had grabbed a heavy stoneware pitcher for a weapon. *If she hadn't been able to call me back to reality, I could have killed her!* Giselle shuddered. The doctor was right. She must be sure she was over these spells before going out into the city.

The day before their arrest, Claude had worried about the possibility of a collaborator in their réseau. He was correct, of course. She could not guess who it might be, so when it came time to leave the hospital, she must be able to function utterly alone. *How long will it be until I can trust myself?*

CHAPTER FIFTEEN

In the hallway of her new home, Jean hurriedly unlocked the door as her scowling neighbor let himself into the next apartment. His remark had set off alarm bells in her mind. How had the previous occupant of her apartment died? Had she unknowingly chosen a location that had been used by a betrayed resistant? Would moving in so soon bring her under suspicious scrutiny? Not being able to guess made her feel vulnerable, as if the hall were full of hidden eyes, watching, seeing right through Marie Fauvre to Jean Thornton.

Maintaining an outward poise, she stepped into her room, locked the door, and leaned her back against it. Without moving, she studied the apartment. Nothing seemed amiss. Tidiness reigned. She chided herself. *I've got a case of the nerves. Anyway, what concierge would leave a clue if there was any foul play?*

She crossed the room, pulled a chair to the window, and sat looking out. Twilight turned colors to shades of gray and darkened the streets. Beyond the courtyard below and the street, the Saône flowed deep and smooth, silvered from the last light in the sky. Jean let out a long breath. At last she was in the same city as Giselle. Tomorrow she would shop for a bicycle. Suddenly she felt too tired to think.

A knock on the door startled her out of her chair. She hurried across the room and listened. "Yes? Who is it, please?"

"The concierge, madame. Perhaps you would like towels since your luggage has not yet arrived?"

Jean opened the door.

The woman stepped inside without waiting for an invitation and proceeded to the bed where she laid two white towels and two washcloths. "I made up the bed, thinking someone without linens might rent the room, but I had forgotten about towels," she said. The concierge quickly glanced at the chair by the window and then back to Jean who had not yet removed her coat. "It is a lovely view, is it not?"

"Yes. Very nice."

"If you wish supper at a café, you will find one at the end of the block toward the bridge."

"Thank you." The woman's eager helpfulness triggered Jean's wariness.

"Did you meet your neighbor next door when he came up?" the concierge asked.

"I saw him. I didn't really meet him."

"A strange fellow. You must not be put off by his talk. I allow him to stay because he is mostly quiet and pays his rent on time, but I wouldn't want him to upset you. He gets to raving, but really he is harmless."

"Raving? He did say the previous tenant in this room had died recently. Is that true?"

"Oh, madame! I am sorry. What a disagreeable fellow to greet a new neighbor with such news. I should have warned you sooner."

"Did the previous occupant die then?"

"Yes. Only two days ago. That is why the room was available, you know. I had just cleaned it. Poor old Gustave was not a good housekeeper, but then a man alone, you know . . ." She gave a very French shrug.

"So he was old and died of natural causes?" Jean inquired further.

"But of course. You weren't thinking of foul play, were you? I manage a quiet, law-abiding establishment, madame. He simply did not come home the other day, and the police finally came to announce they had found him lying dead on the sidewalk. Not a mark on him. The police said his heart had stopped."

"I see. Well, thank you for reassuring me. And thanks for the towels and the directions to the café." Jean moved toward the door.

The woman took her cue and followed. As she left, she

paused. "Don't let Raoul frighten you, Madame Fauvre. I assure you he is harmless, even though he sees an enemy behind every door."

Jean smiled—warmly, she hoped. "I understand."

The concierge smiled too. "If you need anything, I have some extras, and I know where you may purchase a few necessities. Just let me know."

Jean questioned whether her watchful eyes served a simple busybody or a woman with a sinister purpose, but she filled her voice with friendly gratitude. "Thank you, I will." Definitely this was one person not to trust. If nothing else, she talked too much.

For supper Jean walked an extra block to avoid the café the concierge had recommended. Inside the one she chose, most of the patrons were men. One met her eyes boldly and stared. It was her new neighbor from the next apartment, Raoul. She sat at a small table near the window with her back to him.

The serveuse came and announced, "Tonight we have potato soup with carrots and cabbage and bread fresh from the bakery."

"A bowl of the soup, please."

The young woman nodded and added cheerfully, "We also have a custard for dessert." She then whispered, "You have chosen a good café. Our cook, his family has a farm not far from the city. He goes with his bicycle and a big basket and brings back eggs and cheese and fresh vegetables."

"I'm glad to hear that." Jean was also glad when she ate, for the cook knew how to make simple foods tasty.

When she rose from her little table, Raoul also stood up and followed her to the door. She tried to remain inconspicuous, but unfortunately this man and the concierge seemed overly interested in her.

Jean dodged out the door and hurried down the sidewalk.

But the man strode swiftly to her side. "We are neighbors, are we not, mademoiselle, and I owe you an apology for such a gruff greeting this evening," he said smoothly. His low voice reminded her of Georges Crozet, but he seemed more furtive. Was it because of his quick movements and eyes that constantly scanned all directions, in contrast to Georges' solid confidence and penetrating gaze?

"Allow me to introduce myself. Raoul Montaigne, printer by trade."

Georges had told her all people in the communications media either collaborated with the Nazis or were not working anymore in their chosen trade. Before Jean could respond, Montaigne said, "Of course I have not worked as a printer since the occupation. I now have a job on the railroad loading boxcars." He chuckled humorlessly and checked his watch. "Curfew in twenty minutes. May I walk back to the apartments with you?" he asked, suddenly polite.

With only one block to walk, Jean said, "Thank you."

"You are new to Lyon?" Raoul asked.

"Why do you say that?"

"There is a freshness about your face, a lilt in your speech. You look as if you have come from the country, where life is easier."

His mention of how she spoke sent her pulse racing. Was her accent showing too much? She addressed his other remark. "You're right. After losing my husband, I stayed with my aunt near Macon."

"You are widowed. I'm sorry." He fell silent a moment and then said, "And now you want a city job?"

He was asking too many questions. "None of us have much choice, do we?" she responded. At last they reached the door of the apartment building.

He stopped short of going in. "It is better the old gossip does not see you with me. I'll have a smoke before going in. Good night."

While Jean climbed the stairs to her room, she felt, rather than heard, the concierge's door open. She didn't look that direction but strode to the stairs and on up. All the way down the long upper hallway, she felt eyes watching her. At her door she whirled around and confronted all the shadows. No one was there. *Fatigue and my imagination,* she told herself while locking herself in with both the key and the dead bolt.

Giselle fought the metal cuffs fastening her to the chair. The interrogator had left her alone. The man with the scar that pulled his mouth

upward on one side would come next. Hysterically she yanked against the restraints.

He came and stood over her, stretching his ready-made grin to a sneer. "Ah, madame. You struggle. You only hurt yourself." He reached out, gripped her hands in each of his, and squeezed until bones cracked.

Giselle shrieked from the new pain.

He spread his hands in front of her fading vision, hands shining crimson with her blood. The hands grabbed and shook her.

She screamed and screamed.

"Madame Julie! Wake up! Wake up! You are safe. You are having a bad dream. Open your eyes. Look at me. It is Sister Therese!"

Giselle finally focused on the nun's sympathetic face. She threw her arms around her. "Hold me, Sister. Please hold me."

Sister Therese sat beside her and held her in strong, kind arms until she finally stopped shaking.

"It was the dream again," Giselle said.

"I'm sorry. Let me give you some medicine."

"No, I have to be able to wake up!"

"But maybe with the medicine your dreams would be more pleasant."

"No!"

"Would you like for Mother Agnes to come and pray for you?"

"No. Please don't bother her. I'm all right now. Can you bring me a book to read?"

"You need rest. You should try to sleep."

"Please. A book about happy things."

"I'm sorry. I don't have anything. Tomorrow I will look for something."

"Then may I leave the light on?"

"Of course. And I will be right here all the time."

"Thank you."

Giselle lay staring at the high ceiling. Mother Agnes said that this long high-ceilinged room had been a chapel in the old original asylum. Now with the modern hospital built over it, people had forgotten the chapel ever existed. As the catacombs in Rome, it had protected people—many resistants and even entire families of Jews. But now no more Jews came.

If only someone had hidden Claude's family like this. His

mother, father, and young brother had been taken from their farm at the beginning of the occupation. By some streak of fortune—the hand of God, she'd like to think—their records had not connected them to Claude. His new identity had not been questioned. *I must not think about his family now. I must try to relax. I must conquer these nightmares.*

She imagined Jacquie and Angie on the farm playing with kittens and the big dog and maybe a spring lamb or calf.

She remembered the good times when her mother and father had taken her to the Leveque farm when she was Angie's age to show her the animals. Then she remembered the wonderful summers on Uncle Al's small farm in America. In her mind it was always summertime in Oregon, because she had visited only in July and August. She and Jeanie—what a pair they'd made—Jeanie just a little girl but with such a grown-up mind. As for herself, she'd been content to linger in childhood as long as possible, and her parents had not rushed her. It had been a good life. Giselle let the memories warm her, and she began to relax.

In Lyon Jean returned to the same café for breakfast. After eating, she confided to the serveuse that she wanted to buy a bicycle. The girl gave her directions to a shop within walking distance.

The next morning Jean set out, ignoring the black clouds and brisk wind. She hoped it would not rain. If only she could find a serviceable bike quickly. She reined in her impatience. Step by careful step she would find Giselle. Nothing must distract her from taking every precaution. She crossed both the Saône and the Rhône rivers and hurried along the route the waitress had described. Suddenly she recognized a gray stone building across the street, which filled the whole block. Georges had shown her several photos of the Terminus Hotel. There was no mistaking the colonnaded entrance screening a huge inner courtyard. It was the Gestapo headquarters and the place was swarming with Nazi soldiers. She had blundered into the most dangerous part of the city.

Jean attempted to walk normally like the few other pedestrians, with eyes straight ahead or averted. In her peripheral vision she glimpsed a German military bus pull up in front of the ex-hotel. Soldiers jumped out and gestured with their pistols while three disheveled prisoners emerged.

She turned and watched their reflection in a store window. The soldiers herded them into the courtyard. One man limped. Another staggered. Inwardly she flinched but walked on as if seeing nothing. So did the people around her.

Two more blocks brought her to the used merchandise shop. Inside, a variety of household items and tools stood in various stages of disrepair, but she saw no bicycles.

A man appeared in a doorway at the back of the shop. "May I help you, mademoiselle?"

"I hope so. I need a bicycle. Do you have anything?"

"I have three, but only one I have repaired. Would you care to look?"

"Yes, please." She followed him to his workshop at the back of the building. The paint on the repaired bicycle was worn and so were the tires. It would have to do. She bargained a little to get the best possible price and then asked if he could repair another one for her mother.

"Yes."

"How soon can you have it ready?"

"I cannot say until I begin. If you come tomorrow, I can tell."

"May I take my bicycle out this way?" She gestured toward the alley.

The man gave her a shrewd look and said, "Of course. You will find it easier there. Fewer people. Less traffic."

The journey back across the two rivers on the bicycle took so few minutes that Jean's spirits rose. She hadn't been on a bike for ages, but she quickly felt in control. The bike rolled well.

It was early enough in the day that she decided to pedal the fifteen kilometers to Sisters of Mercy Hospital.

To get out of downtown, she had to push the bicycle up the incredibly steep route to the top of the cliff above the St. Jean district. From the summit she could see not only Lyon, but Villeurbanne beyond. The air was clear and clean from the wind and last night's rain. And by the looks of the sky, rain could break loose again before day's end.

She mounted the bicycle and pedaled the streets she had memorized from Georges' map. Going up the hills she had to walk but made up for lost time riding down. An occasional car passed her, but no military vehicles. The homes on these hills lay quietly pastoral, some with yards as large as expensive homes in America. Others clustered into villages with a few local shops. These old houses had only dooryards and stone walls to separate them from the street.

To Jean's great relief, the major landmarks Georges had mentioned were easy to recognize.

After a long ride down a gentle slope into a broadening valley, Jean reached the base of a low rounded hill. The hospital should be on its crest. She pedaled up the narrow zigzagging street until her legs gave out, then pushed her wheels again. At last the climb became less steep. At the top of the hill, a tall stone wall separated her from a thick grove of leafless trees. She pushed on eagerly. Soon she reached an open gate in the wall. Inside the gate at the end of a narrow drive stood the stern facade of Sisters of Mercy Hospital. The upper windows reflected the sky, but the lower ones stared darkly at her. She glanced at her watch. The ride had taken just over an hour and a half. It was almost noon.

Jean walked toward the forbidding front entrance. She needed those few moments to observe the place. At the curb, she leaned the bicycle against an ancient hitching post and climbed the wide stone steps. Tall windows on either side of the entry showed no sign of life. She banged the iron knocker.

After a long wait the door swung open, revealing a nun in a simple gray habit and a wide white nurse's cap. "Good day, Sister. I have come to see Mother Agnes, please."

The sister blinked. "And whom shall I say is calling?"

"Madame Marie Fauvre. She does not know me, but I come with a very great need."

The sister's reserved expression softened. "Please come in, madame. I will tell her you are here." She gestured to a row of high-backed straight chairs along the right side of the entry hall. "Please be seated."

Jean sat. Against the opposite wall stood a sideboard affair that looked as if it belonged in a dining room. Here in the entry it gave guests a chance to glimpse themselves in a mirror, a place to sign the guest book, and a place on the far side to hang coats. The disharmony of a sideboard by the front door was not unpleasant. Beside the long piece of furniture stood a dark, ornately carved wooden hat rack.

On quiet feet the sister returned. "Mother Agnes will see you in her office. Follow me, please."

Jean's street shoes echoed across the marble floor. She calculated one would have to be barefoot in this silent place to walk as quietly as the sister. She followed her guide into an office lined with shelves of books from floor to ceiling. Behind a broad desk sat an older woman dressed in black with only a narrow band of white framing her broad face. Her gray eyes and fair skin reminded Jean of a Dutch master's painting. Her friendly smile enhanced the impression of a kindly housewife.

"Good morning, madame."

"Good morning, Mother," Jean answered.

"You may leave us, Sister Josephine." The nun floated out as silently as she had entered.

The Mother Superior turned to Jean. "Please, do sit and be comfortable. Now, tell me how I may help you."

"I've come to see your patient, Madame Julie Munier." Georges had cautioned her about saying too much before she made certain she was speaking to the correct person.

Without any change of expression, the nun said, "I'm sorry, Madame Fauvre. You are somehow mistaken. We have no patient named Munier. Can it be you have come to the wrong hospital?"

Jean knew she was in the correct hospital. Was this the woman Georges had trusted? "Excuse me, but have you served here long, as head of the hospital, I mean?"

The nun raised her chin in a commanding manner. "I have been here for many years. Why do you ask?"

"I asked to see Mother Agnes. Perhaps the sister did not understand me."

"I am Mother Agnes."

"Martin sent me."

"I know many Martins—"

"The Martin who brought Julie here."

A flicker of emotion crossed Mother Superior's face. She laid down her pen and rested her hand, half-open, on her desktop. "Tell me about this Julie."

Jean pulled the scrap of cloth from her purse and placed it in Mother Agnes's now open hand. "This is from her blouse."

"So"—the nun's smile erased years from her countenance—"you have come for Julie. How glad she will be!"

"Then she is still here? Is she all right? May I see her?"

"The answer is yes, yes, and yes." She raised a cautioning finger to her lips. "But first let us talk for a moment. You must not mention her name outside this room. Let me prepare you. Do you know how ill and injured she was when she came to us?"

"Not really. Mother, I am her cousin. Is she well now?"

"I'm happy to say that she is. However, she is still fragile in some ways. She suffered two episodes of amnesia, and if she were to receive a bad shock, she could lose her memory again. Once the amnesia takes hold, there is no predicting when it will leave. This makes it very dangerous for her to be out in public. Do you understand this?"

"Yes. Then you think she isn't well enough to leave the hospital?"

"I'm not sure. I've been hoping she would remain with us until the war is over."

"But Mother Agnes, she will never be safe here in France. I came from York, England, two days ago. With God's help, I want to take her back with me to England."

Mother Superior's hand flew to the gold cross she wore on a long chain around her neck. "May God help us indeed!" she gasped.

"Mother, I've been trained by professionals," Jean said, "and I was very careful coming here, careful not to attract the attention of the Milice, the Gestapo, or even the curious."

"Of course, of course. It's just such a shock." She cleared her throat. "How did you get here, and how can you possibly take her safely out of France?"

"I can't tell you that. Please trust me. I assure you, I can do it." Jean waited for endless seconds while Mother Agnes silently studied her.

Finally the nun said, "In the years I've been Mother to the sisters here, I've learned much about judging character. I can't imagine how you can do as you say. Yet, however foolish it might seem to others, I do trust you."

Jean sighed in relief. "Thank you! May I see Giselle—I mean, Julie?"

"First I must remind you that her presence here is a secret

even from the sisters. Ignorance of her presence reduces the risk, not only for her, but for everyone else in my charge."

"Yes. I understand that."

"Secondly, you must prepare yourself.... You may not recognize her. She was dreadfully beaten."

Tears rushed to Jean's eyes, and her hand flew to her mouth.

"Can you bear to see her now, or would you like to sit awhile and gather your emotions?"

"Oh, Mother, I want to see her right away!"

"Compose your face then, and I will take you to her."

Jean dried her eyes and again became Marie Fauvre, who had no cousin Giselle.

CHAPTER SIXTEEN

Giselle paced the length of her long room, using the minutes she'd been left alone to exercise, as she had at every opportunity. Pausing beside her bed, she steadied herself with one hand on the metal frame and did several deep knee bends. Her muscles responded quickly and with normal strength. Her spirits rose. When the chance to leave came, her legs would not betray her.

A light rap on her door brought her to attention. Before she could move, the door cracked open and Mother Agnes, in a cautious voice, announced, "Madame Julie, I have wonderful news. You have a visitor—your cousin, Madame Fauvre."

"No!" Giselle gasped. *They have found me! I have no cousin named Fauvre!* There was no place to hide. "Mother!" she cried in anguish.

A woman burst in. "Giselle, it's me—Jeanie!"

Giselle's panic whirled her into near hysteria. Jeanie! How could the enemy know about Jeanie? *Oh, God, help me!* She slumped to her knees beside her bed. "Mother, what have you done?"

"No, no! It really is your cousin. I have proof," Mother Agnes cried. "Please believe me, madame! Calm yourself."

At the same time, the visitor ran to her and knelt facing her. "Giselle. Don't you know me? It's Jeanie!"

The voice! The face! Surely no impostor could be so like her. She whispered, "Jeanie?"

The visitor grabbed her in a tight hug and started to sob.

"Jeanie, it's you? It's really you?" As her senses assured her that she was indeed in her cousin's arms, the wall that she had erected around her emotions crumbled. "You shouldn't have come! Oh, you shouldn't have come." She clung to Jeanie, and Jeanie held her in surprisingly strong arms.

"I've been so afraid for you . . . for so long," Jeanie exclaimed. "Afraid I'd never see you again. Oh, Giselle . . ." She pulled away and gently placed her hands, one on each side of Giselle's face, and gazed into her eyes. Her face was first alight with relief, and then with only slightly disguised horror. "I can't bear to think what they did to you." She grabbed Giselle in a convulsive hug. "It's so good to see you, to touch you, to know you're all right. . . ." Her voice chopped off, and Giselle wept uncontrollably with her.

After a few minutes, Giselle felt a surprising comfort, as if her pain were being washed away by Jeanie's tears. After not even knowing who she was, she now had the arms of a family member around her. How on earth had Jeanie made it into occupied France? Somehow she must be protected until she could be sent out again. Giselle's mind began to wrestle with the problem, and she stopped crying. Finally she pulled away from Jeanie. "How did you get here? Do you understand the danger?"

Mother Superior, whom Giselle had forgotten, interrupted. "Excuse me, please. I will go and keep watch on the driveway and leave you two to visit awhile."

"Thank you, Mother," Giselle said.

After the door closed behind Mother Agnes, Jean dried her eyes and then said in her familiar positive way, "I've come to take you and the girls to England."

"But how. . . ? You are out of your mind!"

"I've been trained by the secret service—the BSE—and your friend Georges. Oh! You knew him as Martin."

"Martin! In England?"

"Yes. He is with de Gaulle's Free French Army. He's been a liaison between de Gaulle and the BSE in France."

"Did he say . . . anything about Claude?"

"Only that he doesn't know where he is."

"I know Claude must be alive. . . . He must be!"

Jeanie's face crumpled, but she brushed her tears away with the back of her hand. "I believe that too. So does Martin. But he insists you must leave France. Your betrayer has not been identified by the Resistance. You can't stay here!"

Giselle reached out and gripped her hand and hung on tightly. When Jeanie didn't say anything more, she said, "I have to keep hold of you to believe I'm not dreaming. Go on. Keep talking. I do understand the danger of staying here."

Jeanie continued. "We are to go north to Macon and meet an agent who will arrange for our flight out."

Giselle tried to listen, but of course what Jeanie proposed was impossible, and even if it was not, she didn't want to go to England. She interrupted. "Did Uncle Al hear anything about Maman and Père since we last communicated with him?"

Jeanie's face gave away the answer. "I'm sorry. He's never been able to confirm where they may be."

"I understand. Look, Jeanie, you must get yourself back to England as soon as possible. But it would be too dangerous for me and the children. Claude ... he will come to Lyon looking for me ... needing me. No. I can never leave France." To her dismay, she began to tremble, and her heart started to hammer against her ribs. The panic was returning.

Jeanie put her arm around her shoulders and drew her close.

"Jacqueline and Angelique are with friends I trust. They will be safe as long as I stay away from them."

Jeanie's arm tightened around her. "I swear to you, I would not have come if I didn't believe we can safely take them to England. You don't know how carefully Martin has prepared me. Listen...." She revealed the details of her training and the plan Martin had devised.

Giselle was amazed at the confidence she read on her cousin's face. She remembered that Claude always had said Martin was the most astute of the men close to him. As Jeanie described her intensive training by the BSE and the plan to disguise Giselle as a grandmother and make one of the girls look like a boy, Giselle's terror eased.

"I've brought identification papers and travel permits for all of us. We can take the train to Macon. From there a BSE agent will deliver us to a safe house in the country where we can wait to be picked up at night by a British plane."

Giselle interrupted. "Did Martin have any notion where Claude is?"

"No one in the Resistance knows. Martin thinks he escaped

and fled south. He hopes he may have joined the Maquis near the Spanish border, but there's been no word."

"Then Claude may not know that I am alive."

"Like you, he would not be certain." Jeanie's gaze met hers piercingly. "If he knew you had this opportunity to take the girls to England, what would he advise?"

This was one thing Giselle did not know about Claude. He had stayed in France even though he risked being identified as a Jew. She stood up and walked slowly to the dresser. Leaning her hands on the top, she studied herself in the mirror. Tentatively she touched the gaunt hollows under her cheekbones and the deep crease between her eyebrows, then ran her fingers through her dingy half-blond, half-brown hair. "I don't even need makeup to look like a grandmother."

Jeanie, so young and pretty, came and stood beside her. "No. We will have to work to make you look old," she said emphatically.

Tears knotted Giselle's throat. "I feel older than Grand-mother ever has looked!"

"She hasn't suffered like you, thank God. The scars can be concealed some. The blond coming back to your hair, of course, we must change."

Giselle smiled wryly. "You almost make me believe. I know how to make my hair brown again, but I'm not sure how to make it gray."

"Then you'll do it?"

Giselle turned from the mirror to Jeanie. "The traitor could still be in Lyon."

"Yes." Jeanie raised her chin with a self-assurance that Giselle could not explain. Somehow her American cousin had acquired the same quality of strength and endurance that so many French women had displayed since the occupation.

"It's true it may be only a matter of time before the Milice or Gestapo find me. I know too much . . . they will not forget me."

"That's why I came." Jeanie said firmly. "Together we can es-cape!"

"But the children . . ." She fell silent at the thought of placing them in the danger Jeanie described. Alone she could go out, do anything, but she didn't want to endanger the little ones. Aloud she weighed the facts. "I'm no longer ill. I was successful when I brazenly deceived the Gestapo. Their arrogance is their Achilles heel. They can't believe a French woman would defy their laws or fight like a man."

Jeanie pressed her to decide. "Then you'll do it?"

"I think I must. God help us! We have to get ourselves and the girls out of France . . . as quick as possible."

Giselle sat down at her desk, picked up a pencil, then realized she must not write down anything, not even a doodle that could be found in the trash and analyzed. "How did you come to the hospital today?"

"By bicycle. I bought a used one in Lyon."

"Can you obtain a bicycle for me?"

"I already asked the shop owner to repair one for my mother."

"We shall go for the girls on bicycles then. It will be a long day's ride, maybe more. I will need to build up my strength."

"As soon as your bike is ready, I'll bring it. Surely Mother Agnes can find a safe place for you to ride."

"You would have to walk back to Lyon. Can you do that and not violate the curfew?"

"I'm sure I can. It took slightly more than an hour and a half to get here this morning. It should take less than four hours for me to walk back."

A tap on the door interrupted them. Mother Agnes let herself in. "Madame, I am sorry to send you away so soon, but it is unwise to stay longer. The wind is promising a storm. Will you come tomorrow?"

Jean got up and glanced out the window at the clouds rolling westward before the wind. "If I don't come tomorrow, it will be because Giselle's bicycle is not ready." She explained the need for Giselle to ride the bicycle to build her strength.

Mother nodded. "That can be arranged."

After Jeanie and Mother Agnes left, Giselle paced back and forth the length of her room, making plans, considering options, trying to anticipate everything that could go wrong. Jeanie could not possibly know all she needed to know to get them out of France safely, but together they would manage.

It took two days for the repairman to finish Giselle's bicycle. Jean went out only to check his progress. She ate in her apartment from the monotonous food she'd purchased at a store and chafed at the delay.

When the bicycle was ready, she placed it beside her own in a storage room at the apartment building where the concierge had granted space.

In the morning she set out while others were going to work in order to conform to the oppressive hours enforced by the German High Command, which required everyone in France to work according to Berlin time.

Riding Giselle's bicycle, keeping to back streets, and circling as far as possible from Gestapo headquarters, Jean crossed to the west bank of the Saône, then peddled along the cobbled streets of old town. She reached the summit of Fourvière and paused beside the great white basilica to catch her breath before heading toward the valley beyond. The weather cooperated by remaining dry, although a cold wind gusted from the northeast.

When Jean reached the hospital, she circled the block and parked the bicycle between shrubs in the back garden. Then she returned to the street to approach the front door on foot. Just as she neared the front gate, a black vehicle carrying men in German uniforms rolled up the street and turned into the driveway. Keeping tight control of her fear, Jean slowly walked down the sidewalk and across the driveway. Out of the corner of her eye, she watched the Germans.

A soldier pounded his fist against the heavy wooden door. Two officers stood arrogantly behind him.

Jean proceeded as slowly as she dared. Just before she lost view of the door, someone opened it, and the officers went in. A dozen questions screamed at her. *Why are they here? Do they have information from a collaborator? Will they search? The bicycle! Will it cause a problem?*

She couldn't go back to Lyon without knowing anything. She crossed the street at the next corner and entered a nearby café that gave her a view of the hospital gate. From her table, the hospital gate remained in full sight. She ordered coffee and bread, eating slowly and watching for the German officers to leave the hospital. After what seemed an interminable time, with no sign of the Germans, she decided she could wait no longer or she wouldn't be able to get to her apartment before the curfew. Reluctantly she left her vantage point, paid the woman who had served her sawdusty bread and ersatz coffee, and left.

By the time Jean reached Fourvière and the basilica, rain was falling with dismal persistence. She arrived at her apartment soaked to her skin and her feet aching from the long walk. At least she did not see and hence was not seen by either the concierge or her neighbor, Monsieur Montaigne.

She stripped off her wet garments, spread them to dry, and rubbed herself briskly with a towel. But she couldn't get warm. Too tired to cook even a potato, she dined on hot water and a chunk of bread with dried salami, then climbed into bed. Despite her lingering chill, she fell into a troubled sleep. After a time, she roused enough once to realize she was warm at last.

In the morning a splinter of sunlight sliced into the room from between the closed shutters, announcing that she had overslept. Her last thought the night before had been of Giselle. Now her first thought was of Giselle. She scrambled out of bed and quickly dressed. Her coat, sweater, and skirt were still damp from yesterday's walk. They would have to do.

Jean ate only some bread with a cup of imitation coffee and hurried to the storage room for her bicycle.

She reached Sisters of Mercy Hospital in record time. The cloistered facade gave no hint of what she might find inside. Again she pedaled to the rear of the building. Giselle's bicycle was gone. She parked her own in a different place, beside the alley entrance, and walked around the block. Watching for any hint of change, she approached the front door. If anything seemed out of line when the door opened, she would simply inquire about a fictitious patient and walk away. She knocked, hoping and praying the Gestapo had come on just a routine inspection, if such a thing ever happened.

The sister who opened the door was not the one Jean had met before. Still, she asked, "If you please, I am Madame Fauvre, here to see Mother Agnes."

After an instant of hesitation, the nun opened the door wider. "Please come in. I will tell her."

Jean stepped into the foyer. It was quiet. More so than before?

The sister scampered away. Her lack of courtesy definitely was different. A quiver of fear ran through Jean. Should she leave now while she could?

Down the hall the sound of measured soft footfalls approached. Mother Agnes strode around a corner. "Madame Fauvre! Do come into my office." She crossed the foyer, opened her door, and beckoned.

Jean could read nothing from her placid expression. She followed, and when Mother Agnes closed the door behind them, Jean burst out, "I saw the Germans come yesterday! Is my cousin safe? Is everything all right?"

"All is well, my dear. They found nothing, not even the bicycle you left. However, I sensed they were not satisfied and will soon be back."

"Then it's not safe for Giselle to stay here!"

"I fear her legs are not too strong, but if she can possibly do it, I think she must leave today. Yesterday afternoon I dressed her as one of the gardeners, and she rode the bicycle around the grounds. This morning she rode again."

Things were progressing faster than Jean had expected. "Let's see what she says."

"Yes, of course." Mother Agnes led the way out the back of her office and down the old hall to the basement.

When Jean entered the hiding place, Giselle rushed to hug her. "I've been so worried about you alone in Lyon for these past days! Mother Agnes found the bicycle and assumed you had seen the Germans. Jeanie, I have to get out of here now! They will come again. I can't stay any longer."

"Yes. Yes, you will come with me. Oh dear, I wanted to color your hair first."

Mother Agnes intervened. "The blond roots must be concealed. I'll see what I can find to do that. Also, I have clothing, although it would be more suitable for an older woman."

"That will be good!" Jean said. "Somehow we need to make her hair look as if it is graying."

When they were alone, Giselle said, "Jeanie, there is one thing. After we leave here, your French ... it is good ... almost flawless, and yet you have a little accent on some words. Most people might not think anything about it, but the Milice ... the Gestapo ... I fear they will know and question you. You should let me do the talking whenever possible."

Jean tried to push away the anxiety Giselle was generating. She had been so careful. "Georges and Eve, my coaches, felt I could pass as native, and all the BSE agents have done so, even though they weren't born here."

"Maybe, but we must not take any risk we can avoid. Please remember and let me talk to others as much as possible."

To ease her mind and because she could be right, Jean nodded. "I'll do that."

Giselle hurried on without even acknowledging that Jean had spoken. "When we get to Lyon, I'll go to our hideaway apartment and get Claude's gun. We can't travel unarmed. Jeanie, I will never be taken alive again by the Germans. And I won't let them take you or the girls alive either."

Shocked, Jean gaped at her cousin. During the ensuing instant of silence, she realized she must not argue with Giselle. Not right now.

CHAPTER SEVENTEEN

Jean could not imagine—didn't want to imagine—experiences so horrible that killing one's own little girls would seem merciful. She wanted to yell, "No!"

From Giselle's desperate and distant expression, she could see her cousin was unreachable, but somehow she must persuade her not to search for Claude's gun. Quietly she said, "I have a gun. They trained me well, and I'm a good shot."

"You? A gun?" Giselle's eyes came back into focus. "But you hate guns!"

"Well, I've learned they have their place." That was partly true. She didn't have to say what place.

"Maybe you should let me carry it."

"Let's talk about this after we get to my apartment," Jean said.

Mother Agnes hurried in. She'd found a bottle of shoe polish. "This should last through rain storms, if not shampoos. Color her hair quickly and go. She will need many rest stops, and you must not be out after curfew. Go out the rear door that leads into the garden. Madame Julie knows the way. I will place her bicycle beside the door."

"Thank you so much for all you've done," Jean said. "When peace comes, I hope I may return to thank you again."

Mother Agnes's swift smile made her look younger. "Nothing would please me more."

"I shall return too," Giselle said, "and find some way to repay your kindness."

"Repay me by taking good care of yourself, my dear. I will be praying for you both. Now good-bye." She left quickly, as she had urged them to do.

Jean lightly applied the shoe polish to Giselle's hair in a streaking pattern, taking care not to touch her scalp. She wiped off the excess, leaving a muddy grayish tint. It set and dried in a short time.

"Not bad," Jean said. Closing the stopper tightly, she placed the bottle in her purse. "I hope that will last until we get out of France."

"Is there enough polish for another application?"

"One more. I'm not sure about two."

Giselle sat in front of the dressing table mirror and grimaced as she lifted limp strands of her dingy hair. "Can you fasten it back into a knot of some kind?"

Jean combed it to the back of Giselle's head and pinned it as best she could. "It's too short for a chignon."

Giselle studied the result in a hand mirror. "It will do. I'll keep it covered as much as possible. Where did you park your bicycle?"

"By the back gate."

Giselle picked up the brown wool coat and black bandanna Mother Agnes had left on her bed. "Then let's go!"

"Wait. You need to carry these." Jean pulled Giselle's forged ration cards and identification papers from her purse. "Here. Memorize your name and ID information. I'll tell you our family history while we walk up the hills and stop to rest."

Giselle studied the cards and then said, "All right. I'm ready."

At the back of the hospital, Jean ran ahead to pull her bicycle out of its hiding place. She felt as if a thousand eyes were watching. Breathless, she pulled her bike from the evergreen shrubbery and waited. Giselle moved with unsteady steps as she pushed her bicycle across the old garden. When she drew near, Jean said, "Are you going to be all right?"

"Yes. Why?"

"You look as if it hurts to move."

Giselle grinned, looking for an instant more like her old self. "I was only acting my age. Remember? I'm a grandmother."

"Oh! I guess I didn't expect you to play the part before we reached the street."

"From now on, my dear child, address me with the respect due your mother. Your père and I taught you better than to remark on how one walks, especially one's elder!"

"Yes, Maman."

"I can assure you the bicycle ride will loosen me, and then you'll have to work to keep pace."

"Yes, Maman."

Several hours later, Giselle was so bone-deep tired that she could not have trudged up one more hill. Her knees quivered like jelly. Fortunately, she was standing on Fourvière and the last few blocks were downhill.

Lyon, stretching out below, monochrome in the late afternoon light, looked as dismal as a gray Nazi uniform. She felt the enemy's evil seep up the cliff and wrap itself around her. With all her will, she pulled her mind away from its dark tentacles and the fear churning in her chest. *I must stay strong. Jeanie needs me.* "I'm rested," she said. "Let's go."

Jeanie coasted ahead of her down the zigzag street. At the bottom of the bluff, she turned into the narrow streets of the ancient St. Jean district. Giselle followed.

At the back of a large old apartment building that fronted on the river, Jeanie stopped beside double doors that must have closed on a stable when the building was new. "The concierge lets me keep my bicycle in here." She propped her bicycle and then took Giselle's. "We'll go in the front door so I can introduce you to the concierge. It's safer not to give her any more time than necessary to speculate on her own. I told her this morning that my mother and two children were coming to live with me. Before she could ask, I paid her double rent. She seemed mollified. Never can tell, though."

"You are so right." Jeanie's suspicion and competence continued to surprise Giselle. That her American cousin could be so attuned to living in France was uncanny. *There's so much I don't know about her anymore.*

She followed Jeanie to the front entrance. While Jeanie knocked at the apartment of the concierge, Giselle leaned against the wall, light-headed from exhaustion.

A buxom woman with a long nose and close-set eyes that

glittered like jet beads came out as quickly as if she had been listening by the door. "Ah, Madame Fauvre, you are back with your maman. Welcome, madame." Her glance darted from Giselle's straggling hair down her figure and lingered too long on her purse. "But where is your luggage? My man will help you with it."

"My daughter has all we need," Giselle said. "Now that we are both widowed, I am so fortunate to have my dependable Marie. We will be fine, thank you."

The woman's shrewd gaze continued to assess her, but her mouth smiled. Like a typical garrulous concierge, she gushed gracious words. "You are indeed fortunate, madame. I wish I could give you more rooms, but ah"—she spread out open hands and shook her head—"you know how it is in these times. You and I, we have seen two wars now. A bad business always. You will need more linens and bedding. I will bring some up immediately."

"No, thank you," Jeanie said. "Tomorrow will be soon enough. We can share the double bed. Then, if you don't mind, please, we will need two cots for the children."

"I will find something for them. Have no fear."

A man entered the front door. As he strode past, he glowered at the concierge, glanced at Jeanie, and stared at Giselle still leaning against the wall. She instantly recognized him—a resistant whom she had met only briefly. She bent her head, searched in her purse, and pulled out a handkerchief. Keeping her face averted, she blew her nose with a noisy old-woman honk. The sound of his footsteps moved down the hall, clumped upstairs, and faded into silence. Had he recognized her despite her disguise and disfigured face? Surely he could not!

The concierge took note of Giselle's condition and exclaimed, "Madame Fauvre, your maman looks ill! Come inside and let her rest before climbing those stairs."

Giselle gave up the support of the wall and shook her head. "Thank you, madame, but I am only a bit tired. Excuse me, please, and I will go to Marie's apartment and lie down." She grabbed Jeanie by the arm and leaned against her. "Come, my dear, do take me up," she commanded. With her chin thrust out and her shoulders slumped forward, she started off.

"Yes, Maman. I will tuck you in and make some nice hot

soup while you rest. Thank you, madame," she called back to the concierge.

The odors of boiling cabbage and onions exuded from apartments as they made their way upstairs. At the far end of the hall, haunted by a sense of watching eyes and listening ears around them, Giselle silently leaned against the wall again while Jeanie unlocked her door.

Inside, with the door shut and locked again, Giselle exclaimed in a low voice, "That old shrew had no business taking double rent from you for this place. She will bear watching, all right." She dropped onto the bed fully clothed and closed her eyes. "I'm so tired!" She felt Jeanie remove her shoes and cover her. *Oh, the bliss of not having to move a muscle.*

The gentle rattle of cooking pans sang her to sleep. The smell of potato soup awakened her.

"I didn't know if you were going to wake up to eat," Jeanie said.

Giselle's stomach contracted with a ravenous hunger pang. She sat up and swung her feet to the floor. "I'm famished, and that smells wonderful!" She stood up and swayed a little. "My legs are complaining. They weren't quite ready for the long bicycle ride."

"Stay there. I'll bring you a bowl."

"I need to be up and moving."

"All right. Eat here at the table, and then it's early to bed for the both of us. We need a good rest before our next move."

The soup was satisfyingly hearty, rich with canned milk, plenty of potatoes and onions, and bits of dried salami for seasoning. Giselle felt strength seep back into her body as her stomach warmed and filled. When she finished, she leaned back. "Pure luxury. Good soup and a full stomach." With the return of her energy, she immediately began to think and plan. "Jeanie, let me see your gun."

Jeanie went to the armoire and returned with the MAB. She handed it to Giselle. "The chamber is loaded, so don't touch the safety."

Giselle's heart sank at the sight of the toy-sized weapon. "Twenty-five caliber. Not much of a gun. But of course they would have warned you about that."

"Yes. I know I have to be close to my target."

"Not much help, but until I get the Mauser, the MAB will be better than nothing. Tomorrow I'll get Claude's gun, and then the next day we can start early to go fetch the children."

"I really think you should forget about Claude's gun. For you to go out into the city where you may be recognized, and for you to carry a German gun are too dangerous!"

"Dangerous?" Sudden, fierce anger stripped away Giselle's control. "I think I know better than you about the dangers here. I *must* get Claude's gun ... unless he has already taken it for himself." That possibility cooled her mind, helped her to think more rationally.

Her next unspoken thought came from Jeanie. "What if the Milice have discovered his gun and are only waiting for you to return for it?"

"I can tell before entering the apartment whether anyone else has discovered our hiding place."

"Please don't go!"

"I must."

"Then I'm going with you."

"No, you—" A small inner voice stopped her. *Anyone looking for Julie Munier will not expect a young woman and her old maman.* "Well, maybe it would be better for you to come."

"Good. So let's go to bed early. The bathroom is two doors down the hall on the right. We share it with several other residents."

This information reminded Giselle of the resistant who had come upstairs just before them. "Did you notice that man who came in while you were talking to the concierge?"

"Monsieur Montaigne? Yes. I try to avoid him. He's been too inquisitive and too friendly."

"I've seen him before acting as a resistant ... but who knows now what he is."

"Do you think he recognized you?"

"I don't see how he could, but he gave me far too much attention. I kept my face turned from him. But do you think he could recognize me by my profile?" She swung a half turn away. "Would you?"

Jeanie's voice came softly, sad, and honest. "No. I wouldn't know you."

In the morning Jean awoke before Giselle. She slipped out of bed and dressed in the dark. By the time she had made barley coffee and laid out the last slices of the bread and a chunk of the dried salami for each of them, Giselle had awakened. They ate by lamplight. It was still too dark outside to open the black-out shutters.

While Jean strapped on her holster she noticed Giselle watching her with the critical eyes of an expert. Jean fumbled awkwardly with the buckles, and once again she dreaded the possibility of having to use the MAB.

Outside the streets were wet, but for the moment no rain threatened.

"We're not far from the place, but we can't go there directly," Giselle said in a low tone. "Turn left and we will climb the hill by the public steps." She moved a step ahead of Jean.

Jean caught her arm. "Do be careful, Maman. The sidewalk can be slippery."

"I was walking wet sidewalks, telling you the same thing, not so long ago," Giselle snapped.

Jean laughed. "Yes, Maman."

Suddenly Montaigne appeared beside them. "Good morning, mesdames," he grunted.

"Good morning," Jean replied, relieved that he didn't linger to talk or even slow down for them.

After he was beyond hearing, Giselle whispered, "We must get out of Lyon as fast as we can."

"Yes! We shall."

Jean followed Giselle's leading, although to anyone watching, it would appear the younger woman was directing the elder. All the way up the hill toward Fourvière, Jean worried about every pedestrian they passed. She should have argued more vehemently against this foolish exposure.

A black Gestapo car drove by, and Jean's heart struck up a frenzied beat. Fortunately, the men inside did not look their direction, and the car moved on. Jean vowed that if they returned safely to the apartment, she would not allow Giselle to take such a chance again.

At last they went down the hill and entered one of the streets not far from where they had started. Giselle opened a rustic door into an ancient rose-colored stone building, and Jean found herself in a spacious rectangular courtyard surrounded by four stories of apartments.

No other person was visible in the Romanesque courtyard or on the colonnaded walkway around the large paved area. Likewise, nobody was out on the covered balconies above.

Jean followed Giselle's gentle tug to the left.

At a door half the distance down the walkway, Giselle paused and ran her fingers along the crack between the door and the frame just below the latch. An anxious expression crossed her face. "I can't find them!" she said. Still leaning on Jean's arm, she moved closer. At last she gave a relieved sigh. "There. Almost turned to grime, but still where I put them, or where Claude put them."

She moved her hand, and Jean noticed a few weathered threads hanging from the crack. When Giselle opened the door, the threads dropped to the paving and became invisible.

Once inside, Giselle let go of her arm and said, "Stand still while I get a light." Jean heard her fumbling in the shutter-darkened room. In a moment, her flashlight revealed a small living room with simple furniture. Giselle bolted the door behind them.

A shivery prickle ran up Jean's spine. She'd never been claustrophobic, but this place felt like a dungeon.

Giselle moved away and disappeared behind an old tapestry on the wall. Jean followed the bit of light still showing and found a concealed flight of narrow stone steps. At the top she saw daylight. She hurried up and into a sparsely furnished room with unshuttered windows.

Giselle had already pulled a cupboard away from the wall and was on her hands and knees with one arm in a hole in the floor. A loose floor tile lay beside her. "I can't find it," she muttered and strained to reach farther. "Ah, the ammunition!" She withdrew her arm and placed a small brown fabric bag on the floor. Lying down on her stomach, she put her arm back in the hole. "There it is! Claude, with his long arms, placed it almost beyond my reach." Giselle removed a bundle wrapped and tied in the same brown fabric as the ammunition. Then she pulled out a leather holster and belt. She carefully replaced the tile and filled the cracks around it with the plentiful grime on the floor.

Jean helped to slide the cupboard back in place. She had been secretly hoping the gun wouldn't be there, that Claude would have taken it.

As if picking up her thought, Giselle said, "I almost hoped Claude had taken it. It would mean that he had come here after our escape and maybe is safe . . . somewhere."

"Georges, I mean Martin, felt sure Claude escaped."

"I too believe." She took the gun and holster to a small table and sat down. "I do not feel he is gone. We love each other so much that I've always believed I would know if he . . . had been killed." She untied the wrapping on the gun. "Surely I would know."

To Jean she looked painfully small and alone, sitting there with light from the window etching the craggy line of her broken nose.

"This apartment, when Claude first found it, when it was safe to leave the girls with friends for the night, we sometimes spent the night here alone. We pretended there was no war. For a few hours it was as if we were on our honeymoon again." She glanced around. "When I am here, I feel close to him."

Watching her, Jean's apprehension began to dissipate. She reminded herself, however, not to let Giselle's nostalgic mood lessen her own watchfulness. She went to the window where she could see the courtyard and the entryway. "You and Claude are fortunate to share this kind of love. Giselle, is there another way out of here besides through the courtyard?"

Giselle's face grew serious. She nodded. "Come. Look out here."

Jean followed and saw the escape stairs down the outside wall of the building and the brushy hillside below. "Have you ever used it?"

"No. But it will serve. Claude tried it." She returned to the gun on the table and began to unwind the wrappings.

Jean picked up the ammunition bag and poured out cartridges and an extra gun clip.

Giselle held up the Mauser. "Now, there is a gun!" she said and extended it out. "Feel the difference compared to yours."

Jean hefted it, handed it back, and said casually, "I know. I had to train with heavier pistols as well as with the MAB." *Why would a German gun look more evil than a British one? No matter. This one did.*

"So if you had to, you could use the Mauser?" Giselle asked.

"Of course."

"You are a wonder! After how you felt losing Jimmy, I never imagined you could do this."

Neither did I! Jean's soul silently cried. "Well, I don't like the fact, but I will do whatever I must to help you and the girls escape to England."

Giselle reached across the little table and squeezed her hand. "My true little sister. I understand something of what all this has cost you. I pray you shall never have to use your gun."

"And I pray that for you."

Giselle nodded and looked away. "I must clean and oil the Mauser before we go out."

So much for my prayer, Jean thought sadly. "I'll load your extra clip and put the cartridges in the belt," she said, picking up the ammunition bag.

The return route back to Jean's apartment was as convoluted as the way they'd come. When they finally reached the river, Jean stopped at a grocery store. They had each carried folded shopping bags for this purpose, so they could lay in food for the children. She purchased as much as was permitted, including the children's allotment of bread, grape sugar jelly, and canned milk for the week.

As they headed for the apartment with full bags, Giselle said, "Only one more day and I'll be with my little ones. Sometimes I thought I would die from missing them."

"Will they remember me, do you think?" Jean asked.

"Oh yes. They may not recognize you now, but I have never let them forget their aunt Jeanie. What a surprise for them! They will think the war is over. I always promised you would come after the war."

At the apartment building they successfully evaded the concierge, but they scarcely had entered the apartment and closed the door when someone knocked. While Jean went to the door, Giselle stepped back the opposite direction.

Jean saw her reach under her coat for her gun. *Oh, dear God, please don't let her panic.* Jean called through the door, "Who is it, please?"

"Raoul Montaigne, madame. I have a small gift for you."

Jean raised her eyebrows at Giselle. Giselle shook her head.

"I'm sorry. I'm not presentable, monsieur."

"No matter. I shall lay it at your door. Enjoy!"

Not wanting to offend or to encourage him, Jean simply called, "Thank you." She then waited several minutes after hearing his door close before opening her own. He had left a worn shopping bag. In the bottom were four thick chocolate bars.

"Oh!" Jean sighed with appreciation and lifted them out to show Giselle.

"Black market. If you were here long enough, you would learn how to barter on the black market." She reached for a bar. "He left enough for us and the children. Did you tell him about the children?"

"No. I only told the concierge. . . ." A thunderhead of apprehension billowed into Jean's mind. "And they scarcely speak to each other. . . ."

Giselle stared back at her, wide-eyed.

CHAPTER EIGHTEEN

For Giselle the bicycle journey to the farm was as arduous as she'd anticipated. Many times she had to rest for ten or fifteen minutes, drastically slowing their progress. Toward the end of the day rain pelted them, soaking through her old coat. She struggled to keep moving but pressed on for the sake of staying warm.

As darkness swept over the hills from the east, Giselle said, "I've heard that the Milice do not enforce the curfew out here so much. I hope that's true. I think we still have a couple of kilometers more." Fortunately the clouds were breaking up and blowing westward. The wet pavement reflected just enough light to reveal the road clearly. After walking their bicycles up a long hill, Giselle was relieved to recognize the farm road that wound upward through more hills to the Leveque farm. "We leave the pavement here. We'll have to walk now. It's too dark to see any ruts and holes, and it's mostly uphill anyway."

Climbing slowly, she stopped repeatedly to catch her breath. Only the thought of seeing her children gave her strength to lift her feet. Jeanie seemed as tired, not trying to talk anymore.

Finally Giselle said, "I think . . . we're . . . almost . . . there. If I'm right . . . the house . . . is around this bend . . . at the top of the next rise." She panted and her heart was knocking against her ribs, but now as much from anticipation as from the climb. Soon she would have her girls in her arms.

The large shepherd dog barked and came bounding to meet them. She hoped he would remember her. Within a few meters of her, he stopped barking and became their tail-wagging escort to the blacked-out house, which stood like a small square fortress silhouetted against the clearing night sky.

The door opened, and a rectangular yellow light framed a broad-shouldered man. "Hello! You are a long way from a public road. Do you need help?"

"Emile! It is Giselle, Jacquie and Angie's maman!"

"What? Giselle! Come in. Come, Evyette!" he bellowed. "Bring the girls! Quickly! Their maman has come!"

By the time Giselle and Jean stepped over the threshold of the farmhouse, the Leveque family—Evyette, adolescent daughter Nannette, older daughter Louisa and her nine-year-old son Pascal—had rushed into the front room. And Jacquie and Angie led the race. Giselle opened her arms to them. They dashed toward her but suddenly halted just beyond reach. Wide-eyed, they stared at her face.

Now the adults were trying not to stare.

"Jacquie? Angie? It is me, Maman. I'm sorry I look so different...." Giselle's voice cracked. She bit her lip and shook her head. She couldn't go on.

Evyette was instantly beside her, holding her in a motherly embrace. Giselle pressed her face against her shoulder and struggled for composure. Evyette murmured, "It's all right. They are just surprised." She gave her a tight squeeze and let go. "Jacquie, Angie, your maman has been hurt in an accident, but she is just fine. Here, come and see. It really is your dear maman."

Jacquie flung herself at Giselle and wrapped her arms around her, crying, "Maman! Maman! You have come!"

Giselle held her close. "Oh, my big girl, I've missed you so much."

Angie still stood unsmiling, peeking out from behind Evyette's full skirt.

Giselle partially released Jacquie and stretched one arm to her. "Angie, dear! I've missed my little angel. Won't you come say hello to your maman?"

Angie approached hesitantly. Giselle dropped to her knees and held both girls close, her cheek against Angie's silky hair. Angie melted against her. "Oh, how you've grown! It's so good to see you and hug you." Then she whispered, "I'm sorry my face frightened you. The doctor has not had time to fix it. Someday I will look just like I used to."

Angie patted her cheek. "Does it hurt, Maman?"

"No. I feel fine. I can't even remember it hurting," she lied.

With an arm locked around her neck, Jacquie asked, "Is Père coming too? Can we go home now?"

"Père couldn't come, but I won't leave you again. We will stay together until Père comes home. We'll talk about that tomorrow. But look! I've brought you a surprise." She loosed their arms, stood up, and touched Jean's shoulder. "Your Aunt Jeanie has come!"

The girls' mouths formed round O's. They had treasured photos of her, but Giselle supposed that only Jacquie could remember actually seeing her.

The mouths of the Leveque family also dropped open in surprise, for they knew about Giselle's American cousin.

Jeanie knelt beside Giselle. "Hello, Jacquie! I'm so happy to see you again. And Angie! You were a tiny baby when I last saw you—and look at you now, a big girl of six!"

"We have so much to talk about, but first, girls, say hello and give Aunt Jeanie a kiss," Giselle said

Although shyly done, their hugs and kisses brought delight to Jeanie's face. Giselle watched with more joy than she had thought possible without Claude beside them.

Evyette suddenly took charge. "You must be starved and frozen! Quick, Emile, bring them some hot tea. Nannette, take them to your room and find them some dry clothes—from the skin out, by the looks of them. Jacquie and Angie, run to the hall cupboard and fetch two big bath towels for your maman and auntie. Louisa, go stir up the fire, and we will make some cheese soup."

Giselle, so tired she felt dizzy, laughed at the jumble of bodies as they all scrambled to obey. Moments later, she and Jean were in Nannette's room, stripped and rubbing their clammy skin dry with fresh-smelling towels. Nannette pulled out wool skirts, blouses, sweaters, cotton undergarments, and even had them try her sabots for size. They fit Giselle, and Jean settled for only the thick wool socks that had been knitted to pad the inside of the sabots.

At last, treasuring the relief of being warm and dry again,

they marched into the kitchen and sat at the trestle table to eat. Everyone gathered around to watch, too excited to let them eat silently. Finally Emile asked how Jean had come to be in occupied France.

Giselle was surprised again at how smoothly Jeanie gave a brief explanation without revealing anything that might be dangerous for the family to know. Emile let the subject rest without any more questions.

After supper Giselle tried and failed to suppress a giant yawn. "I'm so sorry, but I can't stay awake another second. We will tell you our plans tomorrow."

Jean went to Nannette's room to share her feather bed.

Evyette set up a cot for Giselle between the little girls' beds, only an arm's length from them. After the children said their prayers, Giselle tucked them in, then gratefully lay down.

"Will Père come soon, Maman?" Jacquie asked.

"I don't know, dear, but we shall keep praying he will," she answered. She could not keep her eyes open. She was aware of Angie's voice but was too far into sleep to respond.

Jean had known it would take time to prepare the girls for their parts, for them to remember to call her "Maman" and their mother "Grand-mère," but as one day slid into another, she began to grow nervous.

Giselle had made a game of the practice sessions at first. On the third day, however, Giselle turned serious. Jacquie reluctantly submitted to having her hair cut to look like Pascal, and Giselle made them call her "Grand-mère" all the time. Her stern insistence helped them to remember to call Jean "Maman."

By the end of the fourth day, after the children were in bed and the adults gathered at the kitchen table for a last cup of barley coffee, Jean said, "I think we're as prepared as we can be. We should leave in the morning."

Giselle nodded. "I've been thinking the same thing."

Emile meditatively leaned back on two legs of his chair.

Evyette frowned at her husband. "Do set that chair down straight. You will go over on your back one of these days!" Her worried voice expressed the tension they all felt.

He raised an eyebrow but did not obey.

Evyette turned to Giselle. "I understand why you can't tell us your plans, but we're a long way from anywhere. Surely you don't expect to carry those children very far on your bicycles."

Giselle gave Jean a look that said, "You handle this."

"They'll sit behind us when we ride, which will be down hills and on level ground. We'll all walk up the hills. We do have a sizable distance to cover, but we saw an inn on the way where we can stay overnight and make the journey in two days."

Emile thumped his chair legs to the floor. "Now, mesdames, I think this nonsense has gone on long enough. It sounds more risky to stay at an inn than to let me drive you close to your destination. You won't need to tell me any more than where to drop you off, so the little ones won't have to walk for more than a couple of hours. I'll load the truck with our eggs, cheese, and winter produce and go on to deliver our quota to the Germans at La Varenne. No one will question my routine journey. This will be no risk to us and therefore no risk to you."

His proposition worried Jean. It went against Georges' carefully laid plans and also violated one of his cardinal rules that the more people involved, the greater the risk.

While Jean hesitated, considering pros and cons, Giselle spoke up. "It sounds workable and certainly is better for the girls. You may let us off just before entering La Varenne."

"Good. I'll have the truck loaded by the time you finish breakfast." He stood up, shaking his head. "I can't believe you were going to bicycle so far with those children."

Jean interrupted. "Taking two days, it would not be impossible. Also we planned on using the travel time to coach them more before they have to play their parts in front of many people." She stopped short, having given away the fact they were going into a populated area, which logically could be assumed to be Lyon.

"Even so, the truck will be better," Giselle argued. "They will perform best if not too tired."

Evyette agreed. "Giselle is right. They must not become too tired. Emile, the six cheese rounds are ready for the Germans. The chickens still have the winter doldrums and are not laying well, but I think we have enough eggs to satisfy them."

"Do the Germans ever come here to requisition more food?"

Jean inquired, alarmed that she had not thought of this until now.

"We are among the fortunate. They have not been back since the first time," Emile said. "Even if they should decide to raise our quota, they likely would wait for the rains to let up." He rose to his feet. "I will get the truck ready."

On the way up the stairs to their bedrooms, Jean whispered to Giselle, "I don't feel good about changing from our original plan. You and I and two children with bicycles will not attract attention, but on his truck—"

"We can't have a no-risk situation, no matter what. And this will work better for the children. Trust me on this."

"Okay," Jean said reluctantly.

The next morning they rode in Emile's truck, keeping their clothes dry and conserving their energy. He dropped them off close to Lyon.

Without having to hurry to reach the apartment before curfew, they pedaled along easily, and when they walked, they did not have to rush the children. Evyette had packed for them slabs of cheese, a bottle of water, one of milk for the girls, and chunks of homemade bread and butter. They ate while they walked. The girls were good little troopers and practiced the parts they must maintain.

By the time they arrived at the apartment building, people were coming home from work. Jean was relieved to be able to stow the bikes and get into the building and upstairs without having to stop and chat with the concierge.

In the upper hallway she again felt exposed to hidden eyes watching them. Was this just nervousness or an instinctive warning of danger? She searched her memory for any evidence that may have warned her subliminally. No, she could not remember a hint of anything amiss. Nevertheless, she would not feel comfortable until she could get the children and Giselle inside and lock the door behind them. Fortunately the girls were not chattering but instead were clinging to Giselle's hands as if they would never let her go. Their little voices would carry a long way in this mausoleum of a building.

Jean inserted her key and froze. The door was unlocked. She motioned to Giselle to step aside with the children. Should she draw her gun? Or should they just walk away and not open the door? If so, where could they go?

One glance behind her revealed Giselle's reaction. Her cousin's hand inside her coat held the unmistakable bulge of the Mauser.

Jean's moment of uncertainty was broken by the sudden opening of her neighbor's door. Raoul Montaigne raised a finger to his lips and beckoned them to his apartment. When they didn't move, he gestured angrily and mouthed a silent, "Quick!"

Although Jean had no rational reason for doing so, she decided to trust him. She ran tiptoe to him, leaving Giselle with the girls.

"The Milice," he whispered. "They've been in your apartment. You've got to get in here and keep those children quiet. Tell your 'maman' I knew her as Julie. I will help you all escape. Bring her quickly."

"Why should I trust you?"

"You have only my word," he said bleakly. "But Armand saved my parents from the Nazis. I would return the favor. Tell madame this."

Jean raced to Giselle. "The Milice were here and will come again. He knows who you are. He says Armand—Claude—saved his family, and now he wants to help us. I don't know why, but I trust him."

Giselle bit her lip, her face a mosaic of anguish and uncertainty as she glanced at her girls. For a moment Jean feared for her stability. Then Giselle whispered, "All right. You go in first. We'll follow." Her hand remained rigid inside her coat.

Jean pressed a finger to her lips to warn the girls to stay quiet, then led the way into Montaigne's apartment.

Montaigne closed the door behind them, locked it, and leaned against it.

Giselle stepped between him and Jean and the girls.

Jean held her breath. If Giselle's nerves cracked, she might shoot him and attract the *gendarmes*, if not the Milice. Their hope could end here, now, in this ugly small room.

Montaigne relaxed against the door and spoke softly. "You have no reason to trust me, madame, but I hope you will. I owe much to your husband. I would like the opportunity to repay. At any rate, if your gun does not have a silencer, you had best not shoot me here."

Giselle withdrew the Mauser from under her coat but did not lower her aim. "When did Armand help you?" she demanded.

"It was in Loire, September last. The Germans came to our neighborhood to conscript able-bodied men, which meant anyone up to eighty years. We knew they would take old men and the women, grandmothers even, to Germany for slave labor. Armand was able to get my mother and father into the Pyrenees to hide. They are still safe there, doing what they can to help the Maquis."

Giselle slowly lowered the muzzle of her gun. "I remember. He was gone for days. I recognized you, but how did you recognize me?"

"Your beautiful eyes, madame, and if you will forgive me for mentioning, a few scars cannot destroy the graceful lines of your cheek and chin."

She gave him a tight-lipped smile and said sharply, "You talk like an amateur poet, monsieur. I do not believe a word you say."

"I studied to be an artist before the war. When I first saw you, I memorized how I would paint you. That vision of you has not changed."

"How can you help us?" she asked but did not holster her gun.

"I can get you away from here, and I have friends who will loan me a car to drive you to Bourg-en-Bresse. From there you will be on your own."

"Do trains run through there?" Jean asked.

"Yes, as reliably as anywhere."

"Then we would welcome your help."

He turned to Giselle. "And you? Do you agree, madame?"

"I agree. Just remember, I have my gun if you should prove false."

"I would not dream of forgetting. And so may I know the children's names before we leave?"

Relieved that the risk of Giselle panicking seemed over, Jean said, "My son Jacquie and my daughter Angie. Children," she said to the girls, "Monsieur Montaigne has been my neighbor since I moved here, and now he will help us leave the city." To Montaigne, she explained, "Julie is pretending to be their grand-mère, Madame Estelle Du Puy."

"I see. That's all I need to know. Now, we must get you out

of here immediately. Here's the plan. Our apartments face the front of the building, so we do not have fire escapes. However, down the hall beyond your apartment and around the second turn to the right is a doorway to interior stairs and also to a fire escape.

"I will go out the front, as I do every night for supper. You wait here for exactly fifteen minutes. Then take that fire escape down to the alley. I will be waiting there in a blue Renault. If I should not be there, walk quickly to this address in St. Jean." He handed Giselle a scrap of paper. "Another man you can trust will help you leave Lyon."

Giselle read the paper and handed it to Jean.

"Lock the door behind me," Montaigne said and left.

CHAPTER NINETEEN

Jean watched the clock, counting the minutes. *How can we ever get out of the city before curfew?* she worried.

Exactly fifteen minutes after Montaigne left, Jean and Giselle, with the girls between them, darted down the hall and toward the stairwell. They silently guided the girls out onto the old metal fire escape. Jean went first, backwards so she could face Jacquie and keep a firm grip on her arm. Giselle followed and did the same thing for Angie.

At the bottom Jean dropped the eight feet to the ground, then reached up to catch the girls when Giselle lowered them by their hands. Finally Giselle dropped down beside Jean.

As if on cue a Renault chugged into the alley. Montaigne, without getting out, opened its door and beckoned them. As soon as they were inside, he drove on down the alley. "Lie low, so I will look to be alone, as though I'm simply going home from work. And pray we can get up the hill and out of downtown without notice."

Jean crunched herself flat on the backseat, pulling Jacquie beside her. Jacquie cried, "Where are we going now?"

"To another town. We will stay with Monsieur Montaigne's friends and then start out in the morning to meet more friends. You were very brave coming down that fire escape. Your père will be so proud of you."

"Maman, I'm hungry," Angie complained from the front seat.

Jean answered quickly before Giselle could possibly forget

211

she was now Grand-mère. "We will eat before long, dear. Try to be patient."

"Look in the shopping bag on the floor by your feet, Madame Fauvre," Montaigne said. "You will find some bread, cold cuts, and chocolate bars."

"Oh, thank you!" She reached in the bag and passed pieces of bread and meat over the front seat to Giselle and Angie and to Jacquie beside her. "Some for you, Monsieur Montaigne?"

"No, thanks. I ate before you came home. The food, it is for you."

"Thank you," she said again. Her trust for him was growing, even though she knew she must stay wary. She wondered how Giselle felt about him now. She sat very quiet in the front seat.

The children gobbled the food and then took their time on the chocolate. Finally by way of thanks, Angie said, "Mmm, that was good."

"You may sit up now, mesdames," Montaigne announced. "We are out of the city, and I've turned on the running lights. I know a route through the hills to Bourg-en-Bresse that is only used by locals. It will take us several hours, so make yourselves comfortable."

Jean sat up and peered out the window at the dark landscape. Occasionally she could detect the shapes of farmhouses and the rolling hills of vineyards. They passed through several blacked-out, featureless villages. From time to time a church tower rose above other buildings. The car grumbled up hills and bounced along the downgrades on a road that was no better than an abandoned Oregon logging road.

Jacquie dozed against her shoulder, and Giselle's head flopped sideways against the front seat. Angie had disappeared, probably sleeping on her mother's lap.

Above the black skyline, clusters of clouds sailed westward across a sea of stars. It looked deceptively peaceful. In the quiet her thoughts turned to Tom. *I wonder where he is now? On this continent, under this sky?* He could be in Italy now, where she'd heard Hitler's troops were fighting fiercely to halt the Allied drive northward. *Only a few hundred miles away men are dying under these same stars.* She shuddered. *I love you, Tom. Please be careful.*

Abruptly the car slowed. Ahead, a long automobile was parked crossways in the road with blackout lights casting a narrowed dim beam into the hedge on one side. "Keep the children quiet!" Montaigne urged, "and let me do the talking." He kept the engine running and rolled the window down just a few inches.

A man approached the car and, speaking French, said, "Good evening, monsieur. Anyone out this time of night in a Renault is not likely German. You had best identify yourself."

"Edouard Copeau from Lyon, monsieur."

The man bent over, peered in, and beamed his light on the women and children.

"Monsieur Copeau, you are a long way from the main highway. Are you going to visit relatives?"

"As a matter of fact, I am."

"You are aware you are breaking curfew?"

"Yes. We have an illness in the family, so I hoped I might be excused."

The man straightened and guffawed. "No one but a resistant could be so foolish!"

Jean stopped breathing.

The man then leaned forward and said, "As a fellow resistant, let me warn you that up ahead is a railroad bridge that will become dust just about the time you reach it. Are you familiar with this country?"

Jean sighed with relief, glad it was too dark for anyone to see her face.

"Yes," Montaigne said.

"Then take this road to the right." He flicked his light at a narrow intersecting lane. "Stay on it. After three kilometers you'll find a smaller bridge. Take the first left, and it will return you back to this road, safely beyond our project to slow the Germans."

"Thank you, friend. *Vive la France!*"

"Vive la France!"

The man stepped back, and Montaigne turned the Renault as directed. As the night closed around them on the new road, Jean leaned back again. In front of her, Giselle's shoulders shrugged as if she too were rearranging herself. Jean suspected she was holstering her gun and wondered if Montaigne knew.

He spoke. "There are hundreds, no thousands, of small bands of resistants in these hills. I had hoped it was they who blocked the road. Madame Du Puy, I understand your fear, but it would not do to shoot our friends."

"I am aware of the independent resistants," Giselle said coldly, "but I shall take no chances."

Jacquie's hand on Jean's arm tightened convulsively. Jean folded her fingers over the child's and leaned close to whisper, "Don't worry. Everything will be all right."

Jacquie gripped her hand and pressed against her. Just then, above the chugging and rattling of the Renault, an explosion reached their ears. Montaigne turned his head, then waved a hand. "Look! They have blown the bridge. In the moonlight you can see the cloud from the destruction."

Jean followed his gesture and saw a pale cloud rising from the valley floor on the left.

"Not very impressive to look at," he said, "but it will slow the Germans for quite a while."

Jacquie sat up straight and peered out the side window at the lingering gray smudge above the invisible river. "I'm glad those men stopped us."

"Yes," Jean answered. "They don't want anyone to get hurt. They're doing their jobs well." Jacquie had not loosened her grip on Jean's arm. Her small hand telegraphed her fear.

What will our journey do to her, Jean wondered, *even if everything does go well?* A twist of anguish threatened to break her concentration. She caught herself. She must not let emotion distract her. She must stay focused. Her training came to her rescue. "Try to sleep, dear," she said gently. "Monsieur Montaigne is a good friend who will take care of us."

Obediently Jacquie laid her head in Jean's lap, and after a bit she relaxed and fell asleep. Finally Jean dozed too.

She awoke to Montaigne's call. "We are here." The Renault bumped to a stop, and he said, "Stay in the car. Keep your heads down until I make sure all is well in the house." He climbed out and left.

In a few minutes he returned. "You will sleep in the barn, which is not so bad, really. They've done this before and have a hidden room with beds and blankets. And you're in luck for transportation. They have an auto and will drive you to Macon, where the trains are running. From there you will be on your own."

"That will be a help," Jean said, keeping her gladness hidden. No one must know that Macon was her rendezvous destination.

"Stay in the car," he instructed. "I'll drive to the back of the barn."

At the barn door he handed Jean an ancient glass lantern and lit the candle inside. While she held the flickering light, he carried the sleeping children to cots. Giselle and Jean covered them with thick wool blankets.

"Monsieur Montaigne," Giselle said, "I thank you. If you owed any debt of gratitude to Armand, it is repaid in full, and I shall tell him of your kindness to us."

"I am glad to help, madame."

"Will you return to Lyon tonight?"

"Only part of the way. I really do have family not far from here. I will go and wake them and take this opportunity to visit and enjoy a farm breakfast. Rest well and Godspeed," he said, backing toward the door.

"Thank you," Jean said. "Someday I hope I may tell you how much you have helped. Until then, may your kindness be returned to you many times over."

Montaigne touched his béret. "Farewell, my beautiful neighbor. The concierge will not likely be surprised at your disappearance, and she undoubtedly will rent your room in a day." He grinned, winked, and left.

Jean and Giselle lay down on their cots, and Jean blew out the candle in the lantern. After a few moments of darkness, she asked, "When did you feel you could trust Montaigne?"

Giselle's cot creaked. "I am thinking he still could send the Milice to take us. I don't think he will, but it is possible. I don't trust anyone. Do you have your gun within reach?"

"Yes. Under my pillow."

"Good."

The family that hid them did not exchange names with them. A young woman brought them barley coffee, milk for the girls, and bowls of boiled barley topped with a little cream and honey. Then still in the early hours of morning, a man drove a livestock truck to the back of the barn. Over its sides and across the top, he had stretched a canvas tarpaulin. He forked hay into the forward part for them to sit on, then loaded half a dozen goats in the back of the truck. "If anyone stops us, pray they will see the goats and not look further," he said.

The ride was long and blessedly uneventful. When the truck finally stopped, the farmer pulled up the tarp at a forward corner beside them and said, "We are in a woods. The paved road you will see when you climb out. Turn left on it. Macon is about two kilometers from here. If you should need a place to stay overnight there, go to this address and say Louis-Armand sent you."

Jean took the piece of paper he proffered. "Thank you, Monsieur."

He went to the back and helped them climb out around the goats. When they all stood beside him, he said gruffly, "Memorize the address I gave you and then destroy the paper. You go, and I go, and it will be as if we had never met. But my wife, she prays for you."

"Thank you, Monsieur," Giselle said, "and thank your good wife for us. We will pray for your family too. Good-bye."

Half an hour later Jean stood with Giselle and the children looking across the Saône at Macon on the opposite bank. The compact town could be walked from one end to the other in less time than it had taken them to walk from the woods to the river.

Jean reflected that it would not be easy in such a small town to remain unnoticed for long. *We must make contact with the BSE agent right away.* Aloud she said, "Well, let's go."

A brisk breeze whipped their coats as they walked across the bridge and took the first street uphill. "The house where Georges said to stay is down the second street to the right, 25 Rue St. Antoine. Pray we don't have to try the place Montaigne's friend mentioned."

They walked through the old part of town, encountering only a few women with half-empty shopping bags. They soon came to Place St. Antoine. Jean guided them around a small island of buildings and onto Rue St. Antoine.

"You must have a compass in your head," Giselle said quietly.

"I wish. Here we are. Let me go to the door." She climbed stone steps to an ancient porch and knocked on a blue paint-chipped door.

After a brief wait the door cautiously opened. A tall woman with straight black eyebrows, a long nose, and brown eyes that narrowed on Jean, Giselle, and the children all at once, said, "Yes? What is it, madame?" Her tone, in contrast to her quick glance, was expressionless. Her ample body barred any view of the interior.

"If you please, I'm looking for Madame Josephine Vallon. Monsieur Raoul Bertrand sends his regards," Jean responded.

Instantly the woman smiled. "Ah, you must be his cousin, Madame Fauvre," she said. "Come in. Bring your children and your mother. How good of you to look us up." She beckoned for Giselle to come and in seconds had them all inside without seeming to hurry.

With the door closed and locked, she said, "You are fortunate that I have a room for you. Other guests left just yesterday. I must tell you, I only know your names and do not want to know anything more, but you are welcome here until you meet your contact. Are you hungry? I have some soup cooking for lunch, but maybe the children would like a glass of water right away? And some black-market crackers? No?"

Giselle answered, "Oh yes, and so would I, please."

"Come to the kitchen, then, and I will show you your room later."

She led them into a small room at the back of the house, which a coal stove warmed while it kept the soup bubbling. She set out crackers, a small piece of cheese, and glasses of water, then left them alone. The children ate in silence, copying their maman. By the time they finished, their hostess returned and led them to an upstairs bedroom toward the back. Their hostess went to the one window and pulled back the curtains. "Should you have to leave in a hurry, the hillside below is soft and not too far to drop the children if you are careful."

"Yes. Thank you," Jean said.

"Now I have to be gone for a couple of hours. Since you are here, you can keep the coals burning in the kitchen stove. You'll find more coal and a little wood out back in the shed. I glean bits of coal from along the railroad tracks. Please help yourself to the soup as you wish."

Giselle pulled off her coat and laid it on a bed. "I shall watch the soup and the fire. I've had years of experience with such a cooking stove."

"Fine. Then I'll be on my way. Best you keep the children quiet and don't answer the door. I will let myself in with a key." With that she was gone.

Jean studied the backyard from the window. "I will go to my rendezvous location and leave my message. Then all we can do is wait. Let me out the kitchen door and then lock it. When I return, I'll give three quick knocks and then two slow ones."

For Giselle the wait for Jeanie to return seemed endless. She poked the fire, stirred the soup, and held Angie until she fell asleep. She carried her upstairs to their bed and tucked her under a worn but clean comforter. *Poor baby. She looks so tired.*

"Maman," Jacquie whispered from the window, "I see Auntie Jean coming to the back door."

"Good. Let's go let her in."

Jacquie raced for the stairs.

"Wait! Let me go first."

It broke Giselle's heart to see how Jacquie's face twisted with worry. She gave her firstborn a hug. "It's all right. We just have to be extra careful."

From the kitchen window Giselle peeked out to be sure Jeanie was alone, aware of her daughter's wide eyes taking in her every movement and expression. She nodded and smiled at Jacquie. "She's alone. Come. You can unbolt the door."

A cold breath of outdoor air blew in with Jeanie. She headed straight for a kitchen chair and sat down heavily. She sighed.

"Any problems?" Giselle asked.

Jeanie shook her head. "I'm just tired. It's amazing how easily I found my way just from the maps I memorized. Of course this is a small town, and Café Coq Rouge Restaurant is not much more than a back-door kitchen in an old building. Paint's nearly gone from the sign, but from the fragrance of the cooking, I'd guess they have a black-market source for both food and wine. I left my message with the owner, whose photo I also had memorized."

Impressed by her cousin but still quite worried, Giselle poured Jean some barley coffee and sat down across from her.

"Thanks." Jean sipped it, grimaced, and set it down. "Age doesn't improve this at all."

Giselle smiled fleetingly. "So you left your message. Now what?"

"We wait. Every day I will go there at ten in the morning. One morning our man, or woman, will be waiting for me."

"You don't know which?" This kind of uncertainty could lead to deadly errors, but she didn't dare say so. Jacquie was taking in their every word.

"I would recognize either one, and we have our code words for confirmation."

"Of course." Giselle wished it were as simple as that. "Jacquie, please tiptoe upstairs and peek in on Angie to be sure she is covered."

Jacquie left.

Giselle leaned forward, gripping the edge of the table. "How does it really look to you?"

"I know I left my message with the correct person, but he said he had not seen our contact for days and had begun to wonder if he was all right. British agents work very independently and do disappear for periods of time, but this has been a longer time than normal."

Giselle sagged back on her chair. "So it may be up to us to get ourselves out of France."

"No!" Jean snapped. "It won't come to that. You know we couldn't make it alone into Switzerland or Spain, and where else could we go?"

"We could try to join the Maquis in the mountains of southern France. That's where Claude has probably gone . . ." She couldn't finish the sentence, *if he is alive.*

Jean seemed to read her mind. Her face softened. "You're right, and Claude probably is there, but let's not cross bridges unless we have to. I have a lot of faith in the BSE agents."

Jean visited the Café Coq Rouge every day for three days. On the fourth day, the restaurant owner beckoned her through a door to the kitchen and led her into a tiny private apartment. A short man with thinning black hair and a fixed, bored expression arose from a worn couch. He nodded casually, but his eyes, like those of other agents she'd met, seemed to take in everything about her in an instant.

"Madame Fauvre, I am Jean-Pierre Jacquot. I will transport you to your next destination."

She recognized his face, but still she asked, "Monsieur Jacquot, your père hopes you still catch eels in the Saône."

"Only yesterday I caught two. I wish I could send him one."

Satisfied, she responded, "I will tell him."

He smiled broadly. "You will do, and then some! Where did they ever find you?"

"Didn't they say?"

"No. Just that I was to get you to a pickup site and tell them where to land."

"Good. My two children and my mother are ready to leave Macon whenever you are."

He nodded approvingly. "Continue to give no more information than necessary, and you will do well. Can you bring them here ready to go in four hours? LeRoy here will have you wait for me in this room, and then we'll leave by the side alley." He gestured to the door opposite the one by which he'd entered.

"Two o'clock," she repeated. "We'll be here." She stood up, and LeRoy escorted her back into the restaurant.

Outside, with a loose and easy motion, she walked the few blocks back to the hideaway house, paying close attention to the people around her yet taking care not to stare at anyone. Actually the precaution of trying not to appear wary was probably unnecessary. Every French person in France was wary. Without any effort, she was just another one of the crowd.

When she reached the house, Giselle took one look at her face and said, "He was there."

"Yes. We go today. We are to meet him back at the restaurant at two this afternoon."

"Then let's give the girls lunch before we tell them. In the meantime, we can rehearse them again on how to act around others and remind them how important it will be not to forget."

Madame Vallon had gone out again, so when they were ready to go, they left an anonymous thank-you note.

Jean fretted that she couldn't do something to show their appreciation, for the cupboards were nearly empty of food, and all the linens and furniture bore threadbare spots.

Giselle shrugged. "Yes, but it is done all the time. People help and share whatever they have, and it's a favor to her for us to leave while she is out. It's safer for her not to be here."

At the restaurant LeRoy took them back to the tiny apartment and then excused himself.

The girls looked at an old magazine while Jean kept her ears trained on the sounds coming from the nearby kitchen where dishes from lunch customers clattered in a sink.

Suddenly the door banged open. Jean-Pierre, their escort, burst in and exclaimed, "We've got to get out fast! Come!" He rushed across the room, yanked open the door to the alley, paused only long enough to look all directions, and then beckoned them to follow.

An aged, enclosed delivery truck painted in faded shades of green was parked only a few paces away. Jean-Pierre quickly hoisted the children in and told everyone to move to the back and out of sight.

Seated on a makeshift bench, Jean watched him as he mounted the high front seat and fumbled with keys, switches, the brake. Then he began to mumble what sounded like incantations to rouse the dead. For endless moments the truck sputtered and groaned. At last it coughed to life and began to roll.

Jean started breathing again. At least they were moving. "When we finally get out of France, I will never again take gasoline for granted."

"What?" Giselle yelled. At least that's what Jean thought she said. Her voice was lost in the noise of the truck engine.

Gesturing with her hands, Jean tried to communicate "Just talking to myself."

As the truck bounced down the alley, Jean pulled Jacquie close, and Giselle held Angie. They huddled together, listening. Jean doubted they'd be able to hear any sign of pursuit. The end, if it came, probably would be announced by a sudden halt or gunshots.

CHAPTER TWENTY

Giselle had reacted instantly, instinctively, to the urgency in Jean-Pierre's movements and speech. She had fled from danger often enough to recognize the signs of crisis. Shifting Angie from her lap to the floor beside her, she felt for her gun, pulled it from the holster, and taking care that Angie should not see it, rested it against her thigh, ready to raise and fire.

Jean-Pierre drove on for many worry-filled minutes, yet no signs of pursuit materialized. At last he turned sharply, and the truck proceeded down a rough unpaved country road. Then he slowed down. Above the noisy motor, he shouted, "That was close! Just as I got to the kitchen, half a dozen Milice came into the dining room. Only one thing would bring them to the restaurant after the normal lunch hour—a surprise search for resistants. Fortunately LeRoy stalled them long enough for us to get away."

Giddiness swept over Giselle. Her shattered nerves screamed as she felt her reason slipping away. *Oh, God, please help me!* She must not lose control, not in front of the girls. She made herself breathe deep and slow, and just as slowly the whirlpool of hysteria subsided.

Seated beside her with her arms wrapped around Jacquie, Jeanie appeared unruffled. Giselle knew she had no real idea of what would happen to them if they were captured. And she didn't want her ever to find out.

Jeanie clasped her trembling left hand with a steady grip. Giselle returned the firm pressure with what she hoped was a reassuring squeeze. The Mauser—the alternative escape for all of them—pressed hard against the palm of her other hand. It felt as warm, as if it were also alive.

Jeanie leaned close and said in her ear, "It's all right now. You can put it away." She gave Giselle's hand a final squeeze and let go.

Giselle slowly holstered the gun and draped her coat over it. Angie, who had climbed onto her lap, remained oblivious to the reason for her movements. With renewed determination, Giselle set herself to focus on what her five senses could tell her. She must not let fear rob her of quick, sound judgment, for Jeanie could never manage alone, especially if the worst should happen.

An hour passed. The ride was uncomfortable, but with each passing minute Giselle gave thanks for the unhesitating rumble of the old truck's engine and for the fact that they had not been stopped so far.

The safe house, when they finally reached it, turned out to be a farm much like the Leveques', built in the old style with the house, barn, and stable forming a large U-shaped courtyard. This similarity and its air of agelessness cheered the children and even awakened in her own heart a whisper of hope. They were now another day closer to escape, and maybe here she could rest enough to be able to think more clearly.

Giselle felt about to collapse, almost unable to take in where they were. After meeting their hostess, she asked if the girls might lie down for a nap before supper. When they were led to the hidden room in the attic, she tucked them in and then slumped exhausted onto a cot beside them. She was tired, drop-in-your-tracks-tired, as if she had run on foot the whole way from Macon. She was afraid if she fell asleep, she would not wake up for days.

She closed her eyes just to rest, and in a few seconds fell into a deep sleep.

Downstairs in the large kitchen, Jean helped the farmer's wife, Madame Cuvillon, prepare supper. As she peeled and washed potatoes under the single tap of cold water, she asked, "Do you often hide people?"

Madame Cuvillon's ready smile dimpled her plump cheeks. "Whenever needed. We are isolated. Our children are grown and gone...." A cloud of sadness erased her smile. She turned to tend the stove. "With this large house and more food than most people have, it's the least we can do." She poked the glowing coals and carefully dropped in another small chunk of wood. Her head, with her set of long braids neatly pinned into a twist on the top, reminded Jean of a younger version of her grandmother. This woman expressed the same kind of enduring dependability.

Jean dropped the potatoes into the cooking kettle on the stove. "But you're doing more than enough! You're risking your lives for strangers."

The older woman shook her head emphatically. "Not for strangers. When we must depend on each other to survive, we see more clearly who is friend and who is the stranger." She banged the iron stove lid into place and said fiercely, "If Hitler wins, the whole world will lose!"

Suddenly someone pounded on the distant front door. Jean jumped and glanced at Madame Cuvillon. "Shall I go upstairs?"

Her hostess nodded and, with unhurried steps, went to answer the summons. Jean ran across the kitchen to the back stairs, closed the stairwell door behind her, and paused with her ear against the door. Men's voices came faintly, then louder. She ran up the steps. Just as she reached the top, the door at the bottom opened.

Madame Cuvillon called, "You can come down. We have four more for supper."

Jean returned to the kitchen. The formerly spacious room seemed crowded now with four men in coats and caps all staring at her.

"These boys are here to go on the same plane as you. Please, let us use our first names. Gentlemen, this is Marie." Then she gestured toward the men as she named them. "Pierre, Jean-Paul, Yves, and Andre. I remembered correctly, yes?" The men nodded. "I am Jeanette and my husband is Max. He will be in soon from the barn. In the meantime, Marie, please, would you peel four more potatoes? And I will show the men to their rooms."

Supper was an awkward affair. The men eyed Jean from time to time but made no effort to converse, and she didn't want to talk either. She was glad she'd left Giselle and the children to sleep upstairs. If the girls awoke, she'd carry food up to them.

Farmer Max studiously gobbled his wife's good soup and bread, and after a few failed attempts at discussing agriculture, he gave up on conversation altogether and excused himself. The men silently finished and retired to their rooms.

Jean helped clear the table, then poured hot water into the dishpan and dropped in a few shavings of homemade soap.

Madame Cuvillon took the dishcloth from her hand. "My dear, you look about to drop. Go to bed now."

"Oh no. I'm fine."

She shushed Jean and pushed her toward the back stairs. "You may help tomorrow."

Gratefully Jean obeyed.

Giselle awoke to a rooster's crow. The minute she remembered where she was, she sat up and looked to see if the shuttered window showed any hint of daylight through a crack. Yes! She sat up and stretched. For as tired as she'd been, she felt reasonably rested.

Wide awake and hungry, she quietly dressed, felt her way down the dark stairs, and opened the door into the kitchen. As she had hoped, their hostess had a fire going and a pot of barley coffee simmering beside a huge kettle of bubbling porridge. The older woman smiled and, without asking, poured Giselle a cup of the coffee and cooled it with rich cream.

"Thank you." Giselle sat down at the long table to drink it. When her cup was empty, she asked, "How may I help you?"

"You may set the table. We have four more guests, so lay it for ten."

Keeping her voice casual, Giselle inquired, "What kind of guests? Men? Women? Children?"

"Only men. They are on their way to join up with de Gaulle in England. They will go on the same plane as you."

Giselle worked silently. She hated that she could not trust her own countrymen, but she couldn't. She would have to stay out of sight. She'd have to trust Madame Cuvillon and ask her help to avoid the men. Jeanie could carry her meals upstairs. She turned to ask.

At that moment Madame Cuvillon exclaimed, "Ah, I hear them coming now. You must be very hungry after missing supper. Sit down and eat with them. I'll serve the others later when they awaken."

Giselle headed for the stairs. "Excuse me, but I need to—"

She was too slow. The men tramped in. She turned her back to them but not before she recognized the fair-haired one. It was Andre, the one who had stayed with Claude while she and Martin drove the children to the Leveque farm. He gave no sign that he recognized her, which was proof of the damage done to her face and also of the success of Jeanie's makeup work. Nevertheless, she said to the older woman, "Excuse me, please, but I must go lie down again." Without waiting for a response, she opened the door to the stairs, stepped through, and closed it behind her. With her heart thumping hard, as it had done when she was terrified at Sisters of Mercy Hospital, she leaned against the door and closed her eyes, commanding herself to calm down. Slowly her body submitted to her will.

She silently climbed the stairs. The children were still sleeping soundly, but Jeanie opened her eyes and sat up.

"Is something wrong?" she whispered.

Giselle went to Jeanie's cot, sat down on the edge close to her, and whispered back, "The men who have come ... I know the blond one. Not only that, he knows the girls, and they know him."

"Oh no! Can you trust him?"

"Three months ago, I did. I left Claude wounded in his keeping while I took the girls to the farm with Martin. I can't believe he had anything to do with Claude's arrest, but then, how can I know?"

"What should we do? Keep the children up here with you?"

"Yes, but it will be impossible without Madame Cuvillon's help. And how much do we dare tell her? Knowing too much could jeopardize her safety if anything went wrong."

"She's already risking her life just having us here," Jean said. "I'll go down and help her serve the men and then sneak food up for you and the girls. This will give me time to think what to tell her. She's a strong, good woman. I'm sure she'll do whatever we need."

Icy fear ran through Giselle. She grabbed Jeanie's arm. "Every time I hear you use the word 'sure,' I fear for us!"

"I know. I understand. Thanks for reminding me." Jeanie

leaned forward and hugged her, then climbed out of bed and reached for her clothes. "You'd better get into bed to stay warm."

Giselle obeyed.

Jean sniffed appreciatively when she opened the door into the warm kitchen. Could it be ham frying? She peered at the big stove top. No. Only ham fat, apparently, but still a treat as it sizzled around a large omelet. She turned toward the table to be confronted with four pairs of staring male eyes. She smiled. "Good morning, gentlemen."

Two of the men nodded politely. One silently smiled. The fourth, the fair-haired man Giselle knew, already clean-shaven, looked handsome in a navy blue sweater. He spoke.

"Good morning, Mademoiselle Marie. You look refreshed."

"Thank you, I am." She turned to Jeanette. "My children are still sleeping, and my mother is lying down again. May I help you?"

"No, no. All is ready. You sit and eat with the men. Then you may take a plate to your mother. I trust she is not seriously ill?"

"I hope not. A bit more rest and some of your good food will surely help her." Jean sat across from the men, and the older woman placed a bowl of porridge in front of her.

On impulse she bowed her head for only the briefest moment to offer thanks before picking up her fork. When she looked up, Andre, with a curious look on his face, said, "Do you believe in prayer, madame?"

How swiftly he had corrected his mistake about her marital status. This man missed nothing. Given time, he might recognize Giselle, even if he did not see the girls.

"Please call me Marie. Yes, I believe God wants to help us," she said easily. "Do you?"

His one raised eyebrow and slightly lopsided smile gave him a good-humored boyish look. "Sometimes I do. Sometimes I wonder."

Madame Cuvillon placed a plate of fluffy omelet before each of them. The sight and smell of this treat stirred even the most reserved of the men to say thank-you to Jeanette. Andre elaborated. "There must be a kind God in heaven to have given us such miracles as eggs and you to cook them."

Jeanette smiled. Her glance softened. "It is my pleasure."

Without any more conversation, the men dedicated themselves to the serious business of eating. When they finished, Jeanette said, "You may walk outside here. We have no close neighbors to see you. Or if you wish to read, we have a few books in the parlor, and Max has a log burning in the fireplace."

They thanked her, pushed back their chairs, and went their way. All of them chose the out-of-doors, and through the small-paned kitchen window, Jean saw them sauntering, as men do when they are well fed and relaxed.

Jeanette gave them a motherly look before taking a plate for herself and sitting at the end of the table. "That blond one, he had his eye on you until he heard you have children," she remarked with a smile. "I think maybe he still does. Is your husband living?"

"No. He was killed." She stood up and began to clear the table, talking over her shoulder as she worked. "My mother and I—would it be all right if she stays upstairs all the time, and the children too? We have reasons for not wanting to be seen, even by these Frenchmen. . . ."

Jeanette laid down her fork. "Of course, my dear. I will explain to Max. Only we have no stove up there, just the chimney, which gives little warmth."

"They will keep on their coats and wrap in blankets if they have to."

Jeanette nodded. "I will bring up a washbasin, towels, and a slop jar for the necessary . . . oh, and some of my children's old toys for your little ones."

"Thank you so much! You can't imagine how important this is to us."

"My dear, I don't need to. All will be well. Leave it to me."

With a light step, Jean went upstairs to tell Giselle.

Giselle was relieved when Jeanie said neither the men nor Max seemed to think it unusual for an older woman to take to her bed for a few days. If they wondered about the children staying shut in upstairs, well, that couldn't be avoided.

The plan went well except for the pervasive chill that the children had to endure and their need for exercise. From somewhere, Max produced a large scuffed rocking horse, which helped to entertain them.

On the third afternoon while the girls played on the rocking horse, Giselle wrapped herself in a goose down comforter and settled into the rocking chair. Jeanie, in her wool coat, sat beside her on the window seat.

Waiting in seclusion had given Giselle much needed hours of rest. For the first time since they'd left Sisters of Mercy Hospital, she had time to think of something other than daily survival. She confided, "I've been trying to remember more about what happened the last time I saw Claude."

Jeanie gave her an anxious look, no doubt worried about how well she could handle remembering.

"I'm all right. I just keep thinking I may recover some little detail that would show me Claude did escape."

Jeanie cleared her throat. "Why don't you tell me what you can remember. Explaining to someone else usually helps me to see more."

Giselle started slowly, back at the beginning of the occupation. It wasn't difficult to tell Jeanie how she and Claude had worked as the Resistance grew and became an organized movement. But when she came to his arrest and imprisonment, her throat clamped shut. She took deep, slow breaths. She must go over the last time she saw Claude. She gathered her courage to try.

"First . . ." She stalled on the memory of being in the car with the German guards and going again for interrogation. Utter terror filled her. She gasped, "I didn't know how I could survive more torture!"

She stopped and rocked silently for a few minutes. Clearing her throat, she continued. "Before they touched me, they placed me in the cell of a condemned woman, whom I'm sure they kept alive just to show me what lay ahead." Could she speak of it? Jeanie ought to know the truth so she would never hesitate to shoot anyone who tried to arrest them. "The poor soul was nearly insane. The guards would come and tell her the commandant wanted to see her again, and then they would stand and laugh at her hysterical screams. I wanted to kill them for what they did to her. Then after a few days they took her away. It was awful. When they brought her back—" She stopped, struggling again for control. Gulping, she said, "I held her in my arms and prayed for her to die quickly."

"Oh, Giselle," Jeanie whispered. "I'm so sorry."

Giselle closed her eyes and shook her head slowly. The children might hear, and yet she felt compelled to let Jeanie know. "Her dying words were 'I did not tell them anything.' I believed her. Imelda's suffering strengthened me. I swore they would never break me either. And they didn't." She began to tremble uncontrollably.

Jeanie gripped her hand and murmured, "It's over. It's all over. Soon we'll be safe in England."

Giselle struggled out of the horror so she could give her imperative. "Now you know why I can never let them take any of us alive . . . why you must not hesitate to use your gun."

"Yes, yes. Don't worry. I understand. I'm prepared."

Giselle rocked gently, forcing her mind away from the shattering pain of her prison memories. "I still want to tell you what I can remember about the last time I saw Claude. The car taking me from the prison to Gestapo headquarters slowed at an intersection. Then suddenly there was gunfire. The windows shattered. The driver and the guard both fell. A resistant pulled them out of the car . . . and climbed in . . . and he took me . . . carried me . . . to another car. Another man ran and jumped in with us. No . . . there were two. This is a new memory! Maybe more will come.

"They drove us down a side street . . . I don't know where. And then there was more gunfire . . . a lot of gunfire. That was when I saw Claude climbing out of the German car . . . and running!" She closed her eyes, trying to see every detail on the screen of her mind.

"He—" Her voice locked up. She swallowed. "He and three others ran toward an old civilian car. They were almost there when . . . a car full of German soldiers drove up and opened fire with rifles." She choked again. "Two resistants fell. Two kept running! I couldn't see who! I couldn't tell if Claude—"

She gulped again, determined to describe the scene she had never put into words for anyone else. There might be some little thing—something she had previously missed. She searched her mind and found nothing more to glean. Resigned, she shook her head and said, "Then Martin, Claude's closest partner in the Resistance, appeared beside my driver. He yelled, 'Get out! Run!'

"My driver and his companion obeyed. Martin jumped in. He drove me away from the gunfire." She rocked, waiting for more images to come, but none did. Finally she shook her head in defeat. "I can't remember much after that."

Jeanie's smooth face was lined with sympathy. "Did you know you were safe at the hospital?"

"I remember when Martin took me there, and yes, at first I knew I was safe. Then ... I was out of my mind for a time ... thinking Claude had been killed. I didn't want to live. I couldn't remember anything ... who I was ... what had happened. Oh Jeanie," she whispered, "I forgot my own children!" She shuddered and glanced at the two of them riding double on the homemade wooden horse.

Jeanie leaned over and hugged her, then kept hold of her hand. "Don't blame yourself! You had suffered too much! And deep inside you knew they were safe with Evyette."

Giselle clung to her hand as if it were a lifeline. After a moment she could talk again. "Maybe you're right. I do believe we know a lot of things on a level beyond logic. That's why I believe, against all reason, that Claude did escape. I just can't accept that I wouldn't know if he were dead."

Jeanie squeezed her hand. "I pray you're right."

Emotionally drained, Giselle wanted to stop talking about Claude, but one more thing she felt impelled to ask. "Did you know, when you lost your fiancé, David, at Pearl Harbor? Did you sense he was gone before you heard?"

Jeanie shook her head. "No. It was days before we knew, and I simply had denied the possibility of losing Dave."

"Poor Jeanie. It must have been so hard after losing your mother and Jimmy and then having your father leave you."

"Yes. When I lost Dave, only anger kept me going ... for a long time."

Giselle glanced at the girls, who were still chattering to each other and not interested at all in her conversation with Jeanie. "Anger is a harsh companion. I hope you may find love as I did with Claude."

Jeanie's lips tightened, and she frowned. "I thought I did, but I've lost him too."

"Oh no!" Remembering the girls, Giselle lowered her voice. "Killed in action?"

"No. Nothing like that. I betrayed him. He said he forgave me, but in the end he broke off with me." Jeanie wriggled to a different position on the window seat and tucked her coat around her legs again.

"You still love him."

Jeanie nodded. "I can't seem to shake loose from how I feel."

"May I know about him?"

Jeanie didn't answer right off. Giselle was about to apologize for intruding when Jeanie finally answered. "Of all people, you should know. Uncle Al would understand."

"Uncle Al?"

"I was on an assignment for him. I got involved with the Tulelake project to spy on the people who had been interned there. You see, after Japan bombed Pearl Harbor, people on the West Coast were so scared, and there was a lot of prejudice too, so our government ordered everyone of Japanese descent to report to internment camps."

"Concentration camps in the U.S.?"

"Not exactly. The internment camps were like small towns. The Japanese people governed themselves. They had stores, beauty shops, and a daily newspaper, and raised their own food plus enough to ship to the army. They had churches, schools, lots of activities for the young people, and a hospital and fire department, all staffed by the internees. But they were surrounded by barbed wire fences and guard towers where soldiers with machine guns watched them twenty-four hours a day."

"I can hardly believe this!"

"Well, I was as bigoted as the worst of them in the beginning. I hadn't known any Japanese families, and I was scared too. I didn't like the idea of spying, but I was bitter from losing Dave, and Uncle Al was persuasive. In the internment camp I taught the children, and everyone still thinks I was just a schoolteacher. The spying has remained a secret. Uncle Al insists, so you must never tell anyone. Only Tom and his sister Helen know."

"Tom is the one you love?" She supposed somehow Jean had fallen for one of the soldiers on duty.

"Yes. I had to tell him the truth. I had placed his name on the list of men suspected of disloyalty to the United States."

"Oh. So Tom is Japanese."

"Yes. When I got to know him, he became instrumental in helping me find God again. I was so bitter for so long, but he got me to attend one of the Protestant churches in a barracks building the internees had converted into a chapel."

"What did the church people outside the internment camp think about all these people being confined without cause?"

"Some protested. Some sent help. The Quakers built play equipment for the children. The United Brethren churches and others sent presents at Christmastime. Unfortunately, no one roused up to fight against the internment. The Japanese families had to leave their jobs, their businesses, their homes—everything. They lost the work and savings of years. But the worst part was how demeaned the older people felt. Weakened by broken hearts and spirits, the elderly died easily from colds, flu, and pneumonia."

Giselle sighed and shook her head. It was too much to take in and so contrary to all she had learned about America. "How did you, a schoolteacher, get to know Tom, a prisoner?"

"His sister was my teaching assistant. She invited me to a few camp activities, like their harvest festival. At first I went because it gave me an opportunity to spy. Then I helped with the Christmas program at Tom's church. Pastor Ichiba was the wisest, most loving gentleman I'd ever met. He was Tom's spiritual father. Then he became mine.

"From the first time I saw Tom, I was drawn to him. The more I learned about him, the more I was attracted. But I fought the feeling because it seemed like such a betrayal of Dave. Tom was openly very angry at our government, so I went ahead and placed him on the suspect list. Then I began to see through his eyes the truth about the internment. All the internees I met at the Tulelake Camp were quiet, law-abiding people. In the end I forgot they were a different race. I just loved them . . . and I loved Tom."

"So what happened to the list you made?"

"Uncle Al held it. I'd sent it in bits and pieces, and he refused to remove Tom's name when I asked him to. All the men I had named were examined and imprisoned. They took Tom, even though I went in person to stand up for him."

"So he's in a prison now?"

"No, he was cleared and released to join the army."

"What does Uncle Al think about all this?"

"At first he ordered me not to have anything to do with Tom. Then he changed his mind. But he needn't have worried about having a Japanese man for a nephew. Tom doesn't want me. He said it would never work for us to marry and live in the United States. He may be right. At least he didn't love me enough to try."

Jeanie looked drained but added one more comment. "Just before I left England he wrote and asked if we could still be letter-writing friends."

"I'm so sorry, Jeanie. The nerve of him!" Giselle waved both hands for emphasis. "Men! Sometimes they do not know their own hearts until we show them. Tom sounds like an intelligent person. I shall not be surprised to learn one day that he has loved you all along."

"I can't think about it that way. I just can't bear another loss."

"I don't wonder ... but you've come a long way from how you were when you lost Jimmy. You can bear however much it takes for the love of a good man. I know you can."

Jeanie pinched her lips together the way she'd done in childhood to keep from crying.

Giselle felt a stab of remorse over her impulsive words.

"I'd almost as soon come back into occupied France a second time as to test myself on that," Jeanie said without hope.

At that moment Angie called out, "Maman, Jacquie says I can't have my turn. It's my turn now!"

Giselle, forgetting she was Grand-mère, turned simultaneously with Jeanie to answer. They laughed at each other, and it felt wonderful to really laugh.

"After you, my dear Marie!" Giselle said.

Jeanie went and knelt beside Angie. "Let's play a pretend game while Jacquie finishes her turn."

"How, Aunt Jeanie?"

"First close your eyes."

Angie scrunched her eyes shut and immediately exclaimed, "I see! I see!"

"What do you see?"

"Jacquie getting off and giving me my turn."

Above them on the tall rocking horse, Jacquie giggled. "You don't have to pretend that!" She climbed off. "Here. It's my turn to pretend."

Laughing Jeanie grabbed them in a giant hug and received impulsive kisses in return.

Watching, Giselle was suddenly glad for the waiting and the isolation. It gave them time to love and be loved.

At the end of a week of waiting, Jean learned their plane would arrive the next night, weather permitting.

When she ran upstairs with the good news, Giselle reacted with renewed anxiety over Andre. She insisted that Jean give Jacquie a fresh boyish haircut. Then she wanted the roots of her own hair touched up with the last of the shoe polish.

As Jean combed her damaged hair, Giselle's growing agitation began to seep into her own mind and fill her with dread. They were so near the end of their journey. What if something went wrong now? No! It was pure superstition to think they'd had too much success and now the tide could turn.

Giselle kept talking, all worked up, and worrisome or not, Jean had to listen. "We'll stay up here until the last minute," she was saying. "We can sneak out in the dark and meet the men at the car. I'll tell the girls that Andre will be there, but they must not look at him or speak to him. In fact, they'd better not speak to anyone." Fear made Giselle's eyes huge in her thin, scarred face. She glanced nervously at the children as they played a game of marbles on the pattern of cracks in the old floor. She looked near hysteria.

Hoping to calm her, Jean murmured, "We'll manage this, Giselle. Your plan is good, and after all, Andre may well be your friend."

"I dare not think that!" Giselle hissed.

The girls innocently played on, hearing no one beyond themselves.

Jean cringed at the memory of Giselle's hidden gun and her vow never to be captured alive. A shiver ran down her spine.

CHAPTER TWENTY-ONE

On the night they were to leave, Giselle felt a familiar steadiness come over her. It was the way she used to feel when she'd embarked on a mission for the Resistance. Surely this was a sign her nerves were mending. Several times, however, she had to pat her coat and feel the reassuring shape of the gun strapped in its holster, invisible but quickly accessible.

Shortly before their transportation was due to arrive, Jeanette called them downstairs and hid them in the washing room off the kitchen where they could wait comfortably. After a bit she signaled, and they hurried out the door and climbed into the back of the farm truck before the men came out the front door.

Keeping her chin down, Giselle pulled her scarf forward on her head to shade her face from the light of the full moon. She sat down at the front of the flatbed beside Jeanie, who held the children close—facing away from the men who had lined up at the back.

The truck rolled down a country road past gray fields and pastures, reminding Giselle of other nights when she was with Claude on missions for the Resistance while a trusted friend watched over the children at home in their beds. Usually the girls never awakened, so they never missed her or their père. That was earlier in the occupation, when the Nazis and the Milice were not as suspicious. During the past year, she and Claude had gone nowhere together, in hopes that the girls would have one parent left if anything went bad.

The truck finally slowed, turned onto a dirt road, and

followed rutted tracks left by wagon wheels. Upon entering a leaf-less woods, the ruts faded, and the road became a scarcely visible trail. Then the trees thinned, and the truck stopped.

Giselle stood up and glanced all directions. A broad field stretched before them in the moonlight.

The men climbed out, then reached up to help the children down. Andre caught Angie under the arms to swing her to the ground. With her face close to his, Angie smiled, then apparently remembered her orders and looked down, tucking her chin into her coat collar.

Giselle caught her breath. Andre hadn't hesitated in his movement, but did he recognize the child?

One of the other men reached up for Giselle. She gave him her hand. Instead, he lifted her bodily. "Thank you, young man," she murmured, praying he wouldn't recognize her holster belt under his fingers. Then she chided herself. It didn't matter, as long as he didn't know who she was. With her feet on the ground, she assumed her round-shouldered posture and hobbled out of the way for Jeanie to jump down.

The driver strode to the back of the truck. In a stage whisper, he said, "Remember to keep your voices down." In the moonlight he pointed, then continued, "The plane will have to land from that direction and should stop over there." He turned, making a sweeping gesture. "You men take these electric torches and line up from down there to here. You'll aim the beam toward me, so the pilot can know the direction of the wind." He gave the men long flashlights.

Suddenly a light flashed across Jeanie and the children and blinded Giselle.

The driver let out a choice French expletive. "Keep that thing off until I tell you!" To the other three men he said, "Go take your places. When I blink my light three times you turn yours on and shine them toward me. You," he said to the man whose light had flashed on. "You stay here."

He didn't say, "where I can keep an eye on you," but Giselle heard it in his tone.

"When we hear the plane, you'll go the other way to mark the end of the field."

"Right," said Andre's voice.

The driver walked to the front of the truck. Jeanie followed him, but before Giselle could move away from the tailgate, Andre whispered, "Julie! Sorry to have startled you. I only wanted to confirm my suspicions. I will not reveal your identity, even though I believe the others can be trusted."

Giselle felt faint. She took a deep breath. As long as he knew, she could only go along with him. "How did you guess?" she whispered.

"When I glimpsed you that first day, you seemed familiar. Then the fact that you stayed out of sight piqued my curiosity. Madame Marie's children—I wondered why they also hid. And then little Angie, even so bundled up and in the moonlight, I could not fail to know." He paused, then said brokenly, "Your poor face, Julie! I am so sorry!"

Her caution collapsed. Almost automatically she fell back to calling Claude by his Resistance name. "When did you last see Armand? Do you know anything about what happened to him?"

"The last time I saw him was when we were trying to free him from the Gestapo. We had to scatter fast. I could not find a trace of information later. I didn't even know whether you had survived. Now here you are on your way to England. So am I. I'll join up under de Gaulle. I was glad to make contact with the BSE to get me out. Did you hear about any of the others, whether they may be in England?"

"No. I've seen no one and heard nothing."

"So now the BSE is flying you to London too. You must have been very valuable to them."

"No. I am only a French housewife, after all."

"Surely they know about your work with Armand and all of the resistants you have worked with."

"Andre, what happened the day I left Armand with you? Did the Milice come to the apartment? How did you escape. . . ?"

"Escape without Armand, you are thinking. It's a complicated story. I swear I did my best to hide him."

Suddenly the driver called softly. "You with the other light! Get on down the field to the left. I think I hear the plane."

Everyone fell silent. Giselle heard the distant drone of the plane too.

Before doing as the driver instructed, Andre murmured, "It will be good to continue our visit when we get to London."

"Yes," she answered, hoping that somehow in further

conversation, she might learn something from him that would give a clue as to where Claude might be, even though he said he didn't know. He may have overlooked the significance of some small detail.

The driver turned on his flashlight, signaled the others, and then aimed his own light upward in the direction of the approaching plane. While the others kept their lights aimed at the ground marking an invisible landing strip, he blinked a signal to the pilot.

In seconds the black shape of a large plane approached low and dropped swiftly to the field. With a terrifying noise that could expose them all, it raced toward the truck, which now had its running lights on. Speeding beyond the truck, the plane came to a halt somewhere near Andre. Then it turned and taxied back toward the truck, rolling slower and slower until it stopped nearby.

Giselle grabbed Angie's hand from Jean and ran toward the plane. Jean, with Jacquie in tow, followed. By the time they were inside and seated on the bare floor, the men climbed aboard. The engines revved up. The plane shuddered but sat still, as if chained in place. Abruptly the engines cut off.

The pilot scrambled back to them. "We're stuck. The ground has thawed too much. Everybody out."

"The children too?" Giselle asked.

"No. They'll only get in the way of the digging."

All the adults piled off. The men grabbed shovels from the truck as if they had often dug airplanes out of mud. The pilot said, "You women go get branches to set in front of the wheels."

Giselle decided to drop her elderly woman act. She ran to the edge of the woods, keeping pace with Jeanie. As they picked up dead branches, she told Jeanie that Andre had recognized her, but it was okay. There was no time for real conversation beyond that. Panting, they made trip after trip, carrying armfuls of branches and fallen limbs and laying them in front of the plane. With their shovels, the men scooped the thin crust of ice from around the wheels and then dug away the mud and cut a gentle slope upward to the surface of the field. For endless minutes they cleared away mud and sod, and then paved their work with more limbs, creating a makeshift path before each wheel.

Suddenly Andre was kneeling beside Giselle, helping to pack

the branches in place. "It is so good to see you, Julie. I can hardly get over it, that we should meet here. In Lyon I searched and searched for you. Edmund said he last saw you with Martin and that new man, Leon. Armand had told me he suspected both Leon and Martin were collaborators, so I was really worried about you."

Giselle froze. She didn't know a Leon, which may not mean a thing. But she knew Claude would never have said such a thing about Martin unless he was trying to deceive and trap the person he really suspected. Crouching, as she was in the shadow of the plane's fuselage, and without looking up at Andre, she slipped her hand into the front of her coat and closed her fingers around the Mauser. She wished now it were a smaller gun like Jeanie's. It would be difficult in the moonlight to draw without being seen, and she couldn't simply aim it through her coat. She must make her move successfully and fast because he was, no doubt, also armed.

She responded, in what she hoped was a credible tone of shock, "Leon and Martin were collaborators!"

He spoke slowly. "This moonlight is very revealing, Julie. Do not draw your gun. I have mine aimed at your traveling companion, whom you call Marie." Jeanie was on her knees a few meters away, tucking branches tightly into the track the men had opened in front of the other wheel. Andre murmured, "You will be silent and cooperate with me if you care about her life."

"It was you, then!" she hissed.

"Get your hands in the open where I can see them, Julie."

"What do you think you can do with all these people around?" Giselle whispered.

"I'm thinking about that. You and I will board the plane as planned. As an old friend of the Resistance, I will sit beside you and your children. I have my own reasons for needing to leave France, but in England, you will help me resolve that situation. And you will be happy to help me because you want to keep Jacquie and Angie safe.

"Right now you will act as if all is well. You will not make a move or give any hint that I am less than a good and trusted friend because I will stick like a leech to your friend Marie. In fact, I can see she needs help with those stubborn muddy branches. Excuse me, please. And you will give me your gun before I go to her."

"You will not risk fighting me for my gun here," she hissed. "Not with all of these others armed. How far would you get?" She raised the Mauser a bit so he could see its hidden barrel pushing against her coat, aimed at him.

He didn't respond or move for a moment. Then he stood up and went over to Jeanie, who had moved closer to them now. Giselle could hear him whisper something and see Jeanie welcome his help. Her rage turned icy. She would kill him, one way or the other. He must not get on the plane with them. She pretended to be working industriously but kept her focus tightly on Andre. He would slip up somehow, she was certain. *Please God!*

The pilot came under the belly of the plane and inspected the emergency track they had created. "I think it'll do," he said loudly enough for everyone to hear. "I can't risk a full load though. I'll take only the women and children, and maybe not them." He beckoned with one gloved hand. "Come along, ladies. We'll give it a try."

When Jean headed for the door of the plane, Andre stuck to her side. He was going to force his way in! Giselle rushed to the door just as the pilot, who was already inside reaching down, pulled Jeanie up and into the bomber. Giselle threw herself between the open door and Andre. Andre could start shooting, but she didn't think he would. He obviously wanted her alive.

He didn't shoot, but she wasn't strong enough to force him away from the door. Suddenly the truck driver appeared at her side. He shoved Andre and said gruffly, "If you're not going to help her, man, then get back so I can." He grabbed Giselle under her arms and hoisted her upward.

He must still believe she was a grandmother. "Thank you, young man," she said, and reached for the pilot's hand.

She felt Andre's hand on her back, not helping, but pulling on her, secretly slowing her ascent while he said for everyone to hear, "Sorry, madame. How awkward of me. I meant to help." Then as he finally let go, he murmured close to her ear, "I shall be looking forward to meeting you again in England, madame."

Inside the plane, Jean dropped to the floor beside Jacquie and Angie while Giselle climbed in and the pilot closed and bolted the door. He strode to the cockpit. In seconds the engines came to life and blasted their ears again.

Now both girls clung to Giselle, ignoring the pretense she was not their maman without being told they could. Jean patted Jacquie's shoulder to let her know it was all right.

The plane shook and strained. Finally it leaped forward and bounced down the field. With a deafening roar, they rose from the earth and climbed into the night sky.

Once they were airborne, Jean thought about the men they'd left on the ground. Upon reflection, it seemed much safer, maybe even an answer to prayer, not to have any of those men fly with her and Giselle to England.

Then Giselle leaned across Jacquie and said in Jean's ear, "Andre is a collaborator."

Jean drew back in shock and looked at Giselle. She pulled Giselle back close and said, "Are you sure?"

Giselle shouted, "Yes. We'll talk about it later."

Jacquie looked up at both of them and then scrunched herself tightly against her mother.

Jean leaned back, trying to take in the news. She was glad Giselle had not shot Andre on the spot. Surely, once they were in England, Giselle and the children would be safe. But poor Giselle. She reached over Jacquie and gave Giselle the best hug she could manage while stretching so far.

Giselle wrapped her arms around the girls, hoping they were not able to sense her own agony. She bent over and kissed one and then the other. Letting go of them, she tucked the itchy woolen military blankets more snugly around their legs and shoulders. Shouting to be heard, she said, "Try to sleep now. When you wake up we may be landing in England." They obediently laid their heads in her lap, and soon she felt them relax. Their bodies sagged against her, swaying with the frequent turning of the plane.

Giselle was glad that Jeanie didn't try to talk, for their voices would disturb the children even if they didn't talk about Andre. She wondered if Jeanie really understood all the implications of Andre's being a collaborator. He had practically confessed that it had been he who led the Milice to Claude. Could he get to her and the children once they arrived in England?

One thing for certain, she couldn't stay in London. She had revealed that destination to Andre. No city on earth was big enough to safely hide Jacquie and Angie from him if he suspected they were there.

CHAPTER TWENTY-TWO

After the first hour of flight, Jean leaned back and tried to rest. She was extremely tired, but her muscles seemed to be ready to walk a tightrope.

She was headed home at last. Funny that she could think of England as home, but after being in occupied France, the feeling was very real.

The pilot periodically sent the plane into swift changes of altitude—up to avoid the possibility of antiaircraft guns and down to avoid detection from above—while at the same time he zigzagged to avoid being followed. These maneuvers kept Jean ever aware of the fact that they might not make it. With each move her stomach lurched as if on a fast elevator. She hoped that her praying friends—Elizabeth in Wales, Mother Agnes in Lyon, Grandmother in Oregon, and even Tom—were praying for her right now. It was unthinkable that after she'd come this far with Giselle and the girls, they could be shot down. *So stop thinking about it,* she told herself.

Conversing over the noise took more energy than she had left to give, and she thought Giselle must feel the same, for she made no effort. Anyway, it would disturb the girls, who amazingly had fallen asleep.

The news about Andre was frightening, but surely Giselle would be safe in England. It wouldn't be like occupied France where he'd have friends and the military to help him. Hopefully, Georges and Harry could simply not send another plane to pick him up. Forget the other men. Maybe they were collaborators too!

She would reassure Giselle about this as soon as they could talk. Maybe Georges could persuade her not to worry about Andre.

After a while Jean's thoughts turned to Tom, as they seemed to do whenever she was required to sit like this and endure waiting. *Where is he now? God in heaven, have mercy. Please keep him safe.*

The plane rumbled on, banking repeatedly one direction and then the other. Jean wriggled her feet and flexed her stiff fingers to try to warm them. After what seemed an endless time, she noticed that the cockpit was letting in dim light. She wondered if it was still moonlight or the coming of morning. They'd left the ground shortly after two in the morning. In a short while, the April dawn would expose them to the enemy—guns from below and fighter attack from above. The black paint that concealed the small bomber so well at night would soon make them more visible than a normal war plane.

Stiff and cold from sitting on the bare floor, Jean struggled to her feet and made her way to the cockpit. She stood behind the pilot. Below, she spied the silver line of a river and beyond it, a pale expanse—the English Channel! To the left, just like on the maps she'd memorized, was the Cherbourg Peninsula. The city of Le Havre must be on the other side of the plane. The coastline would be fortified by a lot of artillery.

They roared across the harbor flying low. Suddenly the flash of tracer bullets streaked in front of the plane. Puffs of smoke blossomed to the left and right of them. They had been spotted! The pilot banked the plane steeply as Jean stumbled back to help with the children. Giselle had a firm grip on both of them. Jean dropped to the floor and wrapped her arms around the girls also, bracing them against each change of gravity. Although the cover of darkness was fading, she still could see flares of gunfire through the small windows of the cockpit. *Oh, God, save us! Keep us safe. Protect us!*

The plane climbed, but then lunged downward with each tilting turn. Suddenly it shuddered and jerked. Had they taken a hit?

Jean scrambled to her feet and hurried forward again. The pilot was doing something with the knobs in front of him. The engines took on power, and the plane swooped sideways and up-ward, nearly throwing her off her feet. As she caught herself, the pilot saw her and yelled, "Go sit down!"

"Were we hit?" she yelled back.

He ignored her and banked the plane again. This time she saw the sea rushing up to meet them.

She staggered back to Giselle and the girls and threw herself down beside them. Soon she realized the plane had stopped zig-zagging. The flashes from tracer bullets had faded. Now the danger would come from aerial attack. Would they send planes up after them? Every nerve in Jean's body screamed. *Oh, dear God! Please get us to England safely!*

In the gray light she could see Giselle's eyes only as black smudges on the pale oval of her face. Jean clung to the girls and to Giselle. The children were rigid. Jean rubbed Jacquie's back. "It's all right now," she shouted above the plane's roar. "We're almost to England." Jacquie didn't respond. Maybe she sensed Jean's own uncertainty. If they had taken a hit . . . no, she wouldn't think about that. She concentrated on the steady and strong rhythm of the plane's engines.

The attack lifted Giselle out of her turmoil over knowing that Andre had betrayed Claude and the fact that he was free to follow her to England. Now the plane might be in trouble. Jeanie had tried to reassure the children, but Giselle knew they were not at all safe. Any minute a German fighter could attack. She held the children tightly and prayed. *For the girls, dear Lord. Please get us safely there for them.*

After what felt like an eternity, she heard the engines quiet down, as if a race had ended. Maybe they were over England! The plane banked to the right and then settled into a blessedly straight cruise.

Jeanie went forward again and immediately hurried back. "We're over England!"

Giselle hugged the girls. "We're almost there! We'll land soon, and then we will all be safe!" Giselle was grateful the girls were with her now, but where was Claude? She feared for him, since she had heard nothing. *Oh, God,* she prayed, *thank you for getting us out of France. Now, please protect Claude, wherever he is, and bring him safely to us!*

Jean returned to the cockpit to watch from behind the pilot. They must be over Kent. In the first light of morning, she saw the gentle hills and small villages where people would be now awakening. What a welcome sight. She gazed hungrily at the landscape of England. Then she saw a large river ahead, glinting in the sunrise. It must be the Thames, the gateway to London. She could picture German pilots following these same landmarks during the blitz. On a clear night the shining river would have guided them straight into the heart of the city, just as the River Seine and the Cherbourg Peninsula had told Jean where she was over France.

Minutes later Jean felt the plane nose down. The pilot then gestured for her to go sit down. She obeyed. Soon the plane's wheels bumped against the British tarmac.

Jacquie and Angie sat up straight, wide-eyed.

Jean let out a long breath. Giselle and the children were safe in England. It was over. Her mission was complete. She began to shake uncontrollably.

The plane rolled to a stop, and the pilot cut the engines. The abrupt silence made Jean feel as if she'd suddenly gone deaf. Then the thud of the pilot's heavy flight boots gave her ears an anchor in this quieter world. Unlatching the exit door, he beckoned for them to come. "I say, ladies, you have quite a welcoming committee!"

Jean struggled to her feet and helped Giselle up. Together they led the girls to the open door. Hands reached up to help the children down. Jean couldn't stop trembling. Tears of relief and thankfulness spilled down her cheeks. This was no way to greet anybody, but Uncle Al was standing beside the plane. As soon as their feet touched the ground, he grabbed them, first Giselle and the children in one mighty hug, and then Jean.

"Jeanie, don't you ever pull a stunt like this again!" he said sternly. "But I am so proud of you!" He hugged her tight, and his rough cheek against hers was wet also.

"Oh, Uncle Al! I hated deceiving you, but I had to do this. And we made it!" She was ashamed of how badly she was shaking.

He kept one arm tightly around her and reached out again for Giselle, pulling them both close. With a final squeeze he released them and knelt to greet the girls.

From a small crowd of military personnel, two officers stepped forward, one British and one French. It was Harry and Georges.

Jean wanted to hug them but didn't because they both stood at attention and saluted her. Then Harry grabbed her hand and pumped it up and down with more emotion than he'd ever shown. "I say, you are the most welcome sight I've had in a long time. You made it! You got them out! Congratulations on a mission well done, 'Madame Fauvre.'"

"Oh, Harry, thank you for trusting me when you had no good reason. And Georges! Thank you for all your hard work to make me ready. It paid off every day in France. And here she is!" Jean turned and gripped Giselle's arm.

"Martin! Hello!" Giselle exclaimed.

Georges caught both of Giselle's hands in his and said, "Julie! Thank God! You are safe!"

In the excitement of arriving, Jean had momentarily forgotten that Giselle knew Georges as Martin. Now they automatically used their Resistance names. Jean guessed it would take time for them to get over that. While they talked, she turned to Uncle Al.

"I'll walk the children to the car," he said. "We need to get them warmed up. I have a wool car robe that will help."

"I'll come too and let Giselle have a few minutes with Georges."

Giselle was relieved to be able to talk with Martin without the children hearing. First she asked, "Have you heard anything from Armand?"

"No. But I think he may be with the Maquis near the Spanish border. I feel certain he escaped the gunfire when you and I fled the scene in Lyon. The Milice were still searching frantically for him when I left the city the next day. And since then, through my contacts, I've learned that they never have given up their search for him."

"Andre is a collaborator," Giselle said. "He's the one who betrayed us. He as much as admitted it to me." She told him about her last frightening moments in France with Andre.

When she finished, Martin said, "This is disastrous. We must get someone to take care of him in France before he can arrange to come here."

"Can you do that?"

"I must. We have contacts . . . if only we can get a message through in time. The problem is that Andre may already have left the pickup site. He can't take the chance that you might report him here, as you are doing now. He will look for some other way to come to England. From what you say, I suspect he has to get out of France. Other resistants may have grown suspicious of him, or maybe he has displeased his fascist superiors." Martin's face grew increasingly somber as he talked. "Whatever the case, he has demonstrated great skill. He fooled a BSE agent and made his way right to a secret meeting place!"

"He's clever, all right. He had Armand utterly fooled and me too. All the way here, I chastised myself for leaving Armand wounded and alone with that traitor. . . ." She shuddered.

"You must not blame yourself. We all worked beside him and never suspected a thing."

"Oh, Martin, there's so much I want to tell you and ask you, but I must go now. The children are tired, and they've been through so much. When may I see you again?"

"I'll come to your debriefing today, if you feel up to it. But then later we shall talk, just the two of us. In the meantime, I'll try right away to reach our contact in Dijon. But I probably can't reach him until tonight; that's when he normally listens. Go now and try to get some rest before the debriefing."

"Thank you. I will. Until then, *au revoir*."

He nodded and saluted, and Giselle walked swiftly to Uncle Al's car at the edge of the airfield.

They drove several kilometers through the English countryside before coming to the outskirts of London. Upon entering the city, they saw dozens of charred, bomb-gutted buildings. Giselle was appalled to see entire city blocks that had become small mountains of rubble. As the car wove around heaps of broken concrete, stone, and bricks, she wondered how anyone had survived such devastation.

Yet people were going to work, mothers were entering the bleak boarded-up shops with their empty shopping bags, and children marched along with school books. In a few small parks and around buildings that had not burned, primroses and daffodils bloomed. Next to a gaping bomb crater at the edge of a dooryard, a battered lilac shrub burgeoned with purple flowers.

Exhausted as she was, the sight of unperturbed people and tender plants lifted her spirits.

Uncle Al's dignified gray granite apartment building stood in a neighborhood of Edwardian buildings. It displayed an unblemished doorway that was ornately surrounded with marble casing, lintels, and columns. By some quirk, bombs had not fallen within blocks of the place.

Inside, the elevator still worked. When they reached his apartment, he showed them to his extra bedroom. Giselle looked at the pale faces of her children and asked, "Would there be hot water for bathing the girls?"

"Indeed. And for you and Jean also. Have a warm soak in the tub while Mrs. Jones, my cook and housekeeper, prepares a hot breakfast for you. The plan is to let you rest this morning, and then this afternoon Crozet and Lloyd and maybe some others will meet with you for the debriefing."

Jean seemed to notice her exhaustion and said, "Giselle, you look so tired. Why not get your bath first and let me bathe the girls afterward."

"I'm tired, I confess, but I think the girls won't take long, then you and I can really soak and take our time. They'll probably nap after eating."

True to her guess, the children wanted only a short bath. Then they dressed, unfortunately in the soiled clothes they'd taken off, and Mrs. Jones led them to the kitchen to eat.

Giselle ran fresh hot water, feeling guilty about such extravagance. After she climbed in, she called to Jean, "Will you ask Mrs. Jones if I might have a pot of boiling water added to this? Then I'll put some on for you. As long as I can have the luxury of a warm bath, I want to turn pink."

While Jean took her turn in the tub, Giselle, in Uncle Al's pajamas and robe, went to eat. She forced down a few spoonfuls of porridge and then gave up. She pushed it away and sipped the strong black tea that had been mixed with sweetened canned milk. To her surprise, the unlikely mixture soothed her stomach and cleared her head.

Uncle Al came into the dining room. "I've asked my secretary to pick up a change of clothes for all of you as soon as the shops open. While she does this, you can rest. After lunch a man from U.S. Intelligence will visit, and then Captain Lloyd and

Lieutenant Crozet will debrief you at four while we have our tea. And I want one of our army doctors to check you both." He paused, and his gaze lingered on Giselle. "Do you feel up to this? Maybe I could pull strings and make them all wait."

"I'm all right," Giselle said. "I know it's important to do the debriefing as soon as possible." Before continuing, she glanced at the children playing at a small table near the window. They didn't need to hear her anxiety. She carefully lowered her voice. "Uncle Al, Martin—I mean Georges—said he thinks Claude may be with the Maquis. Please, is there any way you can confirm this and get word to Claude that we are here?"

The lines of sympathy on his rangy face sagged. "Our contacts are not set up for this . . . but I'll certainly keep trying."

Giselle nodded. Fatigue moved her dangerously close to tears. She glanced again at the girls to be sure they were neither seeing her distress nor hearing Uncle Al's uncertainty. They were busy with an old game of checkers the housekeeper had given them. She wanted to tell Uncle Al about Andre, but it seem wisest to wait.

Uncle Al patted her shoulder clumsily. "You must keep up your hope, no matter what." Then he startled her by utterly changing the subject. "I want you to know our army doctors can do wonders to repair your nose. When they examine you, they'll explain."

She didn't care about her nose! Not compared to Claude! She hadn't thought about her deformed nose for days except to be glad it helped conceal her identity. Then she caught the flicker of grief on his face and realized that in his own way, he was trying to distract her from her fears for Claude. Nothing could, but she owed Uncle Al, at the very least, appreciation for the effort. She forced a smile.

"Thanks. I'll ask them about it."

The debriefing that afternoon was tiring beyond Jean's greatest imaginings. The U.S. colonel who interviewed them questioned Giselle in the most depth. He obviously was trying to assess what help the Resistance would be when the Allies invaded France. Giselle answered eagerly and lucidly. Jean marveled at her memory for details that must have come from her activities long before her arrest. The colonel also seemed deeply interested in her treatment as a prisoner of the Gestapo. The two men with him made notes at a furious rate while she talked, occasionally asking again for a name and how to spell it.

When it was Jean's turn to talk, all she could offer was observations from her few recent weeks, which were limited to the areas she'd visited. However, after two hours, she felt drained and fuzzy in the head. Giselle, on the other hand, sounded as crisp and clear as in the beginning.

At last the colonel thanked them and left. It was three-thirty, and Harry and Georges were due at four.

Giselle realized how exhausted she was when Georges and the British officer, Captain Lloyd, arrived. After they asked a myriad of questions that dealt with both the Resistance and conditions in France, Captain Lloyd asked Jean about the farm family at the pickup site.

"How many were in the family?"

"Only two, Max and Jeanette Cuvillon. Their children are grown and living elsewhere."

"No day laborers?"

"No."

"Any neighbors that help out?"

"Not that they mentioned. In fact they told the men that they could walk around outside and not worry about being seen. I took that to mean there were no close neighbors."

"And they had no visitors while you were there?"

"No. Why are you asking this?"

"Georges told me about the collaborator, Andre. It's possible he could deliver the Cuvillons to the Milice and expose my agent who set him up for the flight out."

"Oh no!" Jean gasped.

"But if he wanted to do that," Giselle said, "he could have done it while we were there, and we'd all have been arrested."

"You're right," Georges said. "My guess is that he was fleeing his Nazi superiors and didn't want to draw attention to himself. But now that he has seen you, Julie, he may go to his old superiors with this new information to buy his way back into favor. If so, he could also deliver over to them everyone who helped him reach the pickup site, including Monsieur and Madame

Cuvillon. And he could cover his own effort to flee by saying he took the route only to obtain information. I've sent messages to my Resistance contacts, and Harry has left a message for his agents in the area. We can only hope the messages reach them all before the Milice does."

Giselle's mind whirled ahead of him to analyze the possibilities Andre might face. "If he were fleeing his Nazi superiors and then got back into their good graces, they will know I'm in England."

Georges rubbed his forehead with one hand as if he had a headache, then said heavily, "Yes. This could happen."

"Do you think they would try to send someone here to look for Giselle?" Jean asked.

Georges nodded. "It's possible. We'll know more when we hear from our contacts in France."

Giselle's spirits sank. Even in England, the children were not safe.

CHAPTER TWENTY-THREE

The second day in England, British army doctors insisted Giselle must have surgery on her nose and face as soon as possible. Her damaged sinuses could harbor infection close to her brain. The head surgeon said somberly, "Madame, you truly cannot delay this. I'd like to check you into the hospital today."

"But my children! I can't leave them alone so soon. Surely it can wait a few days."

He shook his head. "You've been fortunate so far. Do not trust your luck to continue. If you get an infection, it could quickly become critical, and we can't do the surgery you need in the presence of infection. You wouldn't want to leave your children in a foreign land with no mama."

"Surely it's not that risky!"

"This is my opinion. Two other surgeons who have studied your X rays concur. I cannot be responsible if you delay."

She sighed in frustration. She wanted to get out of London as soon as possible in case Andre found the means to come to England. The doctor, a thin-faced man with the Nordic name of Aarvidson, stood frowning at her.

"I need to go home first and prepare the children," she said.

"Then I will reserve a room in this hospital for you. Please check in at two o'clock tomorrow afternoon."

"Yes, Doctor."

His expression softened. "I don't want you to worry about this. You'll be fine if we can get in there immediately and open up those sinuses." He left the examining room, and a young nurse came and escorted her to the waiting area where Jeanie waited.

She stood up. "What did the doctor say?"

"I must have surgery right away." She suddenly had to get out of the hospital with its institutional look and medicinal smell. She felt trapped, as she had at Sisters of Mercy in Lyon. "We can talk about it later."

Jeanie nodded. "All right."

The soldier that Captain Lloyd had assigned to go everywhere with Giselle stood up, preceded them out the door, then beckoned for them to follow. Giselle was glad for this effort to protect her, but she knew from experience that a bodyguard could easily be outwitted and overcome by a persistent enemy. She maintained her own private vigilance as they proceeded to the army vehicle where a driver waited to take them to Uncle Al's apartment.

Jean wished she could do something to ease Giselle's anxiety but couldn't think of anything more than to entertain the girls while Giselle packed the few personal things Mrs. Jones had purchased for her. Uncle Al finally returned home after the children had eaten their supper and gone to bed. Georges and Harry accompanied him. Seeing the three of them together again reminded Jean of the first time she'd seen the younger men in Govilon, when she'd learned about Giselle's arrest and torture. Now they wore similar stern expressions.

Harry ordered their guard for the night to step out into the hall to stand watch where he couldn't be listening.

Then Uncle Al led them to the dining room and sat down heavily in his chair at the head of the table. "We have news from France. What it means we can only guess. Georges, you tell them what you've learned so far."

Georges leaned forward, one arm resting on the tabletop, his black eyebrows pulled together in a frown. "I've heard from resistants in a réseau near the Cuvillon farm." He met Jean's gaze and then focused on Giselle. "Andre was not at the farm when they went to look. The other men said he had disappeared during the night after they returned from the pickup location. The resistants persuaded the Cuvillons to leave their farm and go into hiding. A neighbor, although some distance away, took their animals. The remaining men, who had planned to fly out, fled, hoping to rendezvous with a plane at a different location. Harry, tell them your part."

"BSE has not heard anything from our agent who had arranged for Andre's flight out. We don't know whether he may simply be away from his radio or whether he has been arrested."

"What about Andre?" Jean asked.

Harry leaned back in his chair and folded his arms across his chest. "Until we hear from our agent or find out what happened to him, we have no way of knowing. The fact that he fled is enough to confirm that he was acting as a double agent, either on his own or officially. If he is in the employ of the Milice or Gestapo, he has connections that would help him go most anywhere."

Georges tapped his fingers on the tabletop in a quiet staccato. "So he may not have been fleeing from France to save his skin. He may have been on an assignment in England. And then he happened upon Julie, for him a fortuitous coincidence. Julie—Giselle," he swiftly corrected himself, "you must assume he can reach England." He turned to Uncle Al. "Mr. Moore, she must go quickly to a village far from London and hide until France is free."

Giselle said slowly, "I've been scheduled for surgery tomorrow, but it can be done elsewhere later—"

"Giselle!" Jean interrupted. She was glad Giselle had told her the gist of the doctor's diagnosis. "Uncle Al, Dr. Aarvidson said she'd be risking her life to delay because of the danger of infection so close to her brain. Her getting a cold could become critical."

Uncle Al nodded. "I know. Dr. Aarvidson called me this afternoon. Giselle, you need the specialists here. The risk is real, and what they propose is quite new. They call it reconstructive surgery. They assured me it couldn't be done anywhere else in Britain. They've learned new procedures from operating on badly wounded men. Furthermore, because of the war there's a shortage of doctors throughout Britain. You must have the surgery here, and you should do it immediately so you can leave as soon as possible."

"We'll post guards at the hospital as well as here to watch over the children," Harry said.

Giselle looked as if she felt trapped, and Jean couldn't blame her. The thought that Andre might find a way to get to London seemed very possible after her own experience of entering occupied France. If she were Giselle, she too would want to leave the city and hope for the best.

Giselle looked from one to the other of the men and finally said, "All right, Uncle Al. While I have the surgery, please find a good hiding place for me."

When Giselle awoke from the anaesthetic, Jeanie was sitting beside her bed. "The doctors said the surgery went fine. Uncle Al and Mrs. Jones are pampering the girls. You mustn't worry about them. They seem relaxed and understand you'll soon be home with them."

Giselle found speaking too difficult. She drowsed back to sleep.

She dreamed she was back in France, in the horror of prison, holding her dying prison mate in her arms, helpless to ease her pain. Giselle tried to scream and awoke abruptly with terror clawing at her reason, her heart pounding as if to escape her body. Then she saw Jeanie still sitting beside her. She gathered her drugged wits and said hoarsely, "I can't believe we're in England. I still expect to wake up in the hands of the enemy...."

Jeanie gripped her hand and squeezed it. "I've been doing that myself. Each morning it's a new experience to remember we're here. One day soon reality will soak in."

Giselle murmured, "I suppose so."

Jeanie went on. "I have to leave tonight for Abergavenny. I got special permission to stay and see you through the surgery. Now they say I must return to work."

Despite her foggy state, Giselle felt a flash of dread. She had come to count so much on Jeanie. The two of them had worked as one. "I thought you could stay longer...."

Jeanie patted her hand. "I know, but the good news is that we'll be together soon. Uncle Al and Georges and Harry all agree that Abergavenny is a good place for you to live. It's a small town, but not so small that you will be noticed as a stranger. It's up in the hills in a quiet Welsh valley. Oh, Giselle, the girls will love it too, and I'm so glad you'll be close to me. Govilon is only two kilometers away."

Giselle, too weary and drugged to talk, let her eyes close. Then the memory of Andre intruded. She flashed awake. "You've got to be careful. When you leave for Abergavenny, watch to be sure no one is following you, just as you did in France."

"I will," Jean said. "Captain Lloyd is sending me in a private army car. We'll leave London under the cover of night. They will bring you to Abergavenny secretly too. And the police and military are watching constantly for Andre, Giselle. Try not to worry."

"Yes." The morphine took over. She could no longer keep her eyes open.

When she awoke later, Jeanie was gone, and through the hospital window she could see that night had fallen. She wished she could talk to Georges. She needed to hear from him that going to Abergavenny was a good idea. She trusted him more than either Captain Lloyd or Uncle Al.

She asked the nurse and learned that only Uncle Al had come and gone while she slept. He'd said he would be back in the morning on his way to work.

Uncle Al came punctually the next day on the way to the embassy and then again on the way home in the evening, but Georges did not come.

The second day Captain Lloyd arrived after lunch. After greeting her, he said, "Georges' assignment to BSE has ended quite suddenly. He's been ordered back into the regular army with de Gaulle. He asked me to give you his good wishes and to tell you he will continue to try to locate your husband."

"Oh no!" she exclaimed.

"I'm sorry. I know you counted on talking with him," Captain Lloyd said awkwardly. "But I'm sure your uncle will also do all he can to help you. And I've got our people listening too for any radio messages regarding your husband."

"Of course. Thank you."

After an effort at small talk, he excused himself, leaving Giselle alone with her fears. With Georges gone and Jeanie in Wales, Giselle felt more vulnerable than when she'd been walking the streets of Lyon under the eyes of the Gestapo. By evening felt she'd go out of her mind if she could not get out of the hospital. She needed Angie and Jacquie within reach of her empty hands. She demanded that the doctors discharge her.

Reluctant at first, they finally agreed that if she checked her temperature frequently and came in daily for the next week, she could safely recuperate in Uncle Al's apartment.

———————⋆———————

A few days later she was sitting in the parlor with a wool blanket wrapped around her legs trying to read a book when Uncle Al returned home from the embassy. He came and sat beside her on the divan.

Tired as he obviously was, his expression hinted at good news. "I know now why Georges Crozet was ordered out of London on such short notice. Today we were informed that, beginning at midnight last night, no one may leave the British Isles, not even our diplomats. Britain is now isolated from the rest of the world."

"But why? And what does this mean for Georges?" Giselle cried.

He put his arm around her shoulders. "My dear, I didn't mean to alarm you. The good news is that this means the invasion of Europe may begin soon. But of course you must not tell anyone I said so. Since I work at the embassy, my opinion could be construed as specific knowledge."

He gave her shoulders a squeeze, then let go and leaned back.

Uncle Al looked exhausted. He had aged so much since she'd seen him last, before the war. She regretted that her own situation most certainly added to his burdens.

Yet, he slapped his hands on his knees and said in a hopeful tone, "Look at how things are going for Germany. The Russians are taking back their land from Hitler's troops. Sebastopol will soon be theirs. Our bombs have nearly obliterated the Third Reich's production capabilities. The time is ripe. The invasion of Europe must come soon, but utter secrecy must prevail."

"Are you still in radio contact with France?"

"Yes. We do not stop listening, and we communicate using coded messages."

"So if Claude tried to reach you, he could."

"Yes. Absolutely."

"Will this limit traveling and make it more difficult for Andre to sneak into England?"

"I think it will."

All Giselle could think was that professional spies could circumvent any martial law. Such was their specialty!

She went to bed that night hoping she could soon leave London. Being with the girls had made her recovery more tolerable, but she knew she was still too weak to protect them. And this latest news terrified her. She couldn't account for such an explosion of anxiety. Rationally she knew she was as safe as possible with Uncle Al and the guards Captain Lloyd had provided, yet her feeling of impending doom persisted. She could lay blame to a letdown after so much stress or even to the new stress created by the surgery, but when she was in Lyon, her ability to sense danger had saved her life several times. She did not dare ignore this familiar warning, and it took all of her energy to conceal her fear from the children.

When Jean first returned to the routine of recreational therapy, she found to her relief that she didn't have to explain her long absence. Uncle Al had written a letter to her supervisor using embassy stationery, saying she'd been engaged in special war endeavors, which could not be discussed. In a staff meeting, the super had made it plain that questions or rumors about where Miss Thornton had been or what she had done would not be tolerated.

Within a week the slower pace in Govilon, after living in constant danger, dragged Jean into a curious downward spiral. At first she felt a little apathetic and laid the cause to fatigue. Then she found herself slipping into a bleak wilderness where nothing mattered. She didn't want to get up in the morning, and exhaustion dragged her down all day.

One day when she was delivering a message to the Red Cross office in Gilwern, she found Mary there with an army nurse, Marge Emerson, whom she'd met on several occasions. Marge greeted her and then stood quietly listening as Jean handed the note to Mary.

"For some reason the super wrote to Colonel Elfstrom, and she seemed urgent," Jean explained.

"Okay," Mary said, reaching for the envelope. "I'll take this to the colonel right away." She didn't move, however. "You don't look so good. Are you feeling okay?"

Jean shrugged. She didn't want to talk about how she felt. "I'm just tired."

Marge moved closer. Jean felt her brown eyes studying her and wanted to walk away. Common courtesy forced her to gaze back at the diminutive nurse. Her short brown curls and uptilted eyes gave her a misleading mischievous appearance. Now she was all business. "You don't look well. Why don't you let me do a quick blood count? You're very pale. I bet you need iron."

"Oh, really, I'm fine. Just a little short of sleep right now—"

Mary interrupted. "Look, Jeanie. Marge is one of the best. And I agree with her. You look worse than tired. Come on and be sensible. You remember how you nearly died of pneumonia at Tulelake."

Jean shook her head wearily. "You two. Will you leave me alone if I have the blood test?"

Mary shook her head. "Not if you need more prods."

"Come on with me to the lab," Marge said. "It will only take a couple of minutes."

"Okay."

"Take good care of her, Marge. After I run this letter to the colonel, I'm going into Abergavenny to pick up a book for Rufe Johnson, who insists on sending it as a gift to some buddy in his outfit in Italy. Can you beat that? Sending a book to a soldier on the battlefront?"

"Oh, Rufe," Marge remarked. "He has unusual ideas, all right."

"See you later, Jean. Do whatever Marge says. She's a sharp nurse."

At the lab Marge drew blood from Jean's arm and handed the vial to the medic on duty. "I'll need a CBC, Sergeant Morgan." To Jean she said, "I'll call you tomorrow and give you the results." Her eyes still studied Jean. "Any other symptoms besides being tired?"

Jean sighed. "I don't know . . . I just feel like nothing is worth doing anymore. I'm feeling gloomy without any particular reason. That's why I figured I needed more rest."

"Mary told me you were gone on some mission that is hush-

hush, and I'm not going to ask you anything about that, but when you came back, did you feel lethargic?"

"No. My weariness has been growing gradually . . . like I said, for no apparent reason."

"Maybe you miss what you were doing before."

Jean almost jumped at the sudden revelation that Marge's words triggered. Slowly she said, "I do feel useless now just minding the personal needs of the patients in my limited way. I keep wondering if this really helps. And then I think about how they'll go back to the battle and maybe get killed. Some of them are only kids, just out of high school. . . ."

"Yeah, it's tough. But I notice the guys' reactions after you and Mary and the other Red Cross women have given them their welcome kits or written letters home for them. I see their faces when you sit and talk with them, and listen. You bring a breath of normal life into the wards. Getting them well isn't just a matter of taking care of their physical wounds. You remind them of home and why they're fighting this war."

Jean forced a smile. "You make it sound good."

Marge walked her out of the lab building and toward the Red Cross office again. She stopped suddenly and gestured toward the nearest building. "Have you been in a mental ward?"

"Yes."

"Would you be willing to stop here for a minute with me? I need to check on Rufe, the man who sent Mary to buy a book."

"He's in the mental ward?"

"Yes, but I'm sure he doesn't belong here. I think he's faking his symptoms. I've seen him when he doesn't know anyone's looking. He is sharp, and I'm sure he's playing a game. Funny thing is, we've become friends in a way. He knows I know but haven't reported him. He's only, as you said, barely out of high school, and there's something about him that makes me want to go along with his game. Does that shock you . . . that I would aid and abet a shirker?"

"I guess I'm not shocked. So what's the future for this boy? Any chance he can go home on a mental disability discharge?"

"Maybe, but then how could he live it down and get a decent job? Employers are funny about mental illness. And so are people in general. Battle fatigue is so misunderstood. I've been wanting my sister to write something about it. My sister Em is a war correspondent for *Newsguard Magazine*."

"A woman war correspondent? That must be rough work."

Marge nodded. "She's had it tough, making a career for herself in journalism. The men don't welcome a skirt in their midst. But back to the subject. Want to come in with me and meet Rufe? I think you'd be good for him."

"Well, sure. I can come say hello if you think it will help."

Inside the ward, most of the men were in bed, some swathed in bandages. They were frozen in all kinds of positions, as if they were dead or wishing to be. Only one looked up when they passed the foot of his bed. His eyes were wide with an expression of horror. Marge stopped and spoke quietly to him.

"Hello, Phil. It's good to see you awake this morning."

The man closed his eyes. "No! NO!" He turned his face away.

Marge went to his side and tucked his blanket over his shoulders. She said softly, "You're safe here, Phil. You're safe now."

He cringed and seemed to shrink under his blanket. Jean's heart felt as if it shrank with him.

Marge left him and then walked down the aisle to the last bed in the ward, where a man lay with a pillow over his head. "Good morning, Rufe. I've brought a friend to meet you."

His muffled voice barely carried to Jean's ears.

"I don't want no visitors."

"You'll be sorry if you don't meet this one. She's a friend of Mary O'Leary's and just as pretty. You'd better at least take a look."

The pillow didn't move. Then slowly the man turned and uncovered his face. His dark hair had been buzzed off in a fresh GI cut, but he had a few day's growth of a black beard. Other than that, he looked like a boy, a handsome kid, but his gaze—Jean stopped her inventory at his eyes. Something about his eyes seemed older than Uncle Al. She instantly saw in him the same attitude of intense awareness that set Georges Crozet and Harry Lloyd apart from the many other soldiers.

CHAPTER TWENTY-FOUR

Jeanie remembered Marge's assessment that this young man, Rufe, did not belong in the mental ward. Facing him, she couldn't help but agree. She saw no confusion, depression, or panic in the sharp look he gave her. She said, "Hello, Rufe. I'm pleased to meet you."

He huffed a sigh. "Sure you are. A guy without a mind to call his own. All girls die for a chance to meet me." He turned his face to the wall.

"Hey, Rufe," Marge said, "if you know what side your bread is buttered on, you'll be nice to this one. She happens to like smart-aleck guys who think they know more than anyone else."

He flopped back over and studied Jean. "Yeah? Well, how about a game of checkers then?"

"Well, right now she's on duty at Govilon and has to get back," Marge said.

"I'd like to come visit on my day off, Rufe. Could we play a game then?"

"Naw. Why bother?" Again he turned his back to them and refused to speak.

When they were back outside, Marge said, "Well, it was worth a try. Thanks for going in with me. Who knows? Maybe he will ask about you later. If he does, would you come? You might get to meet my sister Em too. She'll be here in a few days to interview doctors and nurses and possibly observe some of the mental patients."

"Sure. I'll come if he wants me. I think you're right. He may not need to be there."

On the way back to Govilon, Jean couldn't get the broken men in the mental ward out of her mind. The one who had been so frightened reminded her of the look on Giselle's face the day she said she'd never again be taken alive by the Germans. The others, who had lain like dead men, touched her deeply. She'd felt the way they looked when Dave had been killed at Pearl Harbor. Then there was Rufe. With his whole future before him, he shouldn't have the blot of mental illness on his army record. She'd like to help Rufe if she could, even if it meant he'd go back to the front.

The next day Marge called to say her red cell count was a little below normal and that Rufe Johnson had asked for her to come visit. She could pick up a bottle of iron pills when she came over.

The afternoon that Jean went to see Rufe, she took along a game of dominoes. When she reached the ward, Rufe was up and sitting in a wheelchair. He offered no form of greeting. He just announced, "Marge says we have to go to the rec hall so we won't bother these other guys. They ain't going to notice one way or the other, but I guess I have to go."

"Sure. Marge knows best." Jean gripped the back of the wooden wheelchair and pushed it toward the door. She hoped he really was as well as Marge thought and would not experience a case of nerves on his first time out.

When they were outside on the walkway, he said, "Marge told me to tell you this ain't my first trip out. She took me herself yesterday."

"Good. I'm glad it's a nice day. The sun is warm between the clouds."

He said nothing.

In the rec hall she eased the chair up to a table and sat down across from him. "Do you want to play checkers? I also brought some dominoes, if you like."

He huffed in irritation. "Kid games. How about we play some poker? There're some cards over there." He pointed at a shelf under a window where several decks were neatly stacked.

"I'm sorry. I don't know how to play poker. All I know is rummy."

"Rummy," he snorted. "Where did you grow up anyway? Get me the cards, and I'll show you how."

For the next hour Jean tried to learn poker. He won pile after pile of chips and treated her as if she were hopeless. If he were not a patient, she would have enjoyed telling him off. Finally she said, "I have to be back to Govilon before mess call. How about one game of dominoes, just for me?"

He glared at her for a moment and then said, "Okay. I guess I owe you. You are a good sport."

She wanted to retort, "I didn't think you knew the meaning of the word," but she kept quiet.

Suddenly he grinned. "You got a temper, ain't you? I like that. You know, you're the kind of girl I always wished I could know."

"Rufe—"

"Oh, don't worry." His demeanor changed instantly to self-pity. "I ain't gonna make a pass at you or nothing. What could I do? I'm sick, maybe ruined for life. What girl would ever look at me anyway?"

Jean opened the domino box, dumped it out on the table, and began to turn the dominoes face down. "Rufe, it's not true that no girl would look at you. You're good-looking. And your illness is only temporary. If you treat girls nice, you'll have your pick from a lot of them."

He scowled, and then almost imperceptibly his expression changed. If she was not mistaken, she read sorrow in those canny dark eyes.

"Never a chance," he muttered. He leaned back in his chair. "Take me back to the loony bin. I'm tired."

"Sure, if you wish." She swept the dominoes into the box, laid it in his lap to hold, and pushed the heavy chair back to the mental ward. When she left him with the nurse on duty, he ignored her good-bye. On the way back to Govilon, she chided herself for trying to play amateur nurse, especially with a mental patient.

It wasn't until Sunday when she went to church and saw Nella and Elizabeth that she realized her feeling of gloom had lifted. Her old zest for life was returning, and the change obviously had begun that afternoon when Rufe tried to teach her how to play poker. Now she hoped he would see her again.

On her next day off, she called Marge to see how Rufe was doing.

"He asked about you," Marge said. "I think you did him some good. Want to come again? Em is here. You can meet her too."

"Oh, I'd like to meet her. Tell Rufe I'm coming, and if he doesn't want to visit, I'll just go on to Abergavenny and have tea at the manse."

At Gilwern, she stopped by the Red Cross office to say hello to Mary, but she was not there. So Jean hurried on up the hill to the nurses' quarters to meet Marge and her sister.

They were outside in the gentle sun, waiting. Em Emerson was tall compared to Marge. She had the same uptilt to her eyes, but set in her oval face the unusual angle created an exotic-looking beauty. While Marge tended to dart around, Em moved with confident grace. She was the classic willowy type of woman that Jean had always wished to be.

When Marge introduced Jean, Em smiled warmly. "How do you do, Jean. So you're the one who broke the ice with Rufe Johnson."

"How do you do. Well, I don't know about breaking any ice. When I left Rufe, he wasn't talking. I don't know if he will see me today or change his mind at the last minute, but I thought I'd try."

"Good luck. I couldn't get a word out of him."

"Well, Jean, he is expecting you," Marge said. "He asked to be in the wheelchair again. If you don't mind, I'll let you go meet him while I take Em to the orthopedic ward to talk with some of the boys there."

"Sure, Marge. I know the way. I'm glad to have met you, Em. I hope we may get to visit before you leave."

"Thanks. Me too."

When Jean reached the mental ward, Rufe was sitting in his wheelchair waiting by the nurses' desk. He almost smiled. In a gruff tone he said, "So here's Miss Thornton, the great poker player."

"At your service, sir." She nodded to the nurse. "Does he have a curfew?"

She shook her head. "He would just break it if he did."

Jean wheeled him out into the May sunshine and started toward the rec hall.

"I want to go for a walk," he said.

"Okay, as long as we stay away from hills."

"Oh. Then go ahead and aim for the rec hall."

"Not on your life. You wanted a walk; you're going to have to accept one." She pushed the chair along the walkway, which ran beside a road that led into the heart of the hospital community. Spring had turned the mountains of Wales along the Usk River into a green paradise, that is, if one could overlook the sprawling military station hospital in the foreground. Above the nearby barracks she could see the gentle sweep of pastures on the hillsides across the river. Surely a walk would do Rufe some good.

He rode in silence, looking neither left nor right. When they came to an overlook of the winding river, she stopped and turned the chair toward the view. "I love the view out here. It reminds me of home."

"Home!" He spat the word like a curse. "I got no use for home. You ever lived in a shanty that don't keep out the wind and listened to your old man beat your mother after he comes in drunk? No, I don't guess you have, or you wouldn't want to go on about home."

"I'm sorry, Rufe. I forgot that some people have had such a hard time. My father was a drunk too, but he never beat anyone. Before my mother and brother died, he was good to us. Then he just walked away and left me with my grandmother."

He stared at her with unguarded surprise. "You ain't had it so good neither. I got me a brother too. He's somewhere in the South Pacific, and my mom, she's working in the shipyards. The old man disappeared when she moved out and went to work. I hope to never see him again."

He stopped, and she followed his gaze down to the river.

"It looks peaceful," he said. Then he frowned up at her. "But there ain't no peace. You gotta fight, even to eat."

She waited for him to say more, but his lips closed in a tight straight line across his young face. He stared at the river for a long time, and she felt he wanted her to remain silent.

Finally he said, "Take me back. I'm tired."

"All right."

When they reached the mental ward, Rufe grabbed the wheels of the chair and brought them to a halt. Without looking up at her, he said, "I don't want to see you again. There's nothing but trouble follows me. Don't come back."

"I'll do what you ask, of course. But if you want me, just tell Nurse Marge, and I'll come. Rufe . . . I've enjoyed talking with you."

"Yeah, sure," he muttered in an angry tone.

It made her want to go somewhere and have a private cry. He was so young to be looking so bitter. He let go of the wheels, and she proceeded to wheel him inside to the waiting nurse.

"Back so soon?"

"Yes, he says he's tired. Bye, Rufe."

He did not respond.

"Thanks," the nurse said. "I'll get him back in bed."

Jean left, wondering what would become of him. She didn't know what his plan was, but she felt certain he was not suffering from a true mental breakdown. He was bitter and angry but seemed rational and in control of himself. How had he fooled the doctors? Maybe he'd simply refused to talk.

One morning toward the end of May, Jean awoke to a rumble that sounded like endless thunder. Puzzled, she followed Betty to the door of the squat Nissen hut.

"Will you listen to that? What do you suppose it is?" Betty exclaimed.

"Must be a really big convoy."

"Loudest I've ever heard. Let's get dressed and go out to the highway to see."

Jean pulled on slacks and a sweater for protection against the cool morning air. As they approached the narrow zigzagging highway that ran beside the small village and the military station hospital, the roar became ear shattering. It was tanks! Tanks as far as they could see, up and down the road. Apparently they were emerging from their hiding places in the Brecon Beacon Mountains, as if monsters awakening from hibernation.

"The invasion!" Jean shouted. "They must be heading out to get ready for the invasion of France!"

Betty grabbed her and hugged her. "At last!"

A surge of excitement filled Jean. Surely this was the beginning of the end for Hitler! With so many men in France prepared to sabotage the bridges, railways, and ammunition dumps, and ready to fight when the Allies landed, surely victory was in sight.

Then thoughts of the horrible cost in lives stabbed her. How many men would never come back? How many would be maimed for life? How many minds and spirits would be broken? *Oh, God, be with them all,* she prayed silently. *And please watch over Tom and Claude wherever they are.*

As she and Betty waved to hidden drivers peeking out through periscopes, she exclaimed, "It's a day to remember, isn't it!"

Betty's smile crinkled the corners of her blue eyes. "It sure is!"

They watched the tanks go by until time for breakfast.

All day long while Jean worked, she heard the steady roar of hundreds of tanks. Their noise filled the Usk river valley like a great battle cry. By nightfall the vibrating air grew still. Jean listened to the silence and wondered how long it would be until trains filled with wounded men would begin arriving in this quiet valley.

Each time she went into Abergavenny in the following days, she saw fewer soldiers. Soon only villagers walked the narrow streets. The town looked strangely desolate. No one speculated aloud, for everyone knew the danger of spreading rumors. Shopkeepers, however, greeted Jean with concern about the state of the military station hospitals. "Anything we can do, miss?" they often asked.

She always thanked them but couldn't tell them that the hospitals were completely ready for their intended purpose—to receive thousands of casualties once the invasion began.

More often than before, the appreciative Welsh people brought musical programs to the rec hall and invited the Red Cross women and ambulatory patients to their homes for tea or Sunday dinner.

At last on the afternoon of June 6, Jean froze by the radio in the rec hall when she heard the BBC announce that the invasion of Europe had begun. "Supreme Commander of the Allied Forces, General Dwight Eisenhower, has announced that the Allies, with the largest armada in history, landed successfully this morning in France. Four thousand ships, thousands of lesser craft, and tens of thousands of soldiers, under the greatest air assault ever delivered, are fighting to hold the beachheads."

All the men in the rec hall let out a cheer and crowded around the radio.

After that, as Jean went about her duties, she paused beside every radio she passed, listening for more news and silently praying for the fighting men.

At first patients begged her for the latest reports, but soon they quieted and settled into waiting. By suppertime a few more radios had been set up in the wards, and the men were listening for themselves. Their faces registered tense emotion. Would the Allies be able to hold the beachheads? There was joking too, with comments like "Now we'll show that little paperhanger," their favorite repeatable epithet for Hitler. But in moments of quiet, they looked as if they were praying too.

Before bedtime Jean and Betty listened to the late news in the rec hall. The announcement was optimistic. "Tonight's communiqué just in from D-day invasion headquarters says that Hitler's Atlantic wall is not as formidable as anticipated. Allied troops have secured the beachheads and have advanced nine and a half miles inland. Right now they are fighting in the streets of Caen."

Having come so recently from France, Jean could picture the reactions of the French people. The invasion news probably traveled quickly through the Resistance to all corners of France. In her imagination she was there with Evyette and Emile, Jeanette and Max, Mother Agnes, Raoul Montaigne, Henri and Isabelle, even with the gallant old woman who had befriended her on her first train ride to Lyon. She could imagine their relief, their hope, their determination. Still, nothing was sure yet.

CHAPTER TWENTY-FIVE

The next day Jean wanted to cheer again. According to the BBC, the fierce fighting continued, but now guarded reports said that it would be difficult for Hitler to stop the Allied drive inland. Accounts of blown-up railroads, bridges, fuel dumps, and ammunition stores showed that the resistants and the Maquis were doing their part to cripple the Nazis' ability to stop the invasion.

With the beachheads secured, Jean was able to concentrate more on the work at hand. Soon the first casualties should be coming. She knew the present lack of trains was merely the lull before a terrible storm.

Sure enough, before long, wounded men arrived, not from France but from northern Italy, where the Germans were fighting desperately against the Allied advance. The Govilon hospital received most of the new patients. Jean felt she'd never forget her first impression of them. Swathed in bulky bandages and casts, they looked like a trainload of white plaster statues.

Once admitted, the men needed assistance in reaching their families back home. Jean spent hours writing for those who couldn't write and reading to those who couldn't see. She spent more hours with men who just wanted to talk. A few didn't want to communicate with their families. Then it was her duty to persuade them to let their families know they were all right—injured but alive.

Running personal errands for new patients always took time and meant fewer trips to Abergavenny. She had to miss church on Sunday, so Tuesday she stopped by the manse for a quick hello and to ask Nella to go hiking with her. Wednesday would be her first time off in ten days.

Nella was unusually quiet and at first didn't show much enthusiasm, although just before Jean left, she seemed to perk up. "Maybe it would do me good to get out. I'll come with you tomorrow."

The next day Jean followed Nella through the meadow below the castle ruins. The air held a hundred scents of spring. Jean inhaled appreciatively and began to realize how badly she had needed a respite from her work.

On their way upstream along the river, Nella pointed out blooming wild flowers—yellow marsh marigolds and lilac-colored lady's-smock near the river. In shady places, the bluebells, red campion, and forget-me-nots grew thickly. Some of these Jean had seen in Oregon.

Nella grew quiet, leaving Jean to her own thoughts for a while. When they paused to look at the view across the river, Nella said abruptly, "I'm glad you asked me out. Being out in the midst of wild growing things has always given me pleasure." She lowered her gaze to the path and said hesitantly, "Lately, I've been feeling so worn out and useless, I can hardly make myself move or even think. I know it bothers Mum and Daddy, but nothing much seems worth doing. I still miss Rob, and I can't see any purpose for me. Some days I think I'm no good for Livie, that she'd do better with just her Gamma and Gumpa. . . ."

"Nella, that's not true! No one can ever take your place with her. She needs you more than ever now that she has no daddy."

Nella cast her a troubled look. "Keep telling me that, Jean. I need to be reminded."

Jean felt a twinge of fear for her. "Have you told your father and mother how you feel?"

"No. I've been burden enough for my parents. I dare not show them how I really feel."

Jean said carefully, "I'm sure they would feel less burdened if you let them share your hard times. This is important for you too." Then she told Nella how it had been when she lost her brother and no one would let her talk about it, no one but Giselle. When she finished, she said, "Did you know that new grief can arouse old grief and give you a double dose of pain? Losing your brother has no doubt thrown you right back into grieving for Rob."

Surprise crossed Nella's girlish face. "I hadn't thought of that. So it could be."

Jean responded quickly, instinctively. "There's nothing weak about still mourning the loss of Rob. I can understand how you hate to speak of more pain to your mother when she's still in grief over losing Charles. But will you please talk to your father? For pete's sake, it's his job, Nella! He lets everyone else lean on him. He loves you and would dearly love to have you turn to him."

Nella smiled with a little of her old sparkle. "You could be a preacher yourself, Jean. You're very persuasive. Okay. I'll try to talk to Daddy."

After that Nella perked up and acted as a tour guide again, pointing out more plants and sights along the river. Finally they halted in a pasture where an old stone barn stood facing the river. The farmhouse was nowhere in sight. "Look at the trees beside that barn," Nella said. "See those two pines? They're the only ones here in the valley that I know of. Come and see if they look like your Oregon trees."

Actually the old barn attracted Jean more than did the trees. She moved closer to inspect the hand-hewn timbers and carefully placed stones. Someone had built it solid enough to last for generations. Beside it stood a silo that gave the place the look of a small castle.

Nella handed her a twig of pine. She pinched the fresh needles, releasing their fragrance, a sharp tang of resin. "They don't look like our pines, but they smell as good." She scooped up a handful of the long dry needles from the ground. "I used to make baskets out of these. It might be a good handcraft for some of the men, if I can remember how. Do you think anyone would mind if I came back here for more?"

"Probably not. You could ask. The farmhouse is up the hill, just behind those trees." She pointed. Then said, "The clouds coming over look full of rain. I think we'd better go home now, or we'll get soaked."

As they headed back toward Abergavenny, Jean turned for

one last look at the old stone barn with its silo on one end. "That barn is so beautifully constructed."

"Yes, that's what first attracted me to this place, but I've never seen it used. Must be too far from the present-day roads. If you look off yonder from here, you can just see the white farmhouse atop the hill."

"What a peaceful place to live."

Nella laughed—a welcome sound. "Most folks would say a farm is naught but hard work. But I love it too. Sometimes I wish my father were a farmer instead of a man of the cloth."

They returned to the edge of the high riverbank to follow it back to Abergavenny. The water below swirled darkly, still swift from recent spring rains. Jean glanced down and halted.

"What's that?"

Something was caught in the bushes at the edge of the water. At first she thought it was a drowned animal, but then she realized she was seeing fabric, not wet fur. The pale spot was a human hand floating at the end of a lifeless arm! "Oh, Nella, someone has drowned!"

Nella rushed to her side and let out a horrified gasp, then clamped her hand over her mouth. Her face turned ashen with shock. Jean pulled her back from the edge. "You run to the nearest farmhouse for help. I'll go down to see if he could possibly be alive." She knew he wasn't, but she wanted to get Nella away quickly.

Nella remained frozen for a moment. Then she sprinted across the grass-carpeted pastureland and on up the hill.

Jean scrambled down the bank to the narrow shore of mud, rocks, and bushes. When she drew near the man, she recognized the military station hospital robe and pajamas. She could tell before she reached him that he'd been dead for some time. She couldn't see his face, but his dark hair appeared newly cut—a GI-buzz trim. The side of his swollen, bluish face that she could see did not look familiar. The body was wedged firmly in the tough branches. She didn't try to move him. Queasy and heartsick, she climbed back up the bank to wait for Nella to return with help. While she waited, the first spatters of June rain began to fall.

Before long a farmer arrived with Nella. He hurried down the bank to take a look. Climbing back up, he said, "Body's been there awhile. Before I came down, I called the constable and a doctor." Even as he spoke, the constable arrived. In moments a military ambulance and a jeep sped down the hill and pulled up beside them. MPs had come with a doctor from the Govilon station hospital.

Nella was shaking, despite the warm day, so the doctor told Jean to sit with her in the ambulance while he went to examine the body. All the men disappeared over the riverbank. Soon one MP returned and climbed into the driver's seat. "I need to make a report. Your names and addresses, please."

They gave the information and then answered his other questions as best they could.

"Okay, ladies. I'm going to have my driver take you home in the jeep. I'll go along with the body in the ambulance. If we need more information, I know where to find you."

"Do you think there was foul play?" Jean asked.

He shook his head. "This is just routine. But if it should turn out that he was a victim of a crime, every detail you can remember will be important."

"I see," Jean said. Sitting close to Nella, she felt her shudder. This girl needed to go home. "How soon can your driver take us to Abergavenny?"

The soldier looked up from his notes. "Right now."

By the time they reached the manse, Nella insisted she was all right, and indeed her color had returned to normal.

So Jean rode back to Govilon in the jeep and reported for work. She had to do something to get the image of the drowned man out of her mind before bedtime.

The next day while Jean was on duty in the Red Cross office, Marge called. Her voice trembled with emotion. "I have bad news, but I thought you'd want to know. The drowning victim was Rufe Johnson. It seems he sneaked out at night. I didn't know he was missing until they told me he had drowned. He's not in my regular ward, you know. It's an apparent suicide. The nurses at the mental ward found a note with his personal things."

The news stunned Jean. "But he couldn't even walk to the river. . . ."

"Well . . . I guess I was right when I suspected that he could do more than he wanted us to know. And I was wrong about his mental condition. This is so hard, Jean. I feel I'm partly to blame...."

"No! Of course you're not. You know this can happen despite every precaution."

"I know you're right, but that's not how I feel. I got close to that kid ... I should have known ... but there are so many to watch over ... and he wasn't in my ward...."

After Marge hung up, Jean gulped and tried to keep from crying while on duty. *Poor angry, sad Rufe—so young. What a waste. What grief for his poor mother.* She wished she could write to her, but what could she say? *I met your son, and twice he talked to me and seemed all right, but* ... Like Marge, she felt that if she had tried harder to get in touch with him, he might still be alive.

Half an hour later, when she calmed down, it came to her that her Red Cross work with the patients served an urgent need for some of the men. Raising morale among the wounded could be as important as her journey into France to save Giselle. This was what Marge had tried to tell her.

Poor Marge. It was so difficult to recognize when a man like Rufe was thinking about suicide. And yet she felt to blame. No one could have guessed that he'd consider taking his life. Suddenly Jean remembered how his watchful eyes had reminded her of Georges. His steady gaze had betrayed discipline and confidence, not depression. How could he have suddenly become suicidal?

But if he didn't ... She brushed aside the idea that he had gone for a walk and had accidentally fallen in the river. From what she knew of Rufe, it seemed more likely that someone would have to have thrown him in. Jean shivered at the thought of murder. Then she unconsciously slipped into the alert, defensive mode of Marie Fauvre.

In London Giselle studied her face in the mirror. She was pleased with the reconstruction of her nose. Claude would scarcely notice a difference once the surgery scar faded.

Now that the Allies were fighting to liberate France, she had decided to stay in London a little longer for treatment of the remaining scars. It would be wonderful if Claude wouldn't have to see the worst of those either. She wouldn't let her guard down, though. She still had the soldiers with her constantly. She hoped with the presence of the Allies that Andre might have less need to learn the names of the leaders in the Resistance. Maybe he was lying low to await the outcome.

The girls had begged this morning to go out to a nearby park, and although Uncle Al assured her their bodyguard would make such a jaunt safe, she knew differently. Unless they could all be disguised, it was just too risky. Only one more surgery, then they would all go to the country. The children never had been inclined to pout, but she could see they were on the edge.

Remembering their frustration, she called, "Jacquie! Angie! Come sit in the sun by the window with me, and I'll read to you." Giselle walked to the parlor and pushed the window open to let in fresh air.

Angie brightened and ran to fetch the worn copy of *Alice in Wonderland* that Mrs. Jones had given them. She also brought her new dolls, gifts from Uncle Al, and settled them on the window seat between them.

But Jacquie hesitated, a concerned expression on her elfin face. "Will it make you too tired, Maman?"

Giselle shook her head vigorously. "No, no, sweetheart. I love reading to you. It makes me feel better faster!"

Jacquie smiled and settled beside Angie.

Giselle read to them until her voice grew hoarse, then she sat with them while they played with their dolls. The street below was quiet except for a pedestrian now and again. London was very different from sunny Lyon, but she rather liked the gentler light and warmth. It reminded her of Oregon. Even the bombed part of the city was more pleasant than occupied Lyon, because the people were free. Her heart ached for her compatriots, most of them still prisoners in their own country. The invasion seemed to be proceeding slowly. And her heart ached for Claude. In fact, her whole being ached. *Where is he, God? We are one, and half of me cries all the time for the sound of his voice, a glimpse of his smile, to be in his arms again. Dear God, keep him safe!*

As she watched the children, she clung to one thought: She and they had come through, and so would Claude. She knew it. She prayed he was feeling a breath of late spring wherever he was.

Suddenly she heard an odd humming sound, like the lowest

note on a giant pipe organ. Moments later a distant explosion made her jump. Their guard, Gil, rushed to the window.

"There was no air raid warning! But best to get away from the windows," he said.

He then grabbed the girls and carried them to the center of the room.

Before Giselle could move away, she heard the hum again. "What is that?"

He came back and peered out. "Don't know."

Then she saw it—a small plane with stubby wings, unlike any plane she'd ever seen, just above the rooftops. "Look!" Suddenly the hum stopped and right before her eyes the odd aircraft nosed down toward the city. It wasn't very high to start with, and it was about to crash nearby! She leaped to the girls, shoved them to the floor and tried to shield them with her body. In the next instant Gil landed on top of all of them.

The explosion was deafening.

Gil swore. "Big payload! Where's the RAF anyway? Letting it get through in broad daylight? We'd better get you to the shelter in the basement!" He jumped to his feet and lifted her up with one hand, and then they both helped the crying girls.

Giselle quickly brushed them off. "I'm sorry, Jacquie, Angie. Are you both all right? We didn't mean to hurt you."

They quieted but clung tightly to her hands as they hurried out of the apartment and down the three flights of stairs to the shelter.

By evening Giselle knew what it was. The Nazis had developed huge bombs with stubby wings, pilotless missiles powered by new ramjet engines. Hundreds had been launched over southern England, and although many had been shot down over open land, many more had fallen on country villages and in the city of London, killing people and leaving gaping craters.

When Uncle Al came home, Giselle met him at the door. "I have to take the children away from here as soon as possible."

He nodded. "You're right. I'll tell Captain Lloyd it's time for you to leave. And I'll alert Jean. She'll tell the family you will live with." He wrapped an arm around her shoulder. "I'll try to reach Lloyd tonight."

She tried to control her burgeoning fear but failed. "To have mindless machines bombing at random is more horrifying than bombs from planes."

"That's exactly what Hitler wants us to think."

"Well, I guess he has succeeded."

He hugged her close, and for a moment his fatherly gesture comforted her. "Try not to worry," he said. "Now that the fighter pilots know what they're dealing with, they'll do a better job of shooting down the bombs. But I'll get you out of London right away, hopefully tomorrow night."

Before bedtime the girls helped Giselle pack most of their clothes and a few games and toys. After they were asleep, she cleaned and oiled the Mauser and placed it back in her purse. Then she reached into the back of the wardrobe and pulled out a small bundle wrapped in a sweater. It was Jean's gun, which Giselle had carefully cleaned, oiled, and hidden in her clothes. Jean had been much too eager to get rid of the MAB.

It hadn't been difficult to lift the tiny weapon, holster and all, from Jean's pile of clothing and hide it while Jean bathed that first morning in England. Neither had it been difficult to assume innocence and help her search for it later when Jean tried to return it to Captain Lloyd at the debriefing. Giselle had hated lying, but England was not a safe place, not with Andre unaccounted for.

Now she placed the MAB in the bottom of her suitcase. She hoped she was wrong, but someday Jean might be glad to have the gun again.

CHAPTER TWENTY-SIX

At the end of Jean's day to work in the Abergavenny Red Cross office, just before mess call, Mary telephoned from the Gilwern station hospital. She sounded as if she'd been running. "Jean? I'm so glad you answered. I have news. We've admitted about a hundred new patients, from northern Italy again. I found out that's where the Nisei Combat Team is fighting. Some of them are here. Jean . . . Tom is here."

"Tom," Jean whispered, her voice as weak as her suddenly wobbly knees.

"Are you all right?" Mary asked. "Did you hear me?"

Jean cleared her throat. "Yes! How is he? Are his wounds bad?" She managed to keep her voice steady while inside she was crying, "No, no, not Tom!"

"His arm is all wrapped up from the shoulder down, and he took some shrapnel in his leg, but I don't think there's anything life threatening. He recognized me from when I taught school with you at Tulelake, and—I hope it's okay—I told him you were here too. He asked me to call you. He wants to see you."

Jean's rational thoughts swirled away like water down a drain. Her heart began to race. "I'll come as soon as I can get away. Can you get me into his ward after supper?"

"Can a duck quack? Meet me outside the staff office here at nineteen hundred hours, and I'll have everything arranged."

Suddenly Jean was torn between wanting to see Tom and dreading the emotional consequences. "Oh, Mary, I'm scared."

"If you don't want to see him, I'll just tell him you can't get away right now."

Jean caught her breath. "It's not that I don't want to. I want to too much."

"Trust yourself, kid. I don't know what you were into in that so-called 'war endeavors' the super mentioned, but knowing you, I can guess it took guts and self-control. Tom can't hurt you unless you let him. And I have to tell you, I think he needs to see you. He wasn't his usual arrogant self."

Jean bit her quivering lip. She'd been willing to face the Gestapo for Giselle. Surely she could control her emotions in front of Tom for his sake. "I'll be there at nineteen hundred."

She hung up but couldn't move. Her mind stalled in shock. Tom wounded. Tom here. Was he in pain? Would he be permanently disabled? Her reasoning began to come back. Why had he asked to see her tonight? She hardened her heart against any possibility that his feelings were more than the platonic friendship he had insisted upon. At the same time, she tried to close her mind against imagining how he looked, for always with the memory of his face came emotions she must throttle.

She hurried back to the rec hall to complete preparations for the evening movie.

At nineteen hundred, Jean hopped out of the personnel carrier in front of the staff office in Gilwern and waved good-bye to the driver. She would walk back or hitch a ride with someone else going that direction.

Mary stood waiting, as she'd promised. "No problem about you seeing him. I cleared it officially with the super and his doctor. Come on." She led the way up a long covered sidewalk, past the many rows of brick barracks that served as hospital wards. Far up the slope, near the edge of the complex, she stopped at a door. "He's in bed eight on the left side."

Jean waited. "Won't you come?"

"I think you need to see him alone. Just you two the first time. After that I'll do whatever you think best." Mary gave her a hug and then gently shoved her toward the door.

Inside the ward the rows of beds created a sea of white—white sheets, white bandages, white casts. Upon the sea floated the tan faces of soldiers from the Nisei Combat Team. Those closest to the door turned toward her. She smiled as she always did upon entering a ward, and her eyes moved swiftly to bed eight.

Tom waved his good hand—thank God, his right hand! She hurried to his bedside and stood there wordless. His face was thinner, and fine lines around his eyes telegraphed his pain.

She shaped her lips into a fresh smile. "Hello, again."

"Jeanie-with-the-Light-Brown-Hair." His low voice was steady, if not strong.

She reached for a chair, remembering as she placed it beside the head of his cot the time she'd been the one in a hospital bed, with double pneumonia, and he the one visiting. He, a hospital volunteer at the Tulelake Internment Camp, had roused her will to live when everyone else thought her case was hopeless. She closed her mind to the memory and took control of her fleeing voice. "I'm so glad to see you, but I never wanted to see you here."

He grinned. "I never wanted to meet under these circumstances either." Then he grew solemn and murmured, "You're more beautiful than ever. How can this be?"

The uncharacteristic vulnerability in his look and the warmth in his voice shook her resolve to stay only friendly. She told herself that wounds and feeling helpless did that to the strongest of men, and he probably was not aware of how fragile he was at this moment. She captured her straying emotions and teased him. "Your perception is distorted because you're flat on your back and at my mercy!"

He smiled again, but briefly.

Although she wanted to keep the conversation light, she had to know how he felt. "Are you in pain? Have the doctors examined you yet?"

"Not in much pain. They fixed me up pretty good, even at the front. Mostly my arm needs surgery. Bones shattered and all that. Then I should be good as new."

She burst out, "I prayed for you to stay safe."

He raised one eyebrow, and the etching of pain around his eyes softened. "I am safe. I'm here, aren't I? Sometime I may tell you what God has brought me through. Right now I don't want to think about the battlefront. . . . I just want to look at you." He studied her until she had to look away.

Too often he'd been able to guess what she was thinking, and right now she wanted to reach out and hold him in her arms and never let go. She was certain, for she knew his conflicts well enough by now, that once he was on his feet, he would push her away again. For a moment she wished she had not come to see him right away. Later might have been better for both of them.

"What about you, Jeanie? How are you?" he murmured.

The way he said her name was like a kiss. Her heart flip-flopped. "Me?" she said, fighting for poise. "I'm fine. Just fine." She glanced away at the bed across the aisle where a man lay with his leg propped up and in traction. The man's eyes were closed and his face pallid. Compared to him, Tom looked pretty well.

Tom said in an undertone, "He lost a lot of blood, but he's going to make it. How many of your patients have fallen in love with you, Jeanie?"

Involuntarily her eyes darted back to his. "None."

"I find this hard to believe." His smile was teasing, but his gaze was serious.

She grinned and straightened on her chair. "They're never here long enough."

"So you remain free of attachments."

She nodded, keeping a firm grip on the casual manner she'd achieved. The truth was, after these few moments with him, she knew she would never be free from her love for him. Without him she would carry a disability through life as real as any of the soldiers who had lost legs or arms or sight. But Tom must not know. At least not now, probably never. "Free as a bird. What about you?"

"I'm free too." He suddenly looked very tired. "Why did you stop writing to me?"

"I didn't stop writing. Your mail must not have caught up with you yet. I wrote as soon as I could after—You see, I left here for a couple of months to—Tom, this may sound like I'm brag-ging or something, but it was top secret, and I still can't tell you about it. . . . I was afraid you'd think I didn't want to write any-more."

"That's exactly what I did think. I didn't blame you. I know it was crazy to hope you'd want me for a friend."

"That's not true! I prayed for you every day. I wished I could have told you what I was doing, so you could have prayed for me."

He reached out with his good hand and caught her hand. "I did pray for you. I couldn't forget you."

His touch made her heart race. She longed to smooth his hair and kiss his lips, but instead she said, "I have to go now, and you need to rest."

His fingers tightened on hers. "Will you come see me again, Jeanie? I don't know how long I may be here."

"Of course. My station hospital is only about a mile away." She squeezed his hand. "Good night. Rest well."

At last he released her. "Good night then."

She left him and strode down the aisle. His words, "I don't know how long I'll be here," struck her like a dark prophecy and filled her with dread. She must find out right away exactly how serious his injuries were.

All the way to the door, she felt his eyes on her, but she could not look back to wave. It was a standing rule that no patient should ever see a Red Cross volunteer cry.

Two days later as the rising sun conquered the night over Wales, Giselle awakened in the front seat of the army auto Captain Lloyd had provided for her escape from London. She turned to check on the girls in the backseat. Gil, seated beside them, smiled and nodded a silent good-morning. Angie lay sleeping across his lap, and Jacquie slumped the other direction with her head resting against the side of the car.

Giselle returned Gil's smile and straightened to look at the land that would be their home for the duration of the war. It was hilly country. Farms spread out, flowing over the rolling contours. Hedgerows neatly separated field from field and field from pasture. They drove through a village, just a cluster of houses with a church in the center and a few small shops and a pub facing the highway. In a moment they left the village, and more farmland bordered the road.

A few minutes later the driver gestured toward the view before them.

The highway dipped into a broad valley surrounded by very

high conical hills. A river curved in the middle of the valley, and on the far side of the river, a town nestled against the gentle slope to the hills. She raised her eyebrows at the driver, and he mouthed, "Abergavenny."

She said aloud, "We'd best waken the children now." Turning, she called, "Jacquie! Angie! We're almost there. It's time to wake up!"

The children stirred and sat up, blinking.

After a moment, Jacquie said, "Will Aunt Jeanie meet us?"

"She said she would if she could get off work. We'll be staying with friends of hers."

They crossed a river and entered the outskirts of the town. A hill led down past a long row of old stone mansions. Giselle felt like an alien, which, of course, she was. The great houses, although obviously built by wealthy people, bore a look of stern frugality. Constructed of blocks of dark gray stone, the window frames and entries contrasted harshly, outlined with blocks of pale tan stone. The straight lines and squared corners gave a fierce appearance, so different from the warm stone, red tile roofs, and Italianate curves in much of the architecture in Lyon. But there were flowers everywhere despite the privations of war.

They turned to the right and went up a narrow street past a large church. The sign proclaimed it to be St. Mary Cathedral. The business district seemed to branch out on the left.

"Oh look, Maman! Horses pulling a wagon right in town," Angie exclaimed. A farmer's wagon, filled with milk cans, clopped up a side street.

"It's like a doll's town, it's so small," Jacquie remarked. Her face looked composed and thoughtful.

The driver, who had been stationed in Abergavenny until recently, told the girls, "This is a market town. All the farmers come here from the outlying villages to sell their animals and produce and to buy what they can't grow on their farms. Look. Down that street on the right are the stables for the farmers' horses. They park their wagons in town but take their horses to the stable to rest and eat. That way the farmers' wives can shop and easily bring purchases back to the wagon."

"This is not so much different from France, but the girls haven't seen many small towns," Giselle said.

A few blocks farther along, the driver slowed and stopped at the curb in front of a large gray-stone house. Creeping vines covered much of the front. The dooryard was a riot of color—rose bushes heavy with pink, red, white, and yellow blossoms, magenta hollyhocks, blue delphiniums, and other plants Giselle could not name. A fair-skinned woman with graying hair hurried out to greet them, followed by a pretty young woman. A toddler stood at the open door sucking on one finger.

The older woman cried, "Welcome, welcome! I'm Elizabeth MacDougall. And this is our daughter Nella Killian. Jean is coming, but she was delayed. We're so glad to have you and your girls." She turned to Angie and Jacquie with a warm smile. "I hope you'll be happy here in Abergavenny. We have a yard out back for playing with a swing and a spot for your own little garden if you wish."

The girls smiled shyly, but Giselle could tell they liked their hostess.

Angie spoke up first. "I like gardens. At Auntie Evyette's, I got to feed the chickens."

"We have a few chickens. You can help me with them. Livie is too small to gather the eggs. But do come in. You must be tired from that long train ride." She led them inside. "Nella, please show the men to the side door so they can carry the luggage directly up. When they've finished, breakfast will be on the table for everyone. Giselle, you come with me, and I'll show you and the children where you can wash up."

"Thank you. That sounds wonderful after driving all night."

"Good. This way then."

The girls paused to talk to Livie, but the baby refused to say hello. She smiled, however.

Before they sat down to eat, Jeanie arrived, breathing as if she had run the whole way from the hospital, wherever it was. Giselle rushed to hug her.

Jeanie held her tightly and then backed away to hold her at arm's length. "It's so good to see you! And your nose! It looks great!"

What with her fear of the bombs and of being seen by Andre whenever she left Uncle Al's apartment, Giselle had forgotten all about the success of her surgery. Grateful to be reminded, she rubbed the straight bridge of her nose with one finger. "They did do a good job on it, didn't they? And you look so well! This country life must agree with you."

"I guess it does. Better than London for sure. How is Uncle Al? I hate that he's there with all those bombs flying in."

"He says it's his job to stay in London."

"Yes. He would."

Elizabeth then interrupted. "Well, now, you two come have your breakfast while it's hot. One of our parishioners brought us a bit of bacon to go with our eggs and muffins."

"It smells wonderful," Jean said.

Giselle introduced Jean to the men, and then Elizabeth introduced her husband, Reverend Ian MacDougall, who had just come in. He was fair like Nella, but his curly hair was mostly gray.

They sat down to eat, and Reverend MacDougall thanked God for the food and for his guests. He was a man of few but well-chosen words. Giselle listened to his calming voice and felt as if she had stepped into a very different world, one free of terror. She instantly cautioned herself. She must not let down her guard.

After breakfast and good-byes to the men, Giselle followed Jean upstairs to unpack. The girls started down the outside stairs to explore the backyard. Giselle's heart jumped in alarm. "Wait! Don't go out alone. In a few minutes we can go with you!"

"Oh, let them go, Giselle. They're safe here," Jeanie insisted. "Besides, look. We can see them from the windows, and the yard is enclosed by a high stone wall."

Giselle walked to the window and scanned the yard, all of which was visible. "All right, girls. Go play. Just stay in the yard where I can see you."

As she and Jeanie unpacked, putting clothes in drawers and wardrobes, she frequently returned to the window to check on the children.

While they worked, Jeanie chattered on like a schoolgirl. "You're going to love the MacDougalls. Nella's a widow. Her husband was killed in action in the RAF, so she came home with her baby, Olivia. Elizabeth and Nella have made this apartment so cozy. Last time I saw it, it didn't look so homey. It was built originally for visiting missionaries and other guests to the parish. The MacDougalls really brightened up at the idea of having you and the children."

"How can I thank them enough for taking us in like this?"

"No need to feel that way. You'll see. They truly live by the golden rule. I've never known such happy Christians . . . well, almost never."

"The Japanese pastor you knew at Tulelake?"

"Yes. Oh! I haven't told you yet! You'll get to meet Tom too. He's here!"

"Your Tom here? In Abergavenny?"

"Yes. He was wounded in northern Italy and arrived just a few days ago."

Giselle couldn't tell whether Tom's arrival had brought happiness or pain, but Jeanie seemed more like her old self. All the tension from those days in France was gone. She listened to her cousin and wondered, *Have we truly left danger behind?* She went again to look out the window at the children playing below with the baby, Livie.

Spying her big leather purse on the divan, she picked it up, pressing the comforting bulk of the concealed Mauser against her ribs. If it was not safe here, she was as well prepared as possible. She wouldn't mention having the gun right now. It would only worry Jeanie. She took her purse to the smaller bedroom, which she had chosen for herself, and laid it on the bed.

When the unpacking was finished, Giselle settled into an overstuffed chair by the window. Jeanie took the window seat beside her, tucking her feet up as she used to do when they were in her childhood tree house on Uncle Al's farm. Giselle smiled at her memory of little Jeanie in pigtails, thinking big thoughts. Now she had become a strong woman, still inclined to think big thoughts . . . and to do big things. She deserved the best. "Now, cousin, tell me about Tom. Is his presence here good news for you or bad?"

Jeanie straightened and pulled her knees to her chin while she gazed out the window. Her face, in the soft light of the room, looked very young and troubled. She sighed, and Giselle knew the answer.

"I was . . . overjoyed to see him alive, even though wounded. And then I was scared. I didn't want to hurt anymore, and I'd been able to back away from craving to be with him. Actually, when I was with you in France, when I had to keep my mind on how to survive, I almost got over missing him." She pressed her lips together and shook her head. "Now I think I probably never will. With him here, so close, I almost live for the moments when I can be with him." She no longer looked girlish.

"I'm so sorry. Does he ... is he aware of how you feel?" Giselle asked.

"No! I'm sure he doesn't guess. I'm a good actress."

"Will he be here long?"

"A little longer than some patients. Probably a couple of months. His left arm needed orthopedic surgery, and we happen to have a fine surgeon at Gilwern, so they did that here instead of sending him to a larger hospital. This means, also, that he's been judged fit to return to the battlefront." Jeanie turned from watching the girls. "You haven't said, so I assume you haven't heard anything about Claude."

Giselle shook her head. There was nothing to say that Jeanie didn't already know. Jeanie would understand her silence.

CHAPTER TWENTY-SEVEN

Jean tore herself away from Giselle in time to have supper in the mess hall. Although she'd been given the day off to meet her cousin and help her get settled, she had arranged for the entertainment that night at the rec hall—a group of singers from Crickhowell—and she needed to be there to meet them and to introduce them at the beginning of the program. Mary was bringing a few ambulatory patients from Gilwern. Unfortunately Tom was not one. He was only three days past his surgery and still had to stay in bed.

That evening, once the program was in process, she left Betty to take care of the closing and hitched a ride to Gilwern. She wanted to tell Tom that Giselle had safely arrived. Well, that was the excuse. She hated for a day to go by without seeing him.

From the gate she went straight to his ward. Inside, the nurse on duty nodded at her and went back to sorting and labeling bedtime medications. The staff had come to accept her comings and goings without questions. She started down the center aisle between the beds. Several patients greeted her, and she stopped to chat for a moment.

At last she was at Tom's bedside. He gave her a morphine-sedated smile.

"Hi," he said.

"Hi, yourself. How are you doing?"

He grinned wider. "Flying high. If I fall asleep on you, feel free to leave."

"Sure. I take it you aren't hurting much."

"Right. So did Giselle get here okay?"

"Yes. She's looking so good. Her nose is back to normal. I never thought it could be. The children seem happy to be here, poor tykes. They've been through so much."

"War's a rotten thing for kids. Makes you want to go out and shoot someone, all right."

Jean didn't quite know what to say to that. It wasn't a typical Tom remark. She waited.

"Jeanie, you're an angel. You're the only good thing that has happened to me in this whole mess. I'd like to fly away with you to some other world where we could—"

Her heart lurched, but she laughed lightly, interrupting him. "You really are under the influence of your medicine."

He grinned easily. "Yes, I s'pose I am. Have you ever heard that morphine works like truth serum?"

"No." She changed the subject. "Do you know how soon you can get up? I really want you to meet Giselle."

He raised his eyebrows. "No one says. Just like the army. You find out where you're going when you get there. I figure I'll give it a try tomorrow, whether or not anyone approves."

From that point on their conversation fell into impersonal subjects until Tom's eyes closed in drugged sleep.

She got up and tiptoed away. Outside the ward she paused and looked up at the clear sky, still pale from the summer sunset. Tom had revealed feelings for her that he most certainly would not acknowledge when he was well. Thoughtfully she went on down the walkway to the entrance. She'd been dangerously close to taking his ravings seriously. How long would she be able to maintain this so-called friendship without her true feelings spilling out?

The singers were on their last number when Jean arrived at the rec hall. As she'd hoped, no one had missed her. She was able to applaud and then see her guests to their cars. As she waved to the last of them, Betty touched her arm. "The super said to tell you your cousin called, quite upset. She wants you to call her. Super said you're free to go if Giselle needs you."

"Oh dear! I hope the children are okay. I'll call her right away. See you later, and thanks!"

In the office she dialed the three-digit number of the manse. "Elizabeth? I got Giselle's message. What's wrong?"

"She's right here. I'll let her tell you."

In the next moment Giselle's voice came on. She sounded as if she were on the edge of hysteria. "Jeanie, he's here! He followed us here. No one believes me. Please come!"

"Giselle, who's there? What do you mean?"

"Andre. I saw him again just a few minutes ago in the garden. Jeanie, I'm so afraid for the children. I have to get away from here. Please come get us."

Jeanie's heart took off in a race of terror to match Giselle's. "I'll be there in a few minutes. Stay downstairs with the Mac-Dougalls. You'll be all right. I'm coming!"

She ran to the Nissen hut and told Betty she was going. Then she ran to the transport depot and requested an ambulance to drive into town, explaining she didn't know how long she would be. As she'd supposed, it was no problem, for no trains were scheduled to arrive.

At the manse she hurried to the backyard and looked all around before knocking on the front door. Nella opened, and Giselle, white-faced, rushed to her. "Jeanie, where can we go? Is there someplace else?"

"I have to think. First, come sit and tell me what happened." She led her to a sofa and sat beside her. "Do the girls know?"

"No. They were already asleep. I went to pull the window shade before turning on the light. I saw him at the far edge of the garden ... in the shadows near the swing. If he hadn't moved, I'd have missed him. He must have guessed I saw him, because he hurried out the back gate."

Nella quietly set a hot cup of tea beside each of them. "Immediately when we heard her report, Daddy and I ran out to have a look. The only thing we found was the gate ajar, and Daddy knew he'd latched it before supper."

So it wasn't Giselle's nerves. Someone had been in the back garden.

Giselle pressed her palm against her forehead as if her head ached. "When we came here we were so careful. I never saw the hint of a car following us."

Jean glanced at Nella, hoping Giselle would not reveal anything about Andre's threats.

Giselle said no more, but dropped her face to her hands and

slowly shook her head. "I so wanted the girls to be able to play safely, as children should."

In all they'd been through together, Jeanie had not seen Giselle so heartbroken. Feeling helpless, she leaned over and patted her shoulder.

They all jumped when Reverend MacDougall threw open the front door and called, "Well, I've found the culprit." He stamped into the parlor. Behind him a large man stepped into the light, filling the room with his unusual size. "'Tis Robert." He took the man's arm and led him over to Giselle. "This is Madame Munier, Robert. The little girls belong to her. Robert," he explained, "has been a lifelong member of our congregation, and he has a vocation to care for the manse garden. Since war came, he also patrols at night. He's our security guard, aren't you, Robert?"

The big man nodded vigorously but didn't speak. He was obviously simple and childlike. Jean sighed in relief, but when she looked at Giselle, she saw no such reaction. Was she afraid of this mentally disabled man?

Reverend MacDougall seemed bent on reassuring Giselle, and Jean was glad he saw that she was still afraid. He told her, "Robert said he was in the yard to check the swing to make sure the rope is strong for the wee ones. He's sorry he frightened you."

The big man nodded vigorously. "Yeh, lady. Sorry!"

Giselle studied him for a moment and then gently asked, "Robert, did you see any other man near the back garden?"

He shifted from one big foot to the other. "No, not anybody. Sorry."

"That's fine, Robert. I know you meant no harm."

The MacDougalls visibly relaxed, then Elizabeth said, "Come now, Robert, and have a spot of tea with us."

He smiled and sat down on an overstuffed chair. Nella fetched him a cup that looked like a doll's dish in his huge hands.

After a few minutes of casual chatting, Giselle said, "Jeanie, will you come up with me while I check on the girls?"

"Sure thing."

"We'll say good-night, then," Giselle said. "I am tired. Thank you all for calming my fears."

When they got upstairs, Giselle peeked into the girls' room

and then led Jeanie into her bedroom, keeping the light turned off. "Come over here by the window and look."

Jeanie peered down into the back garden. The whole of it was visible. It was dark but light enough to see the various shapes of plants and trees. The longer she stared, the better she could see.

"He was over there, just under the shadow of the big tree. I wish I could be sure it was only Robert." Giselle stared thoughtfully at the dark scene below. Finally she murmured, "I think the man I saw was bigger than Andre, and he did move with a lumbering gait, not swift and confident, as Andre moves." She turned to Jeanie. "It had to be Robert."

Jeanie could not let go of her anxiety. Standing there, she felt she'd seen with Giselle's eyes the horror she must have experienced. Needing reassurance, she asked, "You're very sure that no one could have seen you leave Uncle Al's last night?"

Giselle gave her a troubled look. "As sure as I can be."

They both stared out the window again in uneasy silence.

In the morning Jean felt more objective. As she went about her morning duties, her fears for Giselle the night before seemed extreme now. How, after all, could Andre locate her in London, even if he had managed to sneak into England?

Giselle was a professional at covering her trail and had not detected anyone following her here. Surely seeing Robert in the dark back garden had conjured up an image of what she'd feared most in France. Shell-shocked soldiers went through waking nightmares like this.

Later when Jean called the manse, Giselle admitted she was almost afraid to let the children out of her sight. Hoping to lift her spirits, Jean said, "How about coming to meet Tom this afternoon? He has asked about you. I can get transportation, if you can come."

Giselle hesitated a little. "I'd like that. So would the girls. Will they allow children?"

"I think so. He's to be up in a wheelchair today. We could meet him for a few minutes in the rec hall."

Jean arranged for Eddy to pick up Giselle after lunch and for Tom to be in the rec hall when they came. Then she and Betty set off across the pastures to gather pine needles for a handcraft project for the men.

Jean had woven a miniature sample basket from the needles she'd stuffed in her pockets the day she and Nella had discovered Rufe's body. The super agreed it would make a nice project for the men.

Now she went first to the farmhouse to ask permission. In his thick Welsh brogue, the farmer told them to take as many pine needles as they wished, so they hiked down the hill to the old stone barn and stuffed their cloth bags.

Back at the rec hall during the hour before lunch, Jean showed several of the ambulatory patients how to make baskets. They laughed and accused her of trying to turn them into Camp Fire Girls. Still, they picked up the material and began to work with it. Their continued laughter gave Jean a good feeling. She decided to take her sample basket to show Mary, along with enough pine needles to fashion another sample basket. Mary was always on the lookout for new crafts for the men at Gilwern.

After lunch when Eddy arrived in a jeep with Giselle and the children, Jean was relieved to see Giselle looking more relaxed than she'd sounded on the phone in the morning. Maybe she had calmed down after more time to think. The girls chattered and giggled as usual.

When they reached the Gilwern rec hall and stepped inside, Jean's heart began to gallop with nervous excitement. She so wanted the two people she loved best to like each other. Tom, seated in a wheelchair beside a table, was watching for them. He waved, smiling in the warm way Jean loved.

"You never told me how handsome he is," Giselle whispered.

Jean couldn't respond, for they now were within his hearing.

When introductions were complete, Tom said, "Do you young ladies know how to play checkers?"

"*Oui*—I mean, yes!" Angie exclaimed. She glanced sideways at her sister. "Well, Jacquie knows best, and she tells me what to do."

"Good! I had to fight off ten men to save this game for you." He set the board up on the table beside his chair and handed the box of checkers to Jacquie.

She smiled a Mona Lisa smile, her eyes never leaving his face. Jean detected a glimmer of hero worship in her gaze. "Thank you, sir."

"Please call me Tom. I have a little brother near your age."

She grinned and blushed.

He helped them start the game and then turned to Giselle. "I've heard so much about you that I feel I already know you. I prayed for your safety. And I'm still praying for Claude."

Jean recognized the same surprise on her cousin's face that she herself had felt when she first heard Tom talk about prayer. His manner was utterly unselfconscious, startling in a man who was not a minister.

"Thank you. I really appreciate that." Giselle glanced at the girls and said quietly, "We're still waiting to hear from him."

Tom's face softened in sympathy. "It's a hard way to go," he murmured. He also watched the children. "But it looks like they're doing just fine."

Giselle nodded.

Then Jean said, "Why don't you tell her about your family, Tom. I'd like to hear the latest news too."

So while the children played their game, Tom reminisced. Jean sat in rapt attention, a silent observer, analyzing every word and nuance of emotion passing between Tom and Giselle. In a few moments she decided they were responding as warmly to each other as she had hoped. So she relaxed and simply enjoyed being with the two people she loved most in the whole world. Well, there was Uncle Al too, and Grandmother, and Mary, and Elizabeth and Nella and Livie. . . . She smiled inwardly. She loved them all, but to Giselle and to Tom she was bonded as if . . . as if they were part of her. She didn't know if this was good or bad, but it was true.

The girls finished their game and came back to stand beside Giselle.

"We're all done," Angie said. "Do you have a different game? Jacquie always wins checkers."

Tom laughed and shook his head. "I'm sorry. That's about all I could find for you."

Jean suddenly remembered the little basket. "Here, Angie. Would you like to learn how to make something like this?"

"Oh, a doll's basket. May I have it?"

"Angie, you didn't even say please," Jacquie corrected.

"Well, despite that, she may have it. Jacquie, I'll show you how to make one. I brought these for Mary, but I can bring more to her later. Look, it starts like this." She tied a piece of linen thread around some needles and began to braid and add needles.

"Where did you learn to do that?" Tom asked. "And where did you find the pine needles?"

"In Camp Fire Girls and out on a farm below Govilon," she answered in order. "Nella says the pine trees on that farm are the only evergreens in the whole valley."

Jacquie looked up from trying to braid the needles. "The only place? What if I need more to finish my basket?"

"I'll take you to visit the farm. Actually I'll need to get more anyway. Would you like to go for a hike soon?"

"Oh, Maman, may we? Please?"

"We'll see. Aunt Jeanie is pretty busy with her work." Giselle lost her smile. Jean could tell the anxiety had returned.

Angie held the basket up on one finger and said, "When we get back to the manse, I will take Sybil—that's my new doll— out to the garden and let her gather flowers in her new basket."

Jean glanced at her watch. "Oops! We do have to go. I'm sorry, girls. I wasn't watching. I meant to give you a warning. Now we must hurry."

Tom leaned forward and shook Giselle's hand. "Thanks for coming. It's been a pleasure to meet you at last." Then he took Jean's hand. "Bring her back again, Jeanie. Second to you, she and these young ladies are the best medicine I've had in days."

His grip was strong, but when he stopped smiling she saw tension lines form around his eyes. His pain medicine must be wearing off. It made her ache to just return his smile when really she wanted to hold him in her arms and— She stopped her thoughts with a sarcastic rebuke. *Stupid romantic! As if your embrace could soothe away pain.*

On the way to the parking lot, Giselle said, "I really like your Tom."

Jacquie agreed in her serious voice. "Me too, Aunt Jeanie."

Angie piped up, "Maman, how is he Aunt Jeanie's Tom? Can't he be our Tom too?"

"Friends are to share," Jean said, smoothing Angie's hair where the fine blond strands had slipped from her braid and framed her face. "Of course you can have him for your friend too."

Eddy was waiting with the jeep, as she had requested. They climbed aboard and all the way to Abergavenny the girls smiled, squinting into the wind and holding on with a giggle when Eddy hit a pothole in the road. Jean laughed with them, thanking God again for helping her to bring them to England.

When they reached the manse, the children dashed for the back garden and the swing. Jean glanced at Giselle, but she didn't call them back.

As if responding to her thoughts, Giselle said, "I've been thinking all day. I must give them some freedom, or they'll become victims of my fear. I'll just have to watch over them without their knowing."

Jean gave her a quick hug. "I know it's difficult for you, but I truly believe you and the girls are safe here. It just takes a while to let the fact soak in."

"I hope you're right," Giselle said. "Excuse me, but I really want to go up and sit where I can see the backyard. Can you stay awhile?"

Jean shook her head. "I have to get back." Knowing that Giselle had to live with the memory of Andre's threats, Jean wished she had been more sympathetic.

CHAPTER TWENTY-EIGHT

After Jeanie left, Giselle entered through the side door and ran up the stairs to her apartment. She hurried to the window seat. Jacquie was pushing Angie on the swing. *Oh, Claude, if only you were here, you would know what to do. Are we safe? How can I ever know?*

Claude's answer popped into her mind so clearly, she could almost hear his voice. *"You cannot know; therefore, assume the worst."*

So she went downstairs and asked to take Livie out to play with the girls. Then she sat to watch over them all. Obviously Livie needed someone out with her, so no one would wonder about her staying out with Jacquie and Angie, big as they were.

In the ensuing days and nights, she never again saw any furtive figures in the dark. She never detected a hint of anyone following her or even noticing her when she went shopping for Elizabeth. Gradually, while she stayed out with the children, the warm sun eased the knots of fear in her back and neck. Slowly the gentle ebb and flow of homey activities, interspersed with the worship services at the Presbyterian church, relaxed her. She helped Elizabeth with household chores, cared for Livie so Nella could run errands, and worked with her girls in their victory garden. A few times she actually had to remind herself that danger could lurk behind the quaint stone wall or in the deep shadows of the garden at night.

Also, to her surprise, she found herself falling in love with the Welsh people and with Abergavenny. She wondered if Claude

would consent to living here awhile after the war was over. He probably would need the healing this green valley offered more than she did. She let herself daydream a little and imagined herself teaching French in an Abergavenny school.

One day in late July while on an errand for the hospital, Jean stopped at the manse and found Giselle on her knees in the garden, pulling weeds from around a row of carrots. The children were playing with their dolls and Livie under the big shade tree.

"Aha!" Jean called. "You are getting as sun-tanned as a movie star. You must live out here."

Giselle looked up and smiled. "What better place to live?" She stood up. "I'm ready for a break. Let's go put on the teakettle." Turning to the girls, she called, "Jacquie, Angie, I'm going in now. Keep an eye on Livie and stay in the yard where I can see you."

"Yes, Maman. We will," Jacquie said. Then she looked up and spied Jean. "Aunt Jeanie! I finished my basket. It's too big for my doll, so I'm going to use it myself. It's on the little table in our bedroom."

"Wonderful! I'll go look at it."

As they walked indoors, Giselle said, "I still find it hard to go in and leave them outside. I wonder if I shall ever lose this dread."

Jean wondered too, but aloud she said, "Someday this constant fear will be like a bad dream. Really it will."

Giselle didn't answer. Upstairs she went immediately to the window to check on the children.

Jean kept her word and went to see Jacquie's basket. She picked it up and brought it out to the kitchen for a closer inspection in better light. "You know, she did as well on this as any adult."

"I thought so too. She enjoys working with her hands, so I've started teaching her how to knit."

Jean sat down at the kitchenette table while Giselle poured her tea. Giselle then sat down and handed Jean the tin of milk. "I've been thinking a lot about Claude today ... wondering if he's been trying to get in touch with me. He'd have no idea that I escaped to England.... I've been thinking ... when he can't find me in Lyon, will he think I am dead?"

Jean reached across the small table and squeezed Giselle's hand. "I pray he's believing you're alive, just as you're believing he's alive. Oh, Giselle, how do you stand it?"

"I don't very well. I struggle to stay sane. But I have to for the girls. I pray all the time. Even though I can't understand how God can watch over one man more than others, still I pray. Even when I feel I don't believe in God, I pray."

"Me too." Jean silently considered the uncomfortable fact that German wives and sweethearts were praying too. Surely Hitler had not erased faith in God from the whole nation.

In the quiet pause, they each took sips of tea. Then Giselle said, "Jeanie, what about you and Tom? I saw him looking at you like a man in love. Has he said anything?"

Jean pulled her thoughts back to herself. "No. At first he hinted at more than friendship, but I kept him at a distance. Hospital patients are prone to be overly emotional while they're flat in bed. I couldn't let him say or do something he'd regret after he felt better."

"For whose sake? His or yours?"

For the first time in ages, Giselle angered Jean. She bit her lower lip and looked down into her cup.

Giselle chuckled. "Jeanie, you look just like you did when you were six years old and got mad at me and Jimmy."

Jean simmered for a moment and then relented. "Sorry. I hate to admit I was thinking of myself. I just don't want to be rejected again."

"Dear cousin of mine, if you love Tom, you should take him to some quiet place where you can both forget the war for a few hours. Then let him say what he wants. And don't push him away."

Jean's heart raced with hope and then with fear. She shook her head. "No. I'm done with trying to make things happen."

In Govilon the next day, a new trainload of wounded soldiers filled the hospital wards. Many of the men needed small attentions that the nurses couldn't give, so the Red Cross women worked overtime. With frustration Jean realized Tom soon would be strong enough to return to duty, and she couldn't visit him as frequently as before.

The longer she went without seeing him, the more Giselle's suggestion tantalized her—the idea of spending time alone with him. She wished she could, but there was no way, no time.

One day, however, her supervisor called her into the office first thing in the morning. "Jean, that camera shop in Swansea has received another used movie projector. The owner called and asked if we would like it for the boys in the wards. I've managed to commandeer an ambulance, but no driver. Can you drive a British vehicle?"

"Yes. I've driven one a few times. In fact, they make driving on the left side of the road easier."

"Good. You remember the shop near the waterfront on the road that goes out toward Cardiff?"

"Yes. I can find it all right."

"You're really due more than a day off, but make this trip leisurely if you wish. We'll get along. Just be back here by supper."

"Well, thanks! This will be a pleasant change. Thank you." She took the slip of paper from the super and tucked it into her jumper pocket.

"That's your transportation out at the curb. Don't change your clothes. Your Red Cross uniform will be your credentials, as well as the note. Be sure to convey my appreciation to the man."

"I will. And thanks again."

She ran to the Nissen hut for a sweater. One never knew how it would be along the water's edge in Swansea, and she had in mind to walk on the beach or maybe just sit in the sun for an hour.

Back at the ambulance, she climbed in, stowed her sweater behind her, and turned the ignition key. The engine rumbled to life. Cautiously she put the gearshift in low and eased up on the clutch. The vehicle lunged forward, and with a few adjustments between braking and accelerating, it rolled, or more accurately, it leaped out of the parking area toward the paved road, which ran toward Abergavenny one direction and Gilwern the other way.

At the stop sign she cranked the wheel to the left and headed for Gilwern, batting away each negative thought as it came.

They'll never let Tom go on such short notice. . . .

But it's worth a try. . . .
They won't let him go with only me.
You don't know that!
He hasn't even been released for an outing yet. . . .
Still she drove on, unwilling to give up hope.

At the hospital she ran to the administration office and asked if she could search for Mary. Mary always knew how to work things out. In a few minutes she found her in the rec hall assisting ambulatory patients who wanted to write letters home. Mary looked up, waved, and then came to the door.

Jean blurted, "Do you think I could get permission to take Tom out for the day? I'm driving to Swansea to pick up a movie projector."

"If you'll take over for me here, I'll find the doctor in charge and ask. Come on in." She led Jean to a table with four men sitting around it. "Hey, guys, this is my friend Jean. I've been called out for a few minutes, and she's here to help you until I get back."

"Hello, Jean! Where have you been all my life?"

"Knock it off, Hilmer. Can't you see she's my type?"

"Sorry, boys, I'm already taken." She'd long since learned this was the most effective answer to flirting.

"Okay, you wolves, back off. I need this lady to write me a letter." A man whose fingertips barely showed beyond bandages shoved a piece of paper across the table, and Jean began to write for him. The others wisecracked and teased, but obviously they were buddies, willing to let him be first.

Finally Mary popped in. "Hey, Jean! It's okay! Tom will meet you at the office. Good thing he's been up and walking around for several days. The doc says the trip will do him good."

Jean stood. "Bye, men. Your regular cheerleader is back." She gave Mary a hug on the way out. "Thanks, pal. I owe you."

At the office Tom stood waiting. She hadn't seen him in uniform since they'd parted months ago in the United States. Her heart did flip-flops, and she hurried to his side. Up close he looked too thin.

"Are you sure you're up to a long day out?"

He laughed. "I'm sure. My doctor is sure. Do you want a note from him saying it's okay?"

Laughing with him, she said, "It's just that you don't know how I drive."

"I know these army vehicles, and you can't make them ride much worse than normal."

"Okay. I parked over here." She led the way and climbed into the driver's seat.

He got in without having to use his recovering left arm. She silently blessed the British for making their roads and vehicles "backward." She suspected a U.S. ambulance with the opposite side for passengers would have made the climbing in more difficult for him.

"How is your arm?"

"Doc says all it needs now is exercise to strengthen it. I just have to go at it gradually." He held his hand out palm up and flexed and straightened his fingers. "I've been typing. Pretty poor typing, but the fingers all function."

She reached for the key to turn it on. "You still plan to be a journalist after the war?"

He nodded. "Yep."

She turned on the engine, and with a few abrupt jumps forward—which doubled Tom over with laughter—she herded the ambulance up the hill to the main road and turned toward Newport.

The country road had deteriorated from the constant traffic of heavy military trucks. Although she tried to dodge potholes, she hit one with a bone-jarring jolt. They both flew up in the air. Jean yelled over the noisy motor, "You doing okay?"

Tom grinned and made an A-okay sign with his hand. "I'm fine."

He looked fine. In fact, he looked delighted.

Jean couldn't resist the feeling of their being on a date. She gave in to a giddy sense of happiness. The bright sunshine and the warm wind blowing in the window felt wonderful. It was difficult to talk over the roar of the engine. Of necessity their conversation remained a matter of yelling back and forth in monosyllables. But thanks to her kindly super, they would have time to stop and really talk.

At last they came down out of the mountains, and Newport lay before them. In the city, she turned to the right at the main intersection and drove west until they came to Swansea. On the far western edge of town, near a row of ancient buildings, she spied the shop. Pointing, she yelled, "There it is."

Jean pulled across the highway and parked. "Coming in with me?"

"Sure thing."

It took only a few minutes to acquire the projector, give proper thanks, and stow it in the back of the ambulance.

On the other side of the road lay a beach and smooth water. It looked like a sea but was really Bristol Channel, which connected the sea to the wide estuary of the Severn River. No waves today, just a rising and falling tide, but she longed for a short walk on the beach. She made a U-turn and parked on the seaward side of the road. Despite army trucks and various British lorries rumbling by, it felt peaceful to sit and look at the water with gulls soaring and diving overhead.

"Want to walk on the beach?" he asked.

"Yes! I wasn't sure if you did."

They climbed down a low embankment to the sand. The tide was out, and the wet sand was very fine and brown. Tiny shells lay exposed. Jean picked up one.

"That's a cockleshell," Tom said.

"Reminds me of a nursery rhyme. Did you learn nursery rhymes when you were little?"

" 'Fraid not. We heard family stories. My folks left all of their brothers and sisters in Japan, so they told us about our aunts and uncles and grandparents, and what life was like in Japan. They wanted us to know and remember, but they also really wanted us to grow up American."

Jean put the shell in her jumper pocket and picked up a stick. She couldn't resist digging a hole to see how fast it would fill. It filled fast.

Tom watched, grinning. "The water table is right under our feet."

She nodded, suddenly feeling uneasy. "This isn't anything like an Oregon beach. It almost looks threatening."

"I think it is." Tom nodded toward a soldier marching toward them from an army truck that had parked behind their ambulance.

Jean straightened up.

The soldier called, "Don't you know this beach is off limits?"

309

When he drew close, his glance took in Tom's staff sergeant bars and the bandage still showing around his left wrist. "Sorry, Sergeant. I guess you're new here. Nobody is allowed to walk the beach."

"Thanks for telling us, Corporal. We'll get right back to where we belong." He took Jean's hand, and they walked hand in hand back to the ambulance. His touch was firm and caring. Jean felt her emotional armor slip.

Getting into the driver's seat, Jean said, "Well, so much for that outing. We should have asked him where we could find a good lunch."

"What about a pub?"

"A good bet for some filling food."

Before they reached the downtown, they stopped at an old black and white pub, the kind with timbers making a jigsaw pattern on the front gable. Inside, Jean was the only woman. Tom ordered hot tea and the sandwich of the day for each of them, which turned out to be made of slabs of yellow cheese. They sat in a booth by a window that would have looked out on the water if the black-out shutters were taken away. They were only partially opened, permitting a narrow, contracted glimpse instead of a view.

Jean glanced up at the low ceiling and dark oak beams still showing the ax marks of the craftsman. A sign over the bar said the pub had been built in A.D. 978. "I can imagine knights sitting here. And sailing ships out there. It boggles my mind to see a place so old still in use. My hometown was only one hundred years old in 1940! And I doubt that there are many original buildings left in Salem."

"The New World," Tom mused. "I can't even imagine what it meant to my dad to come to America where things were so different and free. We enjoy the fruits of other men's labors, and like rich kids, we don't appreciate the cost to the people who came before us." He fell silent, staring out the half-covered window.

She didn't want him to stop talking. "When the war is over and you are a journalist, where do you think you want to live?"

"Oregon. I suppose I'll have to start in Portland. Try to get on with the *Oregon Journal* or the *Oregonian*. But as soon as I can get the money, I'll start my own newspaper."

"In Portland?"

"Maybe. I'd rather be in a small town, but it won't be easy for small-town folks to accept a Jap publisher."

She flinched at the derogatory name so casually crossing his lips. "By the time you're ready to have your own paper, maybe you'll be pleasantly surprised."

He smiled sadly and shook his head. "You are determined to envision what you want the world to be instead of admitting the truth. Come down, Jeanie, to the earth on which I stand." His eyes hardened with anger. "While we were in training in Mississippi, there were comments every time we went into town about 'dirty yellow Japs.' My buddies ended up in the stockade for defending themselves against unprovoked attacks. We were trained by Caucasians. We were sent overseas under white officers despite the fact that numerous men in our division were fully qualified for officer training. We are American citizens, but we've been treated like enemy aliens. How can you think it will be different after the war?"

Her heart sank. This was not the direction she wanted the day to go. "Aren't you fighting to show you're loyal Americans?"

"Yes. But even if we succeed in preserving our honor, we're still the wrong color, and we've come from the wrong nation."

"Then why do you want to get into something as confrontational as running your own newspaper? Why don't you be an orchardist like your father?"

"You know me, Jeanie. I like a good fight."

"You mean a fight for good."

He reached over and clasped her hand. "Sweet little Jeanie. Trying to put the best light on everything, even me!" He squeezed her hand and kept it imprisoned in his. "I lost my two closest buddies in the battle for Italy. They risked everything because they were fighting for their honor and for the honor of their families. I closed the eyes of one and gathered up the pieces of the other for burial. By the time a grenade finally got me, I was covered with more of their blood than my own." He stared at his hand over hers with an expression of agony. "I wanted to die with them. I hated the Japanese code of honor almost as much as I hated the war."

She didn't know what to say. To say anything would sound trite, to her own ears at least. She hoped he didn't want her to look away from his pain. She couldn't. She had to know as much of him as he would reveal.

He straightened his shoulders but kept hold of her hand. "When I came to Wales and found you here, my thinking straightened up. I'm willing, no, I long to go back to the battle, but to fight for freedom, not for honor. But if I live to be a hundred, I'll probably never stop feeling guilty that they died, and I survived."

"I'm so sorry ... so sorry. ..." Jean whispered. She was sorry for him and also sorry for herself, for she knew she could never share this deepest pain with him. Yet she wanted to.

He gave her hand one more squeeze and let her go. "So let's get back to the publishing business. I aim to end up somewhere where there are honest people who are willing to give a hard-working guy a chance. Any idea where that might be?"

She didn't, but it was easy to follow his lead and speculate on the future, even though she wouldn't share it with him. In the back of her mind, underneath the banter, she wondered if she had made a serious mistake in spending time alone with him. The thought of him leaving was more painful than ever, if that could be possible.

CHAPTER TWENTY-NINE

Back in the ambulance, Jean headed for Newport. Soon after they left Newport, they approached a major crossroad. She slowed. "I'd like to take you back to Gilwern by the long way," she said. "We'll stop at a place I've grown to love, Tintern Abbey, if you feel up to it."

Tom raised an eyebrow and grinned. "I'm game for anything you are."

"Good!" With a sense of adventure she turned right, crossed bridges over deep tidal streams with steep banks of brown mud, and headed through the green countryside. She had never approached the Abbey from the south and had no idea what to expect.

In half an hour they reached a picturesque village, Chepstow, clinging to a hillside. Its little shops and row houses lined cozy, narrow streets. On one side lay a huge well-preserved castle. She drove upward through the town and toward the Abbey, which was only a few miles ahead. The road led them through wooded hills, much like those she'd loved in the Willamette Valley. She waved a hand at the scene and called, "It's a lot like Oregon."

With a half smile, Tom nodded. He appeared lost in his own thoughts.

The road fell before them down to the Wye River. The stately abbey ruins rose from the valley floor, filling her again with its sense of timelessness. Or was it, more accurately, a sense of a certain time? She could imagine the abbey before its decline, complete with a solid roof and high arched windows, surrounded by shorter outbuildings. She could almost see robed monks strolling and working in the shade of the massive edifice.

She parked close to the abbey, climbed out, and walked around to stand beside Tom.

Gazing upward and then all around at the wild green hills, he exclaimed, "Some place!"

Jean led the way across a carpet of grass and summer field flowers, through the ruins of the smaller buildings until they stood finally within the roofless walls and columns of the great main structure. The airy gothic windows framed views of the forested hills. A flock of songbirds darted across the blue sky above the open abbey.

Tom said quietly, "Thank you for bringing me here."

"Like stepping into another time, isn't it?"

He thrust his hands into his pockets and spoke without taking his eyes from the high stonework. "I don't know much English history, but I do know the church had its problems. Early on, the conflict was between the Catholics and the Anglicans. Then later, I believe the Church of England had trouble with the Quakers, the Puritans, the Methodists, and a score of others who were seeking the truth. Yet, standing here, I can only feel we're all in the same boat. We all have strayed ... made a mess of things. The men who built this abbey ... they believed in the same Christ we follow, despite our differences. These carefully laid stones are like a bridge of brotherhood to believers of the past."

This was the side of Tom she had hoped to see. The war was a million miles away. "I've felt the peace here," she said, "but I've never been able to put it into words."

He stood close, looking down at her. The bright sunlight reflecting upward from the pink stone floor illuminated his face in soft light. Everything around them glowed with warmth. For an instant she thought he was going to kiss her, but he abruptly turned and walked away, as if studying the architecture.

Once again she wondered if he had read her mind or something in her expression. Was this turning away his silent answer to her unspoken love?

From the distance of a few paces he faced her again. His usually composed face revealed a mixture of emotions she couldn't decipher.

"Jeanie, why did you bring me here?"

His directness caught her totally unprepared. "Why? I wanted you to see just what you have seen—the peace of the place, the timelessness. I . . . I hoped it would be a bit of a vacation . . . away from the hospital . . . away from the war."

He studied her.

She felt her face grow warm. "I hoped you would enjoy it, as I do."

He drew in a deep breath. Through tight lips he said, "It's more than enjoyment, but I—" He jammed his hands into his pockets and glared at her. "Is this all you had in mind?"

Now he was clearly angry. No matter what the cost, she couldn't lie to him. "No, that's not all! But the rest of it is obviously none of your business!" She whirled around and ran for the ambulance.

It took him several minutes to follow her. When he climbed in, she switched on the ignition. He reached over and turned it off. "Jeanie, we need to talk. I didn't mean to come at you the way I did. Please forgive me."

To her horror, she burst into tears.

He slid across the seat and, with his one arm, pulled her close. She felt the warmth of his cheek pressing against the top of her head.

Sobbing, she clung to him. The comfort of his embrace soon stopped her tears. "Do you have a handkerchief?" she asked.

He let go of her, pulled a khaki-colored square from his pocket, and handed it to her.

She wiped her eyes and blew her nose and moved away from him. As he leaned back on his own side of the seat again, a grimace of pain crossed his face.

"Oh, your arm! I hurt your arm!"

Smiling so wide it crinkled his eyes, he said, "You didn't touch it. I strained it myself. When you're around I want to be two-armed." He turned sideways again, facing her. "I don't know about you, but it's wonderful for me to be here with you. If you had that in mind, I thank you. If you didn't, I thank you anyway.

"And I want you to know I wasn't angry at you. I was angry at myself . . . for coming out alone with you, for opening up this possibility . . . that we both have agreed to close. And I was angry at the whole insane world, the war and all the stupid prejudices that separate me from you. Jeanie, nothing has changed! This war will not change the hearts of men. If you and I even date back home, someone will harass you."

"I told you I don't care! It doesn't matter!"

"You're speaking from your dreams. I'm speaking from experience. I couldn't bear to have you hate being married to me. I wouldn't put you or any child through that."

"Will it be so much easier for your children to have a Japanese mother?"

His mouth grew grim. Without emotion, he said, "I can't imagine. But I'm sure it would be easier for a woman to be married to someone of her own race."

Jean wanted to scream and pound him with her fists. Then she wondered what he would do if she threw her arms around him and kissed him instead. He was so careful to keep a distance that she knew he was not invulnerable. But she couldn't play games.

She said with all the coldness she could muster, "You call yourself a realist! The trouble is, you want everything perfect. You want to make everything okay for everyone, and the world isn't that way!"

He didn't answer.

A wave of weariness washed over her. "It's time I got this ambulance back to the hospital." She reached for the key. "Will you let me turn on the ignition now?"

His lips quirked up at the corners in an ironic half smile. With a Japanese bowing of his head, he assented. Facing forward, he gestured with his good hand. "Back to the world, Jeanie."

He didn't try to talk, and she was glad. There was nothing more to say. She concentrated on the heat of the sun on her shoulders and the wind in her ears and tried not to feel anything else. It was just another day, neither worse nor better than any other. After all, nothing had changed. Had it?

Giselle sat at her apartment window overlooking the front sidewalk, waiting for Jacquie and Angie to come skipping home. Reverend MacDougall had taken Elizabeth and Nella to visit an aunt in Hereford for a few days. The girls missed Livie so much that she'd let them visit neighbor children for the first time.

Tommie and Eunice lived only two doors down the street. She'd gladly welcomed the blond brother and sister into her apartment to play with the girls. Then the girls had argued that turnabout was fair play, so she'd finally pushed her anxiety aside and consented to let them go. They had skipped off to the neighbors while she went to the church to roll bandages for the Red Cross for a couple of hours.

Now she fidgeted at the window. They would be coming home soon, but the silence in the manse made her edgy.

The minutes ticked by too slowly while just waiting. She went to her tiny kitchen, opened a tin of canned milk, poured it into a pan, and added water. Methodically she stirred in a bit of precious sugar and powdered chocolate. Summer or not, the girls liked warm cocoa, and it helped them get some milk in a tasty way. She set the mixture aside to heat when they came home and laid the last two thick oatmeal biscuits on a plate.

Back at the window, she peered both directions. Not a sign of the children. Glancing at her wristwatch, she caught her breath. They were nearly half an hour late! Her heart began to hammer against her ribs. She ran down the stairs and hurried to the house two doors away. Mrs. Blake answered her knock immediately.

Keeping a steadier voice than she felt, Giselle said, "I'm sorry to bother you, but the girls must have forgotten the time. They're more than half an hour late—"

"But they left here right on the dot half an hour ago. I wonder where the rascals have gone. Let me ask my Tommie if he knows anything about it." Turning, she yelled in soprano, "Tommie!"

Before Tommie even appeared, Giselle knew what he would say, and she was right.

With a worried expression, he squinted up at her. "They said to me they was going right home."

Suddenly light-headed, Giselle caught hold of the door casing for support. "Did you watch them leave?"

"Oh yes, ma'am. Eunice and me, we stood right here waving to them."

"Did you see anyone in the street nearby?"

"No. . . . Well, there was a car or two parked, but nobody out walking about."

"Thanks. Thanks, Tommie."

Mrs. Blake touched her arm. "Mrs. Munier, you look so pale. Why don't you come in for tea and let Tommie go looking. They're good girls. They won't've gone far."

Again Giselle made herself breath slow and deep. "Thanks, but I think I'd best look. Surely you're right, but I'd feel better looking myself."

"Then let Tommie come along. He can help."

"I . . . thanks, but really . . . that's not necessary. I'll spot them in a few minutes. Thanks. Good-bye!" She hoped her response concealed her deep and growing terror. If Andre had come, she must act alone to be most effective. She feared the worst. Jacquie and Angie would never wander off to explore. She had coached them too well. They were not like carefree Tommie who played all over this side of town.

She remembered the furtive figure in the manse garden. Maybe it had not been large, clumsy Robert. But that was weeks ago. *Oh, God, help my babies! I never should have let them out of my sight!*

In case her instinct was wrong, she searched every dooryard on the block and peeked into the nearby shops. Then she hurried home and rang up the military station hospital at Govilon. She needed Jeanie, and only Jeanie. Good thing the MacDougalls were gone. She wouldn't want them to know. Right away they'd want to call the constable or some other authority. Only Jeanie could understand the nature of the danger and the necessity of not involving local authorities.

To her horror, Jeanie was gone and the woman who answered didn't know how to reach her. On the chance her friend Mary might know, Giselle rang the Gilwern hospital and then had to wait for Mary to call back. Panic threatened to overwhelm her. With the first ring she grabbed the phone.

"Giselle?" Mary said.

"Mary, I have to reach Jeanie, and she's gone. Do you know where she is?"

"Yes. She went to Swansea and took Tom along. She should be back any time now."

Giselle couldn't keep dread from her voice. "Oh, Mary, the girls didn't come home from playing with their friends. Jeanie will understand. Can you make sure she calls me as soon as she returns?"

"Well, sure. I'll watch for her. But Abergavenny is a quiet little town. The kids should be fine."

"Yes, well ... please promise you'll tell her. She will know what to do."

"I promise. How long have they been gone?"

"More than an hour. It's ... it's not like them to do this."

"Maybe you should call the constable—"

"I can't trust the locals. Mary, I can't explain, but Jeanie will understand. Please ... please don't tell anyone else!"

"Okay. Try to stay calm. Remember you're not in occupied France anymore. Surely the girls are fine and will have some childish explanation when they show up."

Giselle's hands were shaking so badly, she had trouble keeping the receiver against her ear. Mary had no idea what could happen if Andre had found them. "Thanks. Thanks, Mary. Tell Jean I'll be waiting to hear from her."

After Mary's good-bye, she hung up and returned to the front window. The street was almost empty in the lengthening shadows cast by the afternoon sun. She went to the kitchen window overlooking the backyard. The swing hung as motionless as death in the shade of the big tree. *My babies! Where are they? Oh, God, please keep them safe!*

The tree's shadow covered the whole yard now. The thought of darkness falling without finding the children threatened her sanity. She couldn't just sit here!

She went swiftly to her bedroom and got out the guns, which she always kept clean and oiled. The Mauser was loaded. She sat on the edge of the bed and slipped cartridges into the MAB.

A bang on her outside door jolted her to her feet as if she'd received an electric shock. Gun in hand, she quietly hurried down the stairs. Bracing herself for anything, she threw open the door. No one was there. A sheet of notebook paper wrapped snugly around an egg-sized rock lay on the threshold.

She ran out, looked both ways, but saw no one. Then she sprinted through the backyard and looked up and down the alley and ran back to the street in front of the manse. The street and walks were deserted. Defeated, Giselle returned to her door, picked up the rock, peeled off the paper, and smoothed it. On the inner side she found a note written in French and signed, "Andre."

CHAPTER THIRTY

When Jean pulled into the parking area at the sprawling Gilwern military station hospital, Tom said, "Maybe you don't want to see me anymore."

"That's not true, and you know it. Of course I want to see you . . . unless you don't want to see me."

He sat silent, staring straight ahead. "Jeanie, I don't know what to say. I'm sure it would be wiser for us to just break off right now and go our separate ways."

She didn't answer. They'd been through this before, and she didn't want to rehash it. She glanced at his profile. He looked as miserable as she felt. She reached over and slipped her hand into his. "I want whatever you want."

He gave her a stricken look. "Don't leave it all up to me, Jeanie."

"Okay. I have one question. Do we have to be wise?"

His fingers tightened on hers. Before he could speak, Mary's voice came between them.

"Jean!" she called. "I'm so glad I spotted you!" She ran from the administration office to their side. "Giselle phoned me, really worried. She said the girls didn't come home from playing at the neighbors. I tried to calm her down, but she was so upset. The girls are probably back by now, but—"

With a rush of anxiety, Jean reached for the ignition. "I'll go see."

"I'll come along," Tom said. "Mary, if that's a problem for my keepers, try to handle it for me."

"Sure thing, pal."

Jean started to argue, but she really wanted him along. If Giselle was suffering the terrors again, he might be able to help quiet her.

As she drove back up the hill to Gilwern, her fear mushroomed. *What if the girls are not home yet? How long have they been gone?*

It felt like forever to drive the four or five kilometers to Abergavenny, and when she finally got there, she had to slow down through town. At the manse she jumped out and ran straight to Giselle's side door. She heard Tom's steps close behind her. After pounding on the door, she grabbed the knob. It twisted in her hand.

Giselle opened it but only partially. With a strained, funny expression on her face, she whisked them in and slammed the door. She had the Mauser in her hand!

"Giselle! What's wrong?"

She lowered the gun and exclaimed, "The girls have been kidnapped! If you are seen here, they could be killed!"

"Oh no!" Jean glanced at Tom. She understood instantly, but knew he would not. "Tell us what you know."

"Come on upstairs." She locked the door and ran up the steps ahead of them. In the parlor she motioned them to the couch and laid her gun on the end table under the lamp. Then she handed Jean a crumpled sheet of notebook paper and an envelope and sat down on a straight-backed chair facing them. "That is fabric from the girls' dresses and their hair ribbons and hair."

Jean opened the envelope first and touched the strands of soft hair. Her stomach was in her throat, churning with panic. She handed the envelope back to Giselle and smoothed the paper. Her first glance fell on the name *Andre*. She read to Tom a translation.

"My dear Julie,

As I promised, I have come. It was not difficult to change my appearance, to locate the hospital in London that had performed facial surgery on my sister, and to discover the happy news that our American uncle, Monsieur Moore, had come to London. After that it became a challenge to discover your trail to Abergavenny, but as you see, my skill prevailed.

If you wish to see Jacquie and Angie alive, tell no one that I have them. I cannot emphasize this enough. At seven o'clock tonight you will receive instructions.

Your brother, Andre"

Tom gasped. "Brother? Who is this man?"

"Not a brother," Giselle said through tight lips. "In Lyon he betrayed my husband and many others to the Nazis. I didn't know he was the traitor until just minutes before I flew out of France."

"But what does he want from you now?"

"The names of leaders and members in the Resistance. You see, we worked in very small groups and most resistants do not know more than half a dozen other resistants. But Claude and I became leaders. We know many throughout France. . . ."

Jean didn't want Tom's questions about the Resistance to lead into the subject of how Giselle escaped, which might reveal her own activities in France. She asked quietly, "How long have the children been gone?"

Giselle's lips trembled. She pressed them tightly together before saying, "Three hours."

"Despite the threat in the note, you need to get the law into this," Tom said.

"The local law here is inadequate. And I can't trust the military to do the right thing. I can't trust anyone but Jeanie!" Her voice rose to a wild pitch. She jumped to her feet and began to pace.

"Have you been able to keep this from the MacDougalls?" Jean asked.

"Surely Reverend MacDougall would say you shouldn't try to handle this alone!" Tom exclaimed.

Giselle glared at him. "Fortunately, they've gone to Hereford for several days. Jeanie, you've got to tell Tom the truth. It's the only way I can trust him to understand. Tell him what you did during those months you stopped writing to him."

Jean hesitated, thinking of the men who'd helped her go to France and who had sworn her to secrecy. Would telling Tom jeopardize anything now? Glancing at Giselle's tense face, she made a quick decision. "Okay. Tom, this also you must not tell anyone. The BSE, an arm of the British secret service, trained me and dropped me into France to get Giselle out."

He made a choking sound. "Dropped you into France?"

"Yes. Giselle had been injured by the Gestapo. She couldn't escape without help. They had tortured her and would do so again if they could find her. She knew many key people in the Resistance. A trusted friend hid her in an insane asylum run by nuns, but he couldn't go back to help her. I had to get her and the girls out."

Tom gaped at Giselle and then at her. "You went into occupied France?"

"Look. We can talk about that later, but it's true that Giselle may know best how to deal with the kidnapper. At least I agree that the constable would not. And the MPs at the hospitals don't know much more than how to transport drunk or brawling soldiers to the stockade. The fewer people involved at this point, the better. This man, Andre, will kill the children if there is the least slipup."

Tom nodded. "So what will you do now?"

Giselle sank back down on her chair. "Andre is brilliant at what he does—he managed to deceive all of us resistants. He is also a madman. But I can deal with him."

Jean returned to the couch. "He said he would send instructions at seven o'clock. All I saw were the girls' hair and hair ribbons."

Giselle nodded. "There was another note with the hair ribbons. He said he wanted me to think all night about the consequences if I don't do exactly as he asks. I am to meet him tomorrow before daylight." She leaned forward, picked up the gun, and cradled it in her hands. "When I have the children safe, I will kill him."

Tom bolted upright on the couch. "You think you can conceal a German Mauser long enough to surprise him?"

Again Giselle nodded. "I did so in France."

Jean remembered her dread in France over whether Giselle would lose control, shoot someone, and expose them all to the Milice or Gestapo. She had not reacted in panic, but then the children were always with her. Their presence probably helped her to stay focused. Hoping to calm her, Jean leaned forward from her place on the couch beside Tom and spoke quietly. "The main thing is to get the children back." Then her lifelong horror of killing swept over her. She said hopefully, "Once you have the children safe, you can call in the law. You don't have to kill him."

Giselle's cheeks flushed with anger. "You have not lived with the brutality—seen soldiers take away whole families to never be seen again—children, old grandmothers and grandfathers to be killed, for all we know! You have not lost your parents. You have not lost a husband and children. When you do, then you may judge me."

"You're right. I know I can't even imagine how you feel." Yet Jean could not back down. She didn't want Giselle to become a cold-blooded killer. "But to kill him, you will become like him. That's what he would do!"

"You were not in Lyon under the Nazis for four years, Jeanie. You don't know how it has to be to win."

Tom spoke gently. "I too have no way of knowing. I do know vengeance is a two-edged sword. Whenever I've seen it wielded, it always came back against the one who used it. For safety's sake, I hope you'll listen to Jean."

Giselle laid the gun back on the end table. "You are both babes. I know how this man thinks. I know how he was trained. I will do whatever I have to do."

To get Tom to back off, Jean touched his arm. "She's right. She does know best how to handle Andre."

He didn't take the hint. "Then let me go along, stay hidden, and keep you covered. I can get hold of a rifle."

"I can't risk that," Giselle said.

Jean could see Giselle eyeing Tom's stiff arm. She too questioned his ability to fire a rifle. "I agree. So what do you want me to do?"

Giselle glanced out the window. "First you must get that ambulance away from in front of the manse. Tom, drive it back to the hospital but let Jean off in town when no one is watching. She can walk back here and come in through the backyard."

He flexed his weak hand, as if testing its strength and said, "Now, wait a minute. If Jean stays, I stay. We'll get into trouble together."

"No," Giselle snapped. "As I said, I have a plan, and it includes only Jean."

Tom wouldn't give up. "But I can—"

"No! Do you want to kill my children?" Giselle's blue eyes flashed with anger.

"Tom, you must go," Jean said. "Please don't make trouble."

His mouth tightened, and he raised his chin in a familiar signal that meant he would do what he wanted, regardless. But then he looked down at her and said, "Okay. I'll go." He reached out for Giselle's hand. "I'll be praying every second for you and the children."

Her face softened. "Thanks."

"Coming, Jeanie?"

"Sure. I'll be back soon," she called as they started down the stairs.

"Take care about being seen."

"You bet."

Jean climbed in the passenger side of the ambulance. "Are you sure you can crank that steering wheel with your arm still weak?"

"I've driven with one hand before." He proceeded to demonstrate. In the lower part of town, not far from St. Mary Cathedral, he pulled into an alley and stopped.

Before she could open the ambulance door, he said, "Jeanie, I feel as if I don't know you. I'm scared spitless for you. How can I let you do this?"

"You have no choice. Don't fail us. Don't say a word to anyone."

He sighed heavily. "I won't. Assure Giselle I won't." He leaned toward her and quickly kissed her on the lips.

She froze for a second, then said, "I'll tell her." Looking all directions, she opened the door and slipped out into the deserted alley.

When she returned to the manse, Giselle opened the door before Jean could knock and silently ran back up the stairs. Sitting on the edge of the couch, she said, "Are you sure you weren't noticed or followed by anyone?"

"Yes. Positive."

"And you trust Tom to keep all this to himself?"

"He understands. He will."

Giselle dropped her face in her hands and groaned. "Oh, if only Claude were here!" She slowly shook her head. "I don't know. I just don't know. Maybe you should not come. You could be a hazard. Andre controlled me at the plane by keeping his gun trained on you."

Jean sat down beside Giselle and put an arm around her shoulders. "Please don't try to do this alone. We made a good team in France. Let me help now."

Giselle looked up. "You'll have to be as willing to use a gun as I am."

Jean straightened in sudden shock. "I don't have a gun. I actually forgot I don't have a gun."

Giselle rose and went into her bedroom. She returned with a small brown holster and the MAB. She held it out. "I took it that first day in England while you were bathing. I knew you wouldn't keep it, and I was afraid we'd need it."

"You had it all this time? I couldn't believe I'd lost it, but . . ." She took the MAB. As much as she hated guns, the familiar shape and heft of the little gun was almost reassuring. For one thing, it reminded her of all the dangers they had survived without having to use it. "I will do whatever I have to, Giselle. You know you can trust me."

She laid the gun on the couch and went to the phone. She called both the Govilon and Gilwern headquarters, leaving messages in the offices for her super and for Mary that she was staying the night with her ill cousin.

While she was on the phone, Giselle paced the floor, and when Jean rang off, she collapsed onto the couch with a distant look on her face. It was the look she assumed when she was grappling with a problem.

Jean left her and went to the kitchenette. She opened the cooling cupboard and set out some eggs. Not much else there, but they needed to eat. She announced her intention. "We've got to keep up our energy. How about pancakes and eggs?"

A muffled yes came from the little parlor.

When Giselle came to eat, the wild look had left her eyes. This probably meant she'd settled on her plan. "What will you want me to do?" Jean asked.

"I must go alone to meet Andre."

"But you'll need me nearby."

Giselle shook her head. "Not this time. We must not even walk through town together. When I go to meet him, you will leave a few minutes later, go straight to the castle, and hide in the trees at the bottom of the slope. I am to meet him by the river. He said we'd walk to the place where he hid the children.

Whichever direction we go, we will have to cross the pasture below the castle. It should be easy for you to shadow us by staying among the trees along the edge."

"I don't feel good about this. Anything could happen. He could have lied to you about walking and about where he may go. In fact, he probably has."

"I know that, but I'm gambling on his arrogance. He knows I will be near panic about the girls. He knows I won't call in the law. To him, I am just a woman, weaker than he is and definitely not as smart. I shall play the part well when I meet him. If anything goes wrong, I have my gun."

"What if he searches you and disarms you? Surely he intends to make you a prisoner too."

Giselle clamped her hands over her ears and shook her head. "Stop it! I'm prepared for anything. I told you that I'd never be taken alive again, but I will live to free the girls, no matter what it takes."

Her words scared Jean as much as when she'd talked that way in France. Yet she was quite sure Giselle was wise about not asking the constable or the military for help. Her cousin probably knew more than they did about fighting for life and beating the odds in this situation. As for herself, she had no choice but to follow Giselle's lead and pray.

Jean slept in the girls' room on Jacquie's cot. That is, she tried to sleep. As the minutes and hours ticked by, she turned one way and then another, trying to relax. She prayed for the girls and for Giselle. Then she tossed some more. This was worse than being in occupied France. There, at least she had known where to look for Giselle. And Georges, Harry, and Eve had coached her well.

A sound came from the other room. Jean sat up and listened. Maybe Giselle couldn't sleep either. Without turning on a light, she got up and tiptoed out into the parlor. "Giselle?" she called softly, in case Giselle had been stirring in her sleep. All was quiet.

After she got back into bed, she distinctly heard a noise from downstairs, a soft click and thump like a door closing. Her heart gave an adrenaline leap. The MacDougalls were gone. Was somebody breaking in? She rushed into Giselle's room to alert her. "Giselle!" she hissed. Almost before she spoke, she knew Giselle was gone. She flipped on the light. The noise must have been Giselle. She'd slipped out much earlier than they'd planned. She obviously intended to go alone. It was too dangerous!

Barefoot and in her borrowed nightgown, Jean raced down the stairs and outside. The thin, setting moon gave a little light. She ran all the way to the street. Giselle was gone. She hesitated at the gate for only a moment, but before she could turn and run back into the manse, a hand grabbed her and covered her mouth. She fought to break free.

In a stage whisper, Tom said, "Jeanie, it's me!"

He let go of her, but her racing heart didn't quite believe. "What are you doing here?"

"I couldn't go and leave you two alone. I lied a little and got permission to return. I parked the ambulance down the block. I've been on watch, waiting for you. When I saw someone come out the gate, I hurried here, but I was too slow. I decided it was Giselle, so I figured you might come next."

"She fooled me and sneaked out. She promised to wake me. Well, now that you're here, come on in."

Giselle reached the path above the meadow during the darkest portion of the night, just after moonset. Dressed all in black, she wore a loose jacket over her slacks and shirt, and underneath the jacket she'd strapped the holster with the heavy Mauser. As soon as she left the sidewalk, she drew the gun and held it ready. Hurrying past the castle, she wove her way down the slope and across the thick grass to the largest stand of trees beside the river. She stepped into the folds of the bushes at the edge of the copse and waited with every sense alert. She would have to make the first move and do it right. She would not get a second chance.

Taking in the surroundings, she had to admire Andre's clever choice of a meeting place. He would have been able to see her approach from any direction and from quite a distance, despite the darkness. Already her eyes had adjusted, and she could see for several meters.

She must not get sleepy or let her fingers get cold and stiff. She flexed both hands and then slipped her right hand, gun and all, under her jacket against the warmth of her body.

She expected Andre to arrive early for their appointment. She hoped they'd be gone from the meadow before Jean discovered her absence. After sleepless hours of reviewing the possibilities, she was positive Jean would only have added to her risk.

In a breathtakingly short time he came as silently as a cat. He approached from upriver instead of from town. He was disturbingly close when she caught his movement in half impressions. Then he stopped next to the very shrubs that concealed her.

"Andre," she said steadily. "Do not move. I have my Mauser steady on you."

He was silent. She had succeeded in surprising him.

Then he laughed. "You were always a good actress."

"Just try me. I have very good night vision."

"You won't risk shooting. You want your children."

"Oh, I wouldn't kill you. And I don't care if I rouse the constable. Do you?"

He stood silent for moment. "You win."

"Hold your right hand high and with your left hand throw down your gun." Her finger tensed on the trigger.

Andre threw down his gun.

"Now the small gun," she ordered.

He fumbled under his coat.

"Keep that right hand high!"

She heard the quieter thud of his lighter gun.

"Put your hands on the top of your head and start walking in the direction of my children."

He responded as if he believed her threats.

Giselle seized on his insecurity. "If I decide you are misleading me or stalling for time, I will not hesitate to give you a little discomfort from this marvelous German gun."

She knew Andre. His compliance would not last. He'd try to overpower her before they reached the children. Yet she couldn't risk getting closer to search for other weapons.

Gripping the gun in both hands, she followed him across the bumpy meadow, placing her feet carefully. If she stubbed her toe in the dark, her options would be few.

CHAPTER THIRTY-ONE

Jean dressed swiftly and strapped on the gun. When she came out of the bedroom, she found Tom sitting on the couch and holding the envelope that contained the girls' hair ribbons. He looked up, perplexed. "I hoped Giselle might have left the note lying here somewhere, but I found only these. Did she say anything that could tell us where she was to meet him?"

"She told me they'd be walking from near the river below the castle. I was to watch for them and then follow. She left it up to me to decide how to help once they reached the children. Since she lied about the time, she may have lied about walking through the meadow. She really didn't want me to go along...." She pressed her fingers against her lips, suppressing a sudden intense urge to wail and moan as people did in Bible times when they were mourning. "What if she lied? I don't know what to do!"

"Jeanie, I don't know either," Tom said, "but I've been praying a lot. Now, I think we'll just have to start moving, doing our best."

"That's what I did in France." She took a deep breath and tried to steady herself. "France was scary, but not nearly as much as it is right now. We have so little to go on. I feel so unprepared, and there's so little time." She cleared her throat, which suddenly felt parched. "I think the only thing I can do is what Giselle said—hide at the meadow and watch for her." She stood up, then spying the envelope with the hair ribbons on the floor at her feet, she scooped it up to lay it in a safe place for Giselle.

As she did so, bits of dry grass fell into her hand. Curious, she tipped all the contents out. Fine stems of sun-bleached grass were tangled in the lock of Jacquie's dark hair. She shuddered. Had Jacquie fallen, or had she been thrown down in the grass? No . . . the grass was tied in, as if on purpose. Puzzled, she looked at Angie's hair and found none. Suddenly it dawned on her—it wasn't grass. She picked up a piece, broke it, and bruised it with her fingernail. A faint pine smell perfumed her fingers.

"This isn't grass. It's pine needles! It looks as if they were tied into her ribbon. It's hard to believe that Jacquie would have remembered, but whether the needles were tied in the ribbon intentionally or simply caught in her hair, they could only come from one place. That deserted barn would provide an isolated shelter for hiding the children. And if Giselle breaks down and tells Andre what he wants, he might decide to kill them all, and likely no one would discover their bodies for several days."

Tom took some the the pine needles from her and smelled them. "Jacquie is bright enough to think of this. I have no doubt of that."

Jean shuddered again and fought against rising panic. "The only way he can get information from her will be to hurt the children. If that's where they are, we've got to get there first." She stopped, uncertain. "It's true they would have to walk to reach the barn, and if we can see them in the meadow, we'll have a chance to overcome Andre before he can get to the children. I think we must go first to the meadow."

Giselle took care not to let her guard down. Once she jabbed Andre in the back with the gun and then leaped back out of his reach. He had to know she wasn't bluffing. He made no move to turn on her. Obviously he had some other plan.

The lights in town were turned off because of the blackout, yet he marched along the river as if he knew his footing well, and she had to follow faster than she preferred.

"Slow down!" she snapped.

"As you wish."

He slowed so abruptly, she bumped into him. She quickly jumped back, but he didn't try to take advantage. Probably he was gauging her reaction time. "Do that again, and I pull the trigger."

He walked on, leading her upstream and away from town. They were heading toward the old stone bridge and the road that led to the military hospitals and on into the mountains.

She almost wished he would make a wrong move so she could wound him—she so despised his collaboration with the enemy. "What made you turn against your country, Andre? What kind of a Frenchman are you?"

"My country? The Fatherland is my country. My father was a German hero in World War I, and the French killed him. I had a French grandfather who despised me, and my weak-minded mother made our home with the beast. When I was fifteen, I ran away and joined Hitler's youth movement. There I found a true home . . . I'd sell my best friend for the Fuerher."

"And probably have," she said.

"Don't flatter yourself that any of the resistants were my friends."

"Did you betray my husband?"

"Or course," he said calmly.

More than anything, she wanted to kill him right there, but she made herself wait.

Now she could just make out the shape of the bridge. The water, pouring around the stone pylons, seemed loud in the quietness of the night. Suddenly Andre stepped downward and led her toward the river. He was about to take a route under the bridge over wet, slick rocks.

"Stop!" she ordered. "Go up onto the highway and over the bridge."

"You want someone to see us?"

"If we have to cross, we'll have to take that risk."

"Have it your way, but then you may not get to your children."

She paused. "All right. Move on and don't so much as turn your head to look at me." He also had worn black, but she could easily see his face and hands.

He started across, a black shadow set against the darker shadow of the bridge above. Keeping her gun aimed at him, she took one step at a time, testing each place before letting her weight fall on it. Twice she slipped but quickly regained her balance. The noise of rushing water prevented him from hearing her missteps.

At last they were on the other side. He then headed upriver and said, "If you can't walk faster, the sun will be up before we get there. Your girls are very thirsty already."

"You beast. I'd kill you right here if it weren't for them. March!"

At the meadow, hiding in the trees, Jean at first despaired of seeing anything, but soon her eyes grew accustomed to the darkness. She didn't know how long to watch and wait. After a while, she could tell the difference between trees and grass, and the sky seemed to be lighter. Surely by now Giselle and Andre would have met and begun their walk. She must have missed them.

She whispered to Tom, "It's time to go upriver to the barn." Having decided, she felt they couldn't move fast enough. "Come on!"

She had the motor going by the time Tom climbed in. With the running lights on, she carefully maneuvered through the narrow streets, not wanting to attract attention. At the road to Gilwern, she turned left and increased speed as much as she dared. Once they crossed the bridge, she floor-boarded the accelerator, touching the brake before each turn of the curving road.

Giselle listened to Andre's every step and kept her gun steadily trained on his barely visible back. After walking through woods beside the river, they finally came to what seemed open pastureland. Andre still followed the riverbank, however, which seemed to be high at this point. She realized with a shiver that they may be close to where Jeanie and Nella had discovered the drowned man.

Below them, despite the darkness, the ebony water glinted with light it captured from the sky. It was definitely getting lighter. She could see Andre clearly now. She could tell that he was glancing from side to side, for he knew better than to turn fully toward her. Giselle had made him keep his hands on his head, despite his pleas to lower them. She followed close but was careful to stay out of his reach. She watched the pale shape of his hands, his fingers laced on top of his head flexing and stretching. He was becoming more desperate and dangerous now. She must remain calm and stay focused.

Suddenly he stumbled and fell flat. She jumped back, gun steady and aimed at him.

He rolled to his back and looked up at her, hands still above his head. "My shoe came untied. Will you let me tie it?"

"Okay, but keep both hands where I can see them."

He rose to a squatting position and, facing her, fumbled with his shoe. "The string broke. I'll have to tie a knot in it."

"Get up and walk with it broken."

His next move she saw in a blur. Without taking his hands off his shoes, he suddenly launched himself head first at her as if a battering ram. She threw herself sideways and fired, desperately aiming to wound and not kill. His body hit her a glancing blow and knocked her to the ground. He was instantly on top of her, ripping the gun from her hand and twisting her arms behind her back. Her shoulder joints screamed with pain. She arched her back and kicked, but couldn't break free. Her worst nightmare had come true. She was again in the hands of a Nazi.

Andre let go and leaped to his feet, laughing. "You fool! I was trained by the best. Resistants! Bah! Children from Hitler's youth camps could crush your so-called Resistance. Now you will tell me what I need to know to finish my job in France. Their names. Start talking."

She silently clenched her teeth. She'd find a way to get the gun back. And maybe, somehow, Jeanie had awakened and reached the meadow in time to see them and follow. Her gun was small, but maybe it would do.

Without warning, he kicked her in the ribs. Giselle threw her arms over her face and screamed.

He then jerked her to her feet and rammed the gun into her stomach. "Talk!"

The pain in her side took her breath away. She gasped, "You need me alive, you know."

He shoved her away.

She sprawled flat. The pain in her side flared, but she found that a deep breath didn't make it worse. Her ribs weren't broken.

"Get up and start walking," he snarled.

At Govilon Jean parked the ambulance beside the pasture that had been the starting point for her daily walks. They climbed out. After driving with running lights, she was night blind. She had to search a moment for the first stile. She climbed over and turned toward Tom. "Here. Can you see my hand?"

"I'm okay. One-armed works fine."

In a stage whisper, she said, "We've got to get down near the river before it grows light enough to be seen."

She set off at a dogtrot. When she reached the next stile, Tom was several yards behind. She waited.

He was puffing. "I'm sorry. I'm in rotten shape. But I don't want you to arrive there alone. Give me a second to catch my breath, and I'll do better."

The rest did her good too. She set off through the next pasture at a fast walk. Tom kept at her heels.

Half a dozen large pastures lay between the road and the barn owner's home. Resting sheep made pale woolly mounds on the grass. They passed the dark farmhouse undetected by the dogs and hurried on down the long slope toward the river. Jean stopped as soon as the white stone barn came into view. That she could see it meant full daylight was near. "See that tower in the trees. That's where we're going. We've got to approach without being seen in case Andre is there already. This ditch looks as if it runs through those trees on the left of the barn. Let's walk in it."

A small stream trickled in the bottom of the ditch, but there was room to walk beside it. Bending low, they followed the ditch. It gradually became a gully that passed under two fences. When they reached the trees, the banks were steep and extended above their heads.

"Let me scout," Tom whispered.

He didn't give her a chance to answer. He started up without using his hands. At the top he grabbed a hummock of grass with his good hand and clung there, staying low to look around. Then painstakingly, in his one-armed manner, he hoisted himself over the top. "Come on up," he whispered.

Small bushes and tough grass gave her handholds. Kneeling, Tom reached down and gave her his hand for the last few feet. "Lie flat and listen."

She obeyed and, hearing nothing, whispered, "We've got to get inside the barn."

The increasing light would soon place them in full view of

anyone approaching from uphill or down. At least the grass and soft soil muffled their footsteps, and trees grew right up to the barn on this side. When they reached the old stone structure, they froze and listened again. All was quiet. Jean drew her gun from the holster and released its safety.

She led Tom to the only entrance into the barn she had seen, located on the downhill side facing the river. Beside it, the unusual pine trees stood like sentinels, and underfoot, their needles spread a thick carpet that extended to the doorsill.

Tom cautiously cracked open the door and then threw it wide. Jean was surprised at how smoothly it swung outward.

One at a time, they jumped inside and dodged sideways, so as not to be a target against the early morning light. Tom pulled the door shut behind them. Small windows provided dim light, enough to see there was no sign of the children. Her hopes collapsed. She didn't know where else to look. In the underbrush outside? Maybe this location was totally wrong. The pine needles could have been a coincidence. There could be other pine trees that Nella didn't know about. A skittering sound made her whirl toward the left wall.

"Only a rat," Tom whispered.

To her horror she found her gun raised, ready to shoot. What if it had been the children? She snapped the safety back in place. Then her eyes focused on the wall of hand-hewn planks. In it she spied the outline of a small, rough door. A storage room!

"Tom," she whispered and pointed. "The children could be in there!" She called softly, "Jacquie! Angie! Are you there? It's Aunt Jeanie!"

"Aunt Jeanie!" Jacquie's voice quavered. Then it came stronger. "We're here! Let us out!"

"Aunt Jeanie!" Angie wailed.

Behind Jean the outside door of the barn swung open, letting in sudden light. She spun around.

Andre faced them with Giselle at his side. He had a gun in his hand.

Jean's grip on her own gun tightened. Could Andre see she was armed? Tom, standing between her and Andre, partially concealed her. Keeping her gun hand low and out of sight by her hip, she slowly unlatched the safety. Now if only Tom would move.

Andre spoke. "So! This was not smart, Julie. I warned you to tell no one. But then, maybe they will be of value. I shall shoot them one by one. Can you hold out until I get to the children? We shall see, won't we?" Keeping his eyes on Tom, he motioned for him to back away farther. Then he told Giselle, "Get over there by him."

Still keeping his eyes on Tom, he said to Jean, "So, Madame Fauvre, we meet again. Shall you be first or this soldier who is taking my measure while I talk?"

In the growing light, Jean could see his white teeth gleaming in an evil grin. The gun he held looked like Giselle's gun. He still had not noticed Jean's gun, low at her side. She made her voice compliant. "We'll do whatever you want, only don't hurt the children."

He laughed, and the sound reminded Jean of an actor in a horror movie. Andre glanced at her but aimed at Tom. "The soldier first, I think."

Then Jean saw everything as if in slow motion. Giselle lunged across the space, hitting Andre's gun hand at the moment the gun flashed. At almost the same instant, like a human torpedo, Tom hit him in the middle. All three crashed to the floor. They were such a tangle Jean couldn't get a clear shot. Andre broke free of Tom, and before Giselle could get up, he smashed his fist into her face. She screamed and kept screaming, out of control.

Jean saw blood streaming from her nose. Then she saw the Mauser lying on the sod floor of the barn just beyond Andre's reach.

Tom went for the gun, but before he could grab it, Andre kicked him. He doubled up, writhing and cradling his previously wounded arm. Blood stained his uniformed shoulder.

Andre stepped toward the gun.

Jean kept a tight hold on her rage and with a steady hand aimed her gun at Andre's heart. He was close enough that he might be able to jump her, but she only had to exert a little more pressure on the trigger. "Stop! Get your hands up."

Giselle was only moaning now, and Jean realized the children had been screaming too. From behind the wooden wall, they cried, "Maman! Maman!"

Suddenly it took all of Jean's willpower not to pull the trigger and have it over with. She wanted Andre dead.

He had halted at her command and straightened, but he did not raise his hands. His eyes gauged the distance between them. "You don't have the nerve to shoot. I know about you, the American cousin. I know how you watched your brother die—"

"Then you may not know that I've become a very good shot!" she snapped.

He sneered. "You haven't got it in you to shoot me." Keeping his eyes on her, he started to lean toward the Mauser.

Tom, still prone, rolled and twisted to grab the gun. Andre kicked him again, hard.

Jean pulled the trigger.

The explosion left a wake of silence. Giselle no longer moaned. Andre lay motionless on the floor.

Then the girls began to cry again.

Tom staggered to his feet, came to her, and pried the gun from her rigid fingers.

Jean rushed to Giselle, knelt beside her, and wrapped her arms around her. "Oh, he hurt you again!" She started to cry, great gulping sobs that would not stop.

Giselle patted her back, and when Jean could listen again, she heard her saying over and over, "It's all right. Everything will be all right." Except for sporadic shudders, Jean began to quiet.

Tom, now kneeling beside the body, called, "He's still alive. We need to get him to a doctor."

Then Jacquie screamed, "Maman! Maman! Let us out!"

"I'll get the girls," Tom said. "Jeanie, can you clean their mama's face before they see her?"

With a feeling of unreality, she helped Giselle out of her blood-spattered jacket. With a clean corner of the lining, she wiped her face as best she could. "Are you able to stand up?"

"You can bet I will." Giselle struggled to her feet and steadied herself on Jean's arm for a moment.

Tom came out of the storage room with Jacquie on one side and leading Angie by the hand on the other. At the sight of their mother, they ran to her.

She dropped to her knees and caught them both to her and crooned, "Maman is here. You're safe. Everything is all right."

When the children stopped crying, they noticed Tom was tying Andre's limp hands behind his back with an old rope.

Angie said, "Maman, Andre locked us up. He said we were

going to surprise you, and then he left us. He went away and never came back. I was so scared."

"Angie, it's all over now."

"I hate him," Jacquie said, glaring at the unconscious man. "I hope he dies!"

"Jacquie, please. Let's not think about him. Come outside with me." With her arms around the girls, she guided them out into the sunshine.

As if paralyzed, Jean watched Tom use his teeth and good hand to pull the knots tight on Andre's wrists. *I wanted to kill Andre. I aimed to kill him.* A vivid image of her brother Jimmy flashed before her, the way he'd looked lying on the ground beside the fence. Her ears began to ring and nausea threatened to overwhelm her. Jean hurried to the door and leaned against the frame. Her knees felt like leftover noodles, and she began to shake uncontrollably.

Tom followed and gripped her shoulder. "Are you going to be okay?"

She nodded but couldn't speak.

Then she turned and wrapped her arms around his waist and pressed her face against his chest. "Hold me. Please just hold me."

He held her the way she'd always wished, as if he'd never let her go, as if they belonged to each other. She gave her whole self to the moment, drawing strength from him. Slowly the steady strong beat of his heart under her ear healed her trembling.

CHAPTER THIRTY-TWO

"It's over," Tom murmured. "You did the right thing. I know you're shocked, but you did do the right thing. Concentrate on that. You saved the children and Giselle and me too."

Jean slowly released him, and he dropped his arm from around her, grimacing with pain as he did so. In her shock she'd forgotten his new wound. Contrite, she exclaimed, "Andre injured your arm again!"

"I'm afraid so. It's kind of like a bad toothache. I'm okay, but we need to get him to a doctor." He nodded toward Andre's still unconscious form.

Jean stared at the profile of the man she'd shot. "I'm glad he's alive, but I wanted to kill him. All the time I was in France, I was so afraid I wouldn't react fast enough to protect Giselle and the girls. . . . But I didn't fail, did I?"

"You certainly did not."

"And if I had it to do all over again, I'd shoot him again. It will take me a while to get used to this."

"Lord willing, you'll never need to do that again."

Giselle called from beyond the pine trees. "Jeanie . . . Tom . . . I'm going to take the girls up the hill to the farmhouse. I'll call for an ambulance from there."

"Go with her, Jean, and help her calm the girls. I'll stay with Andre."

"But your arm—"

"I'll be okay. Giselle needs you."

"Yes. Of course." She looked at Andre, still unconscious. "Be careful."

"I have the guns."

Their eyes met. She wanted to be back in his arms, but she made herself back away. "I'll see you up at the farmhouse then." She turned and hurried to catch up with Giselle.

On the way up the hill, the children clung to Giselle's hands, but Jacquie turned to Jean and said, "Aunt Jeanie, I just knew you would understand about the pine needles and come find us. I remembered how you said they only grew in one place."

Jean reached for her free hand and squeezed it. "You are so smart and so brave. How did you do it?"

"Well, as soon as I saw the needles, I picked up some and put them in my pocket, 'cause I wanted to show you when we came home. Then Andre took us into the barn and said we were going to play hide-and-seek with Maman. I didn't like that. When I said I didn't want to play, he scared me. He smiled, but his eyes looked mean. Then he cut pieces of our hair and pulled off our ribbons and said it was so Maman would know we were with him. So when he made me tie the ribbons around our hair, I put pine needles in with mine."

"Sweetie, you did exactly the right thing," Giselle said. "Père will be so proud of you when he hears what you did." To Jean she said, "Thank God for your love of nature. I didn't notice the pine needles."

"Well, while we're thanking God, we'd better give thanks for Nella's love of plants too. She's the one who showed me those trees."

"I just thank God for everything," Angie said grandly.

Jean laughed giddily and then stopped. If she let herself go, she would be in tears again, and that would never do. Little girls might not understand crying for relief and happiness.

Because of the shortage of specialists in the local hospitals, Giselle was admitted immediately to the Gilwern military station hospital where a skilled army surgeon operated on her nose. Shortly after her surgery, she learned that Tom also had been operated on within hours of his new injuries.

Jeanie came to visit both her and Tom and brought the news

that Andre had survived surgery and remained in the hospital under guard. Giselle received this news with mixed feelings. Though Andre no longer posed a threat to her and the girls, she couldn't shake her unease.

Finally after ten days in the hospital, Giselle returned to the manse. Elizabeth, Nella, and the children served her a special luncheon and then insisted that she go lie down to rest while they did the dishes.

Upstairs, alone in the apartment, Giselle walked to the window in her small kitchen, and by habit, glanced down at the backyard. Would she ever lose this need to watch out for trouble? She doubted it.

She slipped off her shoes and padded into her bedroom. Freshly cut roses filled a vase on the dressing table. Going to the closet, she reached under the extra quilts on the shelf for the comforting shape of her gun. Jeanie said she'd placed it there. Her fingers closed on the Mauser, and she drew it out.

She'd been relieved when Jeanie didn't argue about the wisdom of keeping the gun. In fact Jeanie had persuaded the authorities to let her keep it. She told them it was all Giselle had left of her husband's possessions, and that he was still missing in France.

Giselle needed the gun. No matter that Captain Lloyd had come to the hospital to assure her that, according to BSE agents in France, Andre had worked alone when he pursued her.

They said Andre had been a devoted member of Hitler's National Socialist Party, but he had bungled a couple of assignments the Gestapo gave him. Then when Claude and Giselle escaped, both the Gestapo and the resistants were becoming suspicious of him. He wisely fled. His unexpected meeting with Giselle must have given him hope for clearing himself with the Gestapo, besides presenting an opportunity for serving the cause of the Third Reich.

Nazis! Giselle shuddered. She carried the gun to the window where the afternoon sun shone in, then opened the chamber. It was empty, but Jeanie had cleaned and oiled every part. From a small cache of ammunition in the dressing table drawer, she loaded the Mauser. Then, with the safety on, she laid it in the drawer beside the head of her bed—within easy reach.

Turning back the top quilt, Giselle lay down in the blessed

quiet of the manse. She closed her eyes and thought about the lovely lunch with her children laughing and having fun.

Sometime later she awoke abruptly. Cautiously she opened her eyes. In the rocking chair by the window, Jacquie sat watching her with a troubled expression.

"Honey. What's wrong?" Giselle sat up and held out her arms.

Jacquie rushed to her, trembling. "Maman, your gun is gone! Aunt Jeanie left it in your closet, and it's gone!"

Giselle caught her breath. "Sweetie, don't be frightened. I have my gun. Right here." She pulled out the drawer to show the gun nested on top of handkerchiefs and underwear. Then her sleeping mind jolted awake. "How did you know where Aunt Jeanie put the gun? She didn't show you."

Beside her on the bed, Jacquie became very still and lowered her chin. "I sneaked and watched her."

"But what made you look for it today?"

"I wanted to ask you to teach me how to shoot."

Her soft voice blurred in Giselle's ears. Surely she hadn't heard right. "You what?"

"I want to know how to shoot the gun."

Horror sucked away Giselle's voice. She gasped, "Jacquie! Have you visited my closet before to look at the gun?"

Jacquie looked down at her hands pressed together in her lap and slowly nodded. "I had to be sure it was there for you."

"Oh, my poor baby." Giselle hugged her close. "Surely you didn't touch the gun."

"I did move it so I could see it easier."

"Did it make you feel safer to know it was there?"

"Yes. But I was scared because I don't know how to shoot it."

"You must promise me never to touch it again."

Jacquie looked away.

Giselle drew away from her, grasped her arms, and gently shook her. "Look at me." When she did, Giselle said, "Promise me you will never, never touch a gun again. Promise."

"I can't! What if I need to protect Angie . . . or you?"

Giselle grabbed her and held her close. "Dear Jacquie, you will never have to do that. I will always take care of you."

"I heard Andre. I heard him hurt you. I wanted to kill him! I hate him! I need to learn about guns. Don't you see ... in case...?"

"No. No!" Giselle smoothed her short curls. "To kill is never the way. Don't think of killing anyone. We must protect ourselves, but we must not be like Andre." She heard herself echoing Jeanie's words because she couldn't think of her own. She too had wanted to kill Andre.

"Jacquie, don't ever give in to hate. Don't ever give in to the wish to harm or to get even...." How could she teach Jacquie in words that she had denied by her actions? She'd worried about what the war would do to her children, but she had been blind to what her own actions were doing to them. She'd always believed that whatever was morally wrong for children was morally wrong for their parents. Now she had accepted a double standard. *But I had to! We've all had to be willing to kill or be killed!*

Jacquie was watching her with anxious eyes, waiting—waiting for what? For her mother to make sense out of a world that had gone crazy.

Giselle silently cried out, *God in Heaven, give me words. Don't let my children be seared by my hatred. God forgive me and help me!*

"Jacquie." Her throat clogged up. She cleared it. "Do you remember your friend Francine in Lyon?"

"Yes. I will never forget Francine."

"Do you remember when she first moved next door and she threw your dolly Annette out the window and then laughed to see you cry?"

Jacquie frowned. "I remember."

"Do you still think she was wrong to break your favorite doll and laugh at you?"

"Well ... yes."

"But you forgave her and became her friend when she said she was sorry."

Jacquie nodded. "Yes. I forgot about the doll. Francine is my best friend."

"But what she did was wrong and mean."

"Yes, but—"

"You forgave her, didn't you? Honey, I want you to remember every day how Francine became your best friend and how much you love her. And remember that she really was wrong, but you forgave her. You hated what she did, but you loved her. I believe this is what Jesus meant when He said we must forgive our enemies. I want you to forgive Andre in that same way, although you will never be friends with him as you are with Francine."

Giselle took Jacquie's hand as she would if she were an adult. "I want you to know that I will do this with you. I want to forgive my enemies—especially Andre. I've never wanted to teach you how to hate. Sweetheart, please forgive me."

"Forgive you? Oh, Maman, I love you!" Jacquie threw her arms around Giselle's neck and cried.

Giselle hugged her and patted her and wondered how she ever could live up to her pledge.

That evening Jeanie stopped to visit. While they sat in the back garden watching the girls play hide-and-seek with Livie in the summer twilight, Giselle told Jeanie about Jacquie and the gun.

"When I heard her say she wanted to kill, I understood how you must have felt when I said the same thing." She hesitated. How could she put her conflicting feelings into words?

Determined, she stumbled on. "I . . . found myself using your words . . . that we become like Andre if we hate and kill. . . . I want you to know that I want to forgive. Right now I can't imagine how. I can't conjure up a drop of mercy or goodwill toward him. I feel that forgiving him will be a betrayal of everyone who has been tortured and killed by the Nazis.

"I despise them! I hate what they've done. I hate what they're doing. I hate what they want to do." She stopped, for the children had wandered closer.

"Of course you do." Jeanie took her hand. "I can't tell you how to forgive. I can't imagine how I could forgive if I'd suffered as you have. But for the sake of the girls, you'll find your way."

Giselle nodded.

They sat quietly watching the girls, but inside Giselle felt anything but quiet. She remembered the contempt and vicious glee on Andre's face when he finally had snatched her gun. The children's terrified screams coming from the dirty dark room where he'd locked them rang in her ears again. Her thoughts tunneled downward to the loss of Claude. Was he alive or had he been dead all these months, and she didn't know? *Please, God, no!*

Suddenly she exclaimed, "You never know what it means to

forgive an enemy until you have one. Pray for me, Jeanie. I can't do this alone."

Jeanie hugged her. "Of course I'll pray."

Angie dashed over. "Maman, look! Is that the evening star?"

"Yes, sweetie. Almost as bright as the moon."

Angie perched on her lap, and Jacquie sat beside her. She wrapped her arms around them both. Jeanie, on her other side, picked up Livie and cuddled her. Giselle felt surrounded by her loved ones, surrounded by love. She was not alone. Somehow, for their sakes and with God's help, she would forgive.

More stars appeared, pale dots and then bright sparkles, pinholes in the dark fabric of the sky. The summer night enveloped her like a cozy comforter. She began to remember the good times. "Angie, when I was your age, your grand-mère told me the stars were candles in heaven's windows, lighted each night by the angels to help us find our way in the dark. When I got older, about Jacquie's age, I knew better. But now, despite all that the science books tell us, I like to think about the angels again."

Both girls snuggled closer.

As Jean went about her daily routine, her rage at Andre cooled. Despite how he'd hurt Giselle, Tom, and maybe even Claude, she was glad she hadn't killed him.

When Jean visited Tom, he always brightened to see her, but then it was as if the closeness she'd felt when they faced death together never had happened. He behaved distantly and fell into silences that made her feel unwanted, yet he seemed to hate to see her leave. Her feelings toward him flipped from one extreme to the other. During the day while working, she felt so angry that she never wanted to see him again. Then in the quiet of night she cried into her pillow from wanting him. No matter how she resented the way he kept her at a distance, when she had time off, she could not stay away from him.

Then Jean learned that Andre's condition, despite a second surgery, had become critical. She began to have nightmares. In the dreams she shot Andre over and over, and then when he fell, his face became the face of her brother Jimmy. She grew afraid to fall asleep at night. A feeling of horror haunted her during the day.

The day Andre died, she went numb. As evening approached she dreaded the coming of worse nightmares. Suddenly the need to be with Tom consumed her. He seemed like an anchor to reality. She had to talk to him.

Jean wasn't sure she'd be welcomed. She hadn't been to see him since movie night when he had been more distant than usual. Well, if he didn't want her around, she could leave quickly enough.

After supper she hitched a ride to Gilwern with one of the ambulance drivers. She had not called ahead, so when she walked into the ward, Tom literally jumped at the sight of her. One glimpse of his face told her he was glad to see her.

He was sitting on the edge of his bed, dressed in army fatigue pants and a shirt large enough to button over the cast on his left arm. He rose to his feet and came to meet her. The bedfast men whistled and made wisecracks.

Jean smiled and waved at them, calling a few by name. When Tom reached her, she said, "If I get a wheelchair, can you go out? It's a beautiful warm evening."

"I could walk a mile, but regulations no doubt require me to ride." They went to the nurses' area, and he sat in one of the chairs parked there.

As Jean pushed him down the outdoor walkway, he said very little. When they reached a quiet place near the edge of the station hospital complex, she stopped, set the brakes on the chair, then sat down on the grass beside him. If they ignored the fence, there was a nice view of the river.

He kicked aside the footrests on the chair, climbed out, and dropped down beside her. With one knee up and his good arm wrapped around it, he lounged so close to her his sleeve brushed her arm. "I've missed you," he said abruptly. "They must be keeping you very busy."

She glanced at him and away. "Yes . . . and I thought maybe you didn't want to see me. . . ."

He answered slowly. "I thought you didn't want to see me. . . . You've been so quiet lately."

"I have?" She had no idea that she'd behaved any differently than usual. She swallowed hard and tried to steady her voice. "I've been upset about Andre, but I didn't think you needed to hear that."

"That's all? You weren't trying to get rid of me?"

She shook her head. "No, but I thought you didn't want me around."

He clasped her hand and folded her fingers around his. "I've had a lot on my mind. The war. My buddies. The fight with Andre brought back a lot that I didn't want to talk about. Guess I should have tried, though."

It had not occurred to her that his frequent silences were not related to how he felt about her. She gripped his hand. Here was the anchor she needed, the reality of his warm touch. Keeping her eyes on their clasped hands, she said, "I've had things on my mind too. Things I couldn't talk about." She had to get it out—as fast as she could, or she'd never be able to say what she had to say. "I killed Andre. He died last night."

He slipped free of her grip and cupped his hand under her chin, turning her so she had to meet his eyes. "Jeanie, you know you had to shoot him."

"I . . . killed . . . a man," she repeated, trying to accept the unacceptable.

"You saved the lives of four people," he said firmly. "Five, counting yourself."

"But if I'd shot sooner . . . I could have taken better aim. I could have only wounded him."

"Andre was, and is, in God's hands."

She choked out, "That bothers me too. If he had lived, would he have turned to God for forgiveness? I feel as if I tried to play God. I judged Andre, and I wanted him dead. If I hadn't wanted to kill him, I might have aimed better and just wounded him."

Tom pulled her sideways against his chest with his good arm and cradled her there. She clung to him and sobbed.

He held her close and gently rocked her, as if she were a child. "I'm so sorry you had to go through this," he murmured. "I know I can't say anything that will make you feel better. But I can tell you that you did what was necessary to save our lives. Try to focus on the fact that you saved us, Jeanie."

She quieted and nodded, sniffing.

He pulled a handkerchief from his pants pocket and wiped her face as if she were six years old.

She smiled shakily. "Will you leave me no pride?"

He chuckled. "That's my girl. I've really missed that smile and that smart mouth." Without warning he pulled her close again and tenderly kissed her. His gentleness blew away her defenses. With a surge of joy she returned his kiss. Finally she pulled away. She couldn't trust herself to speak. She didn't know what to say.

He solved her problem. "Jeanie, in all the thinking I've been doing, I've seen how much I don't deserve even your friendship. I'm so sorry for all the times I hurt your feelings. Can you forgive me?"

They'd been through this before, but she sensed a change in his attitude. Well, they were both different now, and he seemed to need reassurance. "Of course I forgive you," she said. "But you've only been honest with me, which is more than I've been with you. Will you forgive *me*?"

He looked sincerely puzzled and then exclaimed, "Surely you're not thinking of all that stuff in the internment camp! I not only forgave you, but I've forgotten about it. Look, for anything you might imagine, I forgive you sight unseen. Jeanie, I love you so much. Will you marry me? Please?"

She searched his face, so often composed to conceal his feelings. He wasn't hiding from her. His brown eyes were saying "I love you," and love softened every line of his expression. Her gaze stopped at the curved lips she loved to kiss. "If you don't really mean that, you're going to be sorry, because you won't get away from me this time."

He threw back his head, laughing. And then he kissed her again, for a long time.

Epilogue

On August 23, 1944, the day French resistants freed most of Paris, Jean and Tom were married in the Abergavenny Presbyterian Church by Reverend MacDougall. Uncle Al gave Jean away. Giselle served as matron of honor, and Mary O'Leary and Nella Killian were bridemaids. Jacquie and Angie helped baby Livie march down the aisle, casting petals of late-blooming roses in the path of the bride. Three of Tom's friends from the Nisei Combat Team stood with him as groomsmen. For their brief honeymoon, Jean had found a room for let in a picturesque old inn on the road to Crickhowell.

General de Gaulle established the French Provisional Government in Paris on August 30, and at last Giselle learned that Claude was alive. The Germans had surrounded his battalion for a long time. After finally locating Giselle, Claude urged her to stay on in Wales until all of France was free. Jacquie's and Angie's joyous smiles brightened her days. Despite Claude's absence, the girls felt they had their Père again.

On September 1, Tom returned to active duty, and Jean continued to work in the Govilon military station hospital. Since the suicide of Rufe Johnson, her Red Cross work had taken on new meaning—a hope that she could help prevent such tragedies. Giselle also spent more time in volunteer work, both at the hospitals and in the church.

Like wives everywhere, Jean and Giselle threw themselves into the war effort and lived for the day when their men could come home to stay.